D1207156

Curranne
Trueheart

Books by Donald Newlove

Novels
THE PAINTER GABRIEL
SWEET ADVERSITY,
embodying
LEO & THEODORE
and
THE DRUNKS
ETERNAL LIFE
CURRANNE TRUEHEART

Life Study
THOSE DRINKING DAYS
Myself and Other Writers

Curranne Trueheart

Donald Newlove

DOUBLEDAY & COMPANY, INC.
GARDEN CITY, NEW YORK
1986

Library of Congress Cataloging in Publication Data
Newlove, Donald.
   Curranne Trueheart.
   I. Title.
PS3564.E914C8 1986   813'.54   85-10145
ISBN: 0-385-19935-X

Copyright © 1986 by Donald Newlove
ALL RIGHTS RESERVED
PRINTED IN THE UNITED STATES OF AMERICA
FIRST EDITION

Once more, to JACK McMANIS,
who brings back the dead,
and to my wife, NANCY

And to CURRANNE

Contents

PART ONE

King James

W hat could be more hopeless than a madwoman marrying a drunk? But cities have always been full of crazy people and alcoholics who marry. That lasting love can grow from such a union—such a fearful matching of cracks—is a miracle.

My boldest early memory of her is as the girl found sleeping on a roof. But even before that she stood out, an overwhelmingly bright new star, as a Chicagoan moved to King James. When she was nineteen her Marine bridegroom was killed on the Saipan invasion. She'd been living with her mother, who very early one morning found Curranne's bed empty, then went out back looking for her—she sometimes camped out. She wasn't in the yard. She lay head downward on the pitched roof, splayed and naked on rough steep tiles, face up and unmoving in fall sunlight. Her crippled mother, not daring to wake her on such a dangerous slant, called for the nearest hook-and-ladder. Sometime later, firemen lifted her down, a soft wax mute in a blanket.

We lived only a few blocks apart. I'd see her striding about in racing shorts. Strong-boned, not big, but long-muscled. She was three years older than I, so—after screwing myself to it for a half block—I'd barely nod. When she'd passed I'd "forget" something I should go back for, follow her until she turned out of sight, then change my mind and go on. I still remember awakening to an anatomical mystery in the backs of her thighs—how could the *backs* be so oddly attractive? Did she foretell something grand ahead for me, perhaps in high school? When I heard at school about her "nervous breakdown" I felt mild pity. She was the first person I'd ever known to have some form of mental attack. She also became the first utterly human girl in my experience. A creature with eyes that could suffer a soul wound, her body put away, ego-stripped. Even her house bloomed with an added aura for me. After three months I saw her back, going in and out. Healed forever? Then she left town. I made a vow to avoid people like her and not to mess up my life with misfits or women with mysterious imperfections.

The heart plunges back. With Curranne, in the miracle of her last flowering, I would have died for love. But I see instead Jack Trueheart quite alive, hurtling over Third Street in a tomato-stained apron. Chasing his wife's lost wits.

Early summer rain falls on the great stone fort of James Prendergast Free Library. The borrower ahead of me is Curranne. It's now fifteen years since her legendary breakdown on her mother's roof. Released anew, this time from a six-month stay at Gallinger mental hospital in D.C., she is spending her first day back in King James. Once more she's rooming with her mother. You might say she's just walked from her barred ward in Washington into the Prendergast with her mother's library card and is ready to start living.

Her eye takes me in. We've never spoken but I know her baby sister, Cornelle and she knows my older sister, Liz. Nervously, we've been half smiling at each other in the stacks for the past half century. Side-eyed, I watch her reach overhead. Strong-boned, long-muscled. (Stand there! let me touch you.) She has my ears stinging already, not just her legs but her uncommonly fine nose, so straight but birdlike, even haunting. It strikes me as the seat of her sexuality and intelligence. In line I try a polite How are you, a lunch offer beating in my chest. Her body is a bow, despite two children, possessed by brilliant gray-green eyes. She's restless. Even this short line bores her. Her eager smile seems so steeped in men that my skin breathes sex off her. I straighten the tulip knot in my striped silk. She's taking out Reich's *Character Analysis.*

"It's about character-armor," she says. "We all live in steel suits."

"That's pretty bizarre. Do you believe it?"

"I haven't read it yet! Do you like Reich?"

"I faded on *The Function of the Orgasm.*" Look about on orgasm. It's 1958 but the Prendergast still keeps its dirt behind glass.

She's quiet, then eyes me intensely. "I haven't talked with a man since before the Flood."

She hairpins into my ex-wife, then her ex-husband, clearing the air. As we move toward the desk, she plunges into *all* her men. Curranne's up to her neck in geniuses. Her father was a genius drunk who wanted her to be a genius. Her Marine husband who died was a poet genius. Her separated younger third husband, a genius TV producer, is in Chicago, while her two sons by a genius painter, her middle husband, are with their dad in Provincetown. Both living husbands, she insists, are gems. Her dead one was more of an adorable fruit, who joined the Marines to become a man. Her eye shines about him—he might walk out of the stacks any moment, fully empowered (as never in life). She's an English grad with New York teaching ticket. As we talk—pretty boldly for a library line!—I think I intuit a suicide attempt amid her hard times. But suicide and mental problems leave me dumb; I've never met anyone touched by either hardship. I've just turned thirty. Older, she strikes me as hard-focused and self-controlled. Honesty plain-shines from her brow and pulled-back ponytail. Hazel flecks measure my brain weight. Signals crackle, dance, are toying are shy. She raps Reich on her hip, presses him to her pelvis. She's seen in a snap that I'm as strong-willed, bright and—for this town—as bent as she. I take the book.

Just chatting about Reich makes me want to help her. Bring my writer's balms to her service. I'm zilch on mental illness but, who knows, a novelist's advice might be useful. Or so I think, hiding my breath quavers. I watch her wide Irish lip brain-strip and shrink Reich to a husk. Envy shakes me. Shyly, she takes the book back, shutting up. But I sense through her veil, or unveilings, that she is reservedly makable. I invite her to lunch at my mother's a half-block away, where I room (well, cellar), and to hear my Piaf collection. In her smiles I hear a whisper: "Undo me."

"I don't dig Piaf," she says. "All that little-sparrow hopelessness."

My wishful thinking fades. High moldings, runny windows. "Well, she's a great favorite of Cornelle's."

"No sad songs for me, Jack. Life's tough enough."

"But that's her art," I say.

"That's not art, it's money. She's peddling dark cafés and rain. Depression's a *lousy* drug. Too cheap. I don't want to be half conscious with self-pity." A fist for life. "I say give it your best."

"You know, you're not at all like your sister."

"Not much. Should I be?"

The woman ahead has stopped the line for five minutes with questions. Curranne's jaw grits. She draws back her long-pointed umbrella to jab an unguarded buttock. My scalp races. The umbrella pitches hay one straw from the woman's rump. Too close for fun! But Curranne blinks innocently. Chicago humor?—I don't know, but it's too brash for the Prendergast.

The rain dies. In sudden silence our books are stamped. We go out into glowing stone-green brilliance. Robins hop and tug in the grass. Rainswollen angleworms lie drowned on the walk. Her strong fingers shine with bone as I take her umbrella.

"Clearing up," she says. "I want to go swimming. I've been dreaming of it for three months."

"How about Chautauqua? I'll drive."

All clover, she lifts her carryall to show a navy blue swimsuit. *"Super!"*

We walk to my mother's in the after-rain shine. The sky breaks sapphire. Strong heady grass smells boil my sap. Something grave and cold and lilting tells me my day is set. I feel flesh, sandy, damp, blotchy flesh press against me on a sought-out deserted beach. I fear only my ten-thumbed power to seduce. She has such poise! Her nose alone is an ornament beyond my possessing.

I'm a shortish sandy redhead, eleven years out of the Marines, four out of the Air Force, still wideshouldered from a youth spent swimming. I have a good grip. At twenty I was in love with Cornelle. She was playing Ophelia in our Little Theater *Hamlet* while I harsked out a few lines as a spear-carrier. Later, in the Air Force, I married my former fellow student from King James Community College, Thelma. We had a child but lived together less than two years, annulled in five on my failure as a provider. I went hiking about the country and came back to King James at thirty, still unpublished, for a job on the local tabloid. My first small success as a writer. I dress for it: black homburg, charcoal pinstripe, wingtip mustachios. I go at the first draft of my first novel with gusto, but . . . Unfathomably, I'm dying, painfully and depressingly. And ease my blues with steady sips. This town, Jack, such a drain. And yet its weathers sing, its trees have soul-roots, its rain a foresty glower—I'm the most cheerfully intense depressed person I know. Despite my habitual tragic irony, some seed-man in me yearns to split forth, be born. Boundless physical energy!—but I collect overcast photos of black horror, people weeping, a crazed hollow-eyed Stalingrad mother nursing her frozen lump. I savor the deaths of my literary and musical idols, seek out last works in words and music. I've a bland little sex sheaf from nudist magazines too. My years cut me off from our college girls (so I feel), and few singles in King James are willing. Or I've missed them, or they smell bad news on me after noon wine. So meeting Curranne is like striking tuna. I'm serious that I think I can help her. But in fact I'm a dolt at reading people—it takes titanic labor for me to get skin-deep even in my writing—my power of character analysis is more Stan Laurel than D. H. Lawrence. I can't take it in, much less make it up. People pass right through me.

Two huge firs front my mother's house. She's upstairs changing roomers' sheets. Chili simmers in a deep pot on the power stove. In our handsome large living room Curranne eyes my piled manuscript.

"What's it about?" she asks.

"You want my standard vague answer? The god Prometheus visits the States and is the victim of his crime of bringing intelligence to man. In the chapter I'm on now he's tramping around Texas with Jesus and Ike. They're all bums."

"You mean Eisenhower? The real man?"

"Kicked out of office, ha ha!"

"But he's still alive! How can you make up fiction about him?"

"That's what's original. Nobody's ever written about a living President this way. You've heard his news conferences? He lisps and stumbles. Ties himself in knots."

"*He's sick!* You can't make fun of a living man's stroke."

"He's a dummy without the stroke."

"He didn't do badly on D-Day. Is this political?"

"I detest politics."

She fingers the book. "Let me see this, do you mind?"

Hand her the polished new chapter. She zaps three sheets in thirty seconds. Sits back thunderstruck.

"Oh, this is awful stuff! No heart at all. How can you take the time to write it? It's not authentic about anything. Everything's out of your head. Even Texas is fake."

"I take that as a compliment." A stake through the chest.

"I don't mean it as one. Beautifully written, yes. But strawberry-flavored baloney." Lip curling, she skims more. "No attack, all marshmallow. So diffuse. Worse than television. *Ugh!* I want to cry." I wish to Christ she'd stop. But she goes on. "Can't you see nothing *exists* in this? There's not one word felt or alive."

My ribs crackle under her steamroller. "Ike wasn't funny?"

"Oh God. I'd better go. You don't understand a word I say."

"I do, I do!" My head feels like Reich's, very shrunken.

"You need a shock. I cry when I read deliberately sick writing."

I float with embarrassment. Wheeze, "That's what Tolstoy told Shaw."

"Shaw was an idiot. Sending Tolstoy a farce shows how little he understood moral genius."

"Shaw was the devil's advocate."

Her face bloats with blood. "The devil doesn't need an advocate. Argument for argument's sake always favors the devil. An honest man lives by faith and can always be stood on his head by logic. You know that!"

The day tilts. How my hopes waver, fizzling.

My sister Liz, a year older than Curranne, slams in from the porch and calls upstairs. "Let's eat, Mother!"

Curranne rises to leave. "Hi, Liz."

"Well, for God's sake—*Currie!* Your mother told me you were back. You're staying for lunch, I damn well hope."

I say, "That's why she's here."

"Great! We have a guest, Mother," Liz calls upstairs.

"Please to stop shouting," Mother cries below us. "I could hear you hoofing around even in the attic."

"Oh, she's downcellar," Liz says. "Come on."

I follow them down: they're almost sisters in bust and hips, and both have had two sons. A glistening dark-haired force, Liz is remarried, has a fancy place on Lakeview and lives to give parties. "That's Jack's room," Liz waves, then holds her nose. *"Phew!* I don't know how you can bear that soap smell." Cellar windows glow in the concrete laundry where Mother hangs sheets.

"Well, hello!" Mother says.

Before I can introduce Curranne, I'm needled by soap fumes and pinch my nose.

"Mother, this is Carol's daughter Currie," Liz says. "What's your name now, Currie Chaplin? Remember I used to visit Currie when she lived alone on Fifth Street?"

Curranne tells Mother, "Liz was a big lift when I needed her most."

"Well, that was nice of her," Mother says wide-eyed. "Were you ill?"

"She was a young widow," Liz says. "You remember, *Maw.*"

"Oh, my heavens! It all comes back," Mother says, amid sheets. "Why, that was years and years ago."

"I'm all over it," Curranne says. "I'm all over everything."

"But we never forget, do we," Liz assures Curranne. "I lost my first son in his crib."

"I heard! And was so sorry for you."

I nod at Curranne. "We'd like to go jump in the lake."

"What did you say?" Mother asks edgily.

"We'd like to go swimming. May I use the car?"

She's still sensitive about her taillight I ground to sugar last week. She sees now that Curranne's with me, not Liz. "Isn't it a little early to go swimming?"

"Not for seals, ha ha ha!" Liz says.

Curranne says, "I don't care if there's ice on the lake."

Hope tinges my crotch with spring velvet. "Me too. I need a dip."

"Well, it'll be cold," Liz says. "But May isn't too early."

"For seals," Mother says. "Where are you off to?"

"Chautauqua!" Curranne says.

I blush, looking off. Deserted this time of year, Chautauqua's twenty miles farther than Lakewood beach. Mother reads my red face. Through bedsheets I watch her eye recall and weigh Carol's stories about her addled daughter Curranne. Her mouth tightens.

"I'm going out for supper. Try to be back before I leave," she says. Mother prizes her Olds—but me even more.

"I've got to show a house at one. Let's eat," Liz says. She works out of Carol's real estate office.

I trail the three mothers up to the kitchen. As we eat, I pour a lone burgundy. They rake things over. Listening, I despair of my writing. These three are so fertile with dramas, losses, divorces, hospitals, death. I sit silent with my one ex-wife and child apart from me. The wine turns brassy under Mother's chili.

Liz returns from the bathroom, brushed, relipsticked, bright as a dark cat for her house showing. "Well, that was a nice chat. You kids have a good time. Don't do anything I wouldn't do, ha ha ha!"

"That offers some latitude," Mother says.

Tonight's the biweekly meeting in my living room of The Saturday Night Shakespeare and Sharp Cheese Society. So, after lunch I borrow the car and we buy a half-wheel of Cheddar and case of four wine gallons for the reading, then I maneuver Curranne onto my cellar bed for a heavy kiss with Piaf before we change into swimsuits in separate bathrooms and set off for Chautauqua. It's a long, sparkling drive over

May hills to the summer colony's vacant grounds. We turn in at the still unguarded gate. So few summer folk around yet. Coast slowly down to the beach, strip in the car and lay out our blanket near the bell tower. Her aging navy one-piece has a silver-dollar moth hole on the hip. I'm still upset about my bombed novel, but thump to her slim full figure, the harp-line of each hip.

We swim, screw around in the freeze, dry off our gooseflesh in light winds. She suggests we walk over the lower road to look at the houses. Many have spreading wings and balconies. On North Lake Drive I point out Mrs. Lancaster's house. Her son Stu was our Hamlet, ten years ago. *"Let's move in!"* Curranne says, her finger tugging me. The house watches us hold hands. We turn and kiss in our suits. It's sheer hunger for us both, and her more important bones against me send up a cinnamon nova that dances and fades, leaving me half-faint on her shoulder.

Knowing gray-green eyes. She says, "I didn't expect that."

"Bath time."

Walking back to the beach, hand in hand, we both feel bare. I still bulge. She eyes my dry-wet trunks, then looks about at the grand houses, all empty behind tiers of white gingerbread. "This has never happened to me before."

"What hasn't?"

"Public sex."

"I'm not sorry."

"It's nice!"

She's pale and drawn, her hair faintly auburn. The high elms shadow and dapple the road. Our palms lock by the bare animal skin in her moth hole. That hole disturbs me. Shameful, her flesh showing. Chilled and shaking, I lower my eyes to our bare feet, padding on asphalt. The road is chewed and edgeless. If I feel this mortal, how much more must she? Three years older!

We age and the afternoon cools under the bell tower. Beside her, I tremble without stop. The day escapes, face to face on our elbows. Her flowing mind, fearful eye-stammerings, bind me. Hip-rise, bosom-fall. What's dropped into my lap? Since the heavy kiss in my cellar, not one hint of holding back or pulling away. My every grip welcome.

The brassy end of day. "Don't go."

"What?" she asks.

"I don't see how you could ever have mental problems."

"Oh, I'm much, much better"—her deepest voice.

"You know when your husband died? I lived around the corner from you—on Harding Avenue. I'd sit on my porch and watch you jog."

"You did! I don't remember you."

"Well, I remember . . ."—the mysterious backs of her thighs—". . . Carol calling the firehouse . . . to get you down from the roof."

"She did? There's a lot I—" Her hand twists vacantly.

"But what happened this last time was more like a nervous breakdown?"

"No, more like a train wreck. On the bottom of the ocean, ha!"

"But here you are—back again." I sigh, vexed. "You're so well."

She shrugs, wiggling. "But I'm getting better and better and better. I have to prove myself capable of caring for my kids before the court will award me part custody. It's terrible. You have to prove yourself in a vacuum. Without the kids to care for, though caring is what gives you strength. I'll get 'em back." Her jaw marbles at this fixed thought. "First I need a job so I can support 'em." *Fear.* "And I have to show good character and morals."

"That's a problem?"

"Anything could be used against me!" A fear-flash, her finger on my breastbone. "Discreet, right?"

Our walk and standup sex? "By all means." Take her hand. Old Jack, holding his own against the sweetheart of Harding Avenue. *"Don't* go."

"Go where?"

"Away. Not for a while."

"Please, don't. I know you don't mean anything by it—but bullshit upsets me. You're not in real life, d'ya know?"

"I'm not?"

"I know you're trying. But I see your eyes, Jack. One minute you're talking to me and the next you're whizzing off into the next county. Maybe you're composing, I don't know. But I do know when the con starts."

" 'I'll get better and better and better,' I say."

"Hah!" Bats my shoulder. "It won't be easy. You're way out of touch. Your writing is clinical schiz. I've seen a million pages of it."

"Hey, that's first-draft fingerpainting," I lie.

"Yeah, yeah." Turns aside, bosom falling. We lock eyes. "Aha! You've got all kinds of wandering-eye trouble."

"A classic case. Guilty!—lock him up. Whattaya mean my writing's schiz?"

"Wall-to-wall. Every other sentence whips off into a new subject. No focus on anything. Oh, I see the work. Even the typing looks letterpress. And the wording and diction. Don't think I *miss* that stuff, I'm Irish and Welsh. And been married to three geniuses."

"I don't think you miss anything."

"Or the emptiness. I see what you feel, or don't feel—the yearning and lyricism you pour all over it. Have I upset you?"

"No no no."

"I've got to be honest or I'll be as unreal as you are. And may as well kill myself now."

"Don't even suggest that. Hey, supper? You're coming to my Shakespeare reading tonight? Terrific. And no more killing yourself, for God's sake."

"Jack, everybody thinks about that."

"Look, two years from now, you'll look back at this transition and wonder how you were so nervous. Be past all this."

"Two years from now I'll be in court."

"But you'll get those kids!"

"If I can bear two years."

"Something I wanta show you. D'ya know those poplars at Ashville turnoff? Like a Romney painting? Let's go."

She jumps up. "Ha ha ha, you look so frigging together in that banker's outfit you wear! My doctor'd love you."

"Curranne, one second. It's hard to believe. But I want you to know that I am the most well-balanced person I know. Bar none."

She laughs tears. I'm shocked—all's not well with me? I have a sex tic? Some masked or petty flaw I don't know about?

Roll swiftly downlake. Breezing high poplars flank the Ashville lovers' lane. Walk under washing branches, faroff small clouds in rich blue. Hurt of evening. The ground too stiff and brittle for the blanket, we settle into the backseat and go at it half dressed in the chill. Graygreen eyes bore into me. She unrubbers her mane. I wear a sheath.

I hope to feed a year's emptiness in one hard gorging. A burning bush blows me to ashes. I shrink onto her.

"Aghh! I'm sorry."

"Don't be," she says. "It was very nice. Maybe later."

"Keep you to that."

Befogged but hopeful, I kiss earshells through her hair and draw a measureless moment from her cheek.

"That was as good as the other," she says softly.

We drive back quietly. Small pale freckles and milky Irish skin, half shy and bemused. Such a fine brainy brow. I move and see my wine-dark eyes in the mirror. Puffy, sleepless. Can I really interest her? My nose is growing! And yet, my first Welsh-Irish charmer . . .

Whoof! she sighs. "I'm on the mend!"

Curranne showers, then phones her mother that she's staying for dinner and Shakespeare. I lay out the wine gallons and the staggeringly large Cheddar in the living room. Mother makes up at the vanity in her tiny bedroom off the kitchen. Leaving on a supper date with her latest suitor, she eyes Curranne on the couch, ravishing and fresh from the shower, her crossed legs bare. She measures without mercy the brilliant-eyed auburn blonde leafing *Cosmopolitan* in lamplight, and sees nothing that can keep her prince and Curranne apart. I shake her elderly, iron-handed trailer salesman's slab of palm and wish them a peppy evening.

Curranne and I chili-up again, then hear *Transfigured Night* downcellar and neck on my bed until the first guests chime. Last month, hoping to break my loneliness with wine-and-cheese feasts legalized by Shakespeare readings, I ran a squib in the tabloid I work for, announcing the group's first meeting. Two weeks ago, we drank down *Twelfth Night.* Tonight *Hamlet.* I've already cast Ophelia. Curranne stands down the living room, untouched wine in hand, weight on one hip, legs charging me, chatting with Deacon Quince, a gray Buddha-smiling bachelor linotypist from my paper. Seeing her wholly, from a distance for the first time since meeting her this morning, her engaged creatureliness and gestures, fresh ponytail and lipstick, a Chicagoan's easy brass at a King James gathering, stirs my wonder at my luck. Tidal with good feeling, I pour for all. Damp wisps on her neck.

"A drop more?"

"Not for me, thank you," she says. "When do we start?"

"Right you are!" says Deacon Quince. "The night steals on, my boy. At this rate we won't get off the battlements."

Curranne and I pass out paperbacks for those who haven't brought books. Maxie Bonestahl, a tall shriveled new member whose larval face and reared-back magnified eyes have crawled out from under a Lakewood firetruck, follows us about, flat-voiced and taken with her: "Lemme ask your advice, both of you. I've written two unpublished short stories, so I hope to quit the hose company and take up novel writing for a living. But I have seven kids. How should I go about getting an agent?"

"Maybe you should write your novel first," Curranne says.

"Don't quit your job!" I say.

"But if I quit I can write faster."

I whisper, "Stop polishing those fucking trucks and write in the john."

She seconds me, a loose fist just short of bopping him. Maxie's shaken by a freefloating "fuck" before a woman in King James. He implores her, "I'm losing the best writing years of my life."

"They're all good," she says. "If you quit you sink your benefits."

"Henry Miller gave up everything," Maxie says.

She's tightlipped.

"It can be done," he insists.

"Oh Christ, quit," Curranne says. "You might actually experience something."

"Okay, let's start," I say. "Maxie, you're Marcellus. Phil's Horatio."

"Gadfrey! on at last," Phil shouts. "Was that me? Shut me off after the next tumbler."

Phil Newquist is skin-and-bones with an arrested brain tumor that has left him wall-eyed. His first nineteen years have passed like a pistol shot. He has no lovelife. He turns to Curranne, arm shaking wildly, lifts his glasses from a neckstring and jams them at his head. His lenses are chewed, greasy fog.

"Hey, gimme a nudge if I run off too much."

She nudges him, smiling.

"Boy, that was fast," he says. "I can't drink on my medication."

"Neither can I. So I don't!"

"What's that in your hand?" he asks.

"I'm not drinking it."

"Are you on medication?"

"I don't take drugs," she says. "And I hate alcohol. My father died of it."

"Oh, I'm sorry. Mine was going to but recovered. Was yours an alcoholic, may I ask?"

"He sure was! He fell off his ship and drowned."

"Hey, that's too bad. My older brother drowned. Didja love your father?"

"I'm still deciding," she says.

"Pardon me but I think I'm in love with you. But don't worry, I won't be a pest. You remind me of Nastasya Filipovna."

"Good God, who's she?"

"The heroine of *The Idiot.* I'm the hero, but I've been spared epilepsy, thank God. I hope you don't mind sitting next to the village atheist."

"That's better than the village idiot," she says. "I'm an atheist too. Everybody is, but they just won't admit it. I believe that. God is a big political fiction. Family politics, social politics, the church's tax dodge —they all boost the big lie. But if you could hear into people's heads, then you'd hear the truth."

"Spared again!—I can't hear into people's heads. But now I'm sure I love you." Sits back, flushed with recognition.

Deacon Quince tells her, "You've made a conquest."

"I may run off to Manhattan with him." She nudges Phil.

Phil glitters, faint with flattery. "Gadfrey! I've waited so long for this night!"

"Deacon, you be Polonius," I say.

"As you command. But why not Hamlet? Now that I'm really ready at a hundred and eight. Gimme a shot, coach. I'll be the first Zen Hamlet."

I give the Hirschhorns the Ghost and Gertrude. Short, gnomic Henry and buxom Greta are Jews who fled Berlin and the Nazis. Middle-aged Morris and Hedda Beard fill the loveseat. She's stretched out, breathless, hacking quietly. Liquidly dark-eyed Morris sits in cigarette smoke; his parched chuckle travels six inches at best. He's Claudius.

"I'll be Hamlet," Hedda gasps.

"Maybe we can split up Hamlet," I say.

"I am Hamlet," Hedda says.

"Curranne, be Ophelia."

"That ninny."

Sibyl Meadows, severe, invisible spinster head librarian at the Pren-

dergast, is our second Ophelia. A dark, thin sportswriter for my tabloid's rival, Tony Tripi, who claims he's a spy, reads Laertes. Philip
Falcone, balding, debonair fag druggist, is Francisco. As we start scene
one, he reads well, his whole fag life on the line. "Bravo," mutters
Deacon. So, a strong start as Marcellus and Horatio arrive.

"O—farewell—honest—soldier," Maxie intones.

We all wait.

"Who hath relieved you—" Curranne tells Maxie.

"Oh, is that my line?"

I'm Bernardo. "What, is Horatio here?"

"A piece of him!" Phil Newquist cries. "Jesus Christ, I read that
wrong. A piece of him!"

"A great improvement," Deacon sighs.

"What—has—this—thing—appeared—again—tonight?" Maxie
asks.

"Goldarnit, that's *my* line," Phil says. "What! Has this thing appeared again tonight?"

"I—have—seen—nothing."

"No, that's my line," I say. "I have seen nothing."

We all wait.

"This is your line," Curranne tells Maxie. She's pale.

Maxie holds his paperback far off, dead-stopping each line:

> "Horatio says 'tis but our fantasy.
> And will not let belief take hold of him.
> Touching this dreaded sight twice seen of us.
> Therefore I have entreated him along.
> With us to watch the minutes of this night.
> Boy, this acting is hard work.
> That if again this—this—"

"Apparition," Curranne says.

"—this—apparition—come. What's that, a bear?—a lion?"

"It's Hamlet's father's ghost," Curranne says.

"I don't believe in ghosts," Maxie says.

"Well, nonetheless he's coming," Curranne says nervously.

"So is Jesus and I don't believe in him either."

Phil says, "Let's not get off into that garbage."

"Does Hamlet believe in ghosts?" Maxie asks.

"Well, he's afraid his father's ghost may really be a goblin," Curranne says.

"That's fairy stuff." Maxie's face falls. "I thought this was a realistic book, not that salvation crap. This is a famous book!"

We are silent. An oak falls in California. Curranne says quietly, "Let's get on with the play." She's trembling. Her first full night back in King James and it's like the wards.

"While you folks argue, where's the head?" Phil asks, rising, and weaves into the hallway bathroom. Soon back, finger-combed hair soaking his shirt, he locks on his chair intensely, jolts into it with shocked sigh.

Curranne pats his knee. "You're doing great."

"A valiant recovery," Deacon agrees.

"I'm swearing off." Phil lifts his book. "What act are we in? Boy, do I sound fried. Ah! Tush, tush, 't will not appear!"

So we grind on. Brain-fag rises. Scene Two hits with such thanks that I think of calling cheese time. But on we plunge.

Maxie rises. "I think I'll make some tea."

"Bags on the counter."

Philip Falcone lifts his empty glass. "I think I'll wash this."

"Oh, have some more wine," I say.

He draws a brandy half-pint from his inner pocket. Smileless iceblue eyes pin me. "I'll have this. I drink."

He hurries off—I feel warnings, but sudden exhaustion turns my brain to plastic. Rain spatters the screens, sucking out layered smoke. Curranne tamps her shiny forehead. She grips my fingers, turning to me, her eyes wedged with prickles. The life in the hairline whorls of her irises stings me. *Bed, bed!* I think. Lamplight dims the big ceiling. "I'm drowning!" she whispers. We sit embalmed, actors in cotton. Then flagging but unbowed, we gird for Scene Two, the deep redfigured carpet bearing us up.

A smacking kissing sigh from the kitchen blinds me.

"I didn't hear that!" Tony Tripi cries.

A kitchen table leg squeals, dishes shimmying. I boil, gripping my book. Curranne nudges Phil. "Marcellus!" Phil shouts, "it's your line." He starts into the kitchen but is turned back by a rough voice. Sits again.

"Told me to frig off."

"Who did?" Curranne asks.

"I couldn't tell! They're busy making tea."

Sibyl Meadows, our invisible librarian, jumps up. "I must be going."

"But you haven't had any cheese!" I say.

"The wine was plenty, thank you."

"My heavens, don't go," Deacon pleads. "We're all on tenterhooks for your Ophelia, Sibyl."

"I left a light on in my closet."

I too beg her but she's into the hall for her umbrella. "It's been lovely," she says.

I walk her onto the front porch. "It's not always like this," I say, helping her into her coat under the porchlight. As she belts her bulges, I am erotic and want to save her from spinsterhood. She's frazzleheaded and middle-aging fast but her breasts always give me a hardon in the Prendergast. When her hand comes up to shake mine, mine passes up her raincoat. She jerks back, all alarm under the porch globe, and skips a step as she plunges into the downpour.

"I'm sure it's not," she says. Her umbrella shoots.

I know at once I'll not be going into the library for a few weeks.

Comb my florid head in the hallway bathroom, avoiding my mirroreyes, return to the living room stiffly. Everyone's at the cheese.

"We couldn't wait!" Curranne says.

My drear lungs stick wall to wall. Take a plate, still gripped by Sibyl's flit. Watch young Phil hack at cheese. Mutter, "Don't kutcherkockoff."

"I'll try not to."

Guests flop about, nibbling. I become wine missionary, pushing full glasses on all. Soothe my prickle of shame with a half-tumbler. Cry, "I want to get to my experiment!"

Curranne shrinks. "What's that?"

"Funky Hamlet. Wanta hear Ophelia's mad scene to Duke Ellington."

I find her lines for her. She says heavily, "I'd rather not do this."

Ready some records. One drops. The thick blue jungle funk of "Rainy Nights" oozes out. *"Read!"* I say.

"Where is the beauteous majesty of Denmark?" Curranne asks. Cornetist Bubber Miley backs her with a growl. "They say the owl was a baker's daughter. Lord, we know what we are, but know not what we may be. God be at your table!" Her voice, pale and sandy, the muttering cornet impish. "This really is impossible," she says.

All cry, "Go on, go on!"

Phil is enrapt. "Let me off in Harlem!"

After two more wax records, she finishes, glittering. We declare the reading ended. Anyway, everyone's too hazy to take in another word.

I tell Curranne, "I have to drive Deacon home. What shall we do?"

"Would you like to go up to my mother's cabin?" she asks coolly. Too coolly. "She's staying in town tonight."

Farewells are brief. Philip and Maxie, with little waves, part.

"It was very entertaining," Henry Hirschhorn says. "Should I say hotsy-totsy? Usually I'm not electric about Shakespeare, but I found the whole night instructive. There was a certain morbidity which would haff amused Thomas Mann."

"Too bad he couldn't make it," Greta says, winking. "Dare I ask what was going on in the kitchen?"

Before I can answer, Tony Tripi flies up, airborne. "I want to kiss you for this evening! But I won't. We've had enough of that tonight."

We step onto the porch. A cloudburst shatters the walk. A cab pulls up the duck-feathered drive for Morris and Hedda and Phil Newquist.

"Maybe we should do a Viennese *Hamlet*," Hedda says. "He's on the couch with Polonius as his analyst."

"Or in blackface!" Morris says. *"Hamlet in Alabam'."*

"Why not?" Phil asks, climbing in behind them. "Then Trueheart could play his Jolson records."

Soon we are driving Deacon home on our way to the lake cabin.

"Ahh, another evening of cultural despair in King James," Deacon says. "I must say we bring it on ourselves."

"You seemed to enjoy yourself!" Curranne says.

"My dear, I smile with equal beatitude on life and death."

"I hate that." She turns to him in the back seat, gleaming. "I like a position. Now I'm not sure I like you at all."

"Oh, I'll stand like a Greek if I have to. But my spiritual discipline doesn't allow me to discriminate—"

"Come on, say it. Don't sputter behind pomposities," she says.

"Pomposities! You wrong me. This is my little way of holding back the night. Let me pour oil on the waters, so to speak, and say that you read beautifully. Your Ophelia made the whole fiasco worthwhile."

Curranne blows out loudly. We pull up before Deacon's aunt's house.

"Let me not go to my rest tonight, or unrest as it may be, squealing with pain. Forgive old Prolixities, my dear. He'll try to do better."

"Oh, this *is* dismal. Please don't say another word."

"Ah, I'm sad." Smiling-not-smiling, he nods toward her and touches me with a heart-to-heart look of compassionate foresight, saying, "Beware the frumious Bandersnatch, my lad." I shrug to him, shaking his hand. He trudges onto his porch, no umbrella. Soon the porch light goes out.

"Drive, please"—her eyes closed. "I want to scream. He's just like Ned. This has been one of the most painful nights of my life. Ned's all words too, until you want to strangle him. And I know I want to strangle you. It was very unkind of you to insist I read that scene. Especially to that—that—*fungle* music."

"Jungle funk," I say. "What was so unkind about that? Everybody loved you."

"I was hoping to let Sibyl read that scene."

"Sibyl was gone!" But cold waves ripple my back.

"Jack, think. I'm outta the hospital one day—understand? And you want me to sit around imitating a madwoman to that disorienting—jungle sadness." She leans over. "Are you sober enough to hear what I'm saying?"

"It's very muggy . . ." Crack my window, wipe steam from the windshield. "I'm sorry. I apologize for bugging you into it."

"Maybe you didn't know you were being cruel."

"That's kind of you to say. Because I didn't."

"All right. Let's talk about something else."

"I thought Ned made TV documentaries."

"Yeah, but he talks fractured French. You want to kill. He turns you into a joke. You become part of his big joke on life. He'll have to change. All that crap will fall off like a shell, it'll have to. It's too painful to live with. Or maybe I was, and that was his defense. But he's like that with everyone close to him. I think maybe thirty's too late."

"For what?" I ask.

"Change. Do you think a really deep character change can take place after thirty?"

"I wouldn't know."

"Only for the worse, I'll bet," she states.

"Is that why you married him?"

"I was crazy."

I shut up. Her voice has a false note. I sense that Ned is a quite different man from what she says. Earlier today she drew him as wholly loving and giving. A gem.

"You drink a lot," Curranne says.

"The elixir of fluency."

"Bullshit. You're a drunk."

"Well, I chew a lot of gum." And feel an abscess being lanced.

She's quiet. Rain flails the hood, blinds the headlights. I hear my night of love plunging off into the woods. She wipes her cheeks. We're both funky.

"I don't know why I'm out with you," she says. "You're so phony I get knots in my stomach. I'm not talking about bad breath, for God's sake. Just be honest, huh? You drink too much."

That knife again! My nerves whiten. But I withdraw my anger. "Do I seem drunk now?"

Wipes my windshield steam. "I hope you're not. Just don't joke about it. Okay?"

"You don't like phonies. Who does? Even phonies hate themselves. I'll be honest—"

"Don't try. Not if you have to announce it."

I knot from ear to ear. Oh night of sex, slipping off. Then self-pity gusts. I slam the wheel.

"My God!" she says.

"I want to go to bed with you so badly!"

She pats my leg. "Don't worry."

"Make real love!"

She moves closer, arm around my neck. "Sure you do."

"It's not just sex. My whole life I've been waiting for something that never happens." Think twice, Jack. "Christ, that's awful. How could I slip into that banality? I really do want to be honest with you. But I can't *say* anything without attacking myself. Or am I inviting attack?"

Pinches my leg hard. "If I attack you'll know it." Real pain in her pinch.

Wipers thudding. In my daily hormonal madness I've been reading pop psychology books. "Did you nurse your babies?"

"I wouldn't miss that."

Dry-mouthed. "It's that fulfilling?"

"Sure. But I doubt I have the patience anymore. I sleep a lot. I'm back into running. Things pile up. Otherwise, I adore it."

Grind the steering wheel. "You adore breast-feeding?"

"And the affection."

"The *baby's* affection? Forgive me, I'm interested."

"As a writer?" She snorts. "Stop picking my brains."

"That's where your brains are?"

Another hard pinch, with a bruise to show business. I scream, jumping.

We turn off. The dirt road winds a dark half mile, bushes clashing in the rain. *Please* don't scratch the paint job.

"Pull off. Hey, don't drive on the grass!"

"I slid, I swear!"

We plod through swimming grass to the bathroom window. Curranne slides it up and climbs in, then lets me into the kitchen. The cabin is cluttered and small, walled with knotty pine, and reeks of clamminess and heady mouse and skunk. We open both doors for cross breezes and stand on the sill. Rain flogs limbs and treetops in heavy winds, but the chill braces. For safety I've brought a fresh gallon rather than a half-empty and pour two water glasses while Curranne wipes up her bathroom tracks. There's no radio, so we kiss and start stripping. She closes herself into the bathroom. Alone I feel cloven from her, and taste brackish, my eyeballs rolling. Sit in a coarsely Indian-blanketed rocker milking a cigarette, eying myself in the bathroom door-mirror. Draw back lips on purple-parted teeth, check stained tongue from afar. I see a dead-pale fat sex sot. What can she be thinking in *her* mirror, taking her hair down? The room shoots fine red fibers of illicit sex. She's separated, not divorced. I feel drained, banal, and apart from love. It's sheer lust—getting mine again, getting it tonight! I'll make you my love slave, so you'll never let me go. You'll have to kick me off. Then we'll fold up into real intimacy, I'll unroll my carpet of oriental conceits. We'll be uplifted beyond the animal. Flowing, entwined, a moment on the wind, beloved! Is she too bright for this? Boy, I love to squeeze out the heartslops when making love, little spurts of sentiment, threads of agony drawn from old loneliness, long hunger. Sweet little cons, whispered.

Turn out all light but the night-light by the bed and lay back still queasy it's not going to happen. I don't trust fate until I'm six inches in. The car this afternoon? Just skimming the cream. Tongue my acid-sharpened shark teeth. Relax grindingly into alpha. The trouble with sex is women—

. . . Softly she thumbs open my left eye. "Are you here?"

Reddish-blond mane hanging over me, gray-green eyes, shaped wolf-cheeks and hard-cut smile. Her straight fine bird-tipped nose, so wise and sexual I'm senseless, and have been all day and evening. I whisper, "I suppose I should brush my teeth."

"If you'll feel better."

"Well, I know my mother'd want me to."

We laugh. Close the door, finger my teeth with mint paste. I warn my velvet nerves, Pretend we're at the North Pole. Gather energy and return, topping my glass on the way. Hers is untouched. Look at her on the bed, her brilliance measuring me. Go into my Marine swagger.

"That stuff'll kill you." Her face by a small tasseled lampshade.

Clear my throat, sipping on bed's edge. "I'm enjoying myself. How about you?"

"I don't drink. To me, man, a clear head at any time, that's paradise. I detest the whole idea of getting pissed."

"I won't get pissed. I'm too happy." Fall back beside her. "We could have a platonic little tête-à-tête and go home."

"You'd like that?" Curranne asks.

"I might but my hormones wouldn't. They're hopping about like sand fleas."

"That's not very attractive, Jack."

"Well, you are." And I stretch out, drawing her close.

"Now, please! Open your eyes. Look at me. I'm a human being, not a car tire, dig? This is not just a naked carcass."

"It's the rain. Drives us bats batty." Pale sanded freckles, strong shoulders. "Hamlet never had it this good."

"Last warning, Jack. I'm no Ophelia, and I'm not batty. I'm bossy, demanding and aggressive."

"Jesus, I never noticed."

"And I bite." She looks aside, thinking.

"Very funny," I say. "When I saw you in the library today? I said, There's a brainy beautiful sophisticated woman . . . I'll never sleep with her in a million years. Maybe I'm scared of brainy women."

"Shows how wrong you are about so much. Brains aren't everything."

"Women are a swamp to me. Nothing I do or say is right. I lack insight. I'm ignorant—see? And I've never *met* anyone with quite your curve on the ball. Maybe it's—I don't know—what are you? *Neurotic?*"

She covers her face and turns away.

"Hey, buddy. Did I upset you?" I ask.

"No! I'm trying not to laugh. Jack, everyone's neurotic. Some just less so than others. Or at least they don't cop out on everyday life."

"I'm obsessed with writing and I cop out constantly. All my vices are in the name of research."

"It's not the same." Taps her brow.

"What's so special about your head?"

"Little bird gets out, can't get back in again."

I kiss her brow. "Back in now."

"I'm glad you think so."

"I thought your bird got out today," I say. "When you wanted to jab that woman in the library. That shook me."

"Ohh?" She falls silent. Her breath flows from a half world. I watch lungs pump, her breastbone's rise and fall. "What are you thinking?" she asks.

"Chautauqua . . . walking up North Lake Road. It was only this afternoon, but we'll never be those two people again."

"That's a blessing. I wouldn't want to live one hour of my life over again."

She spies a space heater across the room, jumps up and turns it on. *"Violà!"* she cries, over the coil, whose red Martian eye invades the room. She's smaller than I thought. Her carnal white wholeness, hair-flood, head, arms, fingers warming at the orange coil, buttocks, marvelous knee-machines, all balance on the balls of her feet. She beats her hair back from the heater screen, her face orange in the dark, and catches me eying her. "What're you thinking about?" I ask.

"How I hate it," she tells the red eye from Mars.

"Hate what?"

"I couldn't describe it."

"Well, it's not coming again?"

"No one knows. It shouldn't, if I don't get run-down," she says. "Don't get me started on this subject."

"Well, since I don't know what the subject is . . ."

"I'll get angry if I talk about it. Or depressed."

"Damn, I hate that!" I say. "Typical woman's threat. 'I'll get depressed.' Moods! They wave that big stick until I could kill."

"Look, there's nothing I can do about depression. Except stay healthy. It's not a matter of personality or the outer woman, Jack." Curranne looks at the ceiling. "It's not me. It's not my fault. It's some kind of imbalance or flaw. But once you have it you feel at fault. All the way. At fault."

My skin races. I want to help. "If you'd like, I'll listen. Maybe I can see something you don't."

"You can't, understand? I don't need more analysis. I need comfort!" Her fist clenches. "Be nice, you know, just to go to the drugstore . . . 'Some comfort, please.' Or maybe a daily iron transfusion from your husband, as if you were fighting anemia. But it really has to come from you. I've got to give it to me or I'll fall sick again. The doctors only help so much. Recovery is the wrong word for this. It's not like putting in new pistons or cleaning the sink trap. You can sludge right up again if you're not comfortable with your fears. That's not easy. The fears don't go away. You have to adjust to them."

"You're not comfortable?" I ask. *What fears?*

"I've been alone . . . so long. Three marriages, two kids, *poof.* Over and over, shut off." Tears start dripping. I move to comfort her. *"Go away!"*

Sit smoking. Still on her toes at the heater, she sobs into the bones folded over her face. I'm sad but angry, sex fading in a snap. Then my great brain roars that I can help. I move to her side, sit over her.

"Now look, let's be cool. Tell me about it. Maybe it'll go away."

She's wracked. "Go away?"

I hear warnings but plunge on. "Well, try me, for Christ's sake! I've spent my whole adult life trying to dig women so I could write about 'em. I mean it!" And I do.

Radiant contempt stones me. *"You*—understand women? I don't believe my ears. You actually think you might understand anyone? The worst writer I've ever read? Jack, you don't understand *anything* about any human being, not just women. You must be worse than Maxie. You're incredible. You just *shit* on your characters and let them *lisp* through strokes—batter 'em without a second thought. That you think you're a writer is head-spinning."

I look down. Shriveled foreskin—no cock, just balls.

"I think I'm better than Maxie," I say. "But I read you. I'm going out for a swim."

"You can't swim in this weather."

Close the door behind me, squelch to the car with glass in hand. Lie gasping over the drumming hood, my butt soaked, and try to yank the stake out of my chest. "Boy oh boy, have I met my worst critic."

The door opens. She leans on the post. "Hey, Jack? Jack? I didn't mean those things. I was upset. Make up with me. Come on in."

I wave her back. "You may have a knife."

"Hey, man, it's not you I'm so mad at. I was beating up on my second husband."

"I thought he was a gem, Curranne."

"He is! Matthew and Mark think he's the greatest father alive. I hardly rate today. They'd rather be with him. Well, up in Provincetown, you know—he paints a lot of boats. And there's the ocean."

"I'm sorry he has all those advantages. Maybe they'll love you more after you've got 'em back and show you've recovered. Uh, I don't see how they could help liking you," I lie. "They should speed your recovery."

"Being liked has nothing to do with my recovery, Jack."

"I thought it might." Drink leaning back on my elbows then cover my glass from the rain.

"Being respected, yeah," she says. "First I have to get respect. Self-respect before that, even if the whole world stops. It's stupid to think I have to be loved first. Who's loved? Are you? How many people? That's asking for the moon! First concentrate on respect."

Throw my arms wide. "So—respect pouring in while your ass warms an empty nest. That's what you want?"

"Very nice place to be."

She steps out into the big soak. Walks to me . . . a skin-shine that ripples through me, water racing down her. Her arms close on my neck. Some slick dream.

"Were you crying?" she asks.

"Ha ha ha! Who could tell out here?"

"About what I said?"

"I'll tell you, I've got a kid to cry about. If I want a good cry."

"I know how you feel."

She kisses me. Hope springs back.

"I live too much in my mind," I say.

"Where else is there to live?" She kisses me.

"Well, for sure I don't live in a bottle."

Rainy nipples press me. She chills, trembling. Her flesh is rough. I turn her quaking bones against the fender.

"Oh God, it's so cold," she says.

"C'mon." Pull her down into the mush.

We're too raw to connect.

"I've got to warm up first!" she pleads.

I try to lift her slippery body but as I reach for my glass the silk grass bounces us off the hood, raking my shin bloody. I hop with pain and lean on her into the cabin. We towel each other in the bathroom. Sit on the sink, my leg on the closed toilet lid while she daubs iodine down my welt. I'm still red from having failed myself, dropping her so heavily on the grass. How dumb drunk am I?

"This can take the gumption out of a guy," I suggest.

"I have no fears about you, Jack."

We lie on patchwork by the space heater, hip to hip, her hair in tangles. Shake my head as my shin lights up. I groan. Gray-green wonder at my pain.

"You have mermaid eyes. Let's fuck."

I'm a monstrous force and try all too briefly to rouse her before spitting on my sheath and sinking into myself on her. This one's for you, Priapus! Butt and grind into her puzzling spaces. Goat groans climb my windpipe. I force recall of hikes at boys camp, a three-day hurricane at Parris Island as a Marine boot, mess detail and scouring the steel frying ranges, lugging two- or three-hundred-pound garbage cans piled with chicken guts, my Air Force night mess hall in New Jersey, cold grease smells and bacon curled white in warming pans, dog-loneliness watching wings dottled with lights land in the green dawn. Slap and pump into that grin that bore me, sure I bring the fish-out-of-water ecstasy she hungers for. A groan opens my eyes. Her sockets rim with water. She's near, nearer, tears running.

"Oh, it hurts, it hurts! It hurts so much!"

I stop, shocked. How can it hurt?

"Oh, please stop! No more," she sobs. "I'm just raw!"

I rest inside, pained by her tears but not willing to stop.

"Just wait a minute," she sobs.

"You're not enjoying it?"

"No! Ooh, my God, can't you just come?"

I start, without asking, gently.

"Is that better?"—faulty technique. *Women!* I can't believe this.

"Oh! Oh! Oh!" She gags.

"I'm only thinking of you," I lie, believing it.

"Please! *Just come!"*

I will a red fantasy. A cold trickle leaks into my sheath.

"Thank you," I whisper beside her.

Her lips wind in grief.

"Did you come?" she asks, still tearing.

Look at my sagging sheath to make sure. "Yes. Did you?"

She wails at this, turns aside, sobbing. I hop into the bathroom to clean up (as my mother would expect?), laying the condom on the sink while I wash. When I come back she's still sobbing.

"Anything I can do?" I'm not singing.

Her face twists: a Gorgon sucks me out of myself and finds me too disgusting to swallow. I'll never recover from that look, I think. It chills me like snakebite.

"You can't help being utterly without feelings, Jack. Or *insight"*— why not rub *this* in too while she's at it? "You're probably a rapist retard."

Retarded rapist? I'm ready to cry myself blue.

"Curranne! I am not depraved. I'm perfectly normal."

Quiet eyes pierce me.

"I'm too lustful. I apologize. But sex with you is like trying to run a mile wearing handcuffs and shackles."

"Jack, you couldn't run a mile even with Marilyn Monroe waiting for you."

"I see. Well, I'm just not a monster. I'm sticking up for myself."

She's rapt, turning me on eyepoints.

"I have a warm side. Which I thought I was expressing."

I can't believe this injured milksop I hear using my voice. But he goes right on talking.

"This is wonderful," she murmurs.

"The worm turns!"

A sticky-gay agony breaks through. "It's okay, Jack, I feel better."

I sit on the bed's edge and swill a bit. "We could even get to like each other. Like standing up for each other—you know, mutual aid and comfort. I think we could. If we were open . . . Who threw you into the hospital?"

"Nobody threw me in! I committed myself."

"Oh! Because of something that happened to you?"

"Something happened, yes."

"But you don't know what?"

"I can guess."

"So unbelievable."

"Not to me," she says.

"But now you want to know what it is, or was?"

"My God, no!" she says. "I want to *avoid* it. I can't handle it, that's why I committed myself. It's bigger than I am."

"Bigger than you are?"

"Much bigger."

"But you're in analysis anyway?"

"Not right now. I have been. For nearly half my life."

"My God, that seems incredible. All these people grinding your life to pulp. You and Carol and Cornelle and your analysts and three husbands. Just for starters! Milling away at one little life."

She laughs. "It's worse. I have two sisters. I'm the middle one, the outcast." I ask and she tells me her older sister Carrie's in Wisconsin. Happily married and mothering, and the apple of her mother's eye. *One* of her mother's daughters turned out to be a good Catholic bourgeois.

"You're Catholic?" I ask.

"Most certainly not. My father was."

Her mother was a Presbyterian until he left them, then Carol converted and so did Carrie. Cornelle and Curranne went to Catholic grade school in Chicago and took catechism. Went to Mass and all that, but it never really took. Eventually they both married Jews.

"Well, I married a Lutheran and a Catholic first," she says.

"What'd your mother think of you two marrying Jews?"

"She loves all her sons-in-law. It's her two daughters who are the screwups."

"I like Carol. She's awfully sad but I like her. Must hurt raising two renegade daughters lapsed into invincible ignorance."

She punches my chest. "I'm an atheist!"

"You and Camus, huh?" Fall back, reading the rough ceiling.

"You believe in God?" Curranne asks.

"Well, I'm no atheist. Why depress myself all through life denying hope? If I'm wrong, I'll never know it. Will I?"

"Jesus, that's cynical. I like honest atheism."

"You know when you were crouching by the heater, having a long conference with yourself? I saw your spine, notch by notch. I thought, Now there is an ardent young creature. A lot of divine handiwork went into that spine. Believe me! I specialize in this."

"Specialize in what?"

"I read shoes and spines."

"Shoes and spines!"

"For somebody's spirit. I couldn't take my eyes off yours." And pinch her lightly. "When you switched the heater on, and your face turned orange, I saw the old Welsh-Irish shine out. I told myself, That girl is all spirit."

She listens silently.

"Your back is the most spiritual experience I've ever had."

"Well!" A hand encircles my neck. "Maybe you're not quite the knothead I made out."

"Nice tits, too." Jump back from her pinch.

"Rat!" She pushes me over, knuckling my ribs. When I'm crying, she kisses me. Then to my surprise she's touching me.

"No, no, you're too sore."

"Well, then, be gentle."

No sheath, I refrain from my peak. Don't even think of it. We go on and on, barely moving. I dream on my four-year-old naked from his bath and boffing around the living room at our tiny old Ashville cottage. Hurtling on little bow legs, with straight spine and burning eyes. So small, but a full physical being in this "big" room, screaming in joy, weighty and racing on the huge floor as Thelma chases him with a towel. Curranne's wide-eyed, studying me. I nip her lips and draw blood-warmth from her cheek, and linger cheek to cheek, moaning and half-awake. Abruptly, her head chills, she quakes with shock. I watch her pupils widen under a rush of water. She stares into some naked light within her. I have never seen such mad welcome in a woman's eyes. They well and blur. My heart orgasms, her charged being bare to my being.

I'm abandoned to the same grimaces, as glassy as she. At last fall side by side, flesh blended, bones mingled, warm sand figures joined by wind and cooling in late sun, wanting never to wake from this beach.

And so, more kisses and whispering. At last the rain stops, waking us. She rolls off the quilt, dances into her underwear. As her breasts drop into her bra, I fall back on the bed.

"Good God, this is impossible!" she says.

"Panties drive me crazy. They're so snug."

"Get dressed."

"Ah, another day, lad."

"Stop it," she hisses. "Promise me. No more jokes."

Drive back. Under a blue moon glaring in rags. She sits close. Suddenly she shivers. "What?" I ask.

"Just thinking. I hope we really picked up . . ."

"Does Carol smoke?"

"No. Why?"

"My butts are in the garbage. What if she does know? You're adult."

"Yeah, yeah. But shining with good behavior to get my kids back. Right?"

"Right. And getting a job?" I suggest quietly.

"I'll try. But my work history! Pregnant and married. Married and pregnant. I did some substitute teaching in the city between marriages. My mother's been very helpful. Always."

"Your father drowned, I heard you tell Phil?"

"Oh well, we never saw him much anyway. He deserted us after Cornelle was born. Mother raised us. When he died, she converted and decided not to remarry. It left her antimale. And martyred."

"Antimale? She's very warm to me."

"Ha! she's buddies with your sister. You don't really know her. My nut is being the middle daughter. Getting cracked between Carrie and Cornelle. She esteems Carrie for her middle-class blahs and forgives Cornelle everything for her youth. My father and mother both blocked me out. My father hated my temper. And before I really grew up, he was gone. Today my mother buys me off, while wishing I was in Johannesburg. And Carrie and Cornelle are pretty cool characters too. I'm hard to be around, huh? Maybe you noticed? I question everything right to the bone."

"That's just a mask," I say. "You're all heart."

"*Ha!* Hey, Jack, I can't help it, dig? I'm absolutely tactless. I can't bear to hold back."

"You sure swing from the floor."

"I have an enormous temper. That's my earliest memory. Blowing up. I'd get my way or be heartless to everyone. I'd just stand there punching."

"Beating up on yourself?"

"Sure, there's some of that. Inferiority feelings, et cetera, so what?"

"I get a vague gleam of your mother's problems."

She's silent. Something shifts within.

"I've destroyed, I mean estranged, everyone. I know she blames me for my father's leaving. Who'd want to live with me in the house? Never knowing when a drawer's going to come flying."

"If you don't blow off steam you'll go crazy."

"If I *do,* I do."

"Well, you must know. But I haven't seen anything sick in you. You've kept cool with me. Though you have a way with words that's like getting hit by a chair."

"I'm sorry," Curranne says timidly.

"Oh, I deserve every syllable."

The lake is blue silver under a breaking moon.

Peace, peace. We've gone through a lot in the last fifteen hours. I feel caring, but she's keeping back, with little hidden looks. That measuring eye! Then I see some tears and pull off and give her my shoulder. A shadow uncovers the moon. The hood sears. I'm no longer fearful of her, though I don't discount her warning about biting.

We rest face to face. I touch the chipped shine of her temple. She gleams with questions, sees someone I don't know under my skin. My self falls away and I open to her tongue. Her hand shapes my head and neck. We sit cleansed by the moon.

The soft hiss and wind-shear of leaves. She leans against me, listening.

"An angel is passing," I say.

"I thought it was the wind."

" 'Shows how wrong you are about so much.' "

"Oho! That devilish already? I've warned you. You may be in for a terrible shock."

"Why?"

"You really care." She nods.

My heart shakes. "Why shouldn't I?"

"Why should you? You're such an old piece of Marine bootleather."

My sinuses prickle. My soul takes its deepest breath in years.

"I'm pretty thick. Something of a retarded rapist. But at least I don't bite. You do?"

"Monday through Friday."

"But not with your mouth, huh?"

Draw her head to my chest, rub her hair with my cheek.

"Hey-y, you have something in here, Jack. I hear it."

"Right through bootleather?"

"I should!—it's loud enough," she says. "You're all heart. And when you trim that moustache, you'll be on your way."

I stroke her where she's light and feathery. Her arms circle me again, nothing withheld. "Thanks, coach." A bud hardens, pulsing. Those eyes!—no more mad than mine. Clasp and kiss. My brain detaches, floating off.

"I can't believe my luck!" I whisper fiercely. "I like you. Can you guess how much?"

She stretches with a smile. "I'll think about it."

"You look like an opera chorus getting ready to sing."

"Well," she says. "I want to do something. But it feels sinful."

"What's that?"

"That's for me to know," she says. "Are you really single?"

"I have passed through the stomach of the crocodile and emerged a free New Yorker."

"Thelma was a crocodile?"

"I *mean* New York divorce law. Subsection: Annulments."

"Wel-l-l!"—palms flat on the roof. "I feel like swimming. You really think you like me?"

Hold her breast, kiss her ear.

"I wouldn't want to be taking advantage of you," Curranne says.

"How's that?"

"Well, you know. Two kids, twice divorced—almost. You may not even call me tomorrow."

"The phone system may break down."

"With that moustache you must have pretty girls all over the place."

"I'll clear the woods of them."

"Oh, there really are some?"

"Sibyl Meadows. But she won't give me a tumble."

"She must be ten years older than I am. Hmm! Anyone else?"

"Well, your sister Cornelle. But I haven't seen her for ten years."

"Good. Finders keepers."

"That goes two ways. Someone's finding *you.*"

"Yeah-h," she whispers.

Hold her hard, seeing the lissom ridges of her spine by the glowing space heater. My saliva runs like milk into a breast. I hope like a beggar.

"Don't hold back," I say.

"I'm not. That's what's so sinful!"

"Straight shooters?"

"Yep."

"Straight shooter is tough woman."

"Do you think so? Y'know what I want? I want to be a tough, flexible whole human being! *Oh my God.* I've got to get home. My mother'll have the police out."

We drive into the dark town. I'm so happy I want a cigar.

"Your feet make me awfully sexy, Mrs. Chaplin."

"Confess, don't repress." She pats my knee.

"It's your soles. When you were crying on the bed, they looked so bare and arched. Spiritual!"

"I'll never think of them the same again."

"Hey, tomorrow I'm covering a shindig at North Warren State Mental Hospital. The inmates are having a stage show. Like to come along?"

"Oh, I couldn't bear it. I *never* want to see another sanitarium. Even from the air. Have you ever been to a mental hospital?"

"Nope, I'm all virgin." We park at her mother's. "Wonderful night, my love. Thank you. I don't know what we've decided about anything, but I want to be there for you."

She nods, gripping my hand. "I want you there."

I shoot her some staunchness. Her eyes accept. We hug, not kissing. Suddenly her breath is a long sandy outpouring on my ear, a breath that streams over my heart. She goes through shadows to her mother's porch in the moonlight.

PART TWO

North Warren
State Hospital

I awake, Tom Turkey thwacked by a hatchet but not dead. Through sheets drying by my bed, my robed mother talks to me, her tone raw-edged. "There's someone here to see you."

In some long-vanished roomer's castoff robe, I thud blindly into the laundry sinks, rinse crust from bloody eyes, fingercomb flying spikes. Early first light through cellar windows. Brain leakage of any gain from three hours' sleep. Be of good cheer! You have a wonderful day of novelizing to sun in. But yesterday's body costs are great. Robe tight I step onto the front porch for one cold breath in gummy lungs. Not a car abroad, our great firs deep-shadowed. Light needles me. Good Christ. I'll never hit writing stride today.

A bolt strikes. Curranne's mother, Carol, smokes and coffees with my mother at the befogged kitchen table. Carol I know doesn't smoke! *Hello,* I smile wanly, and go straight to the fridge for red-hot sauce. Slurp a chill tablespoon of salt-fire over my shrunken tongue. Focus like Tolstoy on filling a cup with black steam from Mother's chromium electric perk. Descend to the table, barely clinging to waves between tide rocks of mother and mother. Unshaven Jack, naked in faded hand-me-down. The manhood in my eyes a skim of dried eggwhite. "Hi."

Smoke-thick silence.

"Early isn't it?"

"It's seven, my son."

"That's early."

My steam has a husky, woody taste. The Cheddar from our Shakespearean hijinks sits on the counter, hacked and tragic.

Mother announces, "I cleaned up."

"So I saw when I got home. Thank you. I'd've done it."

"Unh! I couldn't face that mess first thing out of bed." She tamps a king-size on the table to pack the already tailormade tip. Lights up. Stands her purple Ronson beside an ashtray fresh with doubled and squashed stubs. Observes my silence. "Or have my guests see it."

"Join you," I say, and light up. Smoke seizes my brain cells. My pupils cramp. Delicious.

My mother's head drops onto her fist, damming her tears. She looks up and glances away quickly, her sigh bursting. I sit Homeric with misdeeds. My nerves sting. On which side will the surgery start? I inventory objects, waiting. My mother's red chenille robe striped with fuzzy cords, her mercilessly judging eight-edged rimless glasses, blowup blue eyes under an unbrushed burst of gray streaks. The age and faded valiance she and Carol share in their worldwide disappointment in men and other weights without end or number. Small, dumpy Carol's plaid suit and tweed bucket, faintly merry cinnamon eyes filmed with heartbreak. She limps from polio but will not carry a cane. Cornelle has her smiling-through-tears rue and spunk. Curranne has the cutting edge. But now Carol's hacksaw eye starts in on my scalp, forehead, nose. It's only 7 A.M.! And already I'm popped inside out, untimely ripped from my mother's cellar, a dirty glove to be soaped and squeezed.

"At this rate." I gulp tobacco fumes. "We may all fall asleep."

Mother's mouth, a brass nameplate. "My young man, we have not been asleep all night—either of us!"

"I'm sorry. I sense that I'm the odd fellow around this watering hole—" Blood climbs my neck.

"We don't need your humor, my son."

Carol lifts her ton of silence. "I don't see anything funny, Stella."

"—and am about to be rubbed to shreds by two moralizing mother elephants." I blaze, shamed to the ears—and brazen.

"You don't deserve it!" Carol asks, or says.

"Or worse!"

"Worse?" I ask.

Mother falls back in her chair, stoned. *"Where in God's name is your horse sense?* Sometimes—ohh!—I can't believe you still have the brain you were born with." Slaps the table. "You take my breath away!"

"What's wrong?" I husk, turning my double-face to each.

Mother sways. "Don't you realize anything?"

"You can get quite a long term for taking advantage of a mental incompetent," Carol says.

"Curranne's incompetent? She's the most intelligent woman I've ever met."

"This is now her second day out of Gallinger," Carol says.

"Right! What was she doing down there?"

"She didn't tell you? I'm surprised. She was committed there at her own request. She wanted to be near that poet at St. Elizabeths."

"Ezra Pound? She didn't mention it."

"Or that they let him out and kept her?" Carol smiles.

"Nope. Why near *him?*"

"They think they're economists."

"Economists? Well, she still doesn't seem deranged to me. No more than most people."

She grunts an unhappy laugh. "She is, Jack. Believe me!"

"She seems to have realistic goals."

"Will you keep quiet and listen?" Mother says.

"As for using my cabin, don't do it again. A repeat performance of last night and you'll go to jail. If I can arrange it."

"What's this about a cabin?" Mother asks me.

Silent longing for the beach at Chautauqua.

"Answer me, buster."

Jesus, I need a shave. Carol waits through my short-winded crackle of phlegm and smoke.

"Oh! We went for a drive up the lake."

Deep tabletop study. Wipe sugar grains into my palm.

"In that storm?" Mother asks.

"Well, it let up. And we wound up at the cabin—for coffee. All very innocent."

Mother droops under crossed palms, then rears back stricken. "This is like something you read about in the paper and wonder where the police were. Do you want detectives showing up here? Can't you think? A woman even a little crazy is—"

"I really didn't know what I was getting into. We just wanted to talk."

"Then why'd you go to that cabin? You could have talked right here in the living room."

"We drove Deacon home. Then there was no other place to go."

"It sounds all very funny."

"We were right there. It was perfectly natural, not like *housebreaking.* Just a literary chat. For an hour. Cleaned up, put the pot away. We left the place spotless, didn't want to worry . . . anyone."

"Well," Carol says. "There are big ruts in my yard—"

"Ah, did we do that?"

"—and you left your empty Trojan foil on the bedstand. That worried me. And the used condom on the bathroom sink."

The trap falls. White shock. Oxygen-starved, my brain shrinks to walnut meat.

The phone rings.

"Oh my God, I can't answer it!" Mother says. "But I must." She marches to the living-room highboy and returns. "It's her."

I walk a bridge of sighs to the phone.

"I haven't gone to bed yet," Curranne says.

I can't speak. I cover the speaker against my chest and slug down a huge half-tearful breath.

"I barely got in and out myself. I'm a little unbalanced. You don't sound tired." My natural voice carries to the pregnant kitchen.

"I sat up writing a poem. Those are my best hours. My worst too, because I should be in bed. I need eight hours minimum. But I think I finished it."

"Terrific. Why don't you lie down for a while and look it over when you get up? Eight hours will give you perspective—poems are sneaky. Very sneaky." All life is sneaky.

"I want to show it to you."

"I haven't shaved." My pulse clogs. "I'm going to North Warren at five. I'm not sure when I'll get back."

"Maybe I'll go with you after all."

A rockslide thickens underfoot. "That's up to you."

"Don't you want me to?"

"You said it might upset you."

"But I want to show you my poem! If you don't want me to come—"

"I do, I do!" I don't, I don't.

"Five?"

"Mm."

"Not before?"

"I should work on my novel."

"You want to pick me up?"

"It's only three blocks, Curranne. Why don't you drift over when you feel ready? And get some sleep meanwhile."

"Five. Maybe I'll be early."

"Up to you. I'm only retyping. I fear there'll be nothing fresh today."

Stare down the living-room depth, recalling her stance, weighing my tie with her. Wringing my spirit for a way out. Such a big bad dream.

"I didn't know you wrote poetry," I say.

"Oh, reams. That's what helps me go on."

"I wish I could say that. It'd be wonderful to have poetry."

"For what?" she asks.

"For life-support. Instead of staggering through novels that are outgrown before they're done. It's more dismal to abandon a novel than a poem."

See her stretching in the library. The nose that enslaves me. Far-seeing eyes, wise smile—reading me to my backbone.

"Are you all right?" she asks.

"Oh, sunny. But this is a long bitch. Great fatigue near the finish line—just when you need absolutely everything going for you. Today I've got fuzzy eyeballs. Is the sun up yet?"

"Oh, I've called you too early!"

"No, no. I have a hook-and-cable that lifts me outta bed every morning . . . to face my manuscript."

"Why are you talking like this?"

"Well, you don't *like* my novel! Four years work hit by a wrecking ball. It leaves me sorta weepy."

"Oh, don't listen to me."

"Ah, but I do. I respect you. Too much! It's like getting blue-penciled by Pound, only the pencil lops off everything after the title."

"I knew him."

"How well I know. Okay, I'm falling back in bed for another hour. Maybe the Divine Wind will slip into my sheets. I dunno if that's a pun or a prayer."

"I'm going to type up my poem."

"Breathe each phrase."

"See you at five?"

"If you wish. I want you to think very carefully about this. I've never been to this place. I haven't the slightest idea what it's like."

"What what's like?"

"Fifteen hundred crazies."

"Why are you going?"

"For the music fest. As I hear it's the first of its kind."

"I doubt that. That's not new at all."

"Fill me in. But right now, bed! Farewell, anon et cetera."

"Wait! Do you still like me? You're not mad, my calling this hour?"

"Yes I do, I'm not. _Bed!_—both of us."

"Okay. I'm happy. See you."

"Bye-bye. But I'm not taking you anywhere unless you get some sleep!"

"See ya."

Kitchen silence. Water falling in a cavern. Sip my coffee.

"Well, I can't absolutely _not_ see her, can I? When she wants to see me?"

"I've told you before and I'm telling you again," Mother says. "You keep that thing in your pants. Do you hear me?"

JACK TRUEHEART JAILED
BOFFS MENTALLY INCOMPETENT
MOTHER OF TWO

"I think I'll go to bed. Maybe this will all—" Silence. "Maybe she won't come!"

Carol studies my pencil-stripe moustache. "And if she does?"

Cross my heart to her and hold up two Scout's Oath fingers. She smiles vaguely and with some part of Curranne's mind sees straight through me. A grievous smile, all my sins raised at a glance.

FAILED NOVELIST HELD WITHOUT BAIL

"Unh!" Mother gasps. "I can't even say that word."

"What word?" I ask.

"I'll say _Trojan_ instead! I suppose we can thank God for small favors."

I get up.

"Sit down," Carol says.

Follow advice. Light up.

"I love Curranne. She doesn't think so. But I do, and right now she's wholly dependent on me. I'll skip the preamble. You've known her one day—"

"And she has a will of steel! That is no weak ego. When she lays into me, I shake."

"Shut up," Mother says.

"—one day! *I've* known her thirty-three years. She's my smartest, no question. She thinks she's a poet and writer, but she burns everything she writes. I don't understand half the stuff anyway. Maybe the poetry, a little. But dizzy tirades about banking and lending, world manipulation by Chase Manhattan, and about Rockefeller, that devil's eyeball, his schemes and frauds—she's as crazy as the next lunatic. I *listen.* But if you touch the wrong spot, she swells up like King Kong. It's the Message. She's got to get it out, but then writes it in code to protect her children. It's not that she can't write. Even after her first breakdown, she made Phi Bete at Columbia pre-med."

"She wanted to be a doctor!" Mother says.

"A profession would be nice," I croak. "Being a doctor sounds like heaven to me."

"She wanted to be White House surgeon-in-residence so she could sterilize the Oval Office daily," Carol says. "She blames the banks for her failure, but really she got married and pregnant. She's been arrested twice in Chase Manhattan for disturbing the peace. She took out a safe deposit at the Bank of America, loaded it with rotting hamburger and never went back."

I jump, smelling that meat. I know nothing about economics but have read *Don Quixote.* Curranne's idealism has appealing logic.

"She's been active," Mother says coolly.

"She's obsessed with credit-banking. Installment buying, illusions of ownership—she'll track blood all over you about 'em." Carol eyes me. "Spengler and Veblen?"

"*Way* over my head. I've never owned a checkbook."

"None of this is real!" Mother makes plain to me.

"It sounds real to me! Okay, she's against credit. And worldly goods, for all I know."

"No, just banks. They let her down," Carol says.

"And her father let her down?"

"Ed drowned."

"She thinks he let her down. It's a big fact to her," I say.

"She feels he did."

"And she gets back at him by attacking banks?" I ask.

"If you're interested, she'll let you know all about it. Don't ask unless you want the Message."

"What message?" Mother asks.

"The gist of it is that usury is the spiritual foundation of America. Or maybe of mankind," Carol says.

Mother eyes me carefully—have *I* got the message?—then taps the table. "What does that word mean, my son? I can bear anything today."

"Usury? Loan-sharking."

"Oh. Thank you. I thought it might mean . . . about women and state lines . . . and *illegal purposes."*

"That's white slavery, Stella," Carol says.

"Don't tell me any more. I'd rather not know."

"I can see how someone might get carried away by usury," I say. "Was Ed in real estate?"

"He was in the merchant marine. But he drowned down in Florida on a fishing trip. Curranne went to his funeral but doesn't remember it. She thinks I lie to her about it. Her idea of when he died can change by ten years from one day to the next. Don't ask about him . . . she can be hard on furniture."

"That I've heard! She warned me herself. But that's better now."

"It's been worse."

"Oh, she'll never do that again," I say. "I can't help thinking well of her. We get along like normal people! Nothing bizarre, no antisocial acts. Well, one umbrella massacre she didn't carry out. I think she values sanity. Really wants to be respected for it. Maybe the worst *is* past."

"You stay out of this!" Mother groans. "I get butterflies just thinking of you two together."

"Wait a minute. You lived with a raging maniac for twenty years."

"We're talking about you, my son. Let's not get sidetracked."

"Yeah, but was he cuckoo or not?"

"Don't remind me!"

"Well, did she force Ed out of the house?" I ask.

"He left for work," Carol says. "He was a sailor. He left and left and left. Sailors vanish for long periods."

"She thinks her temper tantrums drove him out."

"He left over and over and she had tantrums. Two facts, totally unrelated."

"But not to her, huh? You'd think she'd be able to understand this."

"Understanding has nothing to do with it. Not anymore, if it ever did. She's quite sick."

"Oh, you can see it in her," Mother says. "A blind man could see it."

"I must be blind. Do you think she's hopeless?"

"I don't think about tomorrow. I've heard of spontaneous remission in the middle thirties. People letting go of their symptoms. It's not common. I just try to help her bear up today. There's less disappointment."

"Okay, you don't think about tomorrow. But she does."

"I'm talking about me, Jack, Carol Garrity. Curranne is rowing her own boat. She's thirty-three. Someday she'll be fifty. I've been seeing doctors and guiding her through hospitals since World War II. How long can I hold her hand?"

"Well, she thinks you're very generous. I think she has reasonable desires and expectations."

"There are drugs that could help. But she'll always question her mental balance."

"It's the same as mine right now," I say.

"I really don't think so! Hers is quite provisional. I don't think you should see her. You offer a lot of problems." Her palm rises. "Don't ask what they are. Artists make her sick, let it go at that."

"Geniuses?"

"If she can't compete, she'll turn on you. So forewarned is forearmed, right? If she gets out of hand, don't try to stop her. Let it run its course. She's very strong. She could walk up and down stairs on her hands for her father. And when he died, she went into a rage she's never come out of. Not that she wasn't violent before. Sooner or later she'll know you're going to ship out—"

"Ship out?"

"Ship out, skip out. That's when you're on your own."

Mother says, "My God, my head's in a whirl!"

"Thank you. I'll avoid banks."

Carol shrugs, rising. "That should be the easy part. Thanks for the java, Stella. Gotta open my office or I'll be in the poorhouse like a shot off a shovel."

We walk her to the door.

"Let me thank you again, Carol," I say. "I'm sorry for everything that's happened to Curranne."

"Just don't lie to her. She once sat in the tub for a day and a half. She wanted to visit Ed by submarine, I think. I finally got her out by telling her Ed was home. We soon wished she was back in the tub. I haven't lied to her since. Just by omission."

"Oh, I'm frightened of her, just standing here. I shouldn't see her! But she has to see someone. You can't warn off every man she meets. And she will meet 'em. I'd like to ride along for a while. I like her. If I were entrenched in my cowardice, I wouldn't see her. But you know she hasn't a friend in town. And she likes me, for all my faults. I want to help. I don't want it on my conscience that I was too lily-livered to give her a hand. Or that I sent her out sleeping around town until she found some guy who'd put up with her. She's out for help, and there is absolutely no likelihood of her finding a woman friend. I don't know! Maybe I'm wrong. But I don't want to chance it. She reaches me."

She clamps me in a smile. "Everything is against you, Jack."

"Curranne thinks that!" My fist pounds the door frame. "I don't give a damn!"

"I can't do more," Carol says. "The rest is up to you."

"My son will act like a perfect gentleman."

Carol laughs, working sidewise down the front steps, no cane. "I hope not. They're the really sick ones." She limps off jauntily.

Mother takes my arm, standing me back from her. Her face twists. "Such foolishness! Oh, such foolishness! What are you getting yourself into?" She grips me, near tears. "Think of me if you can't think of yourself, John. I see it all now."

"I don't. I'm sorry you feel this way. I'm going to bed."

She goes into her bedroom off the kitchen. I go downcellar. The windows glow as I climb into my sheets, smelling the must and soap fumes. She crouches before the space heater, her long calf and back muscles edged, her spinal ridge the great root of her being. She catches me looking. My heart tries to squeeze out of me. Then I fall through the sheets, sleep like a germ.

Papers rustle. I bolt up, my brow hitting her lip.

"You're here!"

"Oh, I didn't mean to wake you. I wanted to leave my poem on your pillow," she says softly, and sits half dazed on the bed. Her eyes are lively and spent. She looks better than I feel.

I lift the poem. "It's a billet-doux?"

"No! Boy, do you have a big ego." Touching her swelling lip.

"Then I won't read it. Your lip hurt?"

She licks it. "Not bad. I'm sorry I scared you."

"Sorry I clipped you. Where's Mother?"

"I didn't see her."

"Must be sleeping."

Gingerly, she kisses me. I lick her little lip bump. She fingers back my hair. "Pleased?"

"Look," I say, snapping her poem with a nail. "Next time sweet nothings or forget it."

"You're not happy to see me?"

"Not very."

"Why not?"

"That's for me to know. Do I have to have a reason for every little thing?"

A fist rises. "Where d'ya want it?"

I back away. "You can't hit me."

"Why can't I?"

"I haven't shaved. You'll skin your knuckles."

Delight fades to worry. "Maybe I shouldn't be here. The screen door was unlocked."

"For the guests. Have no fear."

Clamp her thigh, drawing her closer. She glances about my window-glower uncertainly. Her smudged lids madden me. Greta Garbo!

"My life has taken a great advance, Curranne Garrity."

"Has it now? What kind of advance?"

"I dream of you."

"Poor thing. What am I doing?"

Shut tight, looking. "Knee-bends; side-straddle hops; touch your toes."

"Well! What am I wearing?"

"A nice smile!" Pull back from the pinch.

Beyond hanging sheets the great squat gas furnace comes on with a heavy *whoof.* Huge asbestos tubes gargle and branch through the dimness. I pull up her bare leg and kiss the knee.

"I haven't brushed my teeth. But your knee can't tell. Can it?"

"It's very sensitive."

Throw back the sheets to get dressed.

"For God's sake, put on your robe."

"Nope."

"I think you have a serious disorder."

We hear Mother's footsteps on the stairs. Curranne throws my brindle robe at me, whispering, "I have to be a model mother!"

Stella carries sheets into the far laundry and starts stuffing the washer.

"Sneak up! I'll see you at five. Get some sleep!"

We kiss. She weighs my face searchingly.

"Measure up?"

"Don't ask disappointing questions," she says.

Loafers in hand she climbs upstairs to the washer's hum. At the turn she looks back, a still marble smile peering into my spine. I fall back, sitting on my bed. She's gone.

"It's nineteen fifty-eight and I'm only a kid of thirty," I say aloud.

"Did you say something?" Mother asks from the laundry.

"Only talking to myself."

"Don't do too much of that!"

Moustache zipped off and poem in hand, sit on the front porch with a burgundy cooler, wet-combed, in white shirt, sharp black chinos and white suede hospital shoes. Hidden are gartered black socks, and boxer shorts for a free swing. Be Ready. After dry spells sex comes in clusters. As with alcohol, accept everything offered. It's research, not hypocrisy. SLOP IT UP! that's my motto. Sipping, eroticized, I'm a magnetic hormonal cloud ready to discharge into the nearest female nervous system. A crippled old granny on the street might be rare apple brandy in bed. I weigh all women, none escape. A blond young well-to-do passing in a Caddie spears me with rosy yearnings. In this pink cloud I am Byron longing for sunset canals, the old whore of Venice. I focus on the sheets on my lap, fall through Curranne's lines.

Goodbye, Captain Hook

When the sea of childhood
took you back, back
away from me,
I wrapped
my stone kisses
in silver foil.

Where are you?
Washed on some beach

of thunderstones?
Or are you
the ghost
of a ghost
of a ghost?

Wanderer,
I dialed you
through the nights
of my night
when the fossil sun
rose behind
cloud cover

when no voice
broke through asking
if the call
was collect.

Wonderfully sane, I think. But only a sketch for a poem. How severe should I be? She's gonna burn it anyway.

At five the chimes tear me from my wine and typing. Tall in heels, she's balanced on one hip beyond the screen, slim and full in a cinched sleeveless turquoise dress. A sky-blue Angora sweater over her arm, she brightens as I open the screen. Gray eyes ringing with daylight, her face bountiful and hair freshly ponied, skin glowing and well slept and cheeks blooded from her walk. Her spirit is naked and thrust forward. She is aflood, her mind flowing. I follow her into the living room, my eyes shut with disbelief at her bloom of hip and show of mountain-spring intelligence.

"Pardon me while I faint. Should I rent a tux for this?"

"I'm overdressed. But I want to be sure. Did you read it?"

"I always judge a book by its cover."

"My *poem!*"

"Oh! Very impressive. Let's talk about it in the car."

She stiff-arms me gently. "Now listen."

"I liked it very much! I want a copy. It's not all there yet . . . some parts I couldn't understand. The thunderstones—what're they? Gravestones?"

"Gravestones? They're the *stones* that fall from heaven in thunder-bolts."

"My God! That's hair-raising. I gotta read it again. I thought it was all more of a catharsis than a poem. It seems so personal."

"If it's not personal, why bother?"

"But then in fifty years it can't be understood without footnotes—if it can even be understood now."

"I'm not writing for universities! Poetry is blood, Jack. That's what's wrong with this one. It's not personal enough. All the literary crud gets in the way. It's pasted over with poeticisms. I work like a bloody demon to get rid of them, but I can't. More roll in! Be honest with me, Jack. You can't be harder on me than I am myself."

"Boy, you have high standards. Is that why you burn 'em?"

"My poems? Who said I burn them?"

"Oh, Carol told me."

"When'd she say that?"

"This morning. I fear she's been out to the cabin. I left an empty Trojan foil on the bedstand."

"I-yi-yi!"

"And a used sheath on the bathroom sink. *Sorry*"—thumping my head.

Her jaw drops. "What'd she say? I won't get angry."

"She was pretty calm. It was my mother who *phfft!"*

"I'm sorry for you," she says. "And I'm embarrassed all to hell. What'd my mother *say?"*

"A lot! But mainly that I did something criminal."

"What? I won't get angry."

"Took advantage of an unstable woman."

"I'm so angry I could scream."

"I wish you wouldn't."

She sighs dizzily, then circles the living room, her hands knotting and unknotting. "I'm not angry. I'm not angry. I will not get angry. I will control myself. Oh my God, your mother will never respect me again! Where is she now?"

"Oh, chewing the rag at Liz's."

"I'll bet. Well, Liz will stick up for me. Won't she?"

I hold Curranne lightly. "I explained to her—and to Carol."

"I can never come here again! What did you explain?"

"My feelings! I said that I liked you very much, very deeply. And that I wanted to be your friend. I was very strong about it. I hit 'em with a hammer."

"But this is my life you're talking about! What right do you have? I will not get angry. I will not blow up. HAHHH! Oh, I feel better. That's amazing. I didn't blow the roofbeam."

"Honey—I mean Curranne, you can get angry if you think you have to."

"I'm sorry. It's your life too. Of course you could say whatever you had to say. I'm okay. I just felt this big emotional leap being made for me. Going public before I'm ready. You really had your back to the wall. I'm very proud of you. She told *your mother* she found a used rubber?" Her tongue flies out. "I think I'm going to cry. Help me."

I embrace and soothe her but her eyes rim, spilling. She clasps me, shaking silently. "You're such a good fella," she says. "I know you stood up for me."

"For us."

"Do me one last favor. Brush your teeth."

"I just did!"

"Well, do it again. And don't drink anymore tonight. I want to faint when you breathe on me."

"Jesus, that's awful. Be right back."

I blush burgundy in the bathroom mirror. Tight-pupiled pink and blues, not the old Trueheart . . . She's sitting straight up, legs crossed, on the couch. I could die for those legs. Sit by her. She smiles but shakes her head.

"It's so unfair," she says, turning, and stares through my brain. "It's so hard for a divorced or separated woman. The goddamn sex cabal. You've got to be an untouchable teenager even for permission to look sexy. I can't risk it anymore, Jack. I could be—something bad could happen. One wrong word, I'm kaput."

"Carol won't throw you out."

"I won't get my kids back! A bad rep is all they have to hear."

I kiss her fingers and give her a hug. Do I want her to get her kids back? "Let's not be late. Better go."

"I'm not going."

"Why not?"

"You don't want me to go. I could tell on the phone."

"Yeah? When you called I was in this elephant stampede in the kitchen. That's why I wavered. But I've made up my mind now."

Hard hug, heavy kiss. She lights up, knuckling my ribs. Then she bites a finger, I think holding back tears. "Christ, that's worth a poem!" she half-weeps.

"What is?"

"That rubber!"

We fall into a jiggling fit, popeyed.

"You should have seen their faces," I say. "A morbidity that would haff amused Thomas Mann."

"It'll be a relief, getting out of King James for a few hours."

Driving out of town we pass a thousand bars where I touched glasses with my first drinking buddies, a comradeship now dark as the Russian empire. I catch sea-brilliant turquoise and blue Angora, breathe her scent, see her womanly knees. Something in me cuts loose, I float in her light. We go up the steep bricks of South Main in the leafy May evening. Cherished songs and faces from old couch passions rise and fall away. World War II and Korea break off, drop into darkness. I feel the heat of a new start in the library and in yesterday's welding at Chautauqua. The sky opens as we crest South Main and enter a passionate twilight dimmed by the windshield's green tint. Venus pierces us, pressing down on far Warren.

"There's your star."

"We're going north?" she asks.

"South."

"Then that's not Venus. You're disoriented."

The earth's edge, backlit with skyglow, lifts a full moon so faint we see the heavens through it. I ride with my love through early evening.

"How do you feel? Do you think you're cured?"

"You're never cured. You adjust."

"But you still need analysis?"

"All my analysis does is put me face to face with the problems. I have to work them out myself. Nobody can hand me the answers, I wouldn't believe them. *I* have to dig them out, and through a lot of pain, believe me."

"Maybe that makes them worth having."

"Well, nobody can *convince* me of anything. But if I take directions I may work my way through. You don't know anything about this?"

"Less and less."

The deep Chadakoin beside us hugs its jungly hillside and sheer banks. We glide restfully.

"It's my best shot, analysis. The doctor I'm supposed to start with in Manhattan is in Europe this summer. He wrote a book on Mahler."

"On Mahler! I dig Mahler."

"I'll lend it to you. Theodore Reik, no relation to Wilhelm. He thinks music helps understand his patients. So I'm on my own."

"He takes vacations from patients who might have breakdowns?"

"They all do. I've got to stand on my own. It's part of recovery."

"He should be shot."

"Cynicism doesn't help, Jack, and I don't give in to it. I just keep writing poems. They help. They really help. Boy, am I hungry. Are we going to eat?"

"We'll find something. I'm happy poetry helps."

"I don't dig in enough. It's the same poem over and over, no matter what I write. The same dumb message comes up."

"Maybe you try too hard. Sometimes when you look away from a problem, the answer sneaks in from another direction."

We pass a tall radio tower in the twilight. It snatches out my soul, plunging me into childhood movie serials.

"Hey, I love talking with you. Do you realize I haven't thought about sex for thirty minutes?"

"Don't flip out!"

"God damn it."

"What?"

"I forgot the wine."

"Are you fishing for praise? Thank you for not bringing it. How's that?"

"Thanks. Maybe I'll grow up one of these years."

She moves closer.

"You're always writing about your father, huh?"

"Yeah."

"Because he skipped off and drowned?"

"I don't know. Gradually he just wasn't there and we all stopped talking about him. He was gone before he drowned. He stopped speaking to me or telling me anything. Then his face sort of vanished, and then he disappeared."

"You never ask Carol anything?"

"Sure I ask. She says he deserted us and may have died at sea. She doesn't know. She makes up stories! But he sure isn't coming back.

The merchant marine lost so many ships during Lend-Lease. I'm certain he was on one."

"There wasn't any telegram?"

"*Nnh.* Maybe he changed his name. Runaway husbands do. Frankly, I wish he'd slipped and drowned in the bathtub. I've never mourned him. I hate him so much I can't mourn."

"Boy, we get bound up in dead issues," I say.

"Dead issues aren't dead, they're killers. You can't just bury them unexamined. They rot."

"You're not suicidal?"

"Oh, man, I couldn't lay that on my kids. Not after my father abandoning us. Hand my sickness on to them? I'm not cruel. Of course, they could get sick anyway. That's not a happy thought. Hah! did you hear that growl? I'm really fading. I didn't have breakfast. Is it much farther?"

"They'll have food at the party. Hang on."

A black Cadillac gusts by and wings into the hills.

"Look at those tailfins. Bastard!" she sneers.

"Sonofabitch! *Confess, don't repress!*"

We glow.

"What'll I do with you in Manhattan? I'm ready to cut my wrists already. I even find your mind sexy—I'm not kidding."

"I know, you think I keep it in my bra."

"I don't mean that. I mean sitting here with you is like having my sinuses suddenly open up."

"You think that isn't sex? How little you know."

"How many of my sex thoughts have any reality at all? Now, breast-feeding. Why am I so attracted to that?"

"Breast-feeding can be a drag."

"I'd find it fulfilling."

"Not if you had all the caring and rashes and sensitivity and muscle fatigue. You drip, you're drained, you smell of bacteria."

"Can't talk me out of it."

"You think I get my rocks off with babies? I'd hate to have to depend on that for my satisfaction."

Frewsburg comes and goes like a scrap. Despite her hunger, the roadhouses we pass don't tempt us.

"I meant that. What'll I do when you leave?"

"We've only known each other two days, Jack."

"Don't try to be reasonable! You know I love you."

"This is pretty sudden."

"Like hell."

"Fight it."

"I don't fight, I confess."

Catch her wedding rings, the dim stones brilliant with the past. Her fingers long and resourceful. What have they held?

"You have beautiful hands. Like a surgeon's."

"Don't remind me. I was going to be a surgeon. Then I hit a couple of hairpin turns—and woke up as someone I didn't know. Twice."

"I'm sorry. I get this yearning to forget everything and start fresh. Wake up new."

"Wake up new!? Not when you wake up nobody. And believe me, not twice! Not when you think other people are thinking you up. People not looking at you, only sideways. And you're nobody anyway. Are you even here? Maybe you don't really exist, except in their minds. You're just a thought! And not worth looking at anyway."

I feel punched. Try to draw her away. "There's *something* I'd like to change," I say through sudden heavy phlegm, my thumb a bottle.

"Hey, I'm not putting you up to that! You're not drinking just for today. That's what I asked. Jack, I don't know how I feel about you. I was so angry with me, I mean you, for not cleaning up the sink that I haven't come down yet."

"You were angry with *me!*"

"Yeah. Why not? You left the rubber. And the foil. And the second time, you came inside me." She holds up crossed fingers. "For that I am responsible. But all in one night you've given me plenty to think about."

"On purpose, huh?"

"Well?"

"I was drunk!"

"Not that drunk. You don't think I have reason to be angry?"

"Well, you weren't angry when you visited me in the cellar this morning. What were you thinking then?"

"I didn't think. I was trying not to."

"Okay, you're right! But why would I want to get into triple jeopardy—the rubber, the foil, and going bareback?"

"Don't ask me."

"Me either. I just hadn't thought that your anger was aimed at me. I mean a half-hour ago in the living room."

"Why should I have been mad at my mother—or your mother? Whether you know it or not, you had a purpose, Jack."

"I don't deny it."

"Forcing me. I don't like that. It's like you leave a gun under the bed. Or a big blade, you know? They're for a purpose, it's not just some idle murder weapon you keep under the bed. I really resent that foil and the rubber. And how you hurt my vagina. Did you think you were in the Olympics? Or have you been reading up on making love slaves out of your girlfriends? Maybe you should slip Sibyl some Henry Miller. Think twice, Jack. I told you I bite."

She's been steaming me open and reading my mind. "I might like it."

She holds up a hand. "I'll tell you, I'm afraid of you. You talk in circles so much, hiding your feelings in feeble jokes. You have no idea when you're lying to yourself. To me you're a rough diamond. A very attractive man who has not emerged yet. You've got good manners, which covers up a lot. What I'm talking about isn't a bit of polish. You're very attractive! But not this public person you show, King James's single intellectual feather, the wino-funk-dodo and black humorist. I really like you, it may not sound that way. But when I think of the stripping down you need, to get at the true Jack Trueheart, I'm paralyzed! You don't mind my being honest? I forget people have feelings. When I teach grade school it takes me ten times the effort it takes other teachers to give positive criticism."

"Oh, say anything. I'm the Invisible Bulletproof Man."

"Only when you drink."

"Now that's ludicrous. That hurts. I'm a perfect gentleman when I drink." I see red. "Even Thelma said so. She *liked* my drinking."

"Oh? She liked you invisible and bulletproof? Not visible and open?"

"Let's keep it simple."

"Okay, you're only stable when you're drunk, or drinking. Otherwise you're driven and bewildered, is that it?"

"How do you know so much how I am not drinking?"

"I've never seen you sober, Jack. So I wouldn't know."

"I'm sober right now."

"Then why are you shouting?"

"Good God! Talk about the urge to murder. Maybe you better just strap me in and pull the switch before you forget."

"You pull it. Does no good if I pull it."

"And saves expenses." Shake my head. "Driving without wine makes me thickheaded."

Silence. She reads the night. Vast decision rises through my haze.

"I'll prove it," I blurt.

"Prove what?"

"That I'm not an incipient alcoholic!" Don't, don't, don't say it, Jack. "I won't drink." My God, I wish I hadn't said that.

"That's up to you. You don't have to show me anything."

"Wait a minute. First you beat me to a pulp, then you're not interested."

She digs my thigh encouragingly. "I'm interested."

"Oh! I feel better already." I light a nervous butt. "Might be nice to have a rest. There might even be compensations."

She lies back, an arm on my shoulders.

"I like that. If you like me better without the stuff, I'll give it a shot."

"It's not my choice."

"Don't say that!"

"I'm not your boss, Jack. Don't lay that on me."

"Well, I sure as Christ am not stopping for myself."

"That's too bad." Her arm withdraws. We drive toward the fat May moon. She's by herself. I leak blood.

"This is the shits!"

"What is?" she asks.

"Growing up, fuck it!"

She rubs my shoulder.

"My God, I hate myself. I must really think I lack moral fiber. How can I *not* stop for myself?"

She covers my hand on the wheel.

I turn to her. "Thank you for everything."

"I haven't said a word," Curranne says.

"Well, I've been toying secretly with the idea. *Unh!*—I can breathe. I've had a choked feeling in my chest for the past year and it just seemed to burst. Ha!"

"Happy birthday."

"Agh, I don't know how happy I'll be. I'll sure make a lot less jokes.

Which, I suppose, would be a relief to certain people. And maybe to me. You know, for all your hardass, I think you care."

"I care for me first. I can't pal around with *anybody* half-poisoned all the time."

We drive by the fence to the grounds and turn in at the gate.

"It's possible. I don't like 'pal around.' But it's possible."

"What is?" she asks.

I kiss her hand.

Not eagerly, she eyes fortresslike buildings. The grounds are big as a village, gray-dark with glowing, heavily screened windows. Curranne falls back, staring ahead openmouthed. A post reads 5 MPH. Far cloudworks drift on the blue night. She is wrenched.

She chokes, her forehead banging my shoulder. She holds me, breaking. I stop as she digs into me and give her what comfort I can. "You're a strong cookie," I tell her, "you can take this." I stroke her head and back. I'm alive, wooing her spirit back. Never better, a giant of health.

"We've got all night. Get it out."

"I don't know what I'm doing here!" Her back is hot. She rears against me, her face falling from a steep place. "I've got chills!"

She's shaking but I'm fearful too, flooded with second thoughts about her body-flashes. Then something groans and gives way in me. "You'll never go hungry again, Scarlett O'Garrity." She reads my face for wisecracks.

Sighs hard, then bucks up, still tearing. "That's your first joke I've liked, Jack."

"It's no joke. I don't care if all Atlanta burns to the ground. I'm for you."

Deep into some mystery on my face. "Rhett, you've lost your moustache!"

"How do I look, my dear?"

I kiss her long. Then her lips are all over me. I hold her ribs and breast like a husband.

She wipes up and I start singing, "Mere alcohol doesn't thrill me at all."

"I get a kick outta you, fella," she delivers, hands on hips.

Great dark stony buildings. Cave dwellers in dungarees and second-hand suits wander the walks and grass. We park in a lot by the auditorium. Right off there's a drumming on the back fender, a haptic walking alone, talking to himself, his fingers shockingly passing over Curranne's window, windshield and front fender.

"Lock your door, my dear," I say.

She swallows a lump. "I wasn't expecting him." Warms the goose-flesh on her bare arms, then twists into her blue angelfuzz cardigan.

We walk toward the door, her fingers knotted in mine. The moon burns on black tar hills. With a great binging of copper cowbells a bus pulls in. A school of girls in Alpine shorts and cone caps pours out, a softly shrieking great breeze from the larger world, their bare knees and tasseled calf-length socks punching me sexily. As their waist-bells tonk, Curranne elbows me with a gay half-grin.

"Goslings!" she says. "They've no idea what will happen to them. They're just breaking out of the egg, all homework and cheerleading. *Whew!*"

We go in amid Alpinettes, eying the backs of their knees and young bottoms. I applaud this bevy already. "I feel splendid!" I tell Curranne, lightly guiding her waist.

"Ha! Don't explain that."

We're backstage. Kids everywhere warm up on trumpets, drums, saxes and clarinets, flushed majorettes practice baton twirls, Rachmaninoff drifts from a boy at the auditorium baby grand. The show's producer, Sarita, a lady in her middle thirties, dressed in pink and a tilted straw saucer of flowers, races from group to group. I latch on to and interview her.

People flood everywhere. We go down to the front row. The auditorium is a basketball court massed with place-set tables. Still more high-schoolers in party dresses hurry about nervously, trying to keep their perfection while guiding patients to seats. The patients are neatly dressed and most of the women have had their hair done. The room is electric, attendants stand everywhere, benignly silent before the gardeniaed girl hostesses. All listen in a charged flaky silence to the Rachmaninoff tidbits, some gassed-looking patients bombed and open-mouthed, wheezing chestily. Others strive for volcanic reserve. Curranne grips my hand, for a moment rubbing her brow on my shoulder.

"Honey—I mean Curranne, I know you're dying. Why don't I try to grab something for you?"

"I'm all right!"

"Maybe they'll keep it short. This is awful."

A little Negro smoking a pinched homemade sits beside her. Beyond him a tall gray craggy-beaked man with part of his jaw caved in and missing sits down. His big stone body and washed slate eyes send a cold trickle down my spine. A ringer for Emerson! Curranne eyes him with shock. "I know that man!" she whispers.

"We may know a lot of people here. This is the nearest mental farm to King James."

"Maybe he's up from Gallinger," she says. "But his jaw wasn't missing then."

"How d'ya know it's the same person?"

"Maybe he's not."

"I'm always meeting lost acquaintances in odd places."

The boy pianist rises to cottony applause and leaves without encores. The craggy man claps loudest in our row and fills with good cheer before falling back into himself. Straight-spined, hands dangling. Beside me sits a fatty in overalls, his dull eyes happy and interested. Among the better dolled-up women in our row are some raggedy-heads with thin faraway smiles and folded hands. A short gigantic shifty-eyed woman in a babushka whom I know from King James talks to herself in Albanian. Her severe lips bite each word like steak. Behind us sit some well-tailored ladies, perhaps not patients, half-smiling and fidgety. Curranne leans past the little Negro and touches the big man's arm. He eyes her slowly from afar.

"Pardon me. Were you at Gallinger?"

He shakes no. Clearly Gallinger doesn't get through.

"Sorry! I thought I knew you." She turns to me. "I'll swear I know him."

The same old man leans forward around the smoking Negro and tells her, "I don't exercise enough!" Then sits back, distant, lofty and grave, thumbing a raffle ticket.

"Thank you," she says, and his large head nods. He leans forward again, eyes gravel-gray.

"But I do ice skate." Sits back, grandly solemn. His Emerson likeness forms into a fiercer, tougher grain, horribly marred by lost jawbone and an entranced piercing emptiness of eye. He has a badly chipped incisor. His huge ropy fingers are very clean and salty. Parted steel-gray hair, engraved flat across his brow. The conch of his ear is enormous. Despite disasters, he seems a man full of days, ready to sleep well. Forever.

All seats filled, all tables. A sudden winding silence greets Sarita as she speaks into a warbling booming mike, thanking the boy who just played and calling him out for a last bow. The skinny swart twelve-year-old scuffs onstage, shamefaced, eyes darkly ringed and fiery.

"He came so far to play for us!" Sarita says. "A big hand for Vladimir Heifetz!"

"Oh, that lovely boy," the old man tells the little Negro, who nods and says: "An' he played many of the right notes."

"We have such a splendid entertainment for you this evening," Sarita says. "I know you are going to enjoy yourselves vastly. But first we have a devilish little opening number by a trick cyclist and trumpet player, Mr. Red Henry, one of your very own fellow patients, who has grandly agreed to get the evening under way with his very lively specialty act that has played all over North and South America and before the crowned heads of Europe. Will you welcome him, please!"

Polite applause. Pocket cornet tucked underarm, a reddish-haired middle-aged mulatto in shimmering black with bow tie wheels out a smallish, brilliantly chromed bicycle and leans it against the baby grand before dragging the mike over and sitting down to the ivories. Vamps a run of pearl notes with melting trill. Thumbs a big gliss down off the keyboard. Mr. Red Henry turns, all teeth and freckles.

"Ladies and gen'men, I gots to warm up before I play my li'l Selmer for you—which is the *good* part of the act! Lemme sorta clear my throat with a li'l medley of good ol' good ones." He eyes the folks slowly. "They sparkle," he says, waiting. "They bubble." He waits, sly and bright, then whispers, "An they gon' getcha in whole lotta mm-mm-mMMH!!"—and leaps into "Them There Eyes," his glossy black heel jumping with rhythm.

Soon he's singing and off into feathers of blue, and turns full face, *WAITIN' for yew!* and jumps into the keys back in his own backyard, and on "Pennies from Heaven" lifts his cornet, blows an arpeggio, then comps a piano bass while fingering his horn with his right hand.

"Go, Red, go!" the little Negro shouts beside Curranne.

"I can't believe it!" I cry. I love horns. "Still hungry?"

"This is worth everything."

Red rises to applause, bows shining, and swings liltingly into "Down Among the Sheltering Palms" and "Dream a Little Dream of Me" and now on his bike begins doing slows figure eights about the stage while blowing "Limehouse Blues" and ends his act racing about on his back wheel romping "Chinatown, My Chinatown" while applause washes over him. Many bows.

"A quadruple threat," the little Negro tells Curranne. "I saw Red's act in nineteen forty-one at the Warner Theater in Erie." He turns to the old man, adding, "He plays *all* the right notes, every time."

"The rest will have to be downhill," I say.

She raises crossed fingers, gritting her teeth.

The hospital's mixed chorus lifts "Shenandoah, I Love Your Daughter" across the wide Missouri, with a heart tug, "The Erie Canal" and a showpiece "Deep River." Applause is polite, the patients' sedatives rolling back in after Red's jump-show. The Delaware Chorus skillfully softens the patients, but response is not inspired, nor is it for the Greenwich students. A ten-year-old brunette plays *The Nutcracker Suite* to a new silence in the room as she varies from daintily marching brilliant sweetness to the poignant treble of the "Dance of the Sugar Plum Fairy" to dreamy Arabian languors and tinkling Chinese and at last the crowning "Waltz of the Flowers," all familiar melodies whose flow of fantasy has patients straining into the notes. As she sits back with a giant breath that shoots her half off the bench, the old man lifts his massive hands and goes POW! POW! POW! and the hall erupts with pleasure.

Billowing in organdy, a rail-thin teenager, her fishy green eyes floating with sex, sings "Amazing Grace" with country sobs ("*She* fits in," Curranne tells me), then a piano, trumpet, clarinet and tenor sax play "Blue Hawaii" and "Trade Winds" and "Red Sails in the Sunset," the patients clapping and singing over the instruments, adrift with mellow moons, breezes and dawns of old Hawaii.

I elbow Curranne. "Dreams come true in blue Hawaii."

"Let's go."

"I prefer Chautauqua." She gives back my sexy glint.

The night's far along as twin redheads come out and stand by the piano. Their reedy voices detach, one rising lyrically, the other undershading, "When shadows fall . . ." All sit rapt, as night covers all. The little Negro sucks his lip, holding his breath at their harmonies. On the chorus the girls change parts, the lead now shading the lower voice and her honey-sad sister dripping with dream toward the strong home chord. The little man's face shrivels. "Nice tune." The twins' encore is "We'll Meet Again" and scattered patients sing along without being asked. No one wants the night to end.

Spilling with fulfillment, Sarita comes out with a box of raffle tickets. She eyes the front row closely, then beckons Curranne.

"My dear, would you come up and pick our winners for us?"

Curranne groans, rising.

"And what is your name again?" Sarita asks into her mike.

"Curranne Chaplin."

"What a superb name! The first number, please."

Sarita reads the ticket Curranne hands her and the short huge woman in the babushka cries out, jumps up and rushes to the stage steps. Sarita hands Curranne a fruitcake.

"Our first lucky winner!" Sarita cries. "And what is your name?"

But the eager woman doesn't hear, grabs the cake from Curranne and, hugging her prize, waddles off without thanks.

Curranne's turquoise sheath, softened by her blue Angora, blazes in stage light. High heels, long legs and stemming spine focus the blue force of her being. The whole hall, I'm sure, envies her radiant health and mental poise. The second winner, a tall tatty stoop-shouldered girl with jumbled undersea eyes, tells Sarita that her name is Jane Jane Jane and stands fixed with her cake. My shining woman, once on that seabottom?

"Thank you," Sarita says, touching her. "I'm so happy for you, Jane."

"Go back to your seat," someone calls unkindly.

Curranne leads her to the steps and when Jane stops at the bottom Curranne comes down, carries her cake to her seat for her, then climbs back onstage as Sarita, masking harriedness, calls the last number.

The little Negro reads the old man's ticket and nudges him. "That's you. Go get your cake."

Wonderstruck, the old man thuds to the steps, so straight he almost topples backward, and with great care climbs up. Sarita sees above her his scooped out half-jaw. "Can you talk?"

"Of course."

"And would you tell us your name, please?"

"Ed."

"Well, Ed, here's your cake."

"I'll save it."

"Well, it'll keep! What are you saving it for?"

"Pennant playoffs!"

"Well, thank you so much, Ed—"

"Garrity."

Curranne steps back in shock. She ignores Sarita's thanks and in a daze follows Ed down the steps.

"Did he say Ed Garrity?" I ask the little Negro.

"He didn't say Kelly."

They walk toward me side by side, Curranne white and staring ahead. Ed holds his fruitcake before him, his smile a rippling twist. When they sit he leans forward, cake in lap, turning to her, his great skull white-hot.

"Thank you, Curranne!" he says and sits back.

Incandescent, Curranne bores into me, whispering, "I think I'm going into relapse." She eyes Ed burningly.

"Did I hear a familiar name?" I ask.

"That's my father!"

Ed catches her look and smiles cheerily. "Wouldja like some?" he rasps. "Sit at my table and you can have a piece. Have all you want. It's not good for my teeth. That's only half a joke because I only have half my teeth. HAW!"

"Hey, great! She's starved," I say, then tell her, "Let's not let him get away."

"Are you kidding? But he's so out of it! What can I ask him?"

A man cries out at Sarita, "This is a gyp! The whole human race! And this raffle too!"

A young woman cries out, "Jesus died for you fruitcakes!"

"Maybe you'll both win next time," Sarita says. "And there's plenty of fabulous food with a mountain of cakes and desserts right after our final presentation."

And now cowbelling Alpinettes lift Swiss airs and harmonies. Spirited patients clap between refrain and chorus, overeager with good will, afraid the singers may fall silent, with an embarrassing lapse before the audience has sounded its passion. Curranne looks poisoned. Echoing mountain yodels and homesick cowbells pour over us. She clamps her cold brow. Girls' voices shimmer, rising ecstatically through alpenrosen and edelweiss. Banked reedy organ pipings float bodilessly. We rise into clear air. At their last note a blast knocks us back as a marching band takes "The Stars and Stripes Forever" and about ten thousand majorettes lift their knees through the singers, razzing their elbows and twirling and tossing batons to three bass drums. What glorious knees! Patients laugh and roll and clap and whistle and hoot. Curranne knots my hand in a deathgrip.

Shake my head happily. "Is this real? What's he doing here?"

"I can't think about it or I'll faint."

"Oh, be kind to your web-footed friends," the little Negro sings, stomping his rapture. *"That DUCK may be SOMEbody's MOTHER!"*

At the last cymbal clash usherettes herd the more swacked patients toward tables. I follow Curranne and Ed and the little Negro. Through their uppers and downers many of the patients did not see the same show we did and had a peculiarly different experience. Singleminded patients mill forward, many in lunar silence, sinking from the musical banquet and now blinkered and fearful. I'm fearful too, gripping Curranne's waist, following a New York Yankee baseball cap in Ed's hip pocket. A small balding man with Mussolini eyes blocks our tide, his hair upcurling in a power frizz. High spirits everywhere mix with long faces and stiff-set mouths.

"Is this worse than Gallinger?" I ask.

"I can't compare them."

"Why not?"

"I'm not a patient."

"Or a prisoner?"

Coming from front row we're last to get table seats.

"They're not prisoners!" she says. "They're not being punished. They're very self-involved visiting aristocrats, ha! But each one is all by himself. Wants to be accepted, you know, but hates to fit in. This kind of socializing is terrific, all the good will from those kids. You couldn't buy that kind of shot for a million dollars."

"They're not as hopeless as they look?" I ask.

"What do you mean? Look at me! I got out. I'm not drugged, I've got my wits, I could take a job tomorrow if I could find one. In some ways Gallinger was the best thing that ever happened to me. I could have spent my whole life a victim and never known what was possible for me. My God, seats."

Our usherette takes our good spirits warily, as if we're patients. We face Ed and the little Negro at a corner picnic table. Curranne looks at the fruit, sandwiches and cakes before us and shuts her eyes with a happy groan. She sits shut-eyed and agape.

"You praying?" I ask.

"Grateful! What if you hadn't brought me?"

Her father turns his homemade fruitcake about, tearing off foil.

"I bet that's five pounds, Ed," the Negro says.

"Enough for a regiment. Feel."

The Negro hefts the browned, cherry-dotted loaf and hands it to me.

"Wonderful. Lift this."

Curranne weighs it, *"Ohh!"* and sets it by Ed. He smiles hugely. "Winning is sweet," she says.

He shakes his palms like a blackface. Ed's used face and steel smile rip me with his sheer experience. His gaze is direct current, his nose ancestral with dignity. In three bites he works a pressed ham and cheese into the better side of his mouth. Even as he chews Curranne sucks a family light from his face.

"When did you arrive?" he asks.

"Just before the show," she says.

He sits back surprised. His friend asks, "You're not patients?"

"We're guests," Curranne says.

"I'm with the King James *Sun.* I'm covering this." But it's hard to swallow my sandwich. Twice being mistaken for a patient, despite my nattiness, makes me think. I mime Ed's stone stare to assure him of my mental health. "I'm Jack Trueheart. This is Curranne Chaplin. You're Ed. What's your name?"

"Ziggy."

"You're Jewish?" Curranne asks.

"I'm not even white. Ziggy's my old basketball cognomen."

"How long've you been here?"

"Seven years."

"How about you?" Curranne asks Ed.

"I dunno. Never asked."

"He's been here a *lot* of years," Ziggy says.

"Don't count 'em," Ed says. "But I'm seasoned timber."

"Well, how old are you?" she asks.

He's baffled. "Thirty-eight, I think."

"An' I'm nineteen," Ziggy says.

"Oh no, that's when I came here. Thirty-eight. The year Roosevelt was elected."

"That's thirty-six," Curranne says.

"Nah, the first time."

"He means nineteen thirty-two," Ziggy says. "Ed's been here twenty-six years. You gonna put that in your paper?"

"Christ, no. This is all anonymous."

"And Ed's family might object," Curranne says. "Where is your family, Ed?"

"My mother's in Olean. The rest are gone fishing. I don't know."

Ziggy says, "Never had a visitor. Not as long as I've known him."

Curranne's moved but zips up her feeling. I'm shocked by the suddenly-struck-blind defensive flutter in her eyes. "Is that why you were so happy to win the fruitcake?"

"I don't follow you."

"Because it was like having a visitor?" she says.

"Maybe. But I like fruitcake."

"Well, you're our hosts tonight," she says. "You and Ziggy. We're your guests!" *Am I dreaming?* her parted lips ask me.

"Well, hooray!" Ed rasps. He grows brilliant with worry. "That's a lot of responsibility."

I sit back, eying the fruitcake. The room smells of floor wax, urine and gardenias. Twenty-six years of ammonia and urine would sour me, paired astringencies I can nose in the wards while sitting right here. I admire the way Ed rises above his ghastly jaw (I was four when he came to this acidic trench!), his spine unbowed and eye cast iron. Ziggy's face is wadded liver, the life punched out of it. But his haughty chin and thin wide mouth lift with pat judgments and jokes and his hooded, droopy yellow-skimmed eyes have an upper-class loftiness or show of education much like Ed's more granite overview of tonight's party. These two are serenely entwined and self-assured. And Curranne and Ed, I see, share the same playful, squinchy, gum-baring laugh, Charlie Chaplin's, though Curranne's is tender and shy and Ed's more the old Irish bully boy.

He drills her. Not backing down, she returns a look of virgin deity, a hardness mirroring his own. They strike sparks from common flint.

Curranne laughs. "Break loose with that fruitcake, Pop."

"Have as much as you want!" Laughs a spiky, loopy laugh, his knuckle nipping the air as if clipping her.

"It's your cake, you cut it!" she orders.

"What kinda host are you?" Ziggy asks.

"Not cheap," Ed says. His plastic knife lops off a half-pound chunk he serves her on a napkin.

"That's too much. We'll split this," she tells me. Actually, that's my size chunk.

"Forget her," Ed says, serving me a chunk. *Ahh!* I cry.

"We can't eat all your cake!" Curranne says.

"Whatcha can't eat, take home," Ed says.

Curranne halves her piece and opens her small purse. "Midnight snack." She sees she's won them.

"This was baked by a *devil!*" I savor candied fruits and walnuts, ringing with sweet. "Catch my feet if I float away."

I try not to watch Ed eat sideways. Ziggy's already done, squeezing up crumbs, and smokes a homemade, purposefully shaving ashes on the table edge. He has no matches. When I started to give him mine, Curranne kicked me under the table. I struck one for him and held out the flame. Ed reads me and exchanges small code with Ziggy.

Ziggy tells Curranne, "You look like you were a WAC."

Stung, I hear wack.

"I thought of the WAVES very seriously—after a boyfriend jilted me! How'd ya guess?"

"You got that put-together look."

"He reads palms too," Ed says.

"Hey, read mine!" she says. Holds out a hand. Ziggy takes it and eyes me. "You don't mind? I always tell the truth."

"Hell, be my guests."

"Well now. Nice hand. Hand of a very brainy person, not so much a philosopher as a woman who knows her business an' could go far on the money side of her chosen field." Ziggy reads her eyes as much as her palm. "This thumb now, it's set low and shows a psychic disposition but also a lot of practicality. I mean more practical than artistic. If you are an artist, you'll be a practical artist and never starve. This line shows a strong will and short temper, ahem! This cushion shows you enjoy but are not knocked out by sex, you take it or leave it."

"Ha!" Curranne says. "You think so?"

"I'm asking you!"

"Okay, I'm not a sex fiend. But I have two children."

"That isn't sex, that's accidents. Really plump thumbcushion means you fight off the thought every minute."

"Ziggy, you've got the wrong hand," I say, holding up mine.

"That isn't sex, that's beer. Think about that."

I think. "What's the difference?"

"Whose hand am I reading? Now this is a very vital and decisive life line. You could live a very long life. But right here, see that early ex, that means you been shaken badly. And up here are two smaller exes which mean trouble. But if you hold on, you'll make it okay. Naturally I'm just reading your character, I don't know about accidents, flood, fire nor acts of God. But your hand is a contract, see? You live right, this is what you got goin for you. Now what you got is a straight-on career line which hit a stone wall, an this break shows self-doubt. Am I right? You gotta tell me or I dry up."

"Right, right. You're reading me."

People down our long table look at our end and watch the black man hold Curranne's hand.

"What I can't do is change you. You gotta do that yourself."

"Do I need to change?"

"You're joking?" Ziggy asks.

"I'm serious!"

"Don't be that, just be open to a hint. You got all the heart line you need. What you need is to mend what got broken in your fate line. I won't say more but am I clear?"

"Yeah, you sure are." She grips me for strength.

"You see why he's my lawyer?" Ed asks.

"How about you?" Ziggy asks me.

"No, thanks. I like mystery."

"It's no mystery to Ziggy," Ed says. "He can read through walls."

From our corner I see a bony, waxy-skinned man beside Curranne who justs sits in place, eating nothing, face lifted to some unseen sunlamp. Our whole table is a strange gauntlet of eye-gleams, stony mutterings, hands weaving over food, fidgets, snickerings and underwater gestures. Our foursome is a marvel of calm, with Curranne its peg. Energy shines as she feeds on Ed's face, and Ed and Ziggy both light up to her wooing, Ed's harsh eyes no longer the old dragon's.

"You ever been to Chicago?" she asks him.

"I was scouted by the Cubs but I stayed with the Falcons," Ed says.

Curranne says, "I teach. But I'm out of work. I just got out of the hospital Thursday. I was at Gallinger in Washington."

"What's that?" he asks.

"I'm a mental case! Just like you. Only I'm on the outside. I was in Gallinger six months. It took the last three, or something like that, just to get up the nerve to leave. One day I saw a squirrel through my window, and I broke into tears of envy. I wanted to kill that squirrel."

Ed pats the table. "They're just rodents."

"It wasn't the squirrel, Ed. I wanted to be free as that squirrel, not locked up in the squirrel house."

"What was your diagnosis?" Ziggy asks.

"That's not important. Paranoid schiz. But I was out of it, man, yeah! I felt I was totally abandoned and alone because I was too angry to live with."

"Christ, who would abandon a beautiful, sensible girl like you?" Ed asks. Sits back, startled at her brilliance before this praise.

"I don't know! Everybody! Everybody did." Her cheeks puff. "Maybe I drove 'em to it. I can't talk about it yet. What means something is that I got my head together and out the gate."

Curranne studies the table, then Ed.

"I was very lucky. My doctor wanted me out of there!" Her eyes mist. "He'd say, 'I can't stand to see a girl with her head screwed on like yours locked up with all these nuts. Let's get your ass on the road before you really get sick.' He really liked me. He wouldn't see me in my hospital gown. He made me wear a dress and hose, wear makeup, fix my hair and be on time for my hours or he wouldn't talk to me. He said it was too draining on him to sit around waiting for nuts wandering around in smocks. He was very demanding. You can't get that kind of care here." She tissues her eyes. "I'm the luckiest nut alive."

"He really loved you?" Ziggy asks.

"Oh, *man!*"

"How can you tell such a subjective thing?" Ziggy asks. "I don't believe in subjectivity."

"Me neither," Ed says. "That's stuff's all in people's heads. It don't exist."

"When I wouldn't shape up, he'd throw me out. He'd say, 'What I like is a presentable patient sitting beside my desk. When I see a hard nut recover, I feel valuable, grandiose, superb—and I sing a lot.' He was tough to fight!"

Ed tells Ziggy, "Sounds like he had funny ideas."

"If I am any judge of character."

"They throw bozos like that outta their club," Ed says, leaning forward, hands locked for business. "You were lucky. Did he make any passes at you? Those guys make me sick." Looks about balefully. "They're all pricks."

She doesn't argue. "What did you do before you came here?"

"You want him taken care of?" Ed asks.

"Don't weasel!"

"I was in pro ball," Ed says. "I led the PONY League two years running in bases earned."

"They had a PONY League in 1930?" I ask.

"Well, they must've."

"What did you do before that?" Curranne asks.

"I was president of Blue Coal. We used to haul it all over the Great Lakes." He looks about sourly. "It was a job. It didn't pay garbanzo beans. I had the power to cloud men's minds. But nobody could afford my services, so I didn't make any money. The company collapsed. Which was all for the best. So I took up managing the Falcons. I forget how many pennants we won, maybe a dozen. I was in good shape, biceps like a shithouse. The Yankees wanted me, the Cubs. I pitched. I had an invisible spitball—I could cloud the batters' minds—but I couldn't hold my temper. I pitched too hard. The catchers were always complaining about my steamball. That was the only ball I had. *ZZHEW!* I couldn't hold back. I didn't have any variety. They'd complain, but when I was really on . . . *Nobody* could hit my ball. But I was totally biceptual and they dumped me, even though I pitched the hardest curve ball ever known. It was unhittable, a curving steamball that disappeared in a cloud."

"Were you married?" she asks.

"Marry! Why should I? Ball player gets everything he wants, beer on the side."

"I'm glad your mother didn't play ball," she says. "You wouldn't have been born."

Waves his big pale hand. "Women don't play ball."

"What are you going to do when you get out?" I ask.

"Who's gettin out?" Ed asks.

"We got more savvy than that," Ziggy says; his nose explodes with a choking gurgle. "Nobody gonna find us out!"

"Find out what?" Curranne asks.

Ed nudges Ziggy. "We're not sick."

Ziggy glitters at the cosmic joke they're playing on the state. "We got no trouble lookin sick if we have to."

"They can't throw us out. We'll fight every foot of the way."

I ask, "Haven't the doctors seen you're not ill?"

"They don't talk with *us* much," Ed says. Feigns a knuckle job.

Ziggy says, "We're fixtures."

"Christ, they hardly know we're here"—Ed, broadly.

"Well, you've found a berth," Curranne says. "Aren't you ever curious about what it might be like on the street?"

"It's like TV," Ed says.

"Big gray place," Ziggy says. "Totally inadequate to my needs."

"We see too much of it already."

"They're all insecure screwballs out there," Ziggy says.

"Who wants to go out there?" Ed asks.

"I do," Curranne says.

"You're a woman," Ed says. "We don't have your advantages."

"Which advantages?"

"Woman can get anything she wants," Ed says.

"Like a ball player?" she asks.

"If she plays ball." Ed smiles.

"Look what you did with your shrink," Ziggy says. "Ran that pillpusher around the flagpole. Got out!"

"Yeah? Well, I have kids to take care of."

"Oh, I had kids," Ed says. Waves 'em aside.

"What happened to them?" Curranne asks.

He shrugs. "Who knows what happens to girls? Here one day, and next year they've lived in six other states."

"Where are they now?"

"Who cares?"

"Don't you?"

"Not if I don't think about it. They're unhappy—or they're dead and buried."

Curranne says, "They're never buried."

"Then they're out fishing!" He clucks, winking. "Or dreaming. They're all dreamers. If more women knew what we have in here, the place'd be packed and all of 'em happily pregnant."

"We got it knocked up," Ziggy admits. He grows serious. "Out there you can't feel anything. Food's plastic, people are robots, everything's planned. From the mortgage to the grave, one long fart. You want the truth? Just thinkin' about the street gives me a terrific helpless feeling. I get queer and unreal."

"Me too," Ed says. "I get tense. How many A-bombs are on those UFOs? Sometimes I can't sleep. Worry about gettin blown outta here. I can't get out of bed. Can't eat. Get constipated, start going blind. That's bad. That's not good."

"Very bad," Ziggy nods.

"Really the shakes. Everything out there on the street or on TV rolls over my bed like a fog and my eyes can't focus. It's the truth."

"So you hang onto your bed," Curranne says.

Ed nods. "I hang onto the bed."

"For days!" Ziggy says. "Or until I talk him out of it. I know what he's feelin'! Do I ever. When I'm nervous, I go into hiding. *Un*identi-fied flying objects, my ass."

"Where do you hide?" Curranne asks.

"Down inside." He points below.

"In your stomach?"

"He's got a great place," Ed says. "Don't tell her!"

"You can tell me," Curranne says. "I've heard everything about hiding places."

Ziggy glitters haughtily. "Whereas I bet you haven't heard this! I got this tree I love. Its roots grow out of my bowels. I go lie under it until everything blows over."

"Why do you love this tree?" she asks.

"You gotta see it to know. I love everything about it. I have been inspecting every inch and limb and piece of bark of that tree since I was a kid. I know it like my own body. I put my fingers in every crevice. That tree is sweet to the touch, like a woman."

"Who won't talk back!" Ed cries.

"Who would want to leave that?" Curranne asks.

This talk makes my scalp race. I'm not just up close but eyeball to eyeball with loonies. I grab her hand under the table. Feel a strong, steady tremor. I ask, "What kind of tree is it?"

"Spring pine. You could kill me then, I wouldn't care. I smell that pine resin and I'm gone, man—I'm in heaven. That is fragrance!"

"Ah," Ed says, wrapping his cake. "I love pine."

"Maybe when we're out this way, we can stop in to see you," Cur-ranne says, rising. Having been the last to sit, we're now the last to leave. "You never have any visitors."

"I have visitors," Ziggy says. "They get on my nerves. Not you, not you! I don't know you and am not supposed to. It's the people I'm supposed to know and don't who make me nervous. I'm getting a writ to have them refrain from visiting."

Curranne asks, "You wouldn't mind if I drop by, Ed? You might want something from outside. I always did."

"Chewing tobacco," he says. "But you'll have to sneak it in. I'm not supposed to have it."

Curranne asks, "Is *that* what it's done to you already?"

"Who knows? They said bone cancer. That's the side I keep my cud, but I don't believe their bushwa. They'll lie through their teeth to get you to leave."

"Why don't you believe the doctors?" I ask.

"Ha! Young man, those people are in a mist! I've always been well. I got a right start, plenty of lake air, hard work, ice skating, swimming, ball, you name it. I hiked. I knew my mountains, the Alleghenies, the Adirondacks. Sometimes I feel more Indian than Irish. I had a fine young manhood!" His eyes swim. "I am impervious to cancer."

We leave the auditorium. My mother's green Olds sits in parking-lot glare.

Curranne waves two fingers by her hip at Ziggy's hand. "What ward are you in?"

Ed barely half waves at my hand. "Just ask for the country club."

"Watch out," Ziggy warns. "Don't step on the boobies."

"Some of 'em bite," Ed tells her. With a deep breath, she grabs his big fingers. "Oh, that's a strong hand."

The two mismatched men in baseball caps amble under streetlamps toward the lighted fronts and dark wards. We are silent, our good-nights linger. Then she looks at me with a blazing inner shine and an anchor plunges to my depths. I am electric with hope under the night stars—for what?

"I want to sing," she says. "What a miraculous night. I feel cured!"

When we reach King James we're both zonked. For a few moments we neck in the car. I walk her to her door. Whispers in lamplight. She has her grand secret now. Looking at her in half shadow, I have mine.

"Are you as afraid of complications as I am?" she asks.

"This is before the complications begin. But I want it all. Even though I know that in September you'll put on your sensible shoes and walk off to New York."

"Will I do that?"

She kisses me.

Carol's voice falls from her bedroom screen. "Will you two butterfly collectors get off my porch?"

Curranne gives me her Chaplin grin and goes in.

I drift with a glass of water beside my bed, her leaf-shadow face before me. Her cheeks are mint. Each breath remembered, remembered mint. Then my blood slows and slows, slipping me into the great family asylum of sleep where we are all mad and alone, and none recover.

PART THREE

The King James Sun

Come September Curranne starts subbing for absent teachers, for a day or two each, hiking about the huge floating hills to grade school and junior high. She worries about doing well. But with work some long-drowned being in her awakes forcefully and doubles her strength. The full woman blooms with backyard exercise. Knee-bends, side-straddle hops, touch your toes—wearing a wolf-smile.

For my education beat I'm doing a series of available-light head shots of children at work—I call it Candid Classroom. She's teaching fourth grade today at Samuel G. Love School. To my dismay, just as our ties deepened during the summer, so the fall finds her cooling, or drawing back by degrees into her harder muscular fitness. Once a week we squeeze in sex, movies, maybe dinner with Carol. Her feelings are on hold. She's delayed seeing Reik until January, and has not been to Provincetown to see her boys. Much hangs on money. Her calls for reassurance, both to my home and office, have built mightily. My mother is frosty, answering so many. An unsettling calm has risen in Curranne after months of upset—I'm not used to dead level with her. Our closest moments are not after sex but on our biweekly Satur-day visits to Ed and Ziggy, with the shared pleasure of caring for these two as she shyly pumps her editorials into them, and with her great secret binding us as we return. Just leaving the hospital is lifegiving and bestows a springy step.

I've not been bulletproof in nearly three months and experience a heady new focus in my work and feelings. Reporting is less frazzling, more intense and fulfilling—my novel's set aside. With long clear sum-mer days of self-possession, I don't goad Curranne into deeper affec-tion for me. I simply know it's there and she's fighting it. Her first days of classwork light her up. I want that light. She too has come into self-possession, a cool heat that tempers our lovemaking.

In the hard blue eternity of 9 A.M. I walk to Love School, my Japanese box-camera slung from a shoulder. Full health in full Sep-tember. At Love, I study the empty schoolyard, listen to singing from open windows and watch clouds pass over cornices. I went to this school. Now my lover is inside, teaching. The clouds' sun-fizzy brilliance lifts me. This sober September, looking into buttery yellow classrooms from the street, I am ecstatic with the life-force which has brought me here, and surrender to its will. I go in, from one heaven to another.

The hectic corridors of 1940 are now dim and cramped. The principal's is just one more small office. I feel clumsy but purposeful in my old padded tweed from pre-Air Force days. My ninth-grade homeroom teacher, Stanley Andersen, is now principal here and as we shake hands I note that I am four years older than he was when my junior high homeroom teacher. I feel a tug of envy for his firm steps upward in the school system while I sit home scribbling unpublishable black farces.

"Well, John, you've done very well," he says. "You must be happy in photography."

"I'm a writer."

"I love those little candids you do."

As we pass a room I see Curranne within and suggest that this would be a good class to shoot for the north light. "I'll speak to Mrs. Chaplin," he says. He is brilliant with idealism and authority. He opens the door for me, his handsome square head aglow with blue eyes, great teeth, sensitive lips. He has the spine of a guardian angel in a three-piece suit. His step is masterful.

"Mrs. Chaplin, this is Mr. Trueheart from the *Sun.*"

"We've met," she says. "How do you do?"

"Fine, thank you. This room has perfect light. If it's all right with you."

"I'd be delighted."

"I'll be a mole. Just ignore me."

Mr. Andersen explains my work to the class and, on a wave of high spirit, fades. I sit in the back row. The class has barely started. She wears an Irish wool cardigan, boxy and unbelted and looking knitted just for her. A jaunty business look, her wrists and hands strong and shapely. With that slim, bosomy figure she could wear armor and look smashing. Something's new about her. Is it the pleated green plaid and suede pumps, the seamed hose shaped to her legs? Her great freshness strikes me, a frank smile and freckled milk-skin as she lowers a shade against a morning sunbolt, the livingness of gray-green eyes under her high brow. How rarely I see her at this distance, flooded top to toe with a night's rest, physically gifted as no one else in this building. I'll never see her again as young and fresh. This does not pass me by! And her favors mine, not Stanley Andersen's. I drink her in.

But I dismiss the thought of taking her picture—all that bloom lost on film. I see she shakes the kids. They've not warmed to her yet, this first day. That naked energy housed in her skull, gazing at them, child by child. I jump each time she includes me in her charge. I feel such undeserved luck, looking out over small heads, at being accepted by this deity. Who will be all mine at least until January. At this small desk, I want nothing else. No one more.

Stretching, Curranne draws down a shade map of North America, surely a place in heaven rounded by blue oceans, its entrance at Chautauqua. She walks under the elms of North Lake Drive, swimsuit in the May sun. What would these children make of her skittery fears, the moth hole on her hip? My hand on her shoulderblades, the small of her back, her hips giving the sun?

"Next year the United States will begin to mount its first census since nineteen fifty. Does anybody know what the census is? Cynthia?"

"It's when we hold a party and elect the President," Cynthia says firmly, her clipped dark hair a chinadoll with wire frames.

"Oh, very good! But that's not the census, that's the national election. I can see how you might think they're the same thing. In the national election we count votes. In the national census we count— what? Herbert?"

"Money!" He looks about, already blessed.

"Yes, in a way, but that's not it exactly. In the national census we do make a big list of what everybody in the country earns. Anybody else?"

A curly blonde raises her hand. "We count houses and dogs."

"Excellent! We do count houses—but not pets." She turns to the map of Elysium. "And we see where people have been moving. From the city to the country or the farm to the city or from state to state or from the South to the North or the East to the West or New York to Florida or even to Alaska or out to Hawaii!" She smiles and the kids moan their understanding. They move all over the universe easily. "In the census we find out the birth rate and the death rate and the sizes of families. How do we do this? We count—"

Two or three mutter "People!" and the room jumps on the word.

"Right! We count people."

I focus my camera on heads and faces about me, then look away. I use no flash. No one knows a picture's being snapped.

"Every ten years the Bureau of Census counts the population of the United States. Why? So we'll know how many people live in every city in the country. In nineteen forty the United States had the largest city in the world. Who knows what city that was?" King James, the mind of God! "No one? That was New York City. But in nineteen fifty the largest city in the world was London, England. How many people do you think lived in New York City in nineteen forty? Billy Johnson?"

Billy wears a tie and suit, looks weightily at London, North America on the map. "About a million and some."

"What would you say, Janice Wynn?"

"Four hundred."

"Charles Sheehan?"

"Two million people."

"Homer Stafford."

"Well, Paris has about two million, so New York must have had a thousand more."

"Janice Hall?"

"It has to be more than Alaska, which is the second largest city in the world and has five thousand people. So New York must have had two thousand. King James is third-largest city in the world and has nine hundred people."

"Well, thank you Billy, Janice, Charles, Homer and Janice. You're all very well informed, I must say. It's a pleasure to teach in this room. King James, by the way, has thirty-five thousand people. Charles?"

"King James can't be third largest, because Buffalo is bigger. I thought Washington was the biggest city in the world."

"No, Washington, in the District of Columbia, is the capital of the United States where President Eisenhower and the Congress and the Supreme Court are governing the country. But it's way down the list, about twentieth. Now since nobody has the figures, ahem, exactly right, let's see what the book says and put them on the board. Eugene?"

"I thought Hollywood was the biggest city. But my dad tells me Dallas, Texas, was more important. So that must mean that Michigan is the third-largest city and Pennsylvania the fourth."

"Thank you very much, Eugene. Why don't we see? First of all,"

Curranne says, drawing down New York State, "we'll have to make clear what cities and states are . . . Here is Lake Chautauqua . . ."

And then, helplessly, as the census winds down and I'm ready to leave, I spend my last five shots on her. She catches me on the last and stiffens, smiling from a cavern of green intelligence. I take down my subjects' names from her seating plan, thank the class and for a moment she goes with me into the hall. The door closes. I kiss her.

"Don't get me fired!"

"Let's have dinner and hit the drive-in tonight."

"Nothing fancy," she says. "I don't want you spending your money on me. What's on?"

"*Niagara* and *The Prince and the Showgirl*. You don't want to miss Olivier."

"And I know what you don't want to miss."

"Your brains are as nifty as hers."

"Not quite!" A knowing arm-bop. "Maybe this'd be a good night. I have something to tell you. But I can't be out late. My bean needs sleep."

"And I have something to tell you. *That's* my ex-wife."

Thelma walks toward us, suited in blue serge and ready for business. As she sees us she looks stabbed, then walks up smiling, laughing, white-knuckled. She pins me, all her old wounds steel-plated.

"Hello, stranger. What're you doing in this neck of the woods? Or shouldn't I ask?"

"Candid Classroom. I just shot Mrs. Chaplin's room. Curranne, Thelma. Thelma, Curranne. What about you?"

"I'm subbing. Somebody's pregnant and decided she couldn't last the morning. So, it's been ages. I hear ya stopped—*uhh* . . . I thought it'd never happen! Good luck to you."

"How's Stuart?"

"I've got to get back," Curranne says. "So pleased to meet you, Thelma. I've heard wonderful things about you."

"All good," I add.

"That's a surprise!" Gulping, she waves blinding clouds from her eyes. "Since you're interested enough to ask, I'll tell you. He's cracking Winnie the Pooh but not into Hemingway yet."

"How old is Stuart now?" Curranne asks me.

"Oh, don't ask him, he wouldn't know. He's four and a half this month. Stuart is, not Jack, ha ha."

"I'll bet he's aging rapidly," I say. "He might like *The Old Man and the Sea.*"

"Not yet, thank you. I hope to help him control any leaning toward gin and fishing." She tells Curranne, "Stuart's middle name is Ernest after you-know-whom."

"Well, I hope he'll never be a beatnik either," I quip.

"He hasn't a Chinaman's chance," Thelma says, then barks a short savage laugh. "Beatnik? I don't know what you are, dude, but it's not that. I'm so happy to meet you at last," she tells Curranne. "And I've heard a lot about *you.* All good, believe me. And if it wasn't, what else could I say? Gotta run. *Ciao!*" She marches off.

"Toodle-oo," I say.

"Goodbye," Curranne says. "I feel bloodied!"

"Cool down, Vesuvius. She's suffering an excess of single parenthood. Unlike you. Seven?"

"Six-thirty. I need my eight hours or I'll be too tired to exercise." As Thelma's heels ring out of sight, she kisses me again, finds something to her liking and grips my arms. "I'm so happy!" And goes in. Lucky kids, I think. I could sit in the back until I had a long white beard and died of joy. Then I recall her self-possession when we make love, the cool-down afterward.

I walk home to my cellar, weighing and reinfused by her "I'm so happy!" Blow some Ellington on my muted trumpet among damp bedsheets. Stare idly at my cracked block of a novel. Chili-up with my mother and go off to work until six-thirty. Work is a one-minute walk downhill. I go in out of the noon gold for the day.

Housed in a vast dim centuries-old loft, the *Sun*—a maverick morning tabloid underwritten by the linotypists' union—has four reporters and two editors, and leans strongly on wire copy and stringers from around the county whose haywire copy the managing editor, Big Jim Lamb, spends hours unsnarling. The top editor, Bill Bierce, writes nothing but boozy, ham-handed, glass-jawed editorials in densely simple English he thinks tough and hardhitting, even witty, and worthy of a Pulitzer he's sure he'll never get—but sure can taste. For Society we have Sandra, our knockout teenage redhead, a *Vogue* beauty always in tailored suits and tams, her smooth hair falling in waves as curved as her copy is frizzed. The very keys jam in dread of her tangles. When she strides through our shafts of *Sun*-dust, to splay in thought before her notes, her hot green eyes burning with gabble over a blank page, our typing dies and all await her first question. "Hey, is eveningwear two words or hyphenated?" "Neither!" cries joyful Jack Kinch, no longer a very old beagle of thirty. "How can it be neither?" "It's one word," Kinch says happily. She types it in. "It doesn't look right. Are you pulling my leg?" "No!" Kinch says, "that wouldn't look right either, Sandy." He applauds himself, *Bravo, Jack, first today.* Kinch is a dark beanpole with monkish skull. With Sam Mittlehauser, a re-formed drinker with steel-gray grenadier moustache, for crime, fire and city hall, our whole staff numbers barely a fifth of the *Post-Journal*'s farther down the hill. But where they cut slabs of granite for readers with the timeless patience of statuary, we are swift and color-ful, a mere jug band beside their church organ.

I type children's names for my captions. *"I'm so happy!"*—and that wise-Athena smile of secret knowledge. *I have something to tell you.* Suddenly I *must* phone her, my mind tickling on the edge of some-thing, but I know she's working. Type on. Hop into the darkroom for my dried prints.

Wall-eyed Big Jim Lamb sprawls in his bullpen, palms clasped on his huge cranium. Sighs and wipes his eyes, bulldog energy awaiting the whip. "Well, let's give it the old Sunday punch, Trueheart. Where's 'Hospitals'?"

"Pronto." I phone W.C.A. and General, type up Births and Deaths. Stare at the box copy on gray pulp. Legs in stirrups, bodies in coolers. All strangers in the King James Version, the Lord opening up wombs, zipping up graves.

Slip Lamb the crap paper. "Before and After."

"Thank you, my son. Take off your homburg and stay awhile."

"I'm of the old school."

Alone in the city room, we work on in silence. No one setting type yet, the pressroom a dead planet. After a moment my ears tingle. I stiffen, unable to read my caption. Motes dance over my wooden desk. A Saharan thirst for beer bleaches my tongue. Run out, Jack, toss down five fat mugs. I stare at fourth-graders in my prints, each softly shaded gray face and unguarded eye. My fingers lock in air over rick-ety keys. My palps run over Cynthia, Janice Wynn, Billy Johnson. Curranne and I, bringing such innocence into the world? That gay health! She's carrying?

After a while I croak, "Do you think the *Sun* will fold?"

"That's a possibility."

"That's the rumor down at the *Journal.*"

"Normally I believe the *Journal*—enough to rewrite it. But my rumor is better. We're being sold. That's just between us. Now that you're off kickapoo, like Sam, I know I can trust your perspicacity until we break the story."

"Will they bring in a new staff?"

"Does a new broom sweep clean? If you learn to double in brass, you should be safe."

"But I don't get hard news assignments. How can I double in brass? I'm just features and visiting banjo kings."

"Maybe you should try matching Alma's Board of Ed pieces."

Alma's my rival at the *Journal.* "But all our stories are one page. We don't jump any story. When she jumps inside she's just warming up! Thousands of words like every Board of Ed meeting is Beethoven's Ninth!"

"Ahh! But that's what impresses the new owners."

"But we don't jump *anything!*"

"That's our style."

"I see. Then give me a shot at the hard stuff. How about overcrowding in the schools? Lincoln Junior High's bursting at the seams. Falling plaster—"

"No more falling plaster."

"—not enough auditorium seats for the assemblies. The R. R. Rogers School boiler is right under the auditorium and there are no sprinklers in the basement. I could do it up like the Triangle Shirtwaist fire is waiting."

"Why not?"

"PARENTS IN ARMS."

"Are they in arms?"

"Not yet. Let's ask Bierce."

"He's not in yet," Lamb says.

I write the feature lead for Curranne's fourth-graders' census and meanwhile develop some blowups of her in the darkroom. That new radiance of eye. I'm sure she's pregnant. Later Kinch comes in and looks at my prints and negatives.

"Hey, not bad, Stieglitz. But they need a boost. Print on high contrast. Ya see my shots of Sandra at the Yarn Box?" He pulls them out of the dryer. She models hand-knit fashions. "Where's that sweater wear grab ya? I couldn't take a bad shot of her standing on my head using a handmirror. In fact, that might even be interesting! Maybe I'll suggest it. This is the teacher? Hey, man, Sandra's photogenic, but this broad's something else. Nothing vacuous here, look how she wears that cardigan. Lemme print these, you've missed half the values. That kind of beauty is awesome."

"That's my girlfriend. She sleeps and exercises."

"Marry her right away. Don't think twice about it."

"Maybe I can twist her arm hard enough."

"This calls for roses and diamonds. Weld that finger with a sparkler."

"Yeah. I could get lucky," I say. "If I were going to shoot a basement boiler with only some bare ceiling bulbs, what setting should I use?"

"You intend to use a flash, I hope?—Boilers aren't art. What're ya shooting?"

"Actually, sprinkler pipes in the Rogers School boiler room. They burst five years ago during Christmas vacation and have never been replaced. The boiler's right under the auditorium and the floor is, as the fire inspector might say, 'fusible.' "

"Well, well, well. You may have something. I get jittery even thinking about kids getting hurt that way. It does something to me. How are ya gonna get permission? I'd get the shots first, then ask—*maybe*. Man, you'll never guess who I have a date with. Alma Anderson!"

"Good God. The *Journal* will allow her to go out with you?"

"We're sneaking into Shea's for *Porgy and Bess*. We'll be alone, ahem, in the loge."

"Well, I like her. She's ten times the reporter I am, really devoted. When we cover the Board of Ed meetings, I have to ask *her* whom I'm writing about. Good luck."

"I swoon with anticipation."

I drop my census piece and the candids into Lamb's basket.

"Bierce wants to see you."

Bierce waves me into his tiny knocked together cube with its ratty desk and gives me his old warrior grunt and grin. He's rather short, brandy-haired and lop-smiling, and rasps and rolls under fifty extra pounds of ego he dismisses with puzzled, stunned eyes.

Soft-spoken, his mouth hand-hidden. "What about the schools?"

I explain and give a pitch.

"How much real danger of fire is there?" Bierce asks.

"They already had one in the auditorium. A spotlight set the curtain on fire just after the Christmas program."

"Christmas! When was that?"

"Nineteen fifty."

"For Chrissakes, Jack, nineteen fifty! That was eight years ago."

"Yeah, but now it's even worse!"

"But this is a dead horse."

"You've got to see that auditorium, Bill. The seats are in splinters. The janitors cannibalize the balcony for replacements. You still get rips in your clothes from the stripped veneers. The place is a tinderbox. One blocked stairway or exit and we have a lot of smoke inhalation, not to mention other possibilities."

"But what's the Board of Ed say about this?"

"They're dragging their feet. They've ordered cost estimates for repairs, but those won't be in until January or February." Curranne's nerviness moves me to copy her. "Say the board makes an on-the-site visit to approve the sprinkler allocation, it can't be before next March. This can't wait, man. Alma may get it."

"But they *are* working on it?"

"Next March, Bill! This is September. The first grade is right near the boiler room. It's a basement classroom with windows way below ground level. If there are flames in the hallway, the only escape for those kids is through the windows. Those first-graders couldn't even climb up to the ground."

The toilet flushes behind Bierce's wall, its pipe tragic with organic disorder.

"Okay, okay, I see it. Lemme think about it."

"Yeah, but I've got to get a shot of that boiler and the burst sprinklers. Before someone puts the kibosh on it. *Comprendez?*"

"What's your thought?"

"I do a Friday afternoon Candid Classroom in the first grade. Leave a window unlocked."

"That's breaking and entering."

"It's entering, that's all."

"This makes me very nervous. We could end up with egg facials."

"You've got to document it."

"Well—put it on the back burner. I'll get back to you in a few days."

"This is hard news."

"No, it isn't. It's scare and conjecture. Sit on it."

Go back to my desk. Stare hotly at my Pharaonic casket of keys.

"What are you working on?" Lamb asks.

"Arson in the city room. Don't phone for hoses, it's just scare and conjecture."

"Oh, I see. Thumbs down?"

"Who knows? It's not hard news."

"Never try to plumb the minds of an editor."

"How can half be plural? I'll deny I said that."

"These are very good." He weighs my census story and pix. "I'll give it page forty."

"Not facing Radio and TV!"

"You can't have everything, Trueheart. Besides, that and Obits are the two most avidly read pages in our esteemed sheet."

"I thought Editorial was. It makes such a nice morning laxative."

"I didn't hear that and you didn't say it. So count a blessing—you'll be read."

His long thin Bing Crosby pipe fuming, he turns back to whaling out his daily twenty-page stint, which takes him two hours, on his latest shot at a novel, his round face slipping into rapt otherworldliness, wall eye adrift and rolling, his huge body hunching and amoeboid as if sucking the typewriter into itself.

Check into my ongoing Debbie Laurel teenage polio saga at W.C.A., my little sisters Linda and Carol cystic fibrosis epic in Falconer, and into a save-the-building fund underwriting the Randolph Children's Home, all my heartbreakers, then race to the mayor's ribbon cutting at the new A&P. On the way I'm haunted by Curranne's radiance this morning and carry Kinch's three blowups. She looks in incredible health.

Carol Garrity and my sister Liz drive off in "Woody," Liz's woodstripped station wagon, as I arrive and ring for Curranne. She's changed to a chartreuse blouse and crème de menthe skirt.

"My God, the Lakewood Drive-In will pay us to attend."

We sit on the porch swing in the rose-and-green dusk, and agree to dine on milkshakes and sandwiches at Fulmer's Dairy, the stamping ground of my adolescence.

"Why don't we ever fight?" I ask.

"Why should we?"

"I miss the old stress and strain of marriage."

"Well! Do you want to fight?"

"When I lived with Thelma there was always something boorish to defend. My drinking, or loud music when she had to sleep. Or my writing time, which was more important than anything she was doing. Always something on my chest to stand up about. You and me, we never have a harsh word. That's probably escaped you."

"No, it hasn't. We're not married. We don't even live together."

"You know, I've never told you that I love you."

"Yes, you have! You think I'm deaf?"

"Not so you thought I meant it."

"Ha! You meant it. Didn't you?"

"I don't know what I meant last week. Today, Curranne, is the day I cleared up. The fog lifted. Whatever I said before, I was only half *compos mentis.* Today I am of sound mind. Can't you hear the difference?"

"You're much too subtle for me, Jack."

"I'm saying what I mean. I've lost fifty pounds of postadolescent *Weltschmerz* in the past three months. Everything's revalued."

"Good," she says. "I'm revaluing too."

"I'm all ears. What're you revaluing? I really want to hear. I take an interest."

"Well, I'll think about it. What's in there?"

"Present. Open it. I'm sorry it's not roses or diamonds."

She withdraws three velvet-rich blowups of her head, two of them three-quarter shots and the third, a creature of singing health, intelligence and self-assurance, musing at the lens.

"My God!" she cries. "This one's incredible."

"Nice tones. I got lucky, the last shot on the roll."

Sucks her thumb in wonder. "These are the best pictures of me ever taken."

"Ah well, miracles of the darkroom."

She bares her teeth. "For me?"

"I have my own set. Mine are better! Let me see that." Hold the front shot beside her face. "It doesn't seem possible but nature outshines art. What makes you so radiant this evening?"

"Have you been drinking?"

"I was tempted, Egypt."

"Really! What tempted you?"

"Well, I wanted to stay as high as I felt after developing these. I may never equal them again. Had to admit it. Jack, this is too much woman for you. Look how she stirs you up. You know she's not committed to you. *Something's* lacking in you. Charm? Talent? Earning capacity? Maybe you lack moustache. Or she sees you're not sensitive enough—even rotten at the core!"

She shakes her head faintly.

"If not, then why does she freeze up when you talk schmaltz? (Even in bed you give her the willies.) What's she afraid of? The marriage mousetrap?" I start shaking. *"Hm!* I'd better slow down." Catch my breath heavily. "She may fear I want a child—"

"What!"

"I might want to have a child with you. After all, you've got everything. Health, mind, guts, beauty. I could do worse. *Aghm,* I'm not saying this right. I'll start over." She takes my hand. "Look at this street. Blue evening. This is a very important moment I don't ever want to lose." Again I shut up, swallow hard. Whisper to keep the words coming. "I want everything I can get from you." Wipe my eyes. "Honey—I mean Curranne—I don't want to go on like this. I want more of you. What can I do to get you to surrender a little more?"

"At last you're not joking tonight."

"All joked out. Is it you don't feel anything for me? I can't believe you'd sleep with a boor. Well, a total boor. Are you afraid to feel? I'm asking! What do you think?"

"I have to think of myself first," Curranne says.

"What's that mean?"

She sorts her skirt, then faces me. "Why am I so restrained? All right, I'll tell you, Jack. If I stay here past my January deadline with Dr. Reik in New York, Jerry may get permanent custody of the boys."

"He has it already."

"Permanent permanent. I should get shared custody after a while. We aren't fighting over the kids. He knows I need that hope. When will I be ready? I can't tell. If I stay I have to get a local analyst . . . maybe in North Warren. That's the nearest one, a Dr. David I've phoned. He has a wonderful voice, yeah yeah, but I can tell he thought I might be too unstable to work with."

"That's such shit. From somebody reputable!"

"Oh, he's on my side."

"So am I!"

"Then act it!"

"Okay, okay. What if you were pregnant?"

She clears her throat. "Well? How's that change my analysis?"

"Are you pregnant?"

"One thing at a time. Let's talk about Dr. David. I'll have to get a car so I can make the trip once or twice a week. And I have to move out of my mother's. I can't live under supervision. Actually I like my mother. She pisses me off, but she cares. I need her love. And I like to give too, though she's more than a little dead in the receiving area. I'm *afraid* to live all by myself in some apartment. I can't face that. It's too draining. I haven't the strength. I'd be whipped in two months, start skipping work, sleeping twelve or fourteen hours a day. On the good days. A lonely apartment could poison me. Loneliness is toxic." Her fingers spiral at her temple. "Then I can't *get* alone, once the symptoms start. Not by pills, not by anything. It's a fever. You go through a long shitty crisis that kills or cures, only it doesn't kill and you're never cured. How could I ask anybody to put up with that? With a relapse hiding behind any extended stress. If I'm in top shape, everything going for me, sleep, exercise, diet, no drugs, no alcohol, no coffee or tea, I mean a kind of Olympic good health, a sound body *hoping* for a sound mind, then I have a good shot at a happy, useful life. And so would anybody else!"

"I'd like it."

"Who'd put up with me, outside of some Swedish gymnast? I'm in training, not just to get well, Jack, but simply to catch up with where I should be. And where everybody else is. Well . . . I can't move out, not if I stay in King James. Down in New York I'd need advance rent, furniture, deposits, steady work. Trouble with subbing down there is they send you to schools where the most absenteeism is. Teachers who can't face their classes, kids with knives and chains who smoke in their seats and rape teachers. I'm not kidding, this is happening. I have to live through that to pay Dr. Reik? And to show I'm able to stand on my own feet and support my kids, after a year of dreading phone calls assigning me to these pits? I don't think I could live a year alone in Manhattan. Or *married!* Not and stay healthy. I can't live in a poisonous atmosphere. I need clear air and clean people around me and lots of uplift. I can't take shit in normal quantities. Can't ride subways. I squirm on New York buses, they're always being robbed. The streets after dark make my hair rise. I'm physically a tough person, but there's so much legitimate fear around down there that I can't tell what's real from what isn't. And all for Dr. Reik?"

"Well, stay here and sub," I say.

"Dr. David is fifteen bucks a shot, maybe twice a week. But I'll need a letter from him sometime for the court. If I can even *face* raising my kids. Frankly, I may not be up to two boys. Weighing everything, I may not be. In just a few years they'll be moving into their first big adolescent hangups. With me worrying about them, I mean in *New York,* as well as myself? That feels like more fear than I can carry." She blows out heavily, holding my hand again. "Jack, there's really only *one* main reason I'd stay here."

"Your father?"

"You!"

"You'd stay for me?"

"I am already." She crushes my hand. "No other reason. I'm staying for you. I'd rather be in Arizona or Wisconsin, someplace sane. My sister Carrie's bland existence really appeals to me. I've had it with geniuses."

White silence.

"What would you say to having two sons for the rest of your life?"

"Three," I say.

She jerks back.

"I have Stuart."

"Oh. Yeah, sure."

"I'd like to try again. I could do a lot better as a dad."

"Ned loved them. He hurt, returning them to Jerry. When I was committed."

I knot up silently.

"What's wrong?" she asks.

"Whoo! I'm wounded, that's what. This is like drawing teeth."

"What is?"

Silence.

"What is it?" she asks.

"Am I angry? No, I'm not angry. It's nothing."

"It must be something."

". . . You still haven't told me and it makes me feel like garbage." She drills me. "Told you what?"

"I can't say it . . . All right . . . That you love me. That's it, that's all. Highly unimportant. But not once, ever. That's disemboweling. How many times have we made love? Ten, twelve times? And I still walk around with my guts in my hands."

"I couldn't. I wasn't free."

"You'll be free in November."

"That's not what I mean, dear heart. It's Matthew and Mark. I have to give them up. For a very long time. That's what staying for you means. And I want to stay."

"Thank you! But I'm confused."

"I don't think you're capable of raising a family. Be honest, you couldn't care less about kids. Thelma saw through you like an X ray and got out. Why should I jump in?—with two growing boys! How could I talk about love?"

"I feel all my flaws coming home to roost."

"I think it's hopeless," Curranne says. "Honestly. Maybe we'd better not see each other anymore."

"Boy oh boy. This is flip-flop night. I come with presents and a blooming heart, ready for dinner and movies. You tell me you're staying in town just for me. And now you show me the gate."

"Should I give up my sons and live with you?"

"Is my track record that horrible? And maybe it's not either/or about your boys."

"Hey, man. I don't believe in overnight character reversal."

"Overnight? I can't believe this. I thought I was . . ."

"You are! But I'd have to be out of my mind to stick myself with a drunk. Three months sober, Jack, that's—" She snaps Nothing.

"You just said I wasn't rotten at the core."

"You're not. You're a typical artist, like Jerry, devoted to your work. You'll want to be alone with your smoke rings again. When your mistress calls, you'll be right back in her lap—where you belong! Jerry wouldn't have the boys now if I hadn't had my breakdown. Ned has legally adopted them but even he couldn't take care of them. Not alone, and working in shows. Twice burnt should be just about enough for me, don't you think?"

"This sounds like your mother."

"*She* was abandoned with three daughters," Curranne says.

"Wait a minute. Is this you or your illness? Am I being found selfish because of what your father and two husbands did?"

"Jack, my husbands were gems."

"I'm happy to hear that."

Look out at the trees and carless brick streets of the mind of God and wonder why I'm sitting here.

"You're not selfish, Jack. You're just what you are." The corner streetlamp floods on. Her green outfit turns purple in leafshadow. "So thank you for everything. Do you want these pictures back?"

"To put needles in? Look, let's drive up to the Peacock Inn at Mayville and eat and rent a room. See what happens."

"I've also had it with goodbye fucks."

"If I went out and got drunk right now, it'd prove everything, huh?"

"Oh, stop."

"I really had the urge today."

"It's your life."

"Jesus, this has been a bad day. And it started like heaven! When I walked into that fucking school this morning, I walked in from heaven!"

"I'm sorry it turned out like this," she says.

"Well, so am I! What's more, I'm reading dark clouds over the *Sun.* The fucking office fell apart today. Then this. It's like getting my fucking thumb caught in a fucking door!" Acting the angry ex-Marine.

"You're hurt, I'm sure."

"Oh ho ho! Well, I don't want you rushing into breakdown over me. Your stamina is ungodly. Honey, you really must have taken a ton of shit before you cracked up the last time. Losing your third marriage *and* your kids. That's a grinder! You must be solid steel. I sit here mending my cracks and you're seamless. Nothing shows! Since our first day together! You've put your best foot forward every moment. And I've been . . . that gorilla who tried to make you in the grass."

"No, you haven't."

"Honey, I traded in alcohol for getting my rocks off steady. Then when I arrive where sex just might be second, it's over. How long've we been going together? Twelve weeks going on twenty years? One last thing, then I'll go."

"I'm in no hurry! Though I am dizzy with hunger. I missed lunch, which is absolutely against my rules. I had a doctor's appointment over the lunch hour."

"Then let's have a farewell milkshake together. In place of anything more exciting."

"Great. I'll close up."

I'm down in a coal mine with a very weak helmet lamp. She turns off lights, lights the porch and, carrying her electric blue Angora, turns the key, her bones braced on the right hip, legs sapping me. We walk over Fifth and stroll arm in arm through Baker Park. During World War II, on a bench in these park bushes, I had my first sex, at fifteen, with a cowy plainjane whose fiancé was in England. Bursting and unbearable, too excited to join her fully, the bushes only deepening the dark act. Now my drifting love and I are here. Half my life later I still want to make that girl again and do it right. I look at Curranne. The large delicious power of the night wakes in us. What divine hand has led me back here? At the dark dry fountain she puts on her sweater and is fluorescent in the dimness. Her starlight passes through me in waves, her shining arm linking with mine.

"You know what I'll miss?"

"I can guess," she says.

"No, you can't. It's driving back from North Warren on Saturdays. That little trip, whatever the weather, it was like all our insanity was set aside. The sheer relief! I always feel healthy and *springy* coming back from there. You can't call it altruism. We get more outta visiting those two than they get out of us. It's like we're really saving our own asses going out there. Go ahead laugh, but I mean it."

She can't stop laughing. I guess in agreement. Said something right?

"I feel that too! But no matter what happens, I need a room of my own," she says. "My own tiny study and typewriter. Or I'll walk into the nearest large body of water."

"First literary suicide in Chautauqua Lake. That's a plot."

"Jack, I'm not joking." Holds out a fist. "I get into such family binds, that there's no me. I'm flat-out—Lady Macbeth, walking the floor at three A.M., wondering where Curranne is. How I abandoned her. I can't allow that to happen again. I'm meant for something and I want to kill when I can't work at it."

"A room is simple enough," I say.

"Where's yours? I've got to get dug in first this time. Before I'm washed away. I can't keep being ground under, over and over. I'm a high achiever but I keep getting torn apart by not having a rock to stand on. This time I'll start at the top. *With* the room. And work outward. What I have to beat first is semipoverty."

"You want to write? Write! I live in a cellar full of soap fumes and hanging wash, yeah, sure—so what?"

"Don't you know how degrading that is? That's why you're driven into those ghastly fantasies. Your newspaper stories are so superior to your fiction. Real people, seen with a writer's eye."

I wave them aside.

"Don't do that!" Her anger shines.

"Do what?"

"'Tear yourself down!'"

"All right, all right. I love my sob stories."

"Ohh! Life isn't a black joke. Why don't you give it a chance?"

"Shape up, Jack," I say.

"Shape up! I'd rather see you peddle fish than writing in a coal bin."

We walk in silence.

"Do you think I'd marry a painter whose obsession is bodies washing up on the shore?" Curranne asks. "Then why should I subject my children to you? Have them grow up in your graveyard? You know, someday I want my kids to say, 'My mother wrote that. She went through hell and came out a woman.'"

"Sounds grand. For you. For me, humanism is just Sunday typing. Doesn't make it."

"Maybe a modest accuracy would be memorable," she says.

"Well . . . I might give domestic romance or family tragedy a shot."

"Jesus, Jack, the world will thank you."

A low blow. More silence. We take a wooden booth in the dairy. Not side by side but facing, against wooden walls, waiting for the firing squad leader to drop his handkerchief.

"Maybe this is the way people talk," I say, "after they haven't eaten for twelve hours. Maybe people should forgive each other for being tired."

Her uncrackable smile wavers. She's weighing me again.

"I speak only in the abstract," I say.

A few hairlines shoot through her ice.

For ornament I add, "Great loves have vanished on an empty stomach."

She nods, power shining, but a tired Helen of Troy in her blue fluff and chartreuse. "People go off half-cocked wounding each other."

"I wouldn't wound you for the world."

"You didn't. You were honest. How can that wound me? Anyway, I like feelings. Even if they do wound me, don't hold back. I don't."

"I know. Nerves of steel."

"That's why I call you ten times a day?"

Our hands meet midtable. I hang on for my life.

"I need you," she says. That plea so rare!

And I so unworthy. "I need you."

Unearthly bird-clear eyes. I want to chain, and double-chain and fuse her to me.

"A light step and an easy heart," she says. "I've never had that."

"—Whitman?"

"No! Margaret Curranne Garrity Gesualdo Chaplin."

"Don't stop! A name like that should march on forever." A sigh of bottomless regard. "And you left out your dead Marine. Doesn't he count?"

She studies her hands. She buries the death that first drove her around the bend? A white-eyed teenager in a blue-and-white uniform takes our order. She doesn't look twice at me. Fifteen years ago I was the Harry James of Fulmer's Dairy. The year of her breakdown. Curranne looks up.

"I admire what you've done for yourself."

"What've I done for myself?" I ask.

"Well, when we met, you know. You had this pasty skin and half-asleep look. Sort of smoky eyes, not quite in focus. And you smelled like a fruit stand."

I burn. "A fruit stand?"

"Well, not now! You always had a film of sweat. And that breath! Your scalp's cleared up. You teeth aren't purple. Your eyes aren't pink."

"And I haven't been in the drunk tank since New Year's Eve." My stomach is a dead flounder. "You were observant."

"Were you arrested?"

"Drunk driving. Bill Bierce bailed me out." My skin's on fire.

"I'm saying I admire you."

"Ahh." I nod. "Well, I seem to have improved, I agree. My ulcer has vanished. My intestinal flora are under control. No nightmares."

"But you need exercise."

"Oh yes."

She reads the floor and walls. Leans on her palm. Doesn't see my shaking.

"Why so pensive?" I ask.

"I don't know. Things I'd rather forget."

"What things?"

"Institutional stuff." Her eyes close. "If you freeze absolutely still, they will turn off the electric chair, or at least not put you in it. If you don't move they won't hurt you. So don't move a hair. And three or four days of just *now* go by."

My scalp crawls. I see her in the wards, gowned. Those eyes— where? My lungs die.

"I'm so sorry for you, Curranne."

"I don't want all that again. But I can't fight every minute of the day. Can I? Do you fight a drink every minute?"

"A few minutes together, here and there. Maybe an hour a day."

"An hour! Oh, I'm not that strong," Curranne says. "I couldn't do it."

"Ha! With your guts?" I'm half alive but give her my best. "Any race, any weather, I bet on you. What'd your father say when you were cheering him up last Saturday? 'I wish I had half your moxie.' Ed, a crazy man, can see it!" She fixes me mutely. "Go ahead, hit me."

"I can still walk on my hands. I'll show you sometime."

"Well, not here. I know how strong you are."

"Yeah, but not the right way. Not like you."

"Look at the photographs I gave you."

"Trouble is . . ." She's quiet, then clenches a fist. ". . . If I allow it, everything looks like a conspiracy. Even those pictures."

"But they're beautiful!"

"Makes no difference, Jack. I can't help it. Something breaks open, I get a hemorrhage. It's like a stroke." Her voice flattens, she bats the table edge. "I shouldn't. You don't want to hear this."

"Not if it upsets *you.*"

"It does. But you should know what you're getting into. Do I *ever* talk about my symptoms?"

"Never," I say.

"Well . . ." Her voice thins out terribly. "They're life and death. I go blah! I'm in a movie I can't get out of—a strange, freakish movie. It's threatening and boring. Like drowning wide awake, without any water. I'm unhelpable. Nothing reaches me. Or I get active, I start faking how much I know. Actually I'm not faking, I really know, I can fit everything with everything, perfectly. If I were given a chance I could straighten out God. Just give me a free hand for one day."

"Or the banks?" I ask.

"The banks are real. That's where I draw the line. I won't talk about the banks if you won't ask me. What the banks do is as real as cancer. Capitalism's only a symptom of a larger breakdown: civilized man's surrender to usury and credit banking. Usury is the greatest disorder in existence, it's worse than war, I'm not making this up. Usury is the stress that gives birth to most medical disorders, like cancer and heart failure and mental illness and alcoholism. Crime and war and the arms race—you name it, it ties in. That's something I can't give up. Usury really kills. I'm getting sick."

"There are worse obsessions than economics. Thanks for laying it out for me. But when you just said that, you sounded remote, as if you didn't believe it anymore. It's rote. Something you've grown out of."

"I don't want to grow out of it! It's not rote. I'm just tired to death of repeating it. When a lot of needles go into you from every direction, Jack, and they're getting bigger, your fears become terribly legitimate. Then if you notice that all the needles are threaded with money some way or another, you try to look behind money to see what's operating against you. Okay? I'm not putting you to sleep? Any obsession, like usury, makes you look odd. It gives you an edge. People see something very sinister about you. You're not being taken in by the shit that's ruling them. Best thing to do is just shut up. But everybody knows about me, I know they do, they only have to look. *'There's* a live kook!' I'd be insane not to worry what people are thinking about me."

"There's no happy balance?"

"Happy balances are in heaven."

"Oh? Because you start including the extraneous?"

"Jack, when nothing's logical, everything's extraneous. I'm spelling it out for you. I don't want any mysteries. I get this leak. My sense of reality turns to gumbo. Why don't other people understand what I understand and see happening right before me? Or hear what I hear?"

"What do you hear that I don't hear?"

"I hear voices, like any nut."

"Please don't call yourself a nut."

"Nut is an okay word with me. It fits," she says.

"You're a nut and I'm a drunk. That's how you see it?"

"I know I'm a nut. You think those hospitals were mistakes?"

"I mean *now.*"

"*I* mean now."

I'm quivering, not happy. "All right, then why?"

"Because it's *life and death.* I go by my track record! I have to, to recover. How could I get well if I didn't know I'm still sick?"

"You still hear voices?"

"Sure. Sometimes. Not often. They're going away, I guess. I hate to give them any importance. They're quite unpleasant. And once they start you can't get away. They're so draining and boring you want to bury yourself, or hide somewhere, anywhere. So you drift off, you vacate. Then suddenly you've switched onto the wrong track and have to go the distance before you can get off again. And by then the world has changed anyway. The period you were in when you broke down is as gone as the Stone Age. Even if it was just three weeks ago. Or three *months??* You start from Go again. So? Are you going to sit around and cry?" She gives a fist. "Not me, Jack."

"That's what being crazy is?"

" 'Crazy' doesn't cover it. It's not describable. I can't tell you the other stuff. It's so boring you go out of your mind with self-pity. And so predictable—you haven't the strength to fight it all over again. Mini-breakdowns, tiny setbacks . . . *chasms* . . . so boringly predictable."

She sips her shake, takes out the straw and drains half the glass. Paleness fades, cold liquid drowsing her. Her pupils widen, eased, and eyes close. Tired bruises line them. She's still a very long time.

I watch her energies rise. What am I into? Couldn't I skip town, have a wonderful life without her? We used to have necking parties in these booths, after closing hours, and on this very floor. Helene of Falconer, the jukebox colors flowing over her, was my goddess. But six years too old, and too engaged to a sailor at faroff Pearl Harbor. For three heavenly weeks one winter, she loved me, a virgin of fifteen. If that was *me,* it must have been a dream! And here I sit, my Helene as real as North Warren, and a demigoddess worth any battle. Skip town? When all that heaven sits before me with a pulsing throat? And needs and desires me?

"Are you asleep?" I ask.

"Listening to my heart beat."

"That'd put me to sleep."

"This talk's okay for you but not very good for me. I feel faint."

Squeeze her hand, close my eyes, still holding her. Something charges from her hand into mine. Focusing, I bring a nervous shot up from my soles and pass it to her.

"Thanks," she says. Bird-pupils looking at me. "You idealize me too much. Not that I don't like it! What does your mother think of me?"

"She's nervous," I say.

"I won't ask about that."

"This is not my old monster tuna sandwich. You're bizarre to her."

"Yeah-h. Do I show bizarre symptoms?"

"No."

"Doesn't matter, huh?"

"You just look overintense. Your eyes are so clear, it's all this right living. Not everybody can bear it. With her, anything you say or do comes under suspicion."

"You're being straight," Curranne says. "My mother likes you and always has."

"She likes you too."

"I'm a vast pain! I try to like her. I admire the way she's stood up. I really see the shit she's put up with. She's not the Soviet bloc, you know? We never got along better. She's a great power of example. But I can't bear that Jesus crap. That's such a sellout. Anyway, she thinks you're a worse threat not drinking than drinking. Too stable and attractive. She says you're a wonderful reporter, so there's not all that much reason to cold-shoulder you. You know, that rubber was less shocking to her than your shaving your moustache. That shook her! This healthy man started peering out of your face. Our screwing around, okay, it's a fact of life. But moral improvement at the same time, that's hard to take. Balling for God isn't what Jesus had in mind, you know?"

"We take precautions." That slips out unbidden. "Uh, would you like dessert?"

"Are you crazy? I just had a junkshake I shouldn't have had."

"I meant coffee. Oh, sorry. I just feel comfortable here."

"You really don't want to hear all this. Right?" Curranne asks.

"Hear all what?"

"About my disorder."

"Look, you're on the upswing. What do I know about nuts? I see your health in your actions, like this morning teaching. That was an hour stolen from heaven."

"That's very important," she says.

"What is?"

"Giving me your true feelings. Everytime you do that I feel it's a gift to me personally." Those eyes! "You help me bear up. So much."

"All right, I'm girded. Tell!" I take her hand but Elvis groans "That's When Your Heartaches Begin." "Oh boy. Let's walk over the bridge where nobody'll hear us."

"Great!"

Third Street's Monday night lies half asleep under elms branching with lamplight. We amble to the quarter-mile span and walk out. Few cars pass. I think of our last Buffalo jaunt for a double bill of *Wild Strawberries* and *The Seventh Seal.* The first depressed her and we left midway through the second while religious flagellants whipped themselves. Curranne was not up to the black plague, nor were the pocked highways and giant power grids of Lackawanna a happy landscape. Now a low moon fills the Chadakoin Valley, silvers housetops below, and gives the river a slate shine.

The breeze lifts her hair. "You know, since you came home, your hair seems silkier and richer. And your skin tone."

"Hormones. In Gallinger, man, I was beat."

"Well, I'm happy it's not all my eager mind."

She bears a hard inward light. "Thanks for telling me."

"My sister wants to sell 'Woody.' "

"She does?"

"The floorboards are rotting, you'd get a wind on your ankles. But it could get you to Warren and back. You do drive?"

"Drive? I've never scratched a fender in my life! I can always bus, if I have to. It depends on how much stress the traffic is. That's a pleasant ride out to Warren. What's she asking?"

"I don't know. I could buy it and lend it to you. I still want to help."

"I'll think about it. Thanks."

"Helping is nice."

"It's better than dying alone by nickels and dimes," Curranne says. "I feel criminal."

"What about? False pretenses? You want to rake through more Freud?"

"Freud didn't treat schizophrenics."

"He didn't? Why not?"

"He treated middle-class Viennese Jewish neurotics. I have an organic disorder. My Freudian side may be frigged up, but it's not my basic illness. If I have a nonorganic breakdown, it'll be *stress* doing me in. That's why I exercise. I need real physical stamina to sweat out mental stress. I could be all wet about this. There may be no tie. Nobody knows! But if I go crazy again, I'm going feeling terrific."

"I'm with you, honey. I love you and I want you. But I don't want to spend my life reading dumb imaginary symptoms into normal behavior. Dig?"

"It's a pretty dumb illness. My behavior constantly gives me away."

"I wouldn't say so," I say.

"You don't live with me, Jack. You see me at my best! How often do I call off a date because I think I should go to bed? How many periods do you think I have a month?"

"You never say it's your period."

"Yeah, but I imply it. Don't I? What was that, wishful thinking?"

"Well, you didn't want me worried."

"About my period?" Curranne asks.

"I could worry about that, yes."

"Have you *ever* seen me cook? There's a reason you haven't. I get two or three pots on a stove and I'm swamped. Overpowered! My very top dish is canned tomato soup with milk. On bad days I can't handle the milk and it's with water. Butter in soup is a mental luxury. Too much to remember. It took me an hour to iron this blouse tonight. I went without even a cracker so I could get through it. See this sleeve? Missed it altogether. You didn't notice in the dark but I just did, sitting in the dairy. I could cry! But then I'd be crying all the time because I'm routinely stupid. Am I going to get better? You bet on it. But overnight? No."

After a while I say, "It's all you, isn't it? I can't help."

"Don't say that. Sometimes you're a powerhouse, Jack."

A powerhouse! I like that, and feel baptized.

"Boy, if Thelma could hear you say that." I'm near tears. "I'm getting *déjà vu*. This talk reminds me of my wedding night. We went to her father's lodge for our honeymoon. We're hardly inside before she sits me down and says over the table, Jack, we are now going to have a serious talk about economics. Before we even went to the bridal bed! Honey, you haven't looked sick to me from the first moment I laid eyes on you. How can your dedication change my mind? Or all that stuff in the psycho bin? I love you right now, here, today. I never address you as anything but sane, do I? I'll take you as you are—and think myself blessed."

"You haven't even asked for me!"

"Somebody's gotta be father to my kid! Why not Jack? Or are you gonna give me a song and dance about not being pregnant?"

"No, I'm not. I couldn't. I don't have the brains for it. Why do you think I haven't said anything so far? It's such a huge problem I can't face it."

"I'll bet it is," I say.

"It's like radiation particles." She bites her lip.

"What did the doctor say today? Happy mothers are married mothers?"

"No."

"What did he say?"

"He said I should have a very easy delivery."

"Well, of course he'd say that. That doesn't mean you need less attention and comfort and pampering. Didn't he ask something really important, like do you love the father?"

"Why should he ask that? I have a wedding ring."

"Well, do you?"

"I think I could, Jack!"

"Boy, is that feeble. I don't think I deserve you—and maybe you don't think so either. But three quarters of yes is better than four quarters of no. Should we celebrate?"

"Not unless you tell me how you knew."

"Are we getting married?"

"We'd better!" she threatens.

"Then, my dear, a man should reserve some mystery about himself, don't you think? If he wants to keep his wife's interest?"

"Hey, man, come clean. Does it show?"

I think of my photographs. "Only in your eyes."

"In my eyes, huh?"

"Well, maybe in your sweater too."

"Now you're being honest." She glances down. "I guess I'm a good trade, huh! You won't feel cheated out of your bachelorhood?"

"Let's just celebrate. You see that bubble up there? That's no moon, that's all your stupid worries floating away. For tonight at least. To-night you're Salome in her seven veils. May I have this dance?"

We waltz on the bridge, wing this way and that. Her body strong and ringing, throwing me a plump little bump, warm breath on my neck. I kiss her ear. She nips my heart with a smile that has teeth in it.

We dance by the light of the moon.

PART FOUR

Little Ikiru

*S*un reporters aren't unionized, and I'm paid less than scale, despite working for a paper floated by the linotypists' union. So I give up the Saturday Night Shakespeare and Sharp Cheese Society, wine I can't drink, cheese I can't afford, and instead thump up a Saturday Night Foreign Films Club supported by its members. My announcement in the *Sun* flushes out about fifty film buffs and soon we hold biweekly screenings in the YMCA gym of Swedish, French, Italian and Japanese movies otherwise not seen in King James. Our Japanese double bill is Kurosawa's *Ikiru* and Ozu's *Early Summer.* "Guess what happened in early summer," Curranne reminds me, patting her bulge. "This little bit of fun."

Curranne is riveted by *Ikiru.* It's the story of a petty bureaucrat with gastric cancer who spends his last months wresting a new park from an unbudgeable bureaucracy. Futureless, he devotes himself to this lonely work without reward, but finds that to live selflessly is truly to live. Curranne's father's bone cancer has flared up and his half jaw too must go. He'll be chinless. A handmade jawbone for Ed is too dear for the hospital to have built before knowing if the cancer has spread. He'll go under the knife a week after our wedding. He may die chinless. The movie cheats on nothing about cancer. We're both shaken by the hero's rebirth, then death, amid postwar chaos.

"I've got to do something for my father," she says. In the movie the dying widower Watanabe—drudging under stupefying bales of documents and spurned by his selfish son and daughter-in-law—awakes after decades of deep sleep and paper shuffling. He tries drink but is too shot to stick with it. A phantomy second childhood with a young girl turns fruitless. But she inspires him to spend his last days helping children. At last he draws daily energy from gray Tokyo sky by overseeing the building of a playground from wasteland and urging on workers through mud and rain. The film fades out in Watanabe's park on a shot upward of a bridge, perhaps from this world to the next. I join Curranne's yearning to help her cancerous father find Watanabe's dignity. "He really should spend his last goddamn years with a jawbone," she says. "Even if it's plastics and ceramics, right?"

"He may not have a year."

She measures his time in my face, then waves at the screen. "He built a whole park in six months!"

"That's movies, honey. And you're not dying, your father is. Or may be."

"He can be helped." She bites a knuckle. "He's going down for the third time, Jack."

"Or the ninth. Well, maybe Carol has some dough."

"Not for that she doesn't," Curranne says.

"Why not ask?"

"I haven't told her and I'm not going to. I don't even know if she knows he's out there. She may, you know. If she does, she couldn't care less. I'm just not going to give her the satisfaction of doing nothing."

"Then you may be denying him his dignity," I say.

"Like hell. She'd let him rot."

"My sweet, Carol is *sure* your father is dead."

"I know she is!"

"I asked her, months ago. She went to his funeral. How surer can you get?"

"Yeah, yeah. She says that. Same bullshit to me too. She can't face his being alive. Don't ask me why."

Early Summer wipes us out all over. An older brother has died in the Pacific during the war, as did Curranne's Marine husband. Now his brother and sisters are grown up, in 1951, with the unmarried twenty-eight-year-old daughter as breadwinner for her parents and grandfather. Curranne replaces them with Ed. If the daughter marries, their home will break up and the old folks have to fend for themselves in the country while her sister and younger married brother with his family do what they must for themselves. She resists marriage over and over. Curranne and I hold hands—we're not resisting marriage. My nose and eyes prickle, though this is not a weeper, it's home drama. Curranne gnaws her lip as the old parents sit in a park and watch a child's lost balloon go up, up, up, carrying with it the parents' disappointment that the daughter will indeed marry and their long home together vanish. Again, the old father goes to the store alone and sits at a train crossing he's sat at a thousand times waiting for a train to pass. Soon, with the marriage, he'll sit there no more. He looks at a midafternoon sky with one fading cloud. We watch the sky. It's just there, emptied of grandeur. Then we watch him lost in cloud-reverie. Then again we watch the sky with nothing else in the frame for sixty enormous seconds while our nerves light from our ankles upward. To that pitiless silken sky, being and loss are one. When the shot ends we groan with gratitude for Ozu's granting us this experiencing of eternity.

"Here are people with overwhelming problems, digging the sky," I say.

"I saw Chautauqua," she says.

After packing the film cases in our rattling station wagon, I drive her home in ripening quiet. Fallen leaves line the gutters, the air nutty with leafsmoke.

She knocks my shoulder with her cheek. "What counts is holding on together," she says. No argument from me. *"Oh, screw!* I don't want to go home yet. Let's go to the apartment."

I've not told her that the apartment I've taken on Chandler Street is the one Thelma's just moved from. When I heard she was remarrying, I phoned to congratulate her and ask about her second-floor walkup. "Believe me, it's only big enough for one big dog, or for one adult and one child," she said. "For twenty-eight dollars a month I can't go wrong," I said. "Oh yes you can! Stay in your mother's cellar, Jack. This is no improvement." "Nah, I gotta get out of that cellar for my feelings of self-worth." "Oh, really? This won't do it. I say stick to your cellar. But it's your throat, Jack. Say, d'ya need a bed? How'd you like to buy my rollout couch? Thirty-five bucks and it's still there. I'll just leave it." "Okay." "Cash ahead. Leave it at my mother's. Tomorrow. I'm supposed to be moved out tomorrow." "Tomorrow? Can I leave a check?" *"You* have a bank account!" "Well, my mother's check." "Oh sure, that's even better. Her check's fine. I was afraid you'd tried to master banking. I'll tell the landlord you're taking it." "Thanks." "Don't thank me. I suppose your mother's relieved to see you go?" "What? She's quite unhappy. I'm getting married. To Curranne Chaplin." "I should hope so." "What do you mean?" "I think it's pretty plain. Or are you the last to know?" "Yeah, well, I wasn't on the top of the list. But I'm very, very happy, considering my part in the matter. I'm ready to try again." "Good luck. Maybe it won't be as painful this time. For either of us." "I hope I've learned something."

"Oh, humble pie! My, my. Well, you won't even have to change the name on the mailbox, just cross out the ess on Mrs. I hope the tool-stamping plant won't wake you up too early. I never had to use the alarm clock myself. *Ciao.*"

Halfway down a black hill, under a busted streetlamp. We pull up before the two-story house, in the low-low-rent district overlooking the woolen mill, the trainyards, the earthquaking stamping plant. Curranne stands on the broken front walk, looking up and down the steep hill, and puffs.

"I'll get *exercise* aplenty."

"Little Ikiru won't mind."

"That's not his name."

"Hardly. Entrance is around back."

"Around back?" She stops at the mailbox. "Hey, your name's here already. You're fast. And there's a letter!"

She takes it out. "It's for Thelma . . ."

"I'll readdress it."

"How did they mix her number with yours?"

"Watch out for these steps. Let me take your arm."

We go around the dark side of the house on a narrow concrete strip. Out back a wooden flight to the second floor rises up the great dim bulk. The trainyards and the stamping plant sit in deep silence.

"I'll go up and turn on the porchlight."

But she's afraid of the dark and, holding the wobbly two-by-four railing, follows me up the moonlit steps. I unlock the back door into the kitchen and turn on the 15-watt bulb that's left. The swept empty kitchen, almost as dim as outdoors, leads to a short shadowy hall, the bathroom and the only other room, a living room with the balding bed-couch. There's no ceiling bulb anywhere.

"It's so small," she whispers in the dark.

"Watch your head."

"Castle Chihuahua."

"There's the closet," I point out.

"Where'll the crib go?"

"Well, it's just for now. We'll find something bigger."

"What's this ugly couch?"

"It's the bed. I'm buying it from the former tenant. It opens up quite nicely. I'll show you."

"There's two and a half of us, Jack. When I'm big we'll be moving about sideways . . ." She bends low and looks out the window at the house's front half. "How many apartments on this floor?"

"I'm not sure. I counted six mailboxes and a forest of antennas. Ah, see, this is a double."

Curranne sits on the unfolded couch where I hide in shadow.

Her small timid voice: "This is it? This is *all* there is?"

Cheapness and chagrin mottle me.

"The crib can go in the kitchen. We'll eat in here off a card table. Ha ha, we need Mr. Watanabe in here to expand the walls."

"This is no playground. But it may give us cancer. Did you look at the other apartments?"

I cough. "This was the only one available in the house." She fails to read my liar's cough and lies back beside me. The low ceiling presses down like slabs angled together.

"Why, for God's sake, Jack, this is the attic. We're on the third floor!"

I look around. It's a lot like "The Pit and the Pendulum" with Poe's walls closing in. Is this where my Japanese family dreams are to come true?

"Sweetie—don't panic. At twenty-eight dollars a month we'll save dough and move out fast. Maybe I'll get a raise if Bierce lets me do that Rogers School story."

Holds up her arms, spanning the living room. "I've been figuring it out and I don't see how we'll save money even if we live in your cellar."

"That'd be unbearable. Truly uncomfortable. This place would loom like the Taj Mahal."

"I had to duck my head just to look out the window. I feel faint." She's breathing hard on the hand in her mouth. "Jack, I think I want to murder you."

"The crib's okay in the kitchen if we winterize the door."

"God, we're lucky I don't have a baseball bat," she says.

"Four or five one-hundred-watt bulbs will do wonders."

"A thousand watts won't light up this dungeon. I'm really dizzy, Jack." Her eyes are wet. "Don't you think we might find a winterized cottage on the lake?" she whimpers. "Or at Chautauqua?"

"Chautauqua would be great. But they triple or quadruple rents in the summer."

"That's only for three months," Curranne says hopefully. "We might get by."

"But that's twenty-six miles. I'd have to drive over three hundred miles each week just to go to work."

Her fist knots over her eyes. She's shaking. "I'd drive six hundred miles a week to be out of this hole!" Sobs against me. "This is like Gallinger!"

"Ah well. Maybe Stu Lancaster's mother's place up there is available. North Lake Drive!—that's nice digs for a prospective Japanese family. I really want to start this marriage right," I remind Jack. "Okay, whatever you say. I'll tell the landlord we heard too many pigeons in the gutter."

She's laughing and crying. "And chains in the attic! Whoever lived here before is still laughing in the walls. Would you do that for me, sweetheart?"

I savor that sweetheart, mull over throwing out my nudist clippings. "Hell, you may have saved our lives."

"You're such a darling. I need ephedrine, I can't breathe. Let's get outta here."

"What about this couch?"

Her hands are knotted on my breast. "Oh please, I want a bed."

Next day Thelma phones about my failure to leave the check.

"We decided against Bleak House for our home drama."

"Home drama? Has that started already? You *don't* want the convertible?"

"We don't even want Crescent Tool's free alarm clock. Thanks but no thanks."

"Oh, think nothing of it. I wouldn't buy your bed either."

And I never tell Curranne about the non-former tenant.

A Volvo pulls up by the church.

"Kinch, you filthy Jesuit. Thanks for coming."

"So, out of the rat race at last, huh? Man, I wish I could get outta single blessedness."

"What about Alma?" I ask.

"Nice kid. Let's leave it at that. Didja see today's *Journal?*"

"Oh, Christ. They didn't announce our wedding?"

"Not if you didn't phone it in to Jennie."

Kinch and I stand on the whitepillared veranda of the Unitarian

Church by the high school. He has his camera. Black eyes glitter above his scaly-gray close shave.

I scan the heavens. "I can read Jennie now: 'The bride wore an elegantly unbelted brown and cream pinstripe that lent her a most pleasing eggplant silhouette.' Do I really want pictures of this?"

"Of course ya do. Or should I shoot around the bride? I thought not. Well, I hate to tell you this, old buddy, and ruin your wedding day."

"All right. What did they run?"

"Alma did the R. R. Rogers School exposé you wanted to do. Pictures, fire marshal reports, Board of Ed minutes, School Community Relations Committee, parents—she interviewed everybody in the county, it's endless. Two full pages like facing gravestones."

Cough into my fist. "That could make a guy pissed off if it weren't his second wedding day. I still have to do my first hard news story. *Wheew!* I'm sure she did ten times the job I could. She's tireless. She cry in bed a lot?"

"Ha ha, dreamer. I can barely waltz her near a couch, if that. It's the curse of the virgin I'm feelin, lad."

"Which of you is the virgin?"

He says something, his tobacco breath dousing me.

"Well!" The sky, rain and ashes. "It's not the end of the world, is it? You bring me a copy? Good. I wouldn't want to read that today. Let's go in."

"Hey, send her a black-bordered telegram: CONGRATULATIONS. Ha ha! She'd like that."

"Kinch, old man, nothing bothers me today." No, no.

We are six at the wedding. Curranne's sisters no longer attend her weddings. My mother and Liz, both with stricken smiles that fade and reappear, Liz's boy, Philip, and my friends Deacon Quince, the Buddhist linotypist, who now has rectal cancer, and half-blind Phil Newquist with his upright stagger, are on my side of the aisle. Curranne's mother alone is on hers. Curranne has no friends in King James and is being given away by Liz. Kinch and I join the small wake down the aisle. I feel stabbed, my raise kaput with the lost story.

Once more I see myself in my mother's cellar this morning, binding my five-hundred-page unfinished novel in twine, then carrying it up to the attic where I put it on ice. Forever? I don't want to see that black bundle again. I remember the four years I've worked on it, the cafés

and beaneries and all-night diners and Salvation Army flops in Dallas
and Los Angeles and hotel bedrooms (my last buck blown on rubber
musky or ash-flavored sherry) and other dark corners across the country where pages were written and the places and pages freeze into a
soft slush in my stomach. Not a single successful short story to show
—just moonlight. Not one strong passage in my novel, everything
singing gray or narcotic marshmallow, my travels worthless. Despite
herculean work spates, every outpouring winy and spineless. A vain
career, not romantic at all, my ego-bound body bloating, kidneys weak
from a tank car of beer, stomach flipping, a bagged fish beating itself
dead. And never any money! Always phoning Mama, from a midnight
pay phone in San Berdoo or Omaha. Mama, always Mama. Now,
walking down the aisle, I try to button my suitcoat. It won't button.
Behind my belt quiver anger and self-hatred. My broad salmon tie
hangs far down to cover as much white shirt as it can. Curranne turns
in her turquoise-striped twilight blue sheath and eyes my approach
with bright, closed, silken smile. She wears an orchid.

Her hair hangs thick and straight and lustrous, without bangs or
curls, and so plain that her full being shines from the bones of her face.
Her figure flows. The mounds of Little Ikiru and her bosom charge
her gray-green waterbright eyes. Her deeps race with intelligence,
light dancing on a stream bed. All is well, all is well. Her shy assur-
ance does not see my unbuttoned coat. This is the woman I've wanted
to marry all my life. I'm half ice cream, but her hope cleaves me. She
wishes the best for me and stands pledging it. With how full a heart?
Full enough. For the moment, my butter does not exist, only the sober
man within. While I was blowing my horn last night, did she not
sneak up and kiss my cheek? Just a little love tap, not for the record.

"Well, my boy," Deacon says, rising delicately from the front row.
"Let me give you away and get this done with. Before I fall dead on
the spot."

I grip his hand in thanks. In his smile, as he is dying, nature itself
offers me her plenty.

"It's still not too late!" Phil warns me.

"I think it is," I whisper, choked.

"Well, I guess you know what you're doing, brother dear," Liz says.
"But you've gone all the way around the bar to get there, ha ha! Or do
I mean barn?"

My mother's face, hiding the worm she sees in the apple of her eye, says she wishes we'd thought of this earlier, much earlier, and even avoided it, but she whispers, "I'm standing right behind you, my son."

Our small black Unitarian minister, Reverend Christopher G. Jaspers, steps up with the Book of Common Prayer ceremony I've requested. Not yet thirty, Jaspers is married to a Cherokee wife with mental problems, has five children still living, and was selected and ordained by the King James Unitarian congregation only three months ago. He has a British West Indian accent. His vague, warmly dazed, shaken eyes have to collect his thoughts even while reading the ceremony. After a dinner at the minister's trailer, Curranne said, "The poor sap is taking on his wife's worst side. He thinks she's some wise old saint when she's only worried out of her mind. He shouldn't take what she says so seriously."

"I'll remember that," I said.

I detach from his words, see his balding and cross-ribbed brow, hear only the finely groping voice, look into the brown wounds of his eyes. A heavy stuffiness grows in my chest as this intelligent man of hardship stares at me from complexities of pain I hope never to know, and asks, "And wilt thou, Jack, love her, comfort her, honor her, cherish her, and keep her; and forsaking all others, cleave thee only unto her, so long as ye both shall live?" The words pierce my stuffiness but my answer feels bolted to my heart. I look at her and bow, speechless. I've caught a terrible cold standing here. My sinuses burst and drain, my face at once a sheet of tears and muck. I have no handkerchief in my freshly cleaned suit. Time passes and passes, choked and dripping. She squeezes my hand for strength. I am two hundred and twenty pounds and five hundred pages into failure and feel blessed with luck unutterable and undeserved.

We drive our Ford station wagon up the lake to Chautauqua and our new home and weekend honeymoon. With our wheezing seat springs, we think "Woody" too high-toned and thoughtfully have rechristened our wagon "Broken Bucket."

"My best wedding," Curranne says.

"Mine too. Clean and sweet."

"But a cliffhanger!"

"Carol looked as if she barely thought it a marriage."

"Yeah, yeah. But she came through. She was there. So do we have any money left?" Curranne asks.

"Not until next Friday."

"How are we going to stay afloat until then?"

"Like yogis," I say.

"Like yogis?"

"Sheer will power."

She studies me. A waking look crosses her. "My God, I'm married again."

The deep gray lake lies below. The setting sun swells between hills, under a heaven-circling cloud cap. Only a strip of sky is clear where the red sun sets. Brandy rays glitter down stone chop.

"Snow?" Curranne asks. "Christ, I felt like a cocktail waitress in this getup."

"I love that dress! And your gorgeous orchid. Sets an erotic new tone for marriages in these parts."

An unglued woodstrip whistles by my door. We're fond of "Bucket's" woody gauds. She's a poor thing but our own. The whiskey-throated heater pitches into cold from rotted floorboards. The loose hood riffles downhill. The thermostat needle sticks in the red. Surely, some revelation is at hand.

"I thought it was a very spiritual wedding," I say. "I was quite moved."

"So I noticed!"

"I felt the past fall away. Did you feel that at all?"

"I thought it was pretty unreal."

"Unreal?"

"Sure. Losing yourself in another person. How unreal can you get? But I felt lucky it was you standing there. You're a good guy. I've always liked you."

"Sold to the woman in blue. But it sounds like you're just settling for the best goods at hand."

"Hey, maybe!" She winks. "And I like my orchid!" Pinches my waist, laughing, then faces me solemnly. "You ready for our talk?"

"What talk?"

"About your economic responsibilities, my bucko. What else could be *impartant* at a moment like this? *Don't think I'm just jumping into the sheets, John!* As I see it, I'm out of work—for obvious reasons—and you have a fixed income. With no prospects."

"Jesus. Let's just drive directly to the bottom of the lake—"

"—and roll down the windows. But with this floorboard we

wouldn't need to." Shivers at gray heavens. "Do you think money talks in the next world? I have no insurance. You have no insurance."

"Little Ikiru has no insurance."

"That's not his name! Stop the car on this hill." Pull over to the crest. The ruddy lake is dancing granite. "I want a hug."

Her cheek, smooth. "Don't want to move. Ever again," I say. "I fear I may not be able to wait for the bridal bed."

"Rub the baby. It may be a girl, you know. I've never had a girl."

"Much too solid. Anyway, what is a girl? A few glands, a couple of kisses. What's all the fuss about?" She takes my lower lip in hers and presses. "Well, they whisper to your soul sometimes."

The sun goes down. Switch on the lamps.

"Is that perfume really legal?"

"Yeah! It's all legal today."

"Well, it's operant. You're some tiger. But you're caged now."

"I won't bite. Well, maybe a little. Don't think I'm a saint."

Rub the baby. "She's not so unreal."

Start up. A few feathers fall, the lakeside silent under fast-appearing flakes, the falling air whitethickening.

Curranne asks, "D'ya think we should get some credit cards?"

"Never had one. Have you?"

"Ned did. He hated it. They're terrible traps. Jerry wouldn't be found dead with one."

"I always pay cash," I say. "But you can't get a cahd unless you has an ac*count* somewheah, Missy Scahlett. Or establish credit with a car loan."

She sighs. "Well, you do have a job and could open a stinking account."

"What'll I put in it? I even paid our rent in cash."

"Put the rent and utilities in it and pay by check. Join the modern age, Jack."

"But that costs the monthly bank charge. That means I work a half hour every week for the bank. Doesn't it? I'm their employee?"

"The point is, it establishes credit."

"Right! But if I get cards I have to pay credit charges, late-payment penalties and whatever else they dream up. Anything I'd put in would go out the same day in bills. I'd never have enough in to be a viable borrower or credit risk."

"Don't be circular," she says. "You're setting it up so you can't ever get credit."

"Yeah—but it's true. I can't meet my debts now, much less want to make new ones. Like the car. On the way to the church, 'Bucket' ran dry and Liz bought me a gift tank of gas. She had to or we'd be walking to Chautauqua. And I still owe Reverend Jaspers for the service—"

"Oh, but he needs that money! You should have paid him."

"Sure. But then *you'd* be making dinner tonight. My God, life is cheaper dead. I can't believe anybody would give me a credit card."

"Please don't say that! I hate the poor-me's," Curranne says. "If there's one thing I hate most, it's self-pity about money. There's no bottom to it."

"Yeah. 'The poor will all always be with you'—J. C."

"I've had two husbands drive me mad about it. David didn't get a chance. There simply has to be a healthier response to life."

"To money, you mean." Shut up. "Why are you worried?"

"Little Ikiru. Oh, horsefeathers." She'd said it! "Baby clothes—I'm starting from scratch again."

"There'll be baby gifts."

"Doctors, vitamins, hospital, bassinet—the works," she says. "Babies don't grow on trees, Mr. Butler."

"No."

"They take you prisoner."

"Still, folks have managed since the Stone Age. Or before," I say.

"No, they haven't. The infant-mortality rate right into this century has been hideous. That's why people had such big families. Now we put more into each child. There's no comparison."

"I'm *glad* we're having our first fight right on our wedding eve."

She grins nuttily. "So am I! Here." Curranne hands me a large package from the small clutter in back. "Present. From me."

"Oh my God. I didn't know we were supposed to exchange presents."

"We're not. This is for you from Tiger."

"I'm very upset. This is awful. I refuse to eat it."

"I hope you won't eat it," Curranne says.

"When should I open it?"

"Right now! Pull over again. This is from Cornelle and me both. I had her get it in New York."

The bloodcolored box under the wrapping says Brooks Brothers. I goggle at a full-length red velvet robe, its pile so rich it catches fingerprints.

"What can I say? I've never owned anything like this. Thank you so much, Curranne. And Cornelle."

Jump out of the car, shuck my coat and slip into sheer luxury. Stride into snow-filled headbeams in the dusk. Turn, the soaring tenor, for Curranne's review.

"You really like it?" she calls.

"Like it? I belong at the Met!"

I stand where the evening slopes into the lake's nightsilver and call out to the giant platter in the dark.

"Lake! Lake! I am the happiest man on earth today! I married a tiger, Lake, and she shall never go hungry again!"

Curranne reels up, popping with gaiety.

"And nothing can take this day away from me! Whatever happens, this day is mine, Lake! My tiger gave it to me!"

Drive home singing in my robe. When we arrive it's raining heavily, too warm for snow. The gates to the summer colony stand unmanned now. The winding tiny cobbled streets are leafless, everywhere deserted and running with rain. We see no one in blocks of empty unlighted houses. Our dark gabled beauty looks out on dripping shoreline. Emptying "Bucket" I'm still rapt by my gift and sing unstoppably: *"I'll be with you in cherry-blossom time!"*

Curranne waits, snuggled into her seat, until I light the porch. As she runs in, packageless, I cry, "Come back out here. I'm supposed to carry you in. *And change your name to mine—"*

"That's apple blossom time, you lug!"

Sweep her up in the living room, carry her out and back in. "I like cherry blossoms." Stand with her aloft, my nose plunged into patchouli until I'm dizzy. She pulls my head into the kiss I've been waiting for since we met last May. I love her weight. She loves to float.

"I think you meant that one," I say.

"I did."

I dance my svelte eggplant about the living room. Rain on the roof is champagne. That turquoise twilight cocktail sheath does something to her, she can't stop kissing me.

"Boy, unreal. Here we are in Loveland."

"Yeah?" she asks. "I've been looking for this place."

"And no one within blocks of us. We can play loud Mahler in the small hours—if you want loud Mahler. Little Ikiru may not groove to Mahler. But he might like a trumpet lullaby. Muted! After he joins us, my pet."

"I've got the best lullaby ever made," Curranne says, lifting a breast. "Knocks boys right out."

"That's superior brain power."

"You'd be surprised where I keep my brains. Let's open the loot before supper."

"That sounds pitifully eager, my little starlet. Start tearing," I say. "Hey, you're not cooking."

"I don't want to. But what's it matter?"

"You are being served this evening, Guinevere. Trueheart's Catering. Open ze loot while I open ze cans."

We have swank digs indeed. I can see Stu of Elsinore staying here during the winter of our *Hamlet* when I was twenty and Cornelle Ophelia. His mother has a piece of a great American circus fortune and is in Sarasota until next summer. Our agreement is to mail her a thirty-five-dollar check monthly, and keep the oil heat flowing through both great floors so the pipes won't burst. We'll leave for our place, wherever that may be, when she returns. Curranne calls the fluorescent bulbs over the bathroom mirrors *moderne*. The well-stocked kitchen is fit for a gourmand. I pull down two cans of Mrs. Lancaster's French soups from the cupboard and mix bisque of shrimp with vichyssoise on the power stove, then dice in onion and bits of bacon and butter. Our dessert will be her leftover pistachio ice cream, and two fortune cookies from a druggist's jar. Laying the table and lighting pearl dinner candles, I hesitate over her wine rack, sigh, and pass on.

"Maybe I'll pop a Pinot Noir the night Little Ikiru arrives," I say.

"Then don't kiss the baby. I don't want him thinking that's what the world smells like the first night he's out here."

"Oh, a little chew of parsley does wonders."

She's quiet, digesting parsley as a wonder drug.

"But you're still a stupid drunk. Aren't you?"

"I jest, I jest!"

"Are you trying to frighten me into an eleven-month pregnancy?"

"I want peaches and cream for you, day and night. That's what I want. Dearly!"

"Yeah. But you weren't joking."

"I was. But I'll never joke again, Curranne. Cross my heart. Not if I frighten you. Hey, do you realize we could have the first nude wedding dinner at Chautauqua and not even have to pull the curtains?"

She rubs baby. "Let's not and say we did. Your mother gave us a toaster oven. I'll leave it in the box until we move. My God! my mother has given us a three-hundred-dollar prepaid charge account at Bigelow's to get whatever we want. Boy, do we need that."

"Damn! I expected a moustache cup." Stop joking, Jack. Stir the potato scum in.

"Too bad we can't cash it in," Curranne says.

"Sounds promising anyway. I think I'll delay my suicide." *Stop!*

"Well, you could charge the rope." Her aloof wolf-smile at this wit. "She'll want to know what we got. What's this thing from Phil? An earth-mother?"

"I'd say it's a genuine pregnancy charm carved by natives at Kenya airport. Put it on the kitchen counter. We'll rub it every morning before breakfast."

"I can't look at that over eggs!" she cries.

"I'm sure it's valuable. He's that way. Do we want it over the bed?"

"It might give me twins."

"I bow to your logic." Towel over arm, turn her chair. *"Madame Vraicoeur, la slop est sur la table."*

As she sits I buckle to my knee in red velvet and kiss the toes of her purple shoe. "May I request the pleasure of remaining down here while you eat?"

"Dine, Jean." Smoothing my collar and shoulders.

"I have a thing for pretty little knees in silk." Kiss both pale bones.

"It's okay by me. But Little Ikiru may get kinky ideas. You'd better get up."

"As you desire." I adjust her to a gold-banded china setting, linen weighted by Swedish silver. Set her orchid into a stem of water between us. Serve the steaming tureen. Turn off the lights. We admire our cheery large-window images and, through candle flame and velvet, study the bleak backyard downpour.

"Mrs. Trueheart."

"Mr. Trueheart."

"And these," I wave at the window, "are Mr. and Mrs. Joseph K, the owners of this little cattle barn. Once in a while you may find them walking around in here."

"I sincerely hope not."

"Pretend they're a dream."

"I'm through with that," Curranne says. "Very hot, watch out."

"Did you feel this was a spiritual wedding?"

"You've already asked me! It was my best," she says. "Poor Chris."

"Hm! We must pay him his ten bucks. Or maybe it won't be legal. Spiritual—but not legal until cash crosses the palm."

"I don't know what spiritual means," Curranne says. "I never experience that about people. Only about nature."

"Well, nature's something. Right?"

"What *I* felt today was sanity."

"Really!" *Not* unreal?

"I felt we were absolutely right in getting married. And against all odds, I might add. When I saw you walking down the aisle, something broke in me. I felt released. From my resistance, I guess." Her eyes close. "I saw a man I wanted with my whole heart."

"Thank you. *Something* flowed between us. I felt my whole life was answered."

We hold hands across the soup. Look into our married eyes.

"The best things in life are free," Curranne says. "Right?"

"I dig. So you did feel some spirit was there in the ceremony?"

She wiggles her bottom. "I was feeling a lot, mister. You looked plenty sexy."

"I did? I sure didn't feel it."

"Well, I *was* worried about you—or for you. And I was happy we were being married by that nut."

"Nut? You're the authority."

"He's been through the wringer, man. Too bad he doesn't have any smarts about it. But he put his heart into it. Even if he is wobbly."

"Me, I just surrendered," I say. "I felt a big breath lifting me. I was seeing this through! I knew I was actually going the distance with this marriage. No copping out. Ever."

She weighs worlds in my ever. "I envy you."

"Envy what?"

"Your feelings."

"You have feelings!"

"Not spiritual. Just maybe poetic."

"You're all spirit. I mean it." Her eyes empty, just hatched from the egg. "Maybe you don't have the courage to admit spiritual feelings because you're so down on institutional religion. I think being just sensible is tragic. I give up. No more tragedy. My tragic sense has been lifted. I dig upward sublimation, God, all that jazz. For me, it works."

Curranne is moved, reading Joseph K in the window.

"The way life is, Mrs K, without God, going crazy is a sane act."

With a restless moan, she pushes her chair back. Looks vexed and timid.

"I only know what I've experienced. When I left Pilgrim State on Long Island, my first commitment, my doctor told me, 'It's going to take you six years to learn to work out your anger nonviolently.' I said, 'Frig you, I'm fine.' I thought he was laying some self-fulfilling shit on me. I was back in three months."

"You've been committed three times?"

We're silent.

"Yeah . . . I told you *twice,* right? I lied. I was afraid you'd think I was hopeless."

"I'm sorry you carried that useless burden. Now you've told me. Do you think I see you differently?"

"Do you?"—her smallest voice. "I would."

"Honey, I'm for you. I married you today with any secret you want to keep. Whatever it is. When you came into my life back in the Prendergast, you stepped down from the moon. I can't believe you've married me. I've been worshiping you since I first sat scribbling about princesses on my kitchen table. Even mooning over my novel for years, that was to earn your acceptance someday. I'm sitting in heaven." A prince in velvet, palm on my heart. "Who needs the Nobel Prize when he's won a moon goddess?"

But my spirits don't lift her.

"I try to bury that second commitment as if it doesn't count."

"Maybe it doesn't. Is there something you *want* to tell me?"

"Yes. No. Oh well. I committed myself. Ned did it at my request. It was the same old trap. I couldn't take it."

"What trap?"

"Money. Servitude. *I needed a room of my own!* There was no me. I felt worthless with Ned and Jerry. So the more inferior I felt the more I tried to lord it. Whatever they earned, *I* felt penniless. If they earned *more,* I felt cheated. If they earned *less,* I felt poverty-stricken. I, loser.

There's nothing more draining than being bighearted to a loser in the house. When we never had enough, either marriage, I'd get nasty about it. I'd get locked into destructive fantasies. Killers! I'd envy the laundry bag and wish I was in it—dead."

"I couldn't follow all that. You wanted to be dead so you could get some recognition from your husbands?"

"Who knows?"

"Well, I get murderous fantasies," I say.

"Yeah? Mine are cosmic. I can't tell you. There's no logic, so don't look for it. I'd just get feeling poorer and poorer and buried alive. I couldn't see any way to earn money for myself. It's like some huge foreclosure. I can't earn one penny, life won't allow it. No matter how hard I try, or dwell on it. I can't even beg a job. Anywhere. I'm too depressed and dumb even to be a prostitute. Wouldn't know how to go about it. Or to set myself up as a call-girl wife. Too complicated. And when I wipe out—I mean feel fully estranged—I bring some kind of basket of snakes down on the planet."

"That's why you hate the poor-me's about money?" I say.

"Wouldn't you? Jack, I loathe what money does to my self-esteem. It gives me wet-brain. Twenty minutes with my bank statement and I rot. Total decay. I collapse."

"I've never had a bank statement. But you don't sound so unusual. You think I should know this, huh?"

"Money makes me stupid."

"Say you didn't have to think about money. Somebody else does that for you. Then what?"

"Well, then there's no growth, is there? And the rot's still there. I know what a hideous economic flop I am. I try to stretch one sliver of liverwurst and a slice of bread into four sandwiches. I do try to accept my flaws and let others help me. But my crazy life finally leaks so much stuff into my sane life that I can't keep them apart. Every room in the house takes on its special disaster or economic delusion. I can't hide. I go into myself. I go to sleep wide awake and wake up on a bus or at a lunch counter. Once I woke up in the Forty-second Street Library reading room, reading Dale Carnegie on how to make friends." Her tears fall. "I'd been missing for a week. *Boy, was I hungry!*"

"I'll bet you were, sweetheart."

"So it's time to recommit. I can see that. And try to have my crazy half pulled out by the roots. I come out *again,* and start over. I'm so far behind! And each time farther and farther. What's funny is"—her pupils drift—"there's another me I never meet, who never got committed, and she's gone on with the Morgans and the Rockefellers and spends her weekends and summers out boating at great camps in the Adirondacks. Or maybe she's become a great writer like Colette, or movie actress like Margaret Sullavan. She's had three kids, you know?"

"No, I didn't. I like her though."

"Do you! I'm so happy. Oh, *she's* been committed. And got her head together and gone back to work. Very plucky woman."

"But Ned and Jerry were considerate of you, huh?"

"Sure, they loved me. They still do, I'm not a bad person. I'm getting nauseous. We always split over stress, not because I was a schiz. Money! I short-circuit. It's a measure of how right I am, or am in tune with life. I swear I deserve the stuff. Money's real, it's part of reality, part of that money out there must be mine. But the credit system has a worldwide lock on it. Nobody sane with any sense of economics can deny that. The Rockefellers sit back in their art collections and phony charities while hiring fancy gangsters to raid the stock market for them. Philanthropy?—they don't give a tithing of their wealth. *Just peanuts!* To feed the world's misery. Maybe I could live with this—if it didn't degrade me! Boy, I'm dizzy."

"Hey, stop. I've heard enough. I think you have an enormous grasp of the whole situation. Let's listen to some music."

"Just because I can think doesn't mean I can defend myself. Not against my feelings, Jack. They rise up and walk. I'm repeating all my mother's errors. I don't want to grow old and unexpressed and damaged. And have to be absolved by Jesus. That's when I want to kill, facing her future. The furniture closes in, man. Is it genes or chemistry? Or *is* it money? Or both? If I had all the money I needed, ha! Would the stress still pop up and twist me where I'm weakest? Ned earned money. But I wasn't all that stable and he was out with crews on location. So I'm alone, and I don't make friends easily. Next thing I'm a phone junkie, chasing him or my doctor or my mother and fighting the phone bills and the phone company the higher the bill we can't meet gets—I mean it's phenomenal. And I'm fighting myself! Is *this* call necessary? This expense? I have to convince myself three times over before dialing. Even if my life's at stake. I mean I'm ready for the bridge."

"Honey, this doesn't sound nutty to me. It doesn't. You're just overscrupulous and conscientious."

"What I am is nauseous. You don't suppose the French soup would spoil in the can, do you? What are their standards over there? I've heard some bad news about vichyssoise. I'll tell you what blah is. They wouldn't let me onto the lawn for my first six weeks at Gallinger. Can you believe six weeks behind screens? You finally twist that around so that you're punishable by law for blinking an eye. A stupor of guilt. You're standing in jelly. Fear blowing over you for nothing. It wakes up on your arm or your back like eczema. But you can't move. All you can do is bear it. Let's shut up about this, what do you say?"

"I'll bet pistachio ice cream would settle your stomach."

"Maybe some music. My God, your spiritual stuff gives me the willies. Turn your problems over to a pipe dream? I would if I could! But for me that would be really flaking out. I don't have the ghost of a belief in any higher being watching over North Warren or Gallinger or Pilgrim State. Or over me. Maybe over you, I sure won't deny you that, even if I could. But he's got a blind eye my way."

"Looks that way, huh?" I say. "I'm sorry for all the shit you've gone through. And I can't argue spiritual stuff with you, that's useless. But I do think your problems can be presented differently so that you might arrive at a safer vantage point."

"Jack, if Christ had ten lives today, he wouldn't have time enough to drive out all the psychoses from all the psychotics."

"No, he wouldn't," I say. "That's why the sick man himself has to help."

"Yeah? Half the sick people I know I wouldn't trust to boil an egg. I have trouble with soft-boiled myself."

"Maybe I don't know shit about it. Huh? Let's hear Mahler's Fourth. Let's have some pistachio. Let's think seriously about going to bed before I go into sex flipout." Big half-smile. "It's not every day I'm sent the waitress instead of the cocktail."

Put on the music. After ice cream we break open our fortune cookies.

"This paints me as El Blando," I say. "YOU HAVE A NATURAL SENSE OF FAIRNESS AND FAIR PLAY. They could have done better."

"Don't fight it! Why d'ya think I married you? For your money?"

"Not at all. You want me to write poems to you."

"No, man."

"Well, my cooking? My station wagon?"

"No! I knew I'd marry you, from the first time we made love. Right out front of this very house."

"Standing up!"

"I saw something in you. And it's been there ever since, despite my being a horse pill and absolutely impossible."

"You're making that up. Do I look like a breadwinner for a horse pill?"

"I saw it at the wedding. And I see it now."

"Christ, you sound serious. What is it? Can I bottle it?"

"No. I saw something I've been looking for all my life," Curranne says.

"My big heart! *HOORAY, TEAM!*"

"I saw that you would never abandon me."

"That's the truth."

"Let's skip the dishes. Have a fire in the fireplace, and get yummy."

"Nope. You can't distract me. What did those Chinese idiots lay on you? Read, please."

Her strip up, eyes fiery. "YOU CAN EXPECT A BOOST IN ASSETS AND MONEY AFFAIRS." She glows hugely.

"Hey, thanks!" I call above.

Her jaw drops. "My God! I think Little Ikiru just had his first belch."

I jump up. "Lemme hear!" She turns to me on my knees. "I don't hear anything. All I hear is pistachio." Lean my ear harder into Little Ikiru. "Boy, people with TV don't know what they're missing."

"Didja hear him?"

"He's blowing scales on his bubblepipe."

"Yeah, yeah!"

"I think it's *Afternoon of a Faun.*"

"Tell me another." Pressing my head to her, digging her chin softly into my hair. "And another, and another."

Rub the baby.

"I dig starting marriage this far ahead."

She raises my face to hers. "Guess who I am," she says.

"Peggy Garrity?"

"Oh, I'm not a child any more."

"Maggie Sullavan?"

Shakes her head.

"Margaret Curranne Garrity Campbell Gesualdo Chaplin Trueheart?"

"Hey-y, not bad! Why don't we just say Curranne Trueheart?"

I nod. "Put me down for a contribution."

PART FIVE

A Day on the Moon

Still haunted by the Kurosawa film, Curranne thinks of Watanabe, frozen to death in the children's playground. Actually he died of bleeding stomach. His cancer must have burst a vein or artery. He bled and froze to death on a swing, like fogging over. Or more painful? All fear breathing outward. Peace flooding in. Leave all behind. I'd be taking Little Ikiru. Save him from my genes, never having seen the light of day. Better never to have been born, says Socrates. With a sound mind and all his gifts, what a nerve! Not a woman. Women have to be mysticized into giving birth. Draw a blind over their future so they don't see the horror. Child senile someday, maybe mad off and on, hospitalized, cancerous like Ed. Mother's polio limp.

She folds the last shirt into her basket, covers the ironing board and carries the basket beside her belly upstairs to the kitchen, heels the cellar door closed, elbows the light switch off, and sideways climbs the back way, a step at a time to the second-floor bedroom's noon brilliance. A wisdom tooth pulses. She has a canker or red welt where she bit the side of her tongue when bolting some salad after forgetting lunch yesterday. Carrot chunks are treacherous. The unwitting hard crunch had her stamping her heels at the table as pain flooded her tongue. Self-hatred, she thinks, punishment, anger at letting myself get so hungry. Anger also at the snow and having to give up her half-hour jog around Bestor Plaza. She now exercises only in the living room but works up a good hot sweat before breakfast. She's still sweating after her shower, can't dry it all off.

Putting his holey shorts away, she sees the jock strap he wears when shorts run out, and recalls his raunchy bedroom dance, the jock a swelling toad. Deaf-and-dumb organ, desire everything, the drop on the tip. Desire is as vascular as anger, she thinks, her own face pink and flaming at times, blowing up, the lips bloating with desire, head swollen, eyes wet with heat, all of her red as a prick at climax and afterward streaming with pleasure. Pricks must run in the family, that's genetics for you. I'm passing on Ed's or Jack's? I'll never know! If Matthew and Mark aren't like Jerry, they must have Ed's. Can it matter if a man's hung like an Irishman or an Italian? Not much. But the woman's organs run in the family too and that's a lot more touchy, more defects possible. Sex is more in the brain for men. Now too sensitive with Jack. I'm too hot and glowy and prickly and it makes him sensitive too. Picks it right up from me. And I'm too wet. Tamp, I get too dry. No happy medium. Lips swollen for hours because of baby. After the birth I'll go back to normal. I'm at my limit, will be getting turned off soon, too fat to think I'm attractive. But he thinks I'm very attractive, can't get enough. I got the flab off after the last kids and I'll get it off after this one. I starve marvelously, Jack. First, don't put it on. And keep my fingers crossed about the varicose veins. Stand ironing. Move a lot, walk, keep blood moving strongly. My peddling on my shoulders exercise, start off with that tomorrow, get my wind up first thing. The faster the second wind comes, the better the whole series, more sweat. The flashes and night sweats after Matthew, the fat dropping off, but so uncomfortable. The damned pads and belts and blood a nuisance. My God, the lotions, cologne, witch hazel, bottles by the dozen, new one every day to buck up your spirit. Like a lush. Jack's doing very well. But so fat. Too bad I can't take it off for him. My hair marvelous. Shall I put it up for a surprise? Yes! Pile it up, the pregnant socialite.

This room brightens her. Backyards joining below and snow trackless. No lunch yet. The hammerblow of money comes. I won't think about money before lunch. Defenseless without energy. Walls close in. Go stupid.

"Stupid!"

She is balling socks as the woman in the dustless bedroom mirror smacks her. Her stance this instant, her charged, impersonal eyes. She chills, caught unguarded. The socks fall, her ear stinging with the echo. *"Stupid!"* She leans into the mirror, spasming. *"Stupid!"* Her heart runs wild. She sees the tub at Pilgrim State, feels the sheet wrapping her, pans of ice cubes pouring down. Don't do it! she warns. Don't come apart. She races to the front window, raises it and, kneeling over the porch roof, packs cold snow and wet ice against her face. Jack's half-eaten plate of fudge in the icebox shows itself. She'll have one piece for a boost, and already feels relief ahead. Slowly her chest thumps dim. Very close, she thinks. Maybe a trank or phenothiazine would hold off these shaky moments. But wobbly or whatever, she's got through it. Sits calming herself with two fists of snow on her brow.

A little imaginary breakdown, not unusual. Nothing happened, nothing serious. I can handle it. Perfectly.

Curranne towels her face on the bed quilt, then—not being stupid—closes the window snugly, smashing ice chips. And thumbs the lock shut, proof of her genetic perfection.

She turns full figure to the room brimming in the mirror and models her head, seeing the hair batched up in pins. A veiled smile, calm and eager breathing. Hello, there. You're no monster, she tells her spirit. Some invisible inner thing looks back through her body. What's your name? Curranne, the spirit tells her. She smiles at her named spirit. But the impersonal, searching eyes return, flaw-seeking. The eyes strip her bare, weighing stretch marks on bust and belly, her hips' broken vessels, the heftier and lighter breast and spreading rings, now dark and stippled. The crinklings of her sex and moonworld of inner organs. Little feet and fingers, waiting for birth. One day out of the gate and I turn myself into this big seedpod. Spring into bed, no waiting, one turn of the earth and I'm pregnant. For luck, for hope, El Stupido? To anchor myself out here! Pregnancy always steadies her like a mold being filled. Plasmic and placid. The need to be dead, from her first weeks at Gallinger, has passed. She forgets her flaws. Queenly, she begets wonder, abuzz with bees crawling on honeycomb. She follows buttocks and bones and ovals undulating up to green eyes whose sharpened pupils never sleep. Her original eyes, the child-shine still there. A stomach shock of pleasure at Brazilian-green irises draws her into the mercury where gray fibers part and smoke her green brilliance. Her skin is silk. She feels supple and dreamless with sheer being, a bare moon by daylight.

Detach, Curranne. No need for flakiness.

She carries the basket down to the living room, puts on *The Children's Corner* and makes lunch to the dancing piano. Lunch is fudge and milk and Chinese leftovers. Strong blues wash over her as Christmas shopping comes to mind. She's pared and pared her list but it still overpowers reason. Her fork sinks to the plate as she drowns under coming holiday and later hospital bills. The dental surgeon in King James and plastic surgeon in Buffalo will not rebuild Ed's jaw for under four thousand dollars. How many years of loan payments and carrying charges is that? If a cosigner were found, the loan even possible . . . The Debussy ends and the player clicks off unheard.

White yards join the whitefrozen lake. The lake and faraway snowy hills ignore birth and cancer. A week after surgery Curranne and Jack visited Ed in the hospital. His chin is a puffy wad, his mouth goofy and eyes enlarged. Her gum pulses. That tooth's gotta go before she's infected. No insurance. One more bill. Would I kill myself if I lost my jaw? Her stomach drops. Granted the money, prosthetic replacement always possible. What about losing your mind for twenty-odd years? Suicide over that? When did she first lose mental health? David's death? Earlier really. Her impacted tooth pulses as she grits her teeth, but she does not falter from looking back. Must she search spiritedly into early suffering? Spreadeagled on the roof, firemen lifting her, carrying her down. So long ago! Jack knows more than she does about it. But even at seven, thoughts of suicide when her mother came home from her polio bout, refusing a cane and limping around the house. Carrie's clothes passed down to her but new ones for Cornelle. Would she suicide over a hip infection that left her crippled? Schiz suicide rate high—but her? Never. Not do that to the kids.

Nor go to Jesus! My God, to bring kids up on that stuff. Oh, His Cross is fleetingly attractive, her pain made plain and given over to Christ. Dr. Joel Goldbaum, her analyst at Gallinger, swore by the Cross. "It's the only way! Don't knock your mother for that. Look what it stands for. Rebirth, a new life, everybody needs that at least once as an adult. Maybe twice. You have already passed through the worst once, been crucified, and come out whole. I mean with your ass really together. Without that really major crisis, the one that shakes you to your soul and crucifies you, you'd go right along living the gray lies. Still unborn. Spiritually without a pot to piss in. You gotta die once! Accept that. Life has got to be too goddamn much to bear, it's got to break you, grind you down like dust, render you utterly humiliated, or you'll never be alive, never trust that life can heal. I don't know, what are you—thirty-three? Maybe you're too young and hidebound. Jesus, you won't understand any of this. I'm wasting my breath. Forget I said anything. Forget it, forget it. Go back to *Being and Nothingness.* Just remember, *one* person took an interest in you. I gave you my best. No drivel, no jargon. Take it or leave it. All this shit should come outta you, not me, or you won't believe it. Maybe it's too subtle. That's why I repeat myself, give it to you on billboards. YOU CAN BE SAVED! You're responsible for your self-therapy, I can't do it all for you. You gotta brainwash yourself outta this nuthatch, Mrs. Chaplin, or you're going to be in here an awful long time. Many snowfalls, like *The Magic Mountain*. There's no pill can reach what's wrong with *you*. Measurably, your recovery's up to you. Oh, we can medicate. I recommend it. But since you are set on doing it the hard way—and with your willingness and intelligence it may be right— you've got to start psyching yourself up in a very, very upbeat manner. Like for winning a race. Read Whitman! You know what he says? 'I stand up for the stupid and crazy.' And in those days the crazy were hopeless, no treatment, no drugs, Freud hadn't analyzed his first dream yet. The crazy were outcasts. It was like Whitman standing up for rapists. So if he can do that, what about you? Don't be stupid, stand up for yourself. Be your own comrade. Start thinking of yourself as getting well. And start loving your mother more. And your sisters. You can't do it alone, you need all the love you can get. Don't put all your eggs in one basket with me or some boyfriend you're going to land or your ex-husband if he wants you back or in your kids. Be open to love. Make friends. You hate all that, huh? It's not worth it? To you it's worth it. You need love-shots, so go out and earn 'em. Act loving and you'll get it back, it'll bounce off of people and they'll return it. You get back what you put out. Put out upbeat, positive vibes and after a while they'll start coming back when you need 'em most. You cannot do it alone! Do you have another pair of stockings? Next time you wear a runner in here you're going to get fifty minutes of total silence from me—at best! If I'm going to break my Freudian oath and unravel my tongue all over the place, I expect you to come in not looking like a horse hit by a house. Here's your diet. Memorize it. Don't sabotage yourself. No stimulants, no coffee, tea, chocolate, candy, sugar, cigarettes, drugs or alcohol, no aspirins, no cold tablets, no diet pills, got it? Absolutely nothing that will interfere with your eight hours' minimum a night. All that shit gives you stress, you don't need it. Your big drug is eight hours' sleep a night, supported with mother love and whatever you can wring out of your sisters. You've got a nice smile. I'll bet you're a winner. You're gonna do okay."

I should write him. And now, Dr. David in North Warren twice a week. Money, *hammerblow*. Must get Jack to go to the dentist with me. *Hammerblow*. Afraid of dentist. Feel me up under gas. Does pregnancy attract perverts?

So hard to part Jack from thoughts of money. He got tight as a spring when I told him the costs for Ed. But didn't try to talk me out of it. Internalized his resistance. Not good. Didn't feel deeply about

him until my fourth month. His health attractive by then, white eyes
and walk. I want his strength, real interest in my well-being. Fourth
month. First I had to accept the baby, no way out, hard, hard, before I
could focus on Jack. No real love at first, or maybe yet. Still resist.
Can't believe that surrender isn't first step toward abandonment. My
feelings knot up against him, despite companionship and his giving-
ness. Real care! But nature wants me to knit all the way, be healed,
and give its baby a safe start. It wants a hard, earned recovery, not soft
feelings, not gush.

Curranne dresses and goes out the kitchen door, scuffling through
unspoiled snow in backyards to the upper road and walks uphill toward Bestor Plaza. The brilliant sky patches over, the thin wind
freezes.

When she'd started writing poetry for therapy, Joel Goldbaum had
given her *The Cantos,* later taken her on a hike to Pound's Sunday
gathering on the Chestnut Ward's lawn at Saint. Pound was silent
about her poetry until he reached some lines about anxiety and the
anaconda of money. "Not anaconda, too stiff," he'd said, "money is
the coefficient of anxiety. Let it expand, explode without end." He'd
been very nervous, rapid-speaking, sometimes loftily witty but mostly
just lofty and dithering. Eleven years at Gallinger and Saint had not
got his wildfire focused. His cunning green eyes, thin nervous mouth,
goatee and bushy gray frizz buzzed from an electric core in midbrain.
His hands rambled and fidgeted through economic theories, certain
that usury and greed were the apocalyptic cancer of the age. She
remembers her trim body beside him, her hair in a psyche knot, the
neat sexy sweater, skirt and stockings which would not disgrace Dr.
Goldbaum. Pound kept forgetting she was a patient like himself.
"Such a breath of fresh air!" he repeated, lounging in his robe and
canvas deck chair, looking at her. But she'd withheld her charm, even
her smile, as she listened, feeling sexuality rise into an air of wisdom,
not smarming the cracked daddy-man ranting through clouds. How
could she be else than serious, fully armed, terrible-eyed, knowing how
much had sprung from him, the geniuses corrected and edited by his
own hand? And now his ceaseless superabundant anger flashed jag-
gedly down on greed, the moneylenders who'd thieved her surgeon's
knife and trustworthy mind. "You must come back, my dear," he'd
said, tapping her hand. "You're sensible."

Walking to the post office, stepping carefully to avoid slipping, she's aware of her body every moment. Her back itches with heat rash, her extra sweater and peajacket bind under her arms and a sailor's blue watch cap prickles her scalp. Her impacted tooth tastes metallic. Right now, pregnant, she feels more girlish than when seated with Pound. Day by day distance sharpens her compassion for the frozen woman she was in Gallinger. Like him, she was there under false pretenses. He'd lived in a curtained alcove, his self-made island away from other patients. "I'm no traitor. Think of me as a respectable horse thief," he'd say, waving at his "cell," "brought to book."

She'd really listened, compelled by his money dirges. *Hammerblow,* her mouth fills with stale rags and dry paper. White flour is not mountain wheat but usury. Property is finance flashed by a card sharp. "Corpses are set to banquet," he'd read to her, "at behest of usura." The memory of his rapt gritty voice deepens the burn of sun on the unplowed street. Her nerves thirst for his sandpaper banter. "Let the slaves die serving their mortgages. Live lightly; save; be you." Did he say that, or she make it up? His quick, sad, wrinkled eyes, a gay seafarer's home from a sea she would never sail. Pound brought news. He'd been twice the age of her father at his then-mysterious sea funeral during the Depression. Perhaps *his* eyes would have had Pound's green cutting edge. Pound's grating terseness had a fatherly ring, "Study money; you'll want it less. It kills, or turns you to cardboard, if you live." She sees herself before Pound, chasing cash at a dead walk, collapsing into kitchen stiffness, long fugues undersea. Mind ash, spirit milled. Wave after wave lapsing tiredly, all action hopeless, then the electric killer snake bolting through her, the hot vain anger curling and weighted in her trunk. Squeezing to save, catch up, the rage of guilts over a misspent penny—and how much yearly on the cat? Now "Broken Bucket" leaks money and has cost twice over its first (unpaid) price. She walks into the wide whiteburning noon plaza in a gigantic funk.

Standing by a tiny food shop on the Colonnade, she counts her cash mentally while looking at three well-bundled women talking before the main entrance. She wants antipasto, her one salty extravagance, but fears she hasn't enough for Christmas card stamps. The three cheery, ruddy faces look in enviable health. Or wealth. Year-round homeowners. In their creamy facial tissue and the way their eyelids droop money, she reads their lives back to the cradle. Pulsing, Little Ikiru glares his anger at them.

"They tried to steal my jaw," Pound tells her. "But I kept right on talkin'."

She walks to the post office. Her box is empty but for a pink rent-due reminder. She taps for the elderly lone part-time clerk. He has a monkish gray tonsure and looks busy. Doesn't like the pregnant jogger in his plaza?

"Isn't this early?"

"We always put it in two weeks early. Can I help you?"

"Hm! When do I have to pay it? I'm short today."

"Before the first, Mrs. Trueheart." A frank woman telling him she's moneyless, her eyes riveted on him. "I'm just beating the Christmas rush."

"Is the rate the same on Christmas cards as regular mail?"

"First class is three cents."

"If I don't seal the envelopes aren't they a penny-and-a-half?"

"Then they go bulk."

"Well, maybe I'll get penny postcards and decorate them. Be back."

Back uphill to the shop window. Her wisdom tooth pulses. A left-over placard announces a summer writing program led by a lady novelist. A sudden massive snowslide of grief breaks loose: she grits her jaw for the writer or poet she might have been. Surely she has a room of her own at last—for most of the day a whole house! But the house only enlarges the standstill of her wits, her wingless heart. The morning hours find her hopeful, but exercise and chores soon skim off high energy. Weaken her focus. She's up to her knees in hardening mud, all her mind's movements stiffening. Noon finds her shaping one end of the couch into a spoon or hatchery. As she empties into the great white freeze of the lake, the nothingness remaining slowly splits her heart.

In the window image she sees one of the trio laugh loudly, glancing at her. "We ought to seal her jaw," the woman says quite tiredly.

"How would you like a boot up your ass?" Curranne asks the image. She sees them look at her back, and turns. "You think I belong to the Deaf and Dumb Society?"

"Why would I think that?" the woman asks.

"Yeah, yeah."

She buys antipasto, goes back into the Colonnade and charges a long-distance call to Dr. David in North Warren. Her nickel returns.

Elderly Dr. David, crisp and Tennessean, says, "My dear, I'm quite busy, I have a patient. Can this wait? I know you're calling long distance and I don't want you to waste your expenditure." He's an absolute owl about money. "How may I help you?"

"Dr. David, you know my impacted wisdom tooth? I've got to have it pulled. But I'm afraid to."

"Why is that, my dear? The anesthetics are quite wonderful these days."

Tears spring. In the hall she sounds under water. "I can't take antibiotics, they'll keep me awake! I can't take anesthetics, they'll put me to sleep!"

"But that's only temporary, Mrs. Trueheart."

"He may knock me out. He may put my jaw to sleep, Dr. David. When I'm asleep I don't know what he'll do to me."

"That's too bad you think that. I'm sure you can find a reputable dentist if you look. Perhaps you should wait until you come to see me —Monday."

"I can't wait. I may infect the baby."

"Well, I can see why you're worried. Perhaps your husband can accompany you to the dentist."

"If I can get a morning appointment tomorrow. I want my father to have my jaw when I die."

"My, my! By all accounts, my dear, your father should predecease you."

"He can't do that! He can't die until I've helped him. I can always get a prosthetic jaw when I've got the money. He needs it now."

"That's all very noble of you, Curranne, and I appreciate your love—"

"It's not *love!* I hate love! I—"

"But don't you think a woman's jaw would be too small for such a robust man?"

"They run in the family, don't they? Like penises? I mean mine might be a little smaller but still fit. I don't know how else to help him."

"Have you thought how your husband might feel about this? Have you discussed it with him? He might not go along with your sense of self-sacrifice. And there's *his* self-esteem to consider. You follow me?"

"Yeah. No, I haven't brought it up."

"Do you want to come Saturday instead of Monday? I might fit you in."

"There's no time. I'm in pain, Dr. David. They tried to steal Ezra Pound's jaw but he got away to Italy before they could gas him. Maybe I should phone him. Do you think he could help me?"

"What about your baby and your abscess? Have your husband bring you in Saturday at five instead of Monday morning and we'll work this out. That's my rest hour but it can't be helped. I really must see you."

"Thank you, Dr. David. I'm sorry I bothered you but I know you're right. I have to think of the baby. I'll try to get a morning appointment in King James so Jack can go with me. Thank you for being there. I love you, Dr. David!"

"That's very kind of you. I know how hard that is for you to say. Be sure to phone me tonight. I'd like very much to speak with John too."

"He won't be home until ten when he gets out of work."

"I understand that, my dear. But I must speak with him to see that you're taken care of properly. You're very fortunate to have his care. Put an aspirin on your abscess and try to rest. Call me first thing when he gets home."

"Thank you, Doctor. I feel awful! But I can't take aspirin. I just can't. It keeps me awake and nervous."

"I'm terribly sorry for you. I understand your concern. But if your tooth is going to keep you awake anyway, then you might as well have the aspirin."

"I can't, Dr. David! I'll be hungover from it and flaky for two days. I know from experience that aspirin rots my brain. I'm extremely sensitive."

"But *I* know how strong you are, Curranne. I've given you my advice. I'll be waiting for your call."

"How's your ear, Doctor?"

"Much better today, thank you. Now I really must get back to my patient, my dear. Goodbye."

He hangs up. She breathes deeply at the phone, then redeposits her nickel and charges a call to the *Sun.* The nickel drops into the box. She bangs the treacherous frozen phone. The *Sun*'s switchboard redeposits her into Jack.

"Where've you been?" he asks. "I've been phoning."

"My tooth is beating."

"I'm sorry. I'm coming home."

"Well, I have to get an appointment first," Curranne says.

"What do you mean?"

"I want you to go with me to the dentist. I'm afraid to go alone. Maybe you can get me an appointment for tomorrow. I'm really dying."

"I don't doubt it. Maybe I can get an appointment for late this afternoon and you can take the bus down."

"I can't take the bus. Warn him that I can't take anesthetics or antibiotics."

"Honey, you want me to drive out and drive back? That's four times I'm driving that road and the gas will be four times the bus fare. *Ie-e!* and this isn't driving weather without chains."

"I don't have the money. I bought some antipasto. I decided to save money on the Christmas cards by buying penny postcards and decorating them by hand. That's much more personal, don't you think? And then I could afford the antipasto."

"But no bus? Look, we've already bought the Christmas cards. Oh, I-I-I can't talk about this anymore. I'll phone the dentist and call you back from my mother's house."

"Call collect. I don't want her mad at me. Why are you going there?"

"I've some very sad news."

"It's not my father!"

"No, Curranne, it's just something personal."

"Well, what is it?"

"I can't tell you here. Not from the office." Sounds near tears.

"Tell me! It's not my mother?"

"No! No. I can't talk. I'll call you from my mother's. I love you. *Goodbye."*

She stands abandoned, white-eyed, fuming at the dead phone. What's the worst could've happened? Skidding into someone, a school kid, a mother? Manslaughter, *hammerblow.* Someone died in his family? Margaret Sullavan in a plane crash?

Instead of walking home she crosses the plaza to a slatted green bench in the center circle and sits in a straightup huddle, the baby not allowing much slump. A stone four-sided memorial shaft rises from the frozen fountain. She's at peace with the great winter silence at Chautauqua, the always empty street and dark windows at night, grand quantities of thinking time. With his working hours, their trips to Dr. David in North Warren, her checkups in King James, and the

biweekly foreign films club, they've not met anyone on the grounds or
visited a single house. She fears anyone noticing her disorder and,
when walking alone, looks ready to bat a stranger who might speak to
her, though she's more relaxed strolling about with Jack. She likes
their walks around the grounds, to the empty piano shacks (too warn-
ing-windowed to pass by alone) or out past the pillared Hall of Philosophy to the far fence on South Fence Drive and back along the frozen
lake under rambling and gabled houses with crooking verandas and
huge white lawns, smoothsparkling at noon, gray at dusk, blue-glow-
ing at night. Liquidlong indigo twilight tugs Little Ikiru, the blue
snow a shoehorn into eternal light. She draws strength from Jack's
arm about her. Quiet, wonderbearing walks, the lake ice flat and sun-
burnt to the far hills. He's never sullen, but may hardline their costs
softly, which she enjoys as if sharing Dante aloud. His rare invitation
to talk money makes her feel adult.

The great calamity is their retarded station wagon. "Made in the
Ninth Circle by Demonic Motors," Jack says. It needs twenty-four-
hour care daily if it's to serve. Vain rage falls on the car, when not on
his sister, for its repeated stark deaths. Curranne races to the kitchen
each morning, as he leaves, but then can't bear not knowing the worst.
She creeps to the door and turns sideways at the window, glancing
through eyeslits. Every morning he circles the dead thing, fists
clenched, stiff-legged as the Frankenstein monster, mouth drawn at
the tragic heap of sprung panels and slow leaks. White lips writhe at
unbudgeable carbon-caked frozen pistons, the drained new battery no
charge can keep alive overnight, faulty wiring and faithfully rotated
bald blowouts. However often this scene repeats, in wet wind slamming from lake ice and whooping his homburg off, each time the final,
lasting disaster beyond miracle, she sinks poisoned to the couch for
the long horror, watching through the picturewindow, her back rippling with pity and fear until hopeless ritual brings the two-ton
iceblock to its first cough, its resurrection melting her pelvis.

When he returns to kiss her goodbye, the motor warming, they are
both too bubbling with nerve poisons to enjoy their victory. His cheek
on her breast, his hand on Little Ikiru for strength. She lifts and kisses
him, then holds him back by both shoulders for inspection.

He groans. "Jesus I'm late."

Wolf smile. "They'll fire you twice."

"I go forth."

She bats his shoulder softly.

"Bring back the bacon."

"No! I feel spinach madness. I *must* have spinach salad tonight."

"Bring back the spinach—and the bacon!"

"I don't even want to go." He presses her bones and mounds to him. "I hate to miss this whole day without you."

He's white-eyed with love. I'll miss you too, she thinks—but lets him dangle.

"They'll fire you three times."

For extra exercise today, she walks down to the lake drive through stinging uphill wind and heads home to North Avenue, the northern-most street on the grounds, off of North Lake Drive, watching a sun-shower on the lake. The sight lifts her, waving gray rain edged by bolts of sun on yellow ice. Then she stiffens, struck by the shakes, and hates Jack for not telling her his sad bad news. She marches home in a ringing huff.

The kitchen wallphone boils under her eye as she jabs her antipasto. Should she call his mother's? She jams the heel of fork onto the table, her face blowing with blood and anger. The phone rings. The chair tips violently, her blood plunging into her bowels. The receiver slips flying from her fingers, bounces from wall to floor. Rather than bend, she pulls it up by its cord with a small wild howl.

"What's happened?"

"I couldn't get you in until nine-thirty tomorrow. Can you hold out? I could bring you home some nerve drops like for teething."

"Nerve drops! That's not what I mean, for Christ's sake. *Give me it straight!*"

"I've been sacked."

"Fired? . . ." she whispers. Her palm hits the wall for support.

"Let go, if you prefer."

"But that's—Christmas is next week!" She hangs over the phone. "We can't live."

His voice quavers. "Go to the head of the class."

"Why are you joking about this, Jack?"

"Because I can't bear what I'm saying. It's not just the money . . ."

". . . How do you feel?" Her eye falls on a nutpick on the breadboard. She yearns for an operation on her genes.

"Pretty raw. My mother's sitting here stunned. Or I'd put it more vividly."

"How did it happen? Lamb and Bierce were in a cabal, right? To stick it to us!"

"What? Oh, what's it matter? It happened. I'll tell you when I get there."

"Why can't you tell me now? You don't have to spare my feelings. Those two guys are open books to me."

"Curranne, keep quiet. Hold on. Your mother? She fell down her back steps—no railing, you know? She's in WCA with her hip inflamed. No bones broken. She'll be all right."

"Oh my God. You said it wasn't my mother."

"Carol's going to be all right! We can see her in the morning. After the dentist. You don't have to come down today. It's *not* cancer."

"Cancer? Jack, I'm getting dizzy. You lied to me!"

"I'm sorry you think so, Curranne. I couldn't talk about anything in the office. I was cleaning out my desk. Lamb read me the death notice. The new owners are cutting back and since I'm the most incompetent person in the office, I go. I'm paid up. Kaput. Finito."

"Paid up? *Today?*"

"My check was waiting. Like some award, ha! But since I'd already drawn a week in advance, my one-week severance gives me a check for a week's pay."

"But that's all spent!"

"The rest is spent. Shakespeare."

"But you're not incompetent. Didn't you stand up for yourself? Were you that stupid? Whose side are you on, ours or theirs?"

"Alma scooped me."

"That's ancient history! I'm going in there with a frigging baseball bat."

"You compare my piddling stuff to hers—it's no show. Well, I'm sorry about your mother. D'ya want those nerve drops?"

"Jack, I don't want to be knocked out with nerve drops."

"These are for babies! *Babies!*"

"We can't afford 'em."

"Don't be idiotic!" He's silent a long time. "I'm sorry, I apologize. Let me bring them as a gift," he pleads. "At least one of us can feel no pain tonight. You have no idea what I went through leaving that office."

"*I want to KILL them all!*" The floor tilts. She grabs the wall receiver.

"Honey, am I drinking?"

"What? What? Of course not. What you don't know—"

"Then thank God for little favors. I'll be home about four-thirty."

She's panting. ". . . It's raining up here . . . Just started . . . Watch the two front tires, they're bald."

"So are the back two. It's raining down here too."

"Jack?" Her voice breaks. Her eyes tighten with suffering. A hand knots her hair overhead, nearly pulling off the glove of her face. "How am I going to do any Christmas shopping?"

"I don't know." He hears baffled disappointment in her silence. "We'll figure it out when I get home. Don't beg me. You're my wife."

"But I have to mail *some* presents to Matthew and Mark. This is the second Christmas in a row I haven't been with them."

"Honey, whatever you want. If it's reasonable. Or even if it isn't. And I promise I won't row out on the lake and pull the plug."

She's crying. "Christ, you'd need a pickax. Thank you, Jack. I'm terribly sorry for you."

"Hold the phone down. Little Ikiru, Daddy's coming right home. Your grandmother thinks I'm crazy, but you take care of Mommy for me. Did he hear that?"

"Yeah."

"I love you."

"Jack, my brain is spurting outta my head."

"I'm sorry for you, Curranne. I know this is a strain. And with your mother. *Don't* phone her, she's asleep. Just hold on, okay? What should I bring for supper?"

"Oh God, don't buy anything!"

"Will you shut up about money!"

"I'm sorry"—a small timid voice. "Buy whatever you wish."

". . . Let me bring you something nice. How about a pizza so you won't have to cook?"

"Cheese is constipating. And it would be completely congealed grease by the time you get here. I can't eat that shit."

"And neither can Little Ikiru. Okay, okay—I give up."

She fights taffy-brain. "Spinach!"

"Spinach?"

"And bacon. How does salad sound?"

"Munchy."

She forgets. ". . . I'm sorry again, Jack."

Hides his surprise. "Thanks."

"I'm saying it because I don't know what else to say."

"Sorry's fine. I love you even when I shout. You know that? Seeya soon."

"Yeah. Thanks."

The windows tink with sleet. White balls bounce from the panes. She sits in the front room, studying melt. Then the Ben Franklin stove in the dining room, its pipe angled into the fireplace chimney. Their oil bill is unpaid. Would wood be cheaper? Their half-grown ringtailed tabby, Perdita, Curranne's only companion, wakes in a daze in the rocker, watching the strange white ice ping and slide down panes. No pets are allowed loose on the grounds. The cat never goes out unless watched and then not until her begging is unbearable. Even then she hides under the front porch, pinning Curranne to the house, for she may run off altogether. If Curranne tempts her with chicken, Perdita will look away, her tiny pasteboard voice calling her an ugly lesbian. "I'll send Little Ikiru under there. He'll pull you out by your tail." Most often she drives the cat out by pounding a broomhandle over her nook. They are not friends.

Curranne lies on the couch to sleep and pulls a knitted green coverlet over herself. Instantly, she's dreaming, before falling asleep—if she is asleep. Dr. David, who has Ménière's disease and spells of nausea and imbalance, has had his jaw removed. He cannot buy a false jaw until Curranne's mounting bill is paid. Her nerves squirt. Far down the sleeted lake she sees a growing speck, Jack driving home on the ice. Her anxiety races about with sexual power, its brightness growing, then buzzes and buzzes.

A knock at the front door. She freezes. The door opens. Elderly, jawless Dr. David comes in, saying nothing, shakes his wet coat and throws it over the rocker. He eyes her on the couch with a disparaging, contemptuous look, then lies down and begins kissing and undressing her. She's naked. His jawless mouth sucks at each nipple. As he enters her the baby turns to ice. After a while he puts on his coat and leaves, closing the door with a backward look. She dresses quickly so she won't be found naked by Jack, then lies down again, stiff with guilt. Curranne whimpers soundlessly through an unmoving mask. When she hears Jack close the car door outside, she looks about the unlighted dark for a towel to wipe up the doctor's tracks but the wet prints have dried. Jack rushes in, steaming from cold rain, and shucks his booze-crazed ex-stepfather's long black Chesterfield. He studies her puffy eyes.

"I'm sorry. Did I waken you?"

"You got here fast. Are you using airplane gas?"

"No. It's four-thirty. Here are the drops. Let's have some light on the subject."

She looks quickly about the couch for sperm traces. "Did you see anyone on the road?"

"No. Why?" Jack asks.

"The baby's cold as ice. I think it's frozen."

"Oh? That's new."

"Well, if you'd ever been raped, you'd know what I'm talking about. It's very funny that we pay people to rape us. But that's the system, Jack. Isn't that the system?"

"What's this all about?"

"What's this all about? That Nazi psychiatrist."

"Dr. David?"

"Yeah."

"You told me he's Hebrew," Jack says.

"Yeah? How he can call himself a doctor—I know what I know. Certain things can't be laughed off that easily."

"What things?"

"Forget it. I've been thinking," Curranne says.

"You're welcome."

"For what?"

"For the nerve drops."

She's aghast. "My God, what you must think of me. That I'd be such a pushover for you and that lampshade artist. You must think I'm a sap!"

He unsnaps the small bottle, puts a few drops on his tongue. "Ooh!" Puckers. "Clove and cinnamon. Numbing!" Sits in the rocker and eyes her, the cat on his lap. "Come over here, will you?" Puts the cat down and pulls Curranne onto his lap. The cat jumps back up onto what's left of her lap. "All right, what have you been thinking?"

"You're very pale," she says. Good guy sells out and can't take it.

"I've drunk stronger things."

"And cold"—feeling his forehead.

"The heater's gone. Believe it or not, I got hailed on my face through the floorboards."

"Now this really is shit. I could kill your sister."

"Get in line. So this is it. I can't get unemployment for eight weeks."

"I'm terribly sorry, Jack."

"Fuck it. What've you been thinking? Make it something about food to take my mind off that drive up. I forgot the spinach, I was so twisted. The windows were streaming like a dam burst from Stowe on."

"How much do you think a cord of wood is?"

"A cord! I don't know."

"Well, what if we let the oil bill ride and burn wood instead? A cord might be only half or less of the oil bill and keep us warm for a month if we conserve it. Then we close off the rooms we're not using. If we slept in the living room we could close off the whole upstairs."

"I don't know," Jack says. "You might have something. We could phone and ask. Haul it in 'Bucket' and save delivery fee. What do we do about hot water?"

"Well, we turn the thermostat down to the bare minimum and stretch the oil we have."

"This may be madness."

She hard-noses him. *"Why?"*

"I don't have the slightest idea. But it sounds too simple and reasonable. Are you sure you thought this up all by yourself?" He nuzzles her breasts. "Aha! What's this? Do I note a little electricity in the pumps?"

"Nobody's pumping anything. Now be serious."

"Dr. Nuzzlehug is always serious."

"You're not helping me think."

"I thought I was. *Don't hit me!* Oh Christ, Curranne, I cannot perform before supper, please don't beg me. I'm so fucking hungry I could eat the couch. Let me be the last to know, whatever it is you're planning."

"Help me!"

"Should I help?" he asks Little Ikiru. "He says I should help."

"He can't talk. Can he?"

"How little you know. To me he talks. You he only kicks."

She goes white. "What's wrong?" Jack asks.

"He hasn't kicked in three hours."

"Of course not, he's like his old man. I haven't kicked you in how long? He's dreaming of the wonderful change of menu when he starts dining on the outside of this glorious confection. *Hey, are you asleep? See!*"

She smiles sleazily. He notices that her lips are growing less defined and more splotchy as if from fruit acids.

"So this is what happened to the American Girl?" he says. "Get up, I'll cook. If we light the kitchen maybe some food will appear. Tell me about your day while I rustle some cans."

"What about yours, Jack?"

"A rest! I can't before dinner. I'll loop into catatonic despondency, complicated by melancholia prolapsis and carbon-caked cylinder head. See what knowing you has done to me? My motor's all seized up —no oil and too much friction."

She collapses onto a fist against the kitchen counter. "You don't have to entertain me." Her eyes half close.

"What about me? I'm just shooting down nightmares before they happen, gang." Jack stares into Mrs. Lancaster's shelf closet of canned foods, loss slicing him. "Just don't believe it! We *gotta* replace this stuff." He empties peas with pearl onions into a can of cream of mushroom on the stove. "Sometimes when I'm at work, or was at work, I'd see you walking up the back stairs or ironing in the cellar or sweeping the porch or washing your lingerie, and the old heartworks would get terribly wobbly. Thinking of you and the little guy in the doghouse."

"Doghouse, huh?"

"I dig your legs."

Curranne nods. "I get that way, thinking of you down at the office. Or I did. I think more of the puppy now."

"I see. Well, I'm fond of him myself."

He unstrips tinned veal pâté with truffles and dices that into the soup-stew. "I like to think of you preoccupied with yourself. To think of you thinking. At the breakfast table alone or walking up North Avenue. It knocks me out."

"My just being here?"

"You being here, yeah. Just being," Jack says. Touch of garlic salt.

"Well, thanks."

"Thank you."

Sniffs the steaming pot, lifts it for her to smell. She gleams. His eye glitters. "This'll give you Chinese restaurant syndrome without one grain of monosodium glutamate."

"And it's 'Together at Last!'" Curranne cries. Lighting up, Jack's old goddess stepping out of a mist. "But now we're going to have each other's enforced company. Maybe we'll find we're wrong for each other?"

"No spark, no magic?" Her searching brightness stabs him. He feels unbounded love for his boggled wife. "Honey, I'm not worried."

"Maybe in a week we'll be racing around screaming for drugs so we can bear each other's company. You know, we haven't really *lived* together. Or you may be out job-hunting? . . ."

"We'll see," Jack says. "I can't see anyone hiring until the new year." Stirs the stew. The backyard splits with green light. "Hey, man, the world's first electric sleet storm." He's caught up by a vivid blue-and-white Dutch dish in a wall holder. "If we ever go into hypnosis, we can use that plate. What are you thinking?"

She splays on the wrought-iron ice-cream chair, then thinks of avoiding blue veins, gets up and walks about. "About Gallinger. How eager I was to get quit and start over. Throw away all my fuzzy crutches and get my head straight. Saggy is horrible, Jack, I'm too sensitive. You wake up in a bale of cotton, if you wake up. It takes two gallons of coffee before one clear thought breaks through—if one ever does. Ya drop things. Can't breathe, walk into doors. I'm not kidding!" Taps her head. "Nothing works."

"I can identify. Fortified zinfandel did that."

"And the tranks are no better. There's no you, only this cow walking around in your body."

Jack rubs her back, gives a hug. "I can tell you haven't fed kitty for three weeks." He digs veal cubes from the stew and puts them on a richly webbed thin blue saucer. "Chow down, Perdita."

Lays the table, stands back judging it, then picks up his horn from the counter—he likes kitchen tones—works the valves and puts it back down. "No zip today, Jack."

Splits English muffins into the toaster. Lights the candles and pulls grape juice from the fridge. "Westfield fifty-eight?" He seats her.

"You wouldn't sell me out," she says. "Would you?"

He nips his napkin through her juice. "Corkage. I'm sorry about the money, but something'll show up. Maybe I can get into advertising or public relations. I can always take a factory job until something breaks. Don't worry about money. I'm hopeful. Cheers, Madame Vraicoeur."

"Hey!" She jumps up. "Feel that?"

"I felt it! Come on, kid, right through the goalposts."

"Yeah! Maybe he's hungry."

"Brave little guy, not even a bankbook. His mother's a toughie too."

The bay window ices them in. The small pendulum wall clock measures eternity. She reads Jack's bruises through his skin of silence—his lids look battered and purple.

"Let's have a concert!" Curranne says.

"After dinner. My heart doesn't cry for music just now. You may not have noticed but I very carefully cook worse than you do."

"That means you can cook better than I do. And you're quite welcome to do your best, Jack. I don't mind being a pregnant princess."

"Well, that's nice. I had a kind of religious experience driving home."

"You're not hearing voices!"—shaken.

"Sure I am. Why not? I had a couple of bad skids on the Hunt Road —the hills were sleet. I got to the first crest past the Lakewood turnoff and was looking down on fields of sleet to the lake. And I thought, This is eternity too. Don't ask what I meant!—because right then a voice said, 'Jack, you're fucked. What're you gonna do?' I still feel raw, see, but worse things have happened to me than being canned. What's tough is incompetence in my chosen field, the humiliation. This is the only money I've ever made from my writing and I'm thirty. I heard myself telling you, 'It's only a job' and you saying, 'Yeah, yeah' and not meaning 'It's *only* a job.' "

"It's only a job," Curranne says.

" 'I know you're not going to cry over money.' "

"No guarantees."

"No, no, that's what the voice said. So I said, 'I think I will.' So I pulled off to the side, pouring tears, looking over this heavenly view of falling ice and gray lake. Really let loose." Curranne bends over, looking up closely into bloodshot eyes—had the tears been just for his job, or were they tears over his life with big dummy?—and begins rubbing Jack's back. "Then the voice was right beside me, and it was Ed, sitting there! No chin. 'Boy, I wish I had your problems,' he says, 'I haven't seen this lake for thirty-three years.' So I told him, 'You know,

I married your daughter? Well, you're going to have an imitation
Japanese grandchild made right here on Chautauqua Lake.' 'Sure, I
know that. You made me very happy, Jack. That's better than prosthe-
sis.' I told him think nothing of it, I had a lot of fun doing it. So then
he looked me straight in the eye—"

"Yes?"

"—with a big glint, and said, *'Make my girl happy.'* 'I'm not sure I
can—she's so damned love-resistant—but I'll try.' And then I pulled
my head off the wheel and drove on." Jack chokes, reliving his vision,
but goes on. "You may not think this was a religious experience. But I
did. Very spiritual. And it'd never have happened if I hadn't been
fired. It's only when you get your nose pushed flat against the wall
that you come most alive. I'd been so wrapped up in money difficulties
that I'd forgotten the main thing."

"What's that?" Curranne asks.

"Helping you feel happy."

"Yeah?"

"Both of you. *All* of us!"

"Happy about what?"

"About being married to me! Love conquers usury, dig? It's your
strong right arm against Moola . . ."

". . . I hope that dream was real and not sick. I mean . . ."

"Hey, hey, hey! I'm being spiritual and you're pissing me off." *Hold
back, don't say it.* "It's my dream, isn't it?" *Don't do it.* "I don't even
think he's your father and *I'm* having experiences about him!" *Don't
let go.* "For Christ's sake!"

Gets up, walks to the counter. Buries his head, breathing heavily.
"That wasn't enough. It's so hard." He puffs and puffs. "I have these
feelings I can't let go."

Sitting quietly. "Why can't you?" she asks.

"I don't believe in busting up like a woman."

"Then bust up like a man."

"I don't like that either," Jack says. "It's too much like Marlon
Brando movies. People raging at each other, bellowing like drunks. I
thought I was Stanley Kowalski with Thelma, an animal. Punching
holes in the bedroom wall. I give it all to the car now. Someday it's
gonna run over me, or slip off the jack on purpose."

"I'm glad you have the car," Curranne says, getting up. She holds
his shoulders again, rubbing his back, then turns him to her. "I'm

sorry you lost your job. I know what it meant to you. And I'm happy."

"Happy about what?"

"That you don't take it out on me," Curranne says.

"Never. Oh, I hope never. I don't want you struck crazy again or dead by your own hand. My conscience couldn't take it."

"You think about those things?"

"For our mutual defense. I don't want to do *anything* that'll hurt you. But I know what I've got bottled up too, you know? It has to come out somewhere."

"Stick to 'Bucket.' Every morning when you bring that car back to life, Jack, I feel like I've had the baby."

"Ha ha. Yeah? So do I." Holds her. *"I love ya!* And I gotta keep my woman happy. Especially, no more wards. *Hm?"*

"No more wards. Not if I can help it." Water stands in her eyes.

"Hey, what's this?" Jack says. "If you can help it? This calls for Sigmund Treuherz."

Jack leads Curranne to the couch and lies down beside her.

"When I'm driving home, I get a whole lot of profound questions to ask you. I develop huge discussions that never get said. All the time, don't you? In this one I'm asking you, What's *right* with your life? You alone I'm talking about. Are you a black woman living in Mississippi? If you have a relapse, God forbid, will you be sent to a segregated second-class snake pit in Jackson? Are you facing crime in the streets in Chautauqua? If you go out at night will you be mugged or raped in the dark like a Detroit housewife? When was the last time you heard a fire siren in earnest? Do you have all the food you need during pregnancy?—unlike mothers in India where the median life expectancy is thirty-five. Will Little Ikiru be born in a fine hospital with the best of care? Do you have an internist? Do you have a doctor for your mental health? Are you going to the dentist tomorrow? Did you get your nerve drops? Is there heat in the house during this fancy weather? What kind of luck has placed you in a palace where your every need has its convenience? Do you have an outhouse or a flush? What kind of rags do you wear? Do you have a sex life? Does anybody at all within a hundred miles love you? I mean if you looked very hard, could you find even one taker?"

"Well . . . *one.*"

"That guy who arrives every night in a split bucket? Now I know all these questions can have cynical answers. But you and me, kid, we don't think that way. Do we? Do you realize that for creature comforts you are in the top one percent of all the billions of human beings ever born? Or that if anyone might ever have a shot at savoring her life, it's you? Or that all of your awful experiences may be enriching you? Or that in days to come you may be the salt of the earth for many people who know you? You can be a powerhouse, I mean a great example to the small circle of people who know you and love you. Every family produces some galvanic figure who gives off current for the rest of them. You've survived the crucible three times, right? You must be getting *some* smarts by now, big mama. People need what you have to give. You're the most valiant woman I've ever met. No improvements are needed. Just keep hanging in there. Are you awake? Well, you see why I never say these things."

She nods. "I'm awake."

"Well, is all this nothing to you . . . when it might be everything?"

Her eyes shut. Her fist wavers and falls. "Where are my children!"

"One step at a time. Right? What do you think about all that?"

"I'm grateful, I guess."

"I'm asking seriously, Curranne. You know, whenever you wake up at night I wake up too. My little driving breakdown wasn't just about losing my job. Your father was talking about something else too. I hear your sighs at 2 A.M. And more at 3 A.M. And then you go down and sit at the living-room table as if you're going to study the house bills and dunning letters but you don't turn the light on. Just when you shouldn't allow cares to eat up your energy."

Biting her lip. "I want to help dig us out."

"Hey, I'll make more money. What else could I do? I don't know how, but I will. But if *we* can't take it, who can? With everything we've got going for us."

"Sometimes I could die when I look at that stack."

"Die? For an oil bill? For a battery charge? Get off it."

"I could kill those frigging, damned—" *The disnamable.*

"Come on, you're upsetting the progeny," Jack says.

"Don't laugh at me."

"What! And lose my equipment? What frigging damned fuckers are you talking about?"

She shuts up.

"Oh. Them. Yeah, well. If wishes were fishes, you'd have ten

A-bombs. I go along with you. Some anxieties are healthy. But just so much, dammit, and no more. Let's keep that stack in a drawer where we don't have it out like a bad-news juju glomming us all day long. On this very productive car ride with next to no *external* visibility, I also thought about the bills. Now that I'll be home, I think we should reserve our money anxieties for business hours, nine to five. Not waste our evenings, you know. Or sit up all night in a black cloud that only drains us. Do you know how much we owe?"

Fright. "How much!"

"I don't know! I know you'd cheat and look at the bills wherever I'd hide 'em, so I don't hide 'em. I thought maybe you'd totaled them up. Trouble is, we never itemize the big bolus. It's always growing so fast we never add it up. It's a big bogey because we don't know what it is. I'll show you, I'm not afraid to add up the fucking money."

"Right now?"

"Oh no no no. That's for business hours. We do that when we come home tomorrow afternoon. And we'll bring a cord of wood, my foxy one. We'll shape up. See where our asses are. Tonight is Happiness Night. We's gonter stomp dat Ol' Debbil Moola. D'ya think our happiness hangs on a buck?"

"We won't let it," Curranne says. "I feel good."

"Okay, let's shrink that fucker down another step. The living-room table. All our financial horror will be reserved for the living-room table alone. Elsewhere, verboten. When we want to go to the mat with Moola that's where we do it. And all stops pulled out, the full sonata. You shout and scream, and I'll kick the table, and we'll work this out like adults. I know, I know, you feel too adult already! So you get an extra scream. And we set the clock for ten rounds. Thirty minutes! That's it. If we can't total it up and portion it out in thirty minutes, we deserve to die. You see what this is all about?"

"Moola!"

"No, no, Mrs. Trueheart. We are bringing two zombies back to life."

"Aren't we smart? We're pretty damn good."

"You're good for me, I know that. Okay, now my spiritual experience. Is there anything I can do to make you happier to be living with me? It hurts to leave myself wide open—but I'm asking."

"There isn't," Curranne says.

"I can take it. Name one thing I personally can do to make you happier. There may be five or ten things. But name just one. I may not want to, but I'll try to do it."

"Maybe less ice cream and sweets. I can't eat that crap and I get nauseous watching you glop down a plate of fudge or quart of ice cream. I'm sorry but I do. I think it's unkind of you to make me watch you kill yourself."

"That hurts. Did you have to pick that? But maybe it's time."

"Pretty soon I'll be able to get into your pants," Curranne says.

"Okay! I'm reeling, but okay."

"You asked for it!"

"I did. On orders from Ed. Now, *this* step is on me. Ask me to do one more thing—within reason."

"Oh, this is fun. We should do this every night."

"Just name it," Jack says nervously.

"I shake every morning when you go out to the car. You turn red going out the front door. I'm afraid you're going to hurt yourself."

"I thought we agreed that was my one therapeutic vice?"

"Not for me," Curranne says. "I start to lose my breakfast, you look so crazy."

"Well, great. Thanks. I'll take the pledge on the porch daily. Maybe a little prayer on the railing. Sanity First."

"Well? What can I do for you?"

"No, no. I'm happy as is. You observe business hours and that'll be a gigantic advance."

"That's not fair!"

"Oh, I dread this. I'll rue this."

"It can't be that bad"—knuckling him.

"I wish you wouldn't say Yeah, yeah to everything I think is spiritual. I get a heavy heart thinking of Little Ikiru being born into a household of stark existential rationality. I hate to think of raising a little periodic atheist."

She's not happy. "What's that mean?"

" 'I'm an atheist. Period.' I'd like to open your mind."

Eye-slits. "What're you asking me to do?"

"Admit that there might be other shoulders than ours helping carry the load. The Life Force, if nothing else!"

"Yeah, yeah. But I don't believe that," Curranne says.

"Hm. Okay, skip it."

"What can I do? I have absolutely no belief. When you talk that stuff, you sound wacko to me. I loathe every word of it. Frankly, it disgusts me to have to listen to it. I get nauseous."

"More nausea. I'll shut up. That'll be three things I'm doing to make you happy. I think I'll play my trumpet while I'm ahead."

Jack sets up his music stand in the living room and blows feebly. Stops. She puts food away in a steadily rising rage. Her eye lands on the Dutch dish on the wall. She snatches it down and hurls it from the kitchen into the living room. *Hah!* she triumphs. But it's thrown badly, lands on the throw rug behind Jack, flips and skitters and doesn't break.

Jack picks it up. "Jesus Christ."

She roars from the kitchen doorway. "Whattaya mean, trying to *change my mind?* You *monster!* You warped sonofabitch! Trying to mindfuck me!" She rushes to the stove, grabs the stainless-steel soup pan. Flies winged to the living room. Slam's Jack's head. Jack falls straight down. When he comes to she's kneeling on his chest, beating his head in. Jack screams, his face whipped with blood drops. Bone buckles inward. He knocks her arms aside. But it's too late. She thwacks him two-handedly and he dims out.

"I'm sorry," she says across the kitchen table. Her teeth lodge in a nectarine.

Holding himself to two tablespoons of chocolate ice cream. "About what?"

"I'm sorry I hurt you."

A minute ago he lay battered to death on the living-room floor. Now he sits before her, completely restored.

"Hey, forget it. Are we going to have Happiness Night? Let's light a fire and lay out a blanket of Mahler."

"You shouldn't love me."

"Now ya tell me! Why not?"

"I may not always be here," Curranne says.

"Oh? Where are you going?"

"You never know. I could just walk out the door." Shrugs. "Never come back."

"Okay, that runs in your family. But it doesn't mean you'll do it."

"What if I can't help myself? Could Ed help himself?"

On his face the blood drops come and go.

"Honey, that was in the middle thirties, if it happened at all. Could Ed help himself? You're really worried about your genes, aren't you?

Look, are we Carol and Ed or are we Curranne and Jack? We'll be extraloving parents as a safeguard. That's all we can do, isn't it?"

A faint smile.

"Just stack the dishes. I'm going to blow a few woodnotes."

Sets up his music stand in the living room and blows. "This one's for you, gorgeous!" Drifts back into the kitchen, horn in hand. Kisses her cheek over the sink.

She's blue. "Thanks."

"The ship's orchestra will now play 'A Lovely Piece.' " Pats her bottom, kisses her other cheek. "I'm desperate for organic therapy, Dr. Reich—a nice, steamy orgone box." She bares her teeth, setting the fatal soup pan into the drying rack, then softly knocks him on the lip with her brow.

"When I left Gallinger I was fit as a frigging fiddle. It's only since I started seeing that Nazi Jew that all this genes shit has been buzzing around the air so that I can't sleep." Slaps an arm hard for winged genes. "I want to be left alone!" Her parrot pupils widen and close at him as she floats in and out of the kitchen in her mind. Her head slowly lies flat on her shoulder, neck broken defenselessly. Wide open to assault, she sneers contemptuous disparagement.

"It's all legal now, Jack."

Waves flood Jack. His nerves bend this way and that. He chokes, shocked breathless, but nods. "I want to help. Believe me."

"No, I can't. It's very hard to when you don't show it."

"How don't I show it?"

"You let that dead pig David go on frigging me. It's your baby too he's killing, not just mine."

"How's he killing the baby? By trying to understand you?"

"Don't be subtle. You call what he does understanding? You're more hopeless than I thought. *David* is a perverted old goat! He gets his kicks by using women's brains as a ray to look inside them. I can feel him pawing my baby. I know he's doing it, he can't help himself. He's got a movie camera in the ceiling to look into me. I watch him every moment to keep him from pressing the buzzer on the side of his desk. He's got another in the floor."

"Another movie camera?"

"Another *buzzer* under the rug! Jesus, can't you grasp anything? I'm giving it to you straight. I can feel the buzzing every time I sit in that ratty old chair of his. Maybe it's wired too. It must be. Maybe—"

"No maybes, please. What if all this weren't true, Curranne?"

"Don't tell me that! Who goes there, you or me? The chair gets overheated! There is an *ionic flow*. I feel it! I know it's *there*. Or I'd think I was in relapse just when I know I've never been healthier. Look at me! Look at my skin. Look at my eyes. I have survived more hospitalizations than Margaret Sullavan. I am the healthiest woman on earth. I can run faster and farther than any *man* alive. And don't you forget—I beat that frigging disease three times. I'm invulnerable. I am up to my ears in antitoxins from my own organs. If I'm not sane, Jack, no one's sane."

"And you're only going to get better. And I've sworn off ice cream so that I'll be worthy of you." He carries his half touched dish to the sink.

She watches chocolate rinse down the drain. "You're not too shot. You could still shape up."

"How can I help you feel even better about yourself?"

"I'm glad I'm getting all this important shit out. I've been holding it in too long."

"I'm happy too."

"It was killing me."

"Hell, yes!" He rubs her. "It's painful to be misunderstood."

She nods. "We'll make out . . . as long as we see eye to eye. But it's hard giving a supersensitive guy like you the straight dope. Just shut up about certain things you don't know anything about. I know everything either of us needs to know."

"Do you love me?"

"Jack, that kinda talk makes me nauseous."

"Maybe you'd get over your nausea if you'd commit yourself."

Eyes fierce and terrible. *"Commit* myself?"

"Well, to the power of love. Don't *I* help you feel better about yourself? That says something about love."

Warped grin. "I suppose it does."

"When you talk with me, you talk with your real feelings, don'tcha? Not some camouflage. Oh, I know you're wicked when you really let go, Scarlett. But you hold back with me—or else I like it. I stand back and take it. Anyway, a little heat brings out the spices, like hot buttered rum."

"Hot buttered rum, huh?"

"And you sing so well!—when you're a little dippy and give way to your feelings. So, you pick, I'll blow. Singer's choice. How about 'You'd Be So Nice to Come Home To'?"

"I thought I was choosing?"

"Sometimes I think of you being three years older than me during World War II. When that song came out." Leafs through a fat book of tunes. "You graduating, thinking of the WAVES and so on. And I get this big thump for you as a young woman. Younger woman! *Girl,* I mean."

Her terrible eyes frisky. "You do, huh?"

"When you were a little filly and bedeviled by hormones."

"I still have a few."

"I see you walking around, digging your life. Widely admired. Your beautiful pins in bobby sox."

She sneers. "My worst years. I'd rather be in the hospital than relive all that heartbreak. At least on the ward you have nothing to lose. My senior year I was voted The Girl Most Men Would Like to Be Marooned with on a Desert Island. While you were jerking sodas at Fulmer's. Yeah! Don't faint."

"Faint? But I've done it! I beat out the senior class! You were the sexpot of King James High School and a horny little ninth-grader won you. Here we are, marooned at Chautauqua. Could I ask for more? Margaret Sullavan with Betty Grable's legs. All my adolescent torture, paid off. My God, life is good."

"Sometimes, Jack, I wonder. Anyway, right out of high school I got engaged. And then I was dumped. Jilted."

"I know that story. Story of your life, huh?"

"So much for sex appeal. It hasn't kept a man yet."

"Honey, one look at you now and I know you deserved that desert-island tag." Jack's eyes close. "There you stand, on the school steps. All sweater and heavenly hips. Balancing your books on your pelvis. If I could just reach out . . ." Reaches for her.

"I'll slug you!"

"All right—you were ugly and bowlegged."

She sneers happily, digging his ribs, and is on him like a cat as he falls. Bestriding and tickling, she locks his hips, her mound on his chest.

"I'm glad you caught me in one of my better humors," she says.

"Jesus, a joke for the family Bible. I think I'll faint. On the other hand I feel awfully organic."

"If you'd been as embarrassed as I was all through school, you wouldn't make jokes. People whispering about my father. I mean, what do you tell people, one day your dad disappears out of the house? Everywhichway *gone,* man. I had to be serious. And when I got jilted I had to be even more serious. And took up premed, so I could grind like a dog and not socialize. College was a relief. I suppose you think I'm too serious?"

"Oh my heavens. You have a wonderful sense of humor . . . under iron control. I flipped the first time I saw you smile. I think it was our wedding night and you were off guard. Giving me my robe!"

"Keep it up, butterball. You think I don't know what a solemn horse's ass I am? Look, mister, I've had some big disappointments. Starting early, dig? Why don't you just blow your horn and shut up."

Jack brings in the lighted dinner candles and switches off the lamp. Curranne, Queen of Baghdad, sweeps about, twirling invisible scarves, and at last sits on his lap by the music stand. An unseen veil over her nose, eyes slick with candleflame.

"Here we are on the moon," Jack says. Puts his mouthpiece rim to her belly and listens through it. "I hope we didn't induce premature labor."

"I'd tell you, Shakespeare."

"Hey, are you up? I guess your dancing didn't wake him."

They sing and play "Come Rain or Come Shine," then "On the Sunny Side of the Street"—she gives *I'll be rich as Rockefeller* the finger. After "Pennies from Heaven" Jack says, "I'm bushed. No more lip."

"No, no!" Curranne cries. "I'm not through. I loved it!" She sits up, startled. "Did you hear it? There! . . ."

Jack listens hard at her belly. Her lips spread flat with pleasure. Her face is a silk sheen.

"Little Ikiru is singing," she whispers.

"In Japanese?"

Her chin marbles blissfully. Jack hugs and nuzzles her. The house creaks. He feels it sink through the lake ice, and digs his cheek into her.

PART SIX

The Marvel

"We'd better get home early," Curranne says, breath steaming the windshield. "The worst blizzard in thirty years and *we're* out. We must be mad."

"You had cabin fever, remember?"

She snorts.

"All right," Jack says. "Maybe the baby said it."

Parks by his mother's lighted porch on Rose Alley, behind Liz's new Chevy. Curranne looks ready to torch the Chevy, her breath exploding.

"When she starts in on me as if I were Liz, it's humiliating. She's not even my mother."

"We'll only stay a half hour." Jack scuffs around the car, opens the door. She grips the door frame with both hands to turn herself as he lifts her legs outside.

"Christ, I'm shivering." Whipping flakes stick to her lashes. "I'm afraid of blowing up, Jack. Warn her. I mean *warn her.*"

"You look lovely." Her clear milk-white eyes search his. "Just a touch of hectic tea rose."

"Stop joking. I'm very depressed."

"You should be. Got every reason. I hope we left enough wood on the fire." They stand in dim porchlight at his mother's door. "How do I look?"

He's dropped ten pounds. "Let's not get lighter-than-thou. I'm not that big," Curranne says.

Thuds his forehead against the door, his hand on the knocker in the Christmas wreath.

"What's wrong?" she asks.

"I'm sorry about the pipes bursting, I'm sorry about the car heater. I'm sorry about God and the blizzard. General apology to cover all my fuckups. Will you forgive me?"

She turns from the wreath, heads back to the car alone. Gets in her side, closes the door. He watches her slide under her blankets.

Jack gets back in. "What's this all about?"

"It's all a mistake. I should never have come, New Year's Eve or not."

He has no answer. "I can't leave you sitting out here, sweetheart. There's not even a heater." She snuggles into her long black coat and square Russian cap with its flaps up. Gives him her big silence.

With both palms Jack washes drivenness from his face.

"I know what you want, Jack. A rip-roaring fight so you can run out the back door, bottle in hand—never to be seen again. And me left with *them*. No thank you. Not on your life."

"I haven't had a drink since last summer."

"Yeah, yeah. So you say. But I see you. That's all you think about, Vasco da Gama off to Florida and the fountain of youth. I see you looking in the mirror. You've got a lot to lose before those beach bunnies give you a tumble. Go in so we can get to the movies."

". . . I'll bring you out something to eat."

She turns aside in nausea.

"You can't go without food."

"I wish I had a fork. I'd get you out fast enough."

Jack starts the car, puts it in low. "Put your foot on the clutch. When I give the signal, take your foot off."

"What're you doing?" Curranne asks.

"I'm going to lie in front of the car. You want to kill me? Kill me."

But as he gets out the motor dies. He faces the dead wagon. Maybe it hasn't the strength to kill him.

"Jack, I really don't like it when you're cynical. I've never heard you talk like this before. You've said some awfully funny things to-night."

He reaches in, switches off the engine. "Right now, dying would be heaven."

"Why don't you wait until morning and start the New Year fresh?"

He takes the keys. "You wait here."

Jack stomps off snow and goes into the house as she rolls down the window and shouts out. "If you leave me here I'll be dead when you come back!" But he doesn't hear.

Her unease is instant. Breath spuming, her life rushes out of her in a *whoosh,* then returns in a hammerblow to the baby. She squeezes on the handbrake so the car won't run off with her. Gray outlines weave through falling snow. She can find no weapon in the car and grinds her boot savagely against the rotting floor's cardboard covering. Wide-eyed she phones Dr. David for help. His phone rings and rings but he will not lift up. She breaks off the call, moaning. A nearing presence invades her, her flesh and baby jelled clear blue. Squinting secretly aside into white waves, she sees God in a big monk's robe shuffle gigantically over the stone fort of the library, lamplight searching up the under-water heights of his dim lower skirts. At first her bones attune to impending miracle, waves of hope that he will see her. One touch, one breath will free her from years of mental cancer. But he turns, is gone into the abandoning silence. Her eyes mist . . . abandonment ripples through her, pricking and pricking her eyes. Barely a breath left in her. She merges with the snow, barren of being, pure and abandoned but for the heavy squeeze popping tears from her eyes. She will take out her baby, pour honey or lye on it in offering, if only he will clap hand to her brain, give her rebirth in this life, skip the extras, just a touch, right here, now. Help me! She knows he can take the baby anyway, if he wishes, and not touch her, leave her ablaze with destruction crashing outward from her. Thumbsucking her peppery evil, gloating on her worthlessness, her power to destroy. Is her infinite emptiness a test, a spiritual trial? "I want you," she says aloud, shut-eyed with bliss of hopelessness. Yearning hammers her. He does not answer. If she freezes, doesn't move, he won't see or punish her. She locks herself in, tries to breathe unseen through her navel; a toad in mud under winter ice. Any movement of her ribs can bring pain.

She knows a bitter, stony lot near Falconer, not three miles from here, so barren, so alluring. Batching it in a wooden crate, slipping through the bars of daily life . . .

"I'm sorry still again," Jack says, starting the car. "I wasn't mad at you, Curranne. When you get savage every word is a knitting needle. I flake out."

She grits her teeth. Hears herself say, "I don't want you to leave me. I'm afraid if you really know me you will."

Her frankness moves him. "Thank you for telling me. This is a cold meat-loaf sandwich I made for you."

She turns the bag between them. "That'll sit in me like a cold frog all through the movies. What'd your mother and Liz say about the pipes?"

"You don't think I broadcast my idiocy?"

The pipes, the pipes. Hammerblow of plumbing repairs. Now they are stuck with woodfire and weak-flowing cold water until they can

pay the plumber and also get the oil bill halved. The plumbing esti-
mate is four hundred dollars; the whole house is damaged. The upstairs flush is shot. The cellar is solid ice four inches deep with the
upright steam iron's tip just showing. Water has loosened a manhole-
size chunk of plaster from the living-room ceiling and rust-stained half
the wall. Mayville Towing refuses further service. *(Hammerblow.)* A
round of bills at town and county groceries, credit cut off, Jack's eye
seeking new stores. Death notices from Bigelow's, Household Finance,
Mrs. Lancaster, stack of monthlies from Curranne's internist, the dentist (she'd had gas but no needle or antibiotics), Dr. David, county
power and gas, the phone's long-distance disaster. *(Thud, thud, thud,
thud.)* She turns to Jack, amused, with a lofty sidelong glance, a cold
floor wind snaking her legs.

Her silence rakes him. "I should gas myself," he says. Silence. "But
I don't dare. Mayville might turn it off in the middle."

Silence.

Curranne laughs to herself, sighing. "Stop being stupid about our
bills, Jack. I can always put my coat on backward and be admitted to
North Warren while you go back to your mother's cellar. You'd be
cozy."

"I think bankruptcy'd be easier. And I don't want to raise Little
Ikiru in a cellar."

For battery tactics they park facing downhill. Jack scuffs the drift
away by her door, gets the film cans, and escorts her into the coffee
shop across from the Y. She takes out orange juice and carrots-with-
raisins salad. In the Y, less than a fourth of the club has shown up for
his bill of Italian neo-realists.

Curranne eyes the sparsely filled chairs. "Christ, you may lose
money tonight."

"King James Infirmary—so cold, so white so bare." But he's caught
by her undrugged, glittering eye and fresh lipstick. *"Komm, mein
Herzchen,* let's not whimper. We asked for it."

Curranne sits spellbound by Rossellini's *Open City:* pregnant Anna
Magnani, unmarried and gunned down in the streets by Nazis. Romans living in shoebox apartments, partisans darting through cellars
and rubble. "That hovel is even worse than ours," Jack says, "if you
can measure these things." She misses the story, seeing an extra film
not there, entering a paradise of bombed emptinesses, broken bricks,
blasted plaster, a bliss of emotional destruction peopled with evil fig-

ures bearing swastikas. Here is metaphysical wreckage, tattered people escaping sight and scurrying into holes and pockets, hopelessness scouring blocks and blocks of godless desolation. She stiffens. Where is *he?* His absence seeps into her, he gives not a breath or touch from his being. She is still as the thought comes: *Nobody believes in God.* The Pope doesn't, Ike is faking it, Jack's Life Force is just words. Nobody does. It's all masks. The priest sacrificing himself to the German firing squad is just an actor, a sentimental sop put in by Jewish usurers. She freezes, entranced and unblinking, cleansed to the bone as the film ends.

Thanking Jack for a great flick, half the room leaves for parties.

"Happy New Year! I love earth mothers," Phil Newquist says.

Curranne laughs, her Chaplin grin.

Phil asks, "Are you going to the Pi Phi dance at the Hotel King James after this soak in Italian depression and get staggeringly polluted? Oh, sorry. You still on the wagon?"

Curranne says blithely, "He's already had a couple at his mother's. That's why he's so gay."

"Gay?" A pall hits Jack. "I begin to wish I had. It was flowing."

She's bewildered. "I don't see why you deny it. I don't keep you from drinking."

"You help."

De Sica's *The Bicycle Thief,* heavy on the gloom. A very poor, honest, hollow-cheeked young father peddles about slapping up billposters of Rita Hayworth. When his bicycle is stolen before his eyes, he's feverish with worry—he'll be fired from his new job without it. Curranne watches his anguish with triumph. He has no more to lose, seemingly. She enjoys his anxiety, fears he'll get his bicycle back, and distances herself from a sentimental letdown. She looks out from a milk bottle on its side, the screen a porthole stretching away from her. He tries to find the thief, with his seven-year-old son tagging along. Matthew's age. Perhaps Dr. David will take Little Ikiru away after she has him, so she can't skip out on her bill. She'll kill the baby first. At last the wretched bill-poster steals a bike himself, but is chased, caught, and humiliated before his son. She twists about. Jack takes her hand. She clamps the baby rigidly within her. Suffering, the damned bill-poster walks home. His son refuses to walk with the outcast. But at fadeout the boy takes his father's hand and they go on walking. Curranne laughs loudly.

Jack is frightened. She wipes a tear of laughter from her eye, saying, "That was so maudlin it was funny."

"I'm happy you weren't bored. I liked it better ten years ago."

She watches from afar as he collects receipts from Phil at the ticket table, pays the projectionist and packs the cans. Phil follows him about stiffly, waving his arms. What's life like with nothing to lose, she wonders. Living with someone worse off, like Phil, attracts her. Giving herself to him would be fulfilling. He's obviously never bedded a pregnant woman. She knows he loves her, and gives him doe-eyed glances, maybe the first he's ever had. He's Jack's only friend she likes, his bumbling is erotic. What she could do for him! They could live in empty lots together. She'd inspire him, love would shrink his tumor, he'd give her the last breath in his body. She strides through town on his arm, Phil reborn in a Joycean eyepatch, his good eye purposeful and shining. Pride fills her at his victorious heart, her breasts are gravid with happiness. This is a hard real family warmth she seldom allows Jack. The freedom to love is a dream, yearning, just past her fingertips. She stands with eyes shut.

"You all right?" Jack asks. "Let's shove off for the ballroom."

Guides her out to "Bucket," locks the film inside. "It's only two blocks. Let's walk."

"How'd we do?"

"Po'ly, Missy Scarlett."

"You'll learn," Curranne says.

"About what?"

"Usury, Jack."

"This is usury? It's a film club trying to break even."

"Please, I'm not poor cow. You may not know it . . . but I am offended by your total obsession with money."

"Oh? Glad you told me. I'll give it up."

"You're going to spend your life groveling for security. And it demeans you! I tell you this for your own good."

"I'm delighted by your interest. It really helps."

"I see your epitaph now. It says ROOM FOR IMPROVEMENT."

"Kind of you to think of my eternal welfare, when you don't believe in it."

Helps her over mounds. Dim snowlight on heaps. The hotel lies ahead in heavy flurries. They hop up and over a drift, faces flakebeaten. Lipstick slick, pale skin splotched with heat. "A real twinkle-toes!" he says.

As they walk he's struck by small flakes winding through marquee glow. Hotel bulbs fix him with hot sicksweet strangeness at the blizzard's limitlessness around himself and this small-boned being on his arm, his pregnant mad wife, with whom he's fighting but not fighting. He stops, turning her to him.

"I don't want to dance tonight," she says. "I'd be grotesque."

"I love you."

"I'm not getting out on the floor, Jack!"

"Kiss me."

Her cold damp cheek and mouth are delicious with snow. He asks, "If you don't love me, what do you think of during sex?"

"Oh? Nice things."

"I'd like to join you sometime."

Smelling liquor, she turns her face away. "I don't know why you do it."

"I love you!"

"You know it's bad for both of us. I go crazy."

"Screw crazy. Anyway, I can't help myself."

"I know you can't. You're so sick, and you were doing *so well.*"

"I'm just normal!"

She laughs hard. "Jack, I'd hate to tell you what people really think of you."

"What do they think?"

"They think you're really scattered. Dr. David is convinced you're a basket case. You'd better start seeing him. I think it's too late, but he thinks there's still a chance. I told him everything about you. He says your real future is as a celibate."

"What about my mad passion for your body?" Jack asks.

"My real worth will be known someday—and it won't be for my body."

"Of course not, it'll be for your brains. Or your spirit! Don't you want me around?"

"It's not up to me. It's what you do to yourself. You're a hopeless alcoholic. Face up to it."

"Sonofabitch!" Jack sees red spots when she brings this up. "Will you stop harping on *my drinking?*"

"I'm sorry, Jack, but that crap affects your brain. I told him about the coat-hangers too."

"What coat-hangers?"

"The ones you wrap around your penis so you can't ejaculate."

"After that tidbit he must think me pretty bizarre."

They cross the crowded lobby of girls in big skirts and orchids and climb to the mezzanine ballroom. Stu Snyder's trumpet plays "I Don't Want to Walk Without You" through the noisemakers. Jack shows off Curranne to his old school chum Harding Olafsson at the door. He's handing out horns, hats and pink and green and black half-masks.

"Welcome!" Harding says. "Go right in. Any wife of Jack's is a wife of mine."

"I hope that doesn't go for babies too," Jack says. "We're not going in. It's time for the lights to go out. We thought we'd stand here."

"Go in if you want," Harding says. His big blond rabbit teeth warm them. "Be my guests. Just nip on in."

"No, no," Jack says. "We'll stand here by the bar."

Cases of scotch and bourbon sit on duck boards by the entrance bar. Curranne eyes them and says, "He thinks you're ready for a nervous breakdown."

"Harding? That's perceptive of him. He may be right."

"Dr. David."

"What gave *him* the first clue?"

Her eye is steady. "Stealing the club money. It doesn't matter that you're ex-reporter Jack Trueheart. It'll be reported in both papers when it gets out. You won't be able to squelch it."

"No, I won't," Jack agrees.

"They'll just hound you. It's going to be pitiful."

"Sure you don't want to dance?"

"I'm a *blimp!*"

"Oh, come on."

Weighing the crowded ballroom—"Wanta show me off, huh?"

"I sure do."

"No." But the sparkling dimness binds her. "I better not."

Harding turns to her pleadingly. "Hey, I'm off! How about one turn? I'm dying for some sex! Well, for a dance—"

"She doesn't feel up to it," Jack says.

"I do so!" She takes Harding's arm, warning Jack: "But I'm keeping my eye on you, mister."

Harding says, "When a beautiful woman says okay, it's *okay*. Thanks, Jack, you're a peacherino."

Still in her black coat and Russian cap, Curranne sinks into the dancers with Harding.

"Ohh, this is fun," she says, taking a Palm Court swirl.

"Wow, you're a lovely dancer!" Thinks twice. *"Drat!* I should have said, Madame, you dance divinely."

"Thank God King James has petrified into the fox trot."

"You're very light on your feet. When are you due?"

"I don't know! Let it come when it comes, I'm in no hurry to be confined. What do you do?"

"I'm a psychiatrist."

"What! I didn't know there was one in King James."

"There isn't. I'm in Rochester. I'm just home to see my family and for the frat dance."

"You're Pi Phi?"

"And Phi Bete."

"Hey, so am I!" Harding's blue eyes are beacons. "Let me ask you a question. What do you think of plastic surgery?"

"Depends. Who needs it?"

"I may want to alter my appearance after Jack is arrested."

"Jack's being arrested? I hadn't heard about that. What for, may I ask?"

"He stole his movie club's funds. It's not all that much, but I'm sure it's over twenty dollars, which makes him open to a jail term." She's happy unburdening herself to a handsome, clearly single psychiatrist, and breathes her winged spirit over him. "That's *malfeasance*, isn't it? He'll be put away and then I'll go to Seattle or Dallas or Rochester and have my face changed." All logical steps.

"I'm sorry you think that might be necessary. I'd really hate to see beauty like yours mishandled by a bungler. That's always a chance you take."

He's so warm. Curranne says, "I don't know what else to do!"

"May I ask, do you have an analyst?"

"Me? Of course not. But Jack's seeing a Dr. David out in Warren."

"Oh, a marvelous man! I know him well. One of the best in the country, if a bit . . . metaphysical. How does Jack like him?"

"I shouldn't say this but I don't think he's much help. Jack associates pretty loosely these days."

"What's wrong?"

"I told him I wouldn't go to bed with anybody sicker than I was. Not that I'm sick! But that does rather upset our marriage. And he's angry that he can't make ends meet."

"Who isn't? That's not enough, do you think, to set him off?"

"Oh, it's the baby too. Heredity fears, that kinda stuff."

"I'm sorry to hear that. I'd never heard of any mental illness in his family."

"Well, his father was a basket case. Hopeless schizophrenic with paranoid symptoms. It's paralyzing Jack. But—we can accommodate ourselves to anything, can't we? Are you going to kiss me when the lights go out?"

"I sure am!"

"Good." Lays her cheek on his. "I need it."

"So do I."

She burns under his cool blue eyes. "I love you."

"What's my fatal attraction?"

"You're a total stranger but I'm drawn, Dr. Olafsson, to your kind of intelligence. I like your eyes. So Swedish but sympatico, ha ha ha!"

Suddenly the band breaks into "Auld Lang Syne" and a roar goes up, horns wailing and balloons popping. As the room drops into darkness, her arms pull Harding. Confetti spiders over them. She kisses him abandonedly. A red ball rises and slips with a liquid burst into her brain, a release so passionate she hopes its streaming will linger, then stretch and deepen and rust like a sunset. No part of the universe is closed to her. A wind parts her limbs, carrying her off. One second of blindness to everlasting pain is ecstasy.

Still in the dark, Harding says, "I think we'd better catch Jack."

As they make their way through bumping bodies, she sees Jack dart behind the bar and slip a full fifth into each coat pocket. When they arrive he's nervous. "Oh, there you are!" he says. "Well, how was that?"

"Marvelous!" She kisses him too, despite the bottles.

"Thanks a lot," he tells Harding. "It's midnight, Sleeping Beauty."

"You mean Cinderella," Harding says.

"That too," Jack agrees.

"Why don't you call me tomorrow? We haven't talked in years."

"Great idea!"

"Be sure to do it. I'm at my mother's on Isabella."

"Wonderful to see you, Harding. Even this briefly. I want to talk with you too."

Jack shakes his hand. Curranne kisses Harding goodbye, and they leave. "We should have him out for supper before he leaves. I like him!"

"So does everybody," Jack says. They go down broad stairs from the mezzanine. "He was president of the student body everywhere he went. That must help in being a shrink. He told you he's a shrink?"

"That's a good word for a friend, isn't it? What do you call your wife? *Broad?* Or something more colorful from the Marines?"

"I could be jealous. But there are some things I'd rather not broadcast around town. Understand?"

"Broadcast? Haven't you heard of confidentiality among doctors?"

"Well, I have to get a job somewhere, somehow, remember? It might be wise to keep my private life private."

"That's the first sensible thing you've said since we left the house. Maybe you should drink more often."

"I'm not drinking, Curranne. Repeat after me: *Jack is not drinking.*"

Suddenly her legs deadlock in the lobby. She's with Prince Harding on the dance floor, then her mouth drops with loathing. She curses to herself, her voice grinding.

"Drunks are the worst liars! They lie, they lie! They take the oath and lie some more!" Her throat cuts each word. She lifts off her Russian cap and clutches it overhead like a flag or brand. "Drunks are the worst! They're worthless, they can't stop lying! Don't trust one farther than you can throw him." Bangs her cap back on sideways. "Such shits, such liars!"

A blonde in a doll gown stands agape, listening to the terrible-eyed mother-to-be in black coat and square hat and flying sweaty hair.

A black mask falls from the mezzanine rail onto a lobby couch. Sucked rigid with shame, Jack bolts into the deep couch and ignores Curranne. Not to be left behind, she sits beside him. He plucks up the mask and, delicately, lifts off her hat, puts the mask over her tearing eyes, and replaces her hat. She sits looking about the lobby, masked. Jack grins at her, all party fun. Such mischief, ha ha.

"What are you doing to me?" she cries, and rips the mask off.

Jack slips the mask over his own face. Looks left and right, hums "I Love Paris."

"They make the worst fathers! The sonsofbitches! What they do to children can't be mentioned in public. What're *you* singing about?"

Horns hoot from drinkers in the Pompeiian Lounge. Midnight streamers from the mezzanine fall and hang over the masked husband and his abounding wife. Handblasts of confetti splatter her hat and hair and coat.

"They hide bottles everywhere! Ya can't tell where you'll trip over one or have it fall on your head!" She glares at the mezzanine revelers.

Even masked, Jack is shame-ridden. He jumps up in a fit and walks off. Stands across the lobby, reads the Pompeiian Lounge's glass-faced standing board. The gay *druggiste* Philip Falcone staggers past him from the lounge, flops onto the couch beside Curranne and pulls her a great sweet stammering smile.

"Mmmmmmma-a-yyyyy I be of some help to youuuuuu, my dear?"

She's trying to place him.

"I-I-I believe we have mmmmmet!"

"Where?" she asks.

"At the Shhakespearre Cheese Society." Studies her hair. "You have come as Ophelia tonight? A *Russian* Ophelia! Brilliant idea. I have come"—he looks about the dull lobby no party can enliven—"as Krogstad the blackmailer."

"Who?"

"Ibsen, my pretty little squirrel." He stares at the masked man by the lounge. "I didn't know this was *un ballo in maschera* tonight. Or is a robbery in progress?"

She spies Jack. *"Where are you going?"* she screeches, and tries to rise from the deep couch, but falls back, holding her stomach. Philip sits open-mouthed and struck stupid.

Jack watches her tear at her gloves, biting one to rip it off. Her hands drop to her side. She sits back, fuming vainly, then her jaw drops with a long wail. She weeps, rocking with both hands on her mound, a creature with no earthly comfort, as Falcone grips her shoulder. Jack walks up the lobby steps, past the taxi booth. Through the revolving door. Out.

Circling under the marquee, he sees his pregnant wife inside clap both hands to the couch rest and struggle to stand as Philip gives her a push up. A cab fights uphill beside Jack, slewing. At last the cab backs downhill. Jack shouts, "I've had it! I want that cab! I'm committing her!"

"Hey, masked man!" Phil Newquist cries, staggering up through drifts. His lenses steam with melt. "What're you doing out here?"

"Hah! Looking for work," Jack says.

"Oh!—safecracking? Where's your better half?"

Jack weighs this. "In the rest room. If she found a diagram. You missed the big pop upstairs."

"Dang! But I couldn't help it. I was out doing the Lord's work," Phil says. "And I was looking forward to a big hug and kiss from Curranne!"

"Well, just humor her. You been all this time getting here from the Y?"

"God, no, I walk faster than that. I met a friend of my dad's, falling all over himself on Fourth Street. He asked me to get him to the A.A. Clubhouse. Hey, there she is! Something wrong with your wagon? She's ordering a cab."

Curranne stands inside arguing with the dispatcher.

"Oh, there you are," Jack says, Phil Newquist following him. "Ready?"

"Have a fast one?" Curranne asks. "I couldn't find you, you fink."

"I had two or three. Let's go."

"I'm not going anywhere with you, you thief. I'm getting a cab!"

"Thief? Thief?"

She looks down at his pockets. "I know what you lifted from the bar."

Jack's blood shoots. "For Christ's sake! I think I'll join A.A. and get put on ice," he tells Phil. "Maybe they have a nice little room where you can beat your head to a pulp."

She turns in tears to Phil. "He's got to be watched every minute and I can't do it!" She looks back at the mezzanine ballroom for her blue-eyed prince. *"Ohh,* who will take care of me now?"

"You've found your man!" Phil says, taking her arm.

"I know what you want. Come on!" Jack says, locking her to him. He bends her to the lobby phone booths, digs out a nickel. "I'll join."

"I can't tell you what to do," she says.

"Now you say it." Still masked, he slides into the booth.

The operator gives him the A.A. number. A familiar voice answers.

"Hey, Sam! Sam, you old arsonist, is that you? Sam, this is Jack Trueheart! What are you doing on this line?"

Sam Mittlehauser rasps, "I've been waiting for your call, Jack."

"For Christ's sake, I didn't know you were in that group."

"Good to hear your voice. Ready for a meeting?"

Curranne watches whiskey leak from the mouthpiece. She reaches out and rips off his mask. "Let them *see* who you are!"

"Yeah, my wife and I think I should give it a shot," Jack says.

"Those guys, they all drink, don't they?" she asks Phil. "Get together like cronies and drink? Look at that guilty face. He's so happy. You'd think he was racing to a bar."

"No, it's not like that," Phil says. "They're sober, believe me."

"He's so pathetic. Just hopeless." She leans in and shouts at the stinking and dripping mouthpiece. "He's got two bottles in his coat pockets!"

"Your wife been drinking?" Sam asks.

"I wish it were that simple."

She moves her belly against Phil. "Will you take care of me tonight?"

"I said I would. But I wouldn't exaggerate Jack's condition."

Sam says, "When did you have your last drink?"

"Jesus, last May, Sam. Can I still get in?"

She kisses Phil. "You're my best friend. You could be James Joyce someday. I don't deserve you. Happy New Year!" Bites her lips blissfully.

"Well, don't cry about it," Phil implores.

"We have a beginners meeting tomorrow night," Sam says. "At seven at the clubhouse. You know, across from the Emerson worshipers?"

"Oh, *that's* what that place is! Okay, I'll be there. Busy night tonight, huh?"

"Not busy enough, Jack."

"Are wives allowed?" He hangs up. "That was Sam! City hall at the *Sun.* I'm gonna see him tomorrow night! I'm stunned. You can come too."

"You may need guidance," Curranne says.

"Did you get your kiss?" Jack asks Phil.

"I could stand another. I may not get a whole lot of them."

"How'd you like to stay overnight with us?" Curranne asks. "I might need help getting Jack into the house."

"I think he'll make it."

She grabs Jack's sleeve with both hands. "You're not going to drink anymore tonight. Are you?"

"Not a drop."

"Good! You've *had* your partying for this New Year's Eve. Let's go home."

Jack's almost whistling as he unlocks the car door for her. She sits with gaze locked as he scrapes fluff from the windshield and digs at ice. In reaching, his foot slides out beneath him and, falling, he catches at the hood. Lies on the street, staring downhill into Chadakoin Valley snowfall. When he gets in she's still stiff but from the side of her eye watches him throw the scraper in back and then lay two squarish fifths of scotch quite openly on the cabin's back rug. Shrinks into herself at his flagrance.

The motor catches. "Thank you, God!" he cries. "This is impossible driving. Maybe we should stay over at your mother's."

"You may be right." She sees him sneaking back to the hotel bar. "But if our fire goes out, we won't have one pipe left."

"Boy, I sure don't look forward to this. I could use some hot sweet Dutch cocoa right now."

"You take my breath away. I suppose you want your last fling?"

Jack asks softly, "What have I done now?"

"You're falling down drunk. Or were you having one under the hood?"

"Curranne, I may murder you tonight. It will be justifiable homicide. I'll be awarded medals and blue ribbons from the Anti-Defamation League. Maybe we should get something to eat before this trek."

"You have plenty to drink. Revelry and driving don't mix, haven't you heard?"

Jack jams the brake to the floor for a lecture but "Bucket" drifts sideways through a red light. "That did it," he says, control back. "My love, accuse me of rape, say anything. Enjoy yourself. One of us should. Crack your window, please? I can't see through this steam." As they pass Carol's he asks, "Are you hungry?"

She sees Jack weaving about her mother's and ghosting out to "Bucket" for nightcaps. "Drive on. If we pass a diner, all right. You need coffee."

"We won't pass one. I think we'd better drive up the other side of the lake. Fewer heavy grades."

And more bars? she wonders.

Silently they round the bottom of the lake, tracking a snowplow for a few blocks, and head out through Fluvanna for Bemus Point. These names are part of Jack's glandular system, helping measure energies and moments of rest. Far out of town, at a nameless dark curve on a hill which he takes at speed to avoid sliding, he loses the road. "Bucket" breaks into a sideskid, two tons of metal drifting on grease. Curranne grabs the dash, the baby lighting up like Christmas bulbs.

"Hang on," he says, trying to turn into the skid and get control.

"Bucket" ignores him. Curranne's side glides brainstruck toward two pumps of a tiny dark gas station. Again, Curranne's life rushes out of her, hovers somewhere and, as the wagon knocks one pump flat, then bends the second, comes back with a *whoosh*. The motor dies. Jack turns off the lights and ignition, his face white and breath heavy.

"Are you all right?" he asks quietly.

She explodes steam. *"You planned that!"*

"Let's make sure we're not going to blow up. Get out my side."

"I'm not moving!"

"I wish you would," he says, outside. "This may be dangerous."

Taking her time, she slides past the wheel but refuses his hand.

"You said you were going to murder me. Sorry you missed?"

"I'm sorry about every fucking thing on earth."

The first pump is down, the other far bent. Snow whistles the gray-glowing hilltop.

She sneers at him. "I was rather interested when you hit the first pump, but the second bored me. Don't tell me that wasn't planned."

"I'm pretty devious, all right. Do you smell gas?"

"You sonofabitch. I know what this is all about."

"I don't dare light a match." He's on hands and knees around the pumps and car. "No fumes, thank God." He eyes the tiny white station cabin. "I suppose I should leave a note in the door. Obviously their insurance will cover this. Though ours will go up—if we report it. I don't know. Should we just drive away and leave it as an act of God?"

"If you think I'm driving anywhere with you, you're bats." Backs up, with a glittery little smile, and starts scurrying downhill.

He pounds a gloved fist against his brow, bringing sparks to his brain. Scuffs after her.

"Hey, if I planned this, I'll go to jail. Turn myself in!"

"Jail? *Hah!* You'd love that, wouldn't you? You must want to fuck off pretty bad."

"Who is this person?" Jack asks.

"What person?"

"You sound like someone else, I don't know who. In fact, you sound drunk. I wish a cop would come and arrest one of us."

She stops, glaring. "This is worse and worse. Now you want out before I've had the baby. After failing to kill me while I'm pregnant."

"All I want is to get home and pass out."

"You are not driving."

"You don't have a license."

"What's that matter? I can drive, for God's sake."

"This road is ghastly. Exhausting!"

"You've done so well. Perhaps I'll pick up your style."

Back to the barren hilltop limbo, Virgil and Dante robed in white flakes. He slides in, then she gets behind the wheel and slams the door. He drapes as much blanket over her legs as will fit.

"Switch on."

She turns. "Who's driving?"

"Sorry."

The motor turns over. She shifts into low and lets out the clutch. "Bucket" bucks. She slams the clutch in, ablaze. *"Well?"*

"That's our fabulous handbrake, the only thing that works."

"Bucket" pulls out smoothly. Both heads work. She enters the white road. He wipes steam from her windshield.

"Please don't breathe on me, I'm gagging," Curranne says.

"I don't smell anything."

"You wouldn't. You're half polluted, judging by your breath. Maybe if you cleaned out the glass, that'd help."

"Oh, sure. Happy to help," Jack says. "Where is the glass?"

"It's right behind me by the bottle that's left."

"Well, I'll look." Rolls off his blanket, hangs over the seat. "I'm looking for a broken bottle? Where is this phantom?"

She stops midroad. "We're going to sit here until you throw out that glass. Am I clear? I'm not moving. You must really hate me to make me sit in this poison." Rolls down her window. *"Agh!* it's all over my boots."

Jack cranks up his patience. "Okay." Gets out, opens the rear. "Aha! Is this some broken bottle I see before me?" Goes through motions of tossing out glass. "I think I got it all. Why don't you check?"

"Throw out the other bottle as well."

"Hell, yes. That's no loss. There! It didn't break, I'm afraid."

Back under his blanket. They start up again.

"Thanks for telling me what was bothering you. Just speak up."

After a few miles she says, "I don't see how you can live with yourself."

"It's not easy. But then I have your companionship. I mean that in a nice way. Did you want to stay at the dance? I didn't drag you out too soon, did I? You seemed to be enjoying yourself."

"Jack, after you put those bottles in your pocket, I couldn't get out fast enough. Neither could you."

"When did I do that?"

"When the lights went out."

"You have terrific vision."

"I could have seen you behind that bar through a brick wall."

"You do have good vision," Jack says. "I'm sorry I did it. I'm swearing off for the whole year ahead. And A.A. should help."

Scotch fumes still gag and dizzy her but she says nothing. They drive many slow miles in silence over trackless unplowed blowing road. After an hour they pass through the deserted midway point at Bemus.

"I can smell that cocoa," he says.

"I'm driving as fast as I can."

"Christ, you're marvelous. You can drive all the time. It's great."

At the Bemus stoplight her head lowers to the wheel, her eyes tearing. She catches a sob.

"Those fumes are upsetting my stomach. I'm going to throw up."

And she gets out, the wagon idling under the stoplight, and heaves her meat sandwich and carrots beside her rear door.

Jack's quickly beside her. "Feeling better? Look, let me take over. I'm cold sober now. You rest. You've done nobly."

Guides her around the heads. Lifts her legs in, spreads blankets. "You've been swell. You better have my blanket too. I'm toasty as a furnace without it."

As he drives on he sees her head against the backrest, lighted by a streetlamp, her chest shaking silently and closed eyes coursing tears. He shifts down to a stop, turns and holds her.

"I'm sorry you're not feeling well. Maybe we should rouse a doctor while we're right here in Bemus? We'd hate to get all the way home and then find out you need one."

"You miserable bastard," she whispers. "I want to kill you, putting me through this."

"You're right, I deny nothing. What about the doctor?"

Eyes closed, she waves the wagon forward. Jack may still outrun *them*. A few miles outside Bemus she wails, "I'm *cold!*"

"No more blankets, dammit. Maybe we'd better go back to Bemus and put up at the inn. Then we could get an early start and make it home before the pipes are too bad. Hell, that log will burn till next Wednesday."

"No. We could get snowed in at Bemus." Glances out the back window. "Then we wouldn't stand a chance."

"I'm willing to do anything. I want you to get warm as soon as possible."

"Just drive! If there's a roadblock, let me out. I'm giving up."

"I don't think there'll be any roadblock."

"I can't go on. They can shoot me like a dog, it doesn't matter." Looks into white blow in the headbeams. "You're safe. They only shoot priests and pregnant women."

Jack slaps the dash. "We're insane to do this. We could go off the road and be in big trouble. If worst comes to worst, at least we have the blankets. I don't think I'm ever going to forgive myself for being so thoughtless already. This really was a shit idea of mine, worrying about those pipes. And the film club. And those films! It's hard to tell whether I'm more of a fuckhead now or earlier tonight."

She says softly, "*I* was worried about the pipes."

"Yeah, but I'm the one risking our lives. Let me tell you, I plan to make it up. You'll have no complaints about anything this whole year. I'm your slave. I mean willing slave. I'm ready to turn back right now."

"Don't say that! We're not turning back." She turns and glares out the back window. "We're halfway to Mayville. We can always knock on someone's door, if we have to."

"Some partisan's?" Jack asks.

She measures him long and thoroughly. "Sometimes I can't believe you exist. Jack, don't you know it's true?—they *really do* SHOOT pregnant women."

"Well, we could put up at the Peacock in Mayville. Too bad we don't have your flying saucer."

"What flying saucer?" Curranne asks.

"The one you came here in. You don't remember?"

Quietly, "Sometimes I wonder which of us got kicked by the mule, Jack."

"We had a long talk about it yesterday. But forget it."

"Oh, man, you were *not* listening. Margaret Sullavan told you that, I didn't. She was talking through the cat. Did you think the cat was talking? Sometimes, Jack, you're so dense it's mind-boggling."

"Right. Perdita can't talk. I should have understood that. Well, now I've got it straight. Thanks for being so patient with me."

"You should give phenothiazine some serious thought. Your drinking has done a job on you. You are addled! I hear every little slip you make."

"Like what?"

"You really want me to say it? I should think you'd be embarrassed. When you were phoning A.A. tonight, it's a wonder you weren't thrown out of the lobby. I heard those pigs squealing in your head. How could you talk through it? I was so ashamed I just wanted to leave you there."

"I'm glad you didn't."

"You think I'd *do* that? You could be in the booby hatch right now. I know about those places. You wouldn't like it, Jack."

"I suppose I should do something for myself."

"You should have seen yourself!" Shakes her head, sighing. "I looked all over for you."

"Thanks again."

"Where do I find you? Hiding in a phone booth. Wearing a mask! I wanted to cry."

"I appreciate your help."

"Well . . ." She covers his hand on the wheel. "I don't want to lose you that way. I respect you. And I have faith in you. If you were in my place, you'd do the same."

Jack clutches the wheel, watching himself stand apart by the Pompeiian Lounge's jolly sign, then slip out like a thief. A fault in his character splits him from brain to fork. He feels cast out from marriage, then reclaimed by a touch. Her trust and affection rise through him, unbearably. He grips her hand.

"Thank you," he croaks. "Miracles do happen."

They drive on.

Occasional lone bulbs at turnoffs, high lamps asway in beating snow. Crossroads fill shoulder to shoulder. The lake is ghostgray. The gas needle wavers at a quarter tank. White hills, white miles slip by.

"I committed myself all three times," she says.

"I know."

"One winter I escaped from Pilgrim State. I was on the street for three days in paper slippers. Jumping around like a Watusi. No more, please," she tells the roof. "I'll do anything."

Jack glances at the line of her nose, senses fissures of unknowable agonies. Lived through, accepted.

"Do you have compassion for the sick person you were?"

"That's all under the wallpaper."

"What do you mean?"

"I mean, how little it takes to wreck you. I can't think about it."

"If you can hold out until after the baby is born, there are some great new drugs which are quite effective."

A long silence.

"I can't breast-feed with drugs in me."

"The baby can get by on bottles. Why tempt fate?"

She reads him for things unsaid. His jaw shakes with cold.

"Can you still smell those fumes?" he asks.

"Yes. Until the day I die."

"I'm sorry. I hope you'll forgive me. Why shouldn't I be hopeful? You felt compassion for your mother when she slipped on the porch steps. That was a change of heart, wasn't it?"

"I should never have done it. I've been in pain ever since."

"I hadn't noticed. What's so painful?"

"It only opens you up to more despair when they fail you."

"I think she's been a gem. Jesus, is that Mayville up there? We may live through this night after all."

"I'm sorry I lied, Jack."

"About what?"

"Marrying you when I didn't love you."

"When'd you lie? You had some strong feelings for me. But I never thought they were love."

"Something's gone. I can't love."

"It's not that you can't, you won't. What can I do about that? I love you and I'll wait. I hope to be worthy of the miracle when it happens."

"It's genetic."

Jack feels a call for showdown. "Ed Garrity is an ex-PONY League ballplayer, just like he says. There are thousands of Ed Garritys. Try the Manhattan phonebook. But this Ed Garrity is not your father. You have no genetic connection with him. That should make you happy. It does me."

"Same old crap." Curranne sighs.

Drive through the gate at Chautauqua. The grounds slope before them, unplowed and markless.

"Thank God," Jack says. "Maybe we can make it to the house. I'd park right here so we can get out again. But I want to get you right into bed, such as it is." They've been sleeping on the living-room rug since sealing off the bedrooms.

"Bucket" buffs and forces its way down to Pratt Avenue and heads toward North. At Evergreen the snow packs up against the fenders. Wagon crunches to a stop. The motor shrugs and dies.

He opens her door and wraps her blankets about her against the frosty rip from lake ice. "It'll be easier if you follow my footsteps."

He hears a cry behind him. She's tripped on the blanket. He raises and cradles her and, side by side, they push on. Her white cheek, and breath streaming on the darkness, move him. He grips her, the bone and flesh he is sworn to.

Through whipping flurries the dim grounds glow around trees and houses in the unbreaking dawn hour. At North they go down to their home, stomp up the porch and into the living room. The cat yawns in its rocker, fangs bare, and shaking its head. Red rays from her eyes study Curranne.

"I said it would burn until Wednesday. I'm putting on hot milk for cocoa. You must be famished. Do you want some food?"

"Let me alone! You don't know how sick I am, Jack!"

"I can guess. I think you'll get better. And I plan to help. Don't forget that in my modest way I've listened to you night and day since you walked out of Gallinger. No time off. When I shave I don't know where you'll be when I get back. The best I can do is know where I'll be. Not that I'm complaining! But a little stability someday will be heaven."

She splays before the fire as he builds it up. "I know where I am now."

"You only know where you've *been*. And then just half the time."

"You really don't know what I've been or where I've been or what I am. So please, shut up."

"Best words all night. I'm sick to death of your sickness. Damn your disorder."

Wonder shocks her dumb.

"Oh, I'm here, when you want me. Just reach out. I'll listen. Spare no detail! We're not hopeless, Curranne, we can improve."

Jack's flaming face fades into the kitchen. She sits by the fire, stroking the cat with a shaky hand. Improving half heartedly. Red rays read her mind. She pushes the cat away but Perdita strides back, sits up.

"I'll melt you!" Something smashes in the kitchen. "What was that?" she cries, jumping.

"Dropped my false teeth," Jack says. "One of those china mugs got away from me. I'm still shaking from the steering wheel. Do you want grape juice or warm milk?"

She hears him sweeping. Sits decoding her life: hot currents wearing and grooving the log into orange char. Nelson Rockefeller took his oath of office tonight. She glances about. What will she answer Governor Rockefeller when he arrives—with his phony smile and checkbook and *Hiya fellas*—to buy their souls? *We're not dead yet, Rocky!*

"I made you warm milk," he says. Sips his cocoa and stretches out. "By the way, I did not have any booze at my mother's tonight. Nor did I steal any bottles from the dance. So no bottle or bottles broke in the car. I'm *not* trying to upset you. But my 'slip' tonight was part of your overwandering imagination. I think you'd rather know the truth. It's one less fear."

The cat rises. Sits by his head, purring at his sleeping face. Looks him over for a sleeping pocket, then rears back prick-eared at the wind.

Curranne is alone. Firelight fountains over sleeping life, tense nerves unstiffen, her veins open and flow with the room. Throwing the Dutch dish and beating Jack bloody has haunted her for the past month. How did Jack recover? Could Rocky have sneaked in paramedics to reconstruct Jack's face that quickly? God knows what kind of secret medical devices *he* has on hand. She eyes Jack intently for evidence of surgery. Maybe she'd actually hit the floor with the soup

pan. But the blood! The bone buckling in. Bringing himself back to life
. . . he must have the power of rebirth. The evidence of her senses
says a full-blown attack, but he hasn't complained once. She's certainly kept him at a distance since then. But her restraint has twisted
him fearfully. His drinking tonight is proof, to bolster his revenge-
slaying—*her* side of the wagon hit those pumps. Jack's an exceptional
driver. He could've pulled out of that skid. His boiling jealousy about
Harding. If she could see *him* behind the bar in the dark, then he
could see her red passion on the dance floor. One more black mark in
his case against her. And in the overwhelming case, since she pushed
over the breakfast table when Carrie was allowed to go off to first
grade with Ed while she was put back to bed. My God, that hasn't
come up in years. But it's more vivid—lying bloated with anger, as a
four-year-old, her stiffness keeping the house from falling in on her—
than the ride home tonight.

Tomorrow check the wagon for glass splinters. Maybe he didn't
throw away the second bottle. And broke that cup in the kitchen
hiding it. She's not smelled his breath since he lay down. Passed right
out! Can't hold it anymore, since he stopped. Just a sip knocks him
silly. She knows about that. One sip and she's a simpering little gig-
gler, knees weaving, no grip on greasy thoughts. Loose logic and slippery stomach, deeply unpleasant. She's no drinker! Hadn't he got her
drunk—or did he?—on the night he knocked her up? Suddenly Jack
rolls over, his blood drops bright and speaking, mouth still: "You got
me pregnant," he says. "Outside my body, of course, but bound to you
as host. I am pregnant in you." Lies back, closes his round eyes. She's
stiff. When he's really out, scout the cupboards! And there's the *wine
cabinet,* a smart place to hide whiskey. Pour, sink.

What about Dr. David's surprise rape? Should she tell Jack that *he*
was raped too? And his baby frozen to death, and then returned to life
by his blowing his trumpet? Hard to fathom her pregnant husband,
though the spirit of his hornplaying always lifts her. And what power!
Bringing the dead back to life, himself, his baby, even impossible
"Bucket." Good man to hang onto. If only he wouldn't try to change
her mind—she turns mean and blue when he nears a tender spot.
Anger gushing. Blackouts flickering, she recalls only bits. Did well the
first three months after Gallinger, despite being a shrinking ninny.
Then the anger gushed more often, overmasteringly, bursts gripping
puppet bones. Seeing Ed, soothing, until his last surgery. Then hard to

bear. She hopes he'll die. If she can't get him a false jaw, she plans to kill him. Many simple, fast-working poisons can be bought over the counter. Her mind races over jars and pill bottles, Ed in tears thanking her.

How does Jack handle his hallucinations? Buries them, very deep. She's gnomic, hides in tight little smiles, a genius at veiling her inmost events . . . but easily tunes in on his. His front hasn't a crack in it. As a drinker he's had flights like hers, or so she imagines from her perils with alcohol—flights never mentioned, a straight face always. His mask of health never flags. But her antennae reach into him, read his dream-fidgets. Half asleep he's painful to watch. She knows just how his mind flits at the threshold of dreams, the thigh muscles clenching, fingers fluttering. Is he dreaming of her? Is he fearful of her or fearful for her? He bluffs: "You made me what I am today, killer." But she catches the reined hysteria behind the whites of his eyes. Youthful, hard-focused, very white eyes, three years less wise than hers. His dark circles and bags are gone. Hardly looks aged or battered at all by booze. He gets most on edge from her flights. Shifty and unsure, faking acceptance. He gets fearful, his voice hoarsens. She knows but—however unreal—she's locked into whatever she's saying. So hard to tell real from unreal! How much of her unreality has infected him? Can he be having the hard road she is? Could he go schiz?

Telling the merely possible from the actual events in her day takes up much of her silences. She's so intense, parting the false from true, it eats her up. Seeing things not there. That happens much less than the voices. Years ago she'd been shaken by her earliest violent dream, of a supermarket she'd torn down shelf by shelf. Just a child, stiff with fright on her bed, holding her breath to stop the melting. Then turning red, spitting out of herself, an unstoppable cannonball ricocheting through A&P aisles, cans flying like alphabet blocks as she crisscrosses the room, madly bouncing from floor to ceiling. Strong as a horse! Powerful . . . In her teens, when the voices began, she was stunned and indignant. Now, like waking dreams, the accusing voices are part of truth. Out of any overheard salad of syllables she can put together a clear and forceful sentence that strikes to her heart. No one need be there for the voices to speak. They speak to the entire woman. Every nerve rings.

She feels savage about lost privacy. Shopping, raking leaves, showering. The voices spell out her cowy worthlessness to the finest fiber.

Even leafmeal on her fingers is guilt. When she was a baby in her crib, and heard her mother's voice, her whole being was invaded by her mother's vibrance, and sometimes now, as in a waking dream, her feet hear the voices. She did not question the voice in the crib, or that spoke to her at her mother's breast. Her virgin unconscious took in rue and barbs dissolved into breast milk, the spoken with the unspoken. Deep spoke to deep. Carol no more could have hidden her feelings from Curranne than from God. Now, the farseeing, farhearing voices have her whole unconscious to emerge from. They rise in waves through her. They stand beside her, seen, unseen. They foreknow her every reply. Defenseless, her anger redoubles. As at the breast, Curranne never questions a voice. But her fear and anger now reply to the spiteful voltage of her abusers. Today she fights back.

She questions the worth of a voice's words. She is indignant at the heavy authority her voices take upon themselves. She has learned to think for herself. She will not just stand there and be told or cajoled. She is in daily battle and resists with logic, abuse or whatever fits. If the voice is lordly she rises to great brilliance and long, fulfilling flights of self-justification. If the voice speaks filth she answers savagely. They are never pleasant. They scorn and blacken, make guilt plain. They think she is nigger-worthless, beneath notice, and plan to leave soon. They do not. They ebb, vanish, return, year in, year out. They adore to make her black-ass self-conscious on the street. They thrill to take her back down a long lonely road. They triumph step by vivid step through a natural history of her loneliness. But now she puts her spine to the test. Year after year her great heart stands up to them. It is such a battle to live with them. Where does their power come from? She is alone and gives birth to her own power daily, hourly, at times moment by moment, hanging on until drained witless. In sleep she sees her faceless self strong and unbeaten. She is never black with self-consciousness in dreams, but is a ball of virgin consciousness who can no more see her own face than can a baby in a crib. Her world awake is often much the same world as asleep but she is less strong. Being weaker she is ready to smash her way to success where logic or swearing fail. Taking or holding the high ground demands superhuman energy. She is superhuman every second, alone, with Jack, watching movies, drying dishes. She dries dishes with a sense of ordering herself for battle, braced and supple, eye watchful for lint or smudge. She is a bloody wolf about physical care and exercise. She likes racing blood, deep breathing, a heavy sweat. Her will staggers Jack. "Am I manic?" she asks him. "Hell, no. You make me want to join the human race. I thrive on pregnant women with mental problems. When I grow up can I be like you?"

Thrice lost, she fears fourth commitment. This could be for a very long time. The very thought brings memory-twinges of her emotions falling off, her shying away from all work, lack of interest in Matthew and Mark, in much of anything that will bring on the pain of guilt for wrong actions, wrong thoughts. Trees, the houses on the street, the whole outdoors are baleful with warnings. If she fails at anything, everything will be taken from her and everyone leave. Best not to go anywhere, move anything, not a bone or muscle. Energy straggles, fades, dies. All life is inner, the past in pieces. Every moment is spent in a disorderly attempt at strict review and judgment . . . that only scores her failure, deed by deed.

She looks out at the dawn.

Jack's harsh, loving invective returns. She thinks it over, his urgency giving hope. If he wasn't lying about the bottles, she's willing to take him to heart. He is so asleep, fallen in battle. And in the morning he will rise, quick with work in the kitchen, overactive on caffeine. Since losing his job, he serves her in every way possible, with her breakfast in bed unfailingly. She now exercises before lunch. He does not write. He turns over work thoughts, a beaver at the want ads. Evening he devotes to her good cheer. "I'm your drug. Count on me. I work." He types up moral and spiritual passages from the Bible. "This is inspirational stuff—it works. It's like bran flakes for the blues. Where's it been all my life? Some sonofabitch has been hiding it away in hotel drawers. I hope my reading doesn't offend you? If some weasel-eyed prognosticator had told me six months ago that I'd be sitting on my ass in the snow today, typing up Bible homilies, I'd've said he was insane." "Why should I care what you read?" "Oh, I won't bore *you* with any of it! You might throw me over the roof. But I get continual help from God. God knows, I need it!"

She looks through cupboards, the wine rack, around the cellar stairs. Digs through the laundry basket, lifts the lid off the toilet. She's getting ragged. If he has it, it's hidden in the walls. She's relieved not to find it though. A deep breath. Thoughtfully, she glides to her peajacket and sailor's blue watch cap on the couch, then softly out the kitchen door. This will be quick, then she'll sleep. She stops, having forgotten her gloves in her silence, but does not go back for them. The path she and Jack scuffed home is filled waist-high. She goes by summer homes in radium. Heavy flakes weave and fix to her in driving chill. Ahead at Pratt and Evergreen the wagon is a white hump. She leans into the work of getting there, it's farther than she thought, as if dwindled. Everything seems farther apart, the houses more removed from the street. Trees stretch to be apart. She turns and walks backward against scooping wind, hands in pocket slits. At last there's "Bucket," no aeration possible under its thick egg-white, though the driver's door still shows under the roof's airflow. She opens it with a crunch and slides in, slamming the door with a fluff. A flood of scotch fumes gags her. Her eyes rim with water. Her breath bursts from her in red anger and waves of blood. She is shit, lied to by all. But she doesn't want to kill Jack. She wants to kill herself.

With a choked wail she looks for broken glass. He cleaned it out really well. Maybe the pieces were big pieces. It's so hard to believe he lied. Is this a dream? Throws herself out the door, her stomach in dry heaves. You're so beautiful but you've got to die someday. She wretches on sex and beauty. As she gags at her floppy bust and brilliant gray eyebulbs—all parts of her separating and swelling outward and in at each breath—murder is one of her kinder thoughts. Bloodstains and human beef fume from the floorboards. She hasn't eaten in twelve hours, nor has the baby kicked or moved. That song has ended in a hump of ice. This time nothing will bring the frozen near-bastard back. Her last faint faith in Jack fades: it does not return. The first light, drained utterly, is bleak chain steel. Nothing glows but the pain in her eyeballs. Her scalp feels adrift. Her neckbones part. Jack has given her the hardest blow of her life. Face wet, Curranne freezes in thought. She looks back on today from tomorrow. For her this day will be very short. As Jack will measure it for her. The day she ended. For her it will be nothingness. She will carry this lightless light as far as she can. Then never write her name again. A woman's life is steam wiped from glass. Nobody to help me, all by my nothing.

Or will she be back in the sun? We all came from the sun, Jack says. The whole soup that made us is back there. Big tug for the sun. But even the sun will die someday. Implode and blow up. While everyone jumps for joy? No likelihood Jack's Life Force will end well. What *is* all this germination! Something she can't deny sticks to her mind, some potency in this big milky seedpod she becomes. And now some part of her is Jack. Jack, pregnant in her. She can deny for herself but not for Jack. So she will lend one atom of faith to Jack. If she gives that atom one last test, will the atom awake?

"Bucket" sits deserted, its roof whipping and snow-ridge deepening. Only small clear window patches let in light. The lapped car sinks as day brightens dimly. The car joins the flowing yards and buried porches and is now a mere white hump. The sun is wholly blitzed from the heavens, without even a pearl glow. The risen day at its strongest is gray and dead. Inside the cold car nothing breathes or moves where Jack and Curranne have sat side by side for months trading their life-breath.

The log shifts. Jack rolls over, then bolts up, checking the sparks. Perdita looks up drunkenly.

"Curranne? Hey, where are you? I'm cold. Christ, maybe I should learn to sleep under blankets."

Gets up, wanders about the house looking for her. The pendulum-swinging wall clock measures ten-twenty.

He calls, "Jesus, haven't you gone to bed yet?"

Empty rooms.

Checks the sealed upstairs rooms, finds frost on a long-leaved forgotten amaryllis. "My God, are we crazy?" Carries the plant down to the living room to thaw. May she have gone to the grocery? All services are closed New Year's Day. Her mittens lie on the living-room floor.

He sighs. "Okay, search party."

Dressed and scarved, Jack trudges through backyards and finds his and Curranne's once more filled path in midroad at Pratt. As he nears the station wagon's boxy hump his stomach begins shaking and he prays wordlessly, not admitting his fear. When he opens the car door, his heart leaps at the emptiness within. Breath fails him. He leans on the roof. Slams the door and scuffs over Pratt toward Bestor Plaza, following her faint path. As he rounds the Colonnade Building he sees her far beyond, seated on a bench under the fountain's frozen stone peak. The whole large long plaza, windsmooth blankness. And she, so still in the white-blow, such a white rigidity. Fear thuds into a shocked hot column in his trunk. Drained nerves squirm. A wail shakes him at the terrible marble wife who waits on the bench.

"Curranne!" he calls, walking toward her.

Her lakeside is deep white. Jack is running.

"Curranne!"

He stands gasping before her. She is unmoving, her bare hands crowning her knees. Locked under crusts of ice, the fingers are liver-purple with blood-drain. Her belly keeps her upright, the stiff backbone lifting her small figure ever straighter. Her face is white clear wax. A yellow strand whips over her sightless gray stare and breathless half-open mouth.

He beats snow and ice from her face, crying, "My poor honey! My poor baby!"

Jack buckles to the seat beside her, clawing a gloved hand over her unopenable fingers, freeing the crusts. His heart ravishes her face as it would never dare in life. The stone-blue lips, the fine-edged nose cut for breath. A clear ear-shell no word can woo. All life dried from cloudshatter pupils. A flake sticks to her eyeball, unmelted.

"God help us!" Jack shouts. His head falls into his gloves. He leans on his knees, sobbing. The brute body beside him waits. Last night his bright-skinned bride, her small-boned arch stepping from the shower, a wet-haired, brilliant-eyed goddess, breasts flushed, body in bloom, a questioning look in cheekbones of ivory. Toweling herself, muscled, firm. And when his half-shaven face turned to ogle, threatening him with towel snap and elbow to the ribs. Loss empties him. His spirit cracks. He sobs without stop.

The ice-stiffening wind molds his boots. His coat turns to white flax. He groans with the rolling and hooping plaza winds. Where is she in that wind, the torn woman? He can not look at the spirit-empty flesh beside him. Where is Little Ikiru, lost to the warmth Jack and Curranne breathed into him, one rainy May night? He sees his flannel-gowned pregnant wife on their tossed blankets and living-room floor. The cat yawns dizzily at the fire, mortal and waiting to be rubbed. Not a breeze disturbs her. Staring over the roiling plaza at his measure of eternity, Jack's wits shrink to hot tears, the blood prickling his ghastly elasticity of chest.

"Oh Lord!" he moans. "What have I done?"

He looks up, begging. The heavens are dead.

His sob deepens. He is wracked with howls as more and more of his living wife appears and is ripped from him. He sees the booting foot of Little Ikiru push up a knob on her belly. Grief cleaves him further.

"God, please God!" he cries out. "Isn't there some way I can pay, not her?"

An arm crosses his shoulder.

My God, he thinks, I'm crazy.

"What're you crying about?" a breathless voice rasps.

His lungs gush, his breath hoses her face. She looks into him. Her still half-dead eyes tighten against painful daylight. The hairline leaves of her irises pulse under glaze. Fluttering, her lids flush with stinging salt, wetting the windburned whites. Curranne coughs, then coughs again, and begins to sob with breath, with fast, deep gasps and small wild howls of happiness.

"My God, oh my God!" Jack screams joyously. "I thought you were dead! *Dead!* Ohh! Ohh! Thank God, oh thank you, God!"

Her arm hugs him.

"How could I die?" she whispers.

"Oh, how couldn't you!"

He tears off his gloves to feel her face.

She groans, her cheek on his. "Not when I have you."

"Oh, Jesus in heaven!" Jack cries.

"To bring me back."

The marvel charges them. In the plucking of a string, they blend into one being. She hangs from his neck, her mouth on his face. His breath wets her cheeks as he grips her. Her hot life pumps over him. She leans back, spuming and spuming, her fist slowly beating from her breast to his, to and fro, to and fro with a little laugh, for the first time putting her heart out to Jack, and pulling at his.

He lifts the fist, kissing it. Rubs her icy fingers on his cheek. His eyes are in her head, her eyes are in his head. They are one pregnant body. His hands cup her blue watch cap, broad flat fingers pressing love into her skull. Squeals fill her head, then all her ills lift and detach and flow off. She gasps, achingly fresh and wonderstruck, her saliva running as from a pulled tooth. Her lungs at last fill to the brim. Curranne gazes with half-lidded ecstatic hunger at the blue-eyed Jack before her, the life-adoring husband drunk with her spirit. She forgives all. She gives everything.

"Not when I love you so," she says.

PART SEVEN

Dymphna the Midwife

My chemistry is up! Little Ikiru is here! My first daughter. Little Guzzler's a week old, feels like a month. Feeding schedule a grind. Her name is Avon. Jack calls her "Judith of Avon" (Shakespeare's daughter).

Writing this for mental exercise. In a 10-lb ledger Jack gave me for Xmas. Threatening to use it himself if I don't. I love this ledger. If only I could lift it! How intrigued I was when it was wrapped, and Jack's cat-smile. I dread the day when Avon weighs this much.

Can't take my eyes off J. Sticky w/sex, raw, male lust, can't keep his hands off me. Swooning to Mahler on my boobs. I mean *lust*. Good, healthy, sane lust. No intercourse for nearly . . . a month? I'm not sexy. But that doesn't stop him. Takes his treats where he finds 'em! (NB: Work on your Precambrian sense of humor.) When not looking gave him a big squirt in neck and hair. That got to him.—DON'T STOP I LOVE IT! Poor J., so starved, alas.

Any little coo drives him silly. Lights up like a bulb. He looks cracked, helping with A.'s bath, holding up her head while I sponge soft little waving legs. But tells me,—I wish you treated me half as well as I treat you. I'd be in heaven on earth. Well-1, I was out of it last year, getting buggier by the day and afraid to surrender. After I give in, they all leave me. The pattern—when I really love, anxieties go up like flags, stress buzzing, rooms underwater, then hopeless, hospitalized, can't bear to start over. Not with someone who's seen me at my mingiest. Fly-bitten, spotted with emotional measles. Stale ward fodder, my cheeks and eyes puffed up like a boxer's. *I'd* find it hard to love most of the schizzes, paranoiacs and depressives I've known. Surrender to a kook? Sexually, spiritually, our relapses boiling away underfoot, how could I? Supersensitive, growing an alligator skin, feel not worth loving. So HARD to love, take *or* give! Me especially, can't bear reaching out, people frightened of me, their hands damp. My face made of woodbark. Watching life through a pinhole. Don't open the pinhole up, let them in! But J. loves me, no matter how I cool him out.

He sticks. Swears I'm what he's wanted all his life.—*We are going to live forever!* Some masochist he is.

New Year's Day had spiritual experience, first ever. J. laid his hands on my head and suddenly I felt sucked clean. All my pigs and snakes vacuumed out hissing and squealing. Maybe it was force built up holding back since we became lovers last May. J. not lovable then, so callow. All literary dishwater. And now really incredible—world class, standing right by me. Never lost faith in me, though I did in him. When the bugs got me. But he dug me out. He's some wonderworker. Has the touch. We *contact.* I love him, talk about miracles! It's a low-grade fever that keeps my tongue dry. Is that love or lactation? I still keep a *little* veil handy, my safety mask.

I'm writing this to buck me up when I come back from North Warren. Where I don't want to go. *I* don't think I need it. I *don't* need the side effects. I know I really can handle myself without medication. *But* I want at least one year of lasting security. That insurance. So I'm committing myself to the new mothers' ward while Dr. David balances my dosage. Turns out that PHZ in mother's milk is harmless. Treatment could be done at home but he wants me under his eye. When I get back I'll have this to read while fighting the groggies. PHZ is a sleepyhead. At first, anyway. Couch analysis is all empty calories, but psychiatry zips me up. No flying strands with that bear-grease. PHZ Fights Dandruff!

But it's all I've got. I'm sick of suffering. A century from now schiz will be corrected in the womb. Drugs and dream analysis 20th-century casting of bones. My Big Problem: frazzling and wearing out friends, until I think I've never had any. My *turmoil* would erode granite. Well, mother sticks, and Cornelle. Ned and Jerry are good guys. They'll write if I do. They're beautiful.

New Year's morning on the bench was what J. calls direct prayer, when my sickness was lifted. Direct prayer lifts your heart straight up to HP (A.A. for God, or Higher Power). J. points out certain passages in Bach, Beethoven and Mozart that are direct prayer. Some last bars are held in suspense while the composer thanks God for having allowed him to write the piece. During B's *9th,* J. jumped at sudden slow passage at the very end—Listen! Listen! B's talking with God! Enormous discovery for J. Big moment for me too, even I could hear it—right in my scalp. This ledger is direct speech. To J.'s HP to keep my sickness lifted. HP works. But can HP fight flawed genes forever, central nervous system breakdown, chemical panic-spurts, short circuits, blown fuses (everything wavy and marbled), voices from the unknown, hallucinations, deep-rooted worthlessness, guilts, help, help my brain is attacking me, bills, household stress, postparturition blues, atom bomb anxieties, and a depressed station wagon? Can love? Or only PHZ?

Are these even real questions?

My attraction to J. is scary. Pulled himself inside out. Nothing like the person I met last May. Hiding a ton of worry but won't let on it's there. All self-confidence, healthy ego, energetic (but driven), full of sexy smiles, never avoids eye contact, and gentle, getting slim, dressing well but not dressy (despite hardup), full of compliments about my education (he's self-educated) *and* desirability, funny, always thinking of me, listens, is passionate—and has itchy fingers 24 hours a day. He's always at my side, and elsewhere, ahem.

Keep it SPICY, C., so you won't fall asleep rereading it!

Just bathed A. Still can't believe she's such a feather aft Matt and Mark. Not a body but a grin. Miss the little bag and nozzle. She answers all my little touches with thoughts and smiles but J. gets the big gurgle. Does A. like me? Is there some dead or hidden spot in me she senses? Shouldn't be, I'm all here, maybe too much so. Or *not* enough? That wet pink under my fingers, so sensuous! Oiling and dusting her featherweight, I remember how she came into me on a wave, last summer, something self-aware out of eternity. And here she is! If not wholly mine. Something is withheld, some half I can't possess. J.'s? I feel A. holding back. She's terribly beautiful. J. and I both experience that. Our lives, given a heartbeat apart, fingers and feet. Tiny ribs a bellows on the spark. And already a great beauty. It hurts to look at her! Like some blood-drop fallen from a cut, drawing you in while the throb still pulses. A spellbinder, even asleep, not only waving and suckling. I know how Mama Bear feels, her eye on her cub, wanting to lick her all over.

(NB: One reason I don't feel sexy, aside from new-mother low sex drive, is that J.'s daytime hanky-panky in the living room or kitchen opens me right up to schizy visits. Just when he's charging my buzzer and sparks are leaping, some friendly idiot will walk into the room and start talking to me about clothes or old song lyrics. Half-awake sex state too similar to breakdown but less vivid. I get too distracted to climax, genitals go numb and rubbery. Hiss like a bitchy goose at J., can't help it. Then plunge feebly into housework for an hour, to steam off being swollen and unsatisfied. Subliminal visitors no good for this recovered schiz. I don't want to romance breakdown even for a second. Trouble is the dreampeople actually interest me with idle, friendly chat, a guitar or new piano pops up out of nowhere, and we hash over my future career as a music teacher—for which I'm totally unqualified. But that doesn't seem to stop me! Sometimes when J. plays a record the room slows down and I experience music like a sunken lightning rod. But that doesn't mean I can teach it! Keep both tootsies on terra firma, C., at *any* cost.)

This morning at the sink here comes this hand.—Hey, are you comforting you or me?

J.—The baby! She needs every attention. That's why I keep this glorious set of pumps polished.

—I'm sure Avon will praise you.

—What we need here at Chautauqua is a slide lecture on the Song of Solomon in the Hall of Philosophy. I'll suggest it! You pose, the tasteful Madonna with Avon. I read Solomon. Bring it all home, y' know? With a big breast-feeding climax, real steamy biblical stuff.

Look out at the snow.—I think I'd get goosebumps.

Suddenly J. is sober, even bitter.—If we'd make love, maybe I wouldn't talk so dumb. That drinker's vulgarity is such a rote response!

It's true, with not eating, not drinking, and not making love, J. is shriveling (or growing) into a new man.

We're in deep Feb. Until this week the grounds seemed to belong to the 2½ Truehearts but for an idle figure here and there. Houses empty, street after street bare of people. No window lights. Short days. My mind knitting w/winter. Windy days, weeks of silence. Refreshing! I'm reborn, and really hate the idea of drugs. But avoiding PHZ is Russian roulette. I'm not suicidal.

In the deli last Saturday (today is Saturday) we met Leopolda Dymphna, just arrived from Corfu. Swept in in a big black Astrakhan and lamb half-cape. Instant envy (the hat, the cape). Tall, thin blonde (sexy); frantically depressed; two women at once, first imperial, then sidemouthed, half-finished questions, gasps, mini-breakdowns. Very dramatic. She's Laurence Olivier's alter ego. Always hamming. Has owned her own theater in London's West End.—The Great Thing about being Larry is that then I can be anyone else I want to be. She was drooling over a giant antipasto. Picked up something about me, we instantly exchanged symptoms and life histories. Astounding pair of paranoiacs. She says PHZ is like a phantom limb that works. J. shocked. Afraid of her effect on me, seducing me into heavy dissociation. At first I was sympathetic to a fellow sufferer worse off than I am. Then I found we were hitting it off because she felt that way about poor pregnant me, and full of cast-iron sanity beside my little slips.

I want this to be factual, not a lot of schizy angst and chopped-up imagery. So far I feel strong. If I sink into half-formed half-tormented poetic grasping at fragments, I'll miss the whole point: keeping alive my strengths. I don't know what PHZ will zap me with, but am already squeezing myself to keep active. This spring I'll be running. I need Leopolda's iron. I dig her. We'll have our own little iron mine.

J. & I talk on a plane of very high seriousness. I have absolutely no sense of humor. J.—You're the greatest straight man ever born. *And* you'd make a good wooden Indian.

—I like it! he adds. He means my pain-in-the-ass loftiness. I can feel it form on my face. Masking my rage with myself. My jokes aren't worth making and only strengthen my sad-ass side. C.'s no good. She'll never grow. But snakes and lizards shed their skins when they grow. Maybe I'll shuck my mask.

So L.'s writing a whopping check in the deli for antipasto and half the store. With a fat black-and-gold pen. J. bug-eyed with envy at her writing tool.

—That's the Rolls-Royce of pens. With that I think I might write again.

L.'s reddish-blond, widens her eyes with smoldering Italian-starlet eyeliner, has English accent. Skin fabulous almond-pearl that holds light, her eyes rainy brown, moody and blithe and wounded, and nuts. She smokes Gauloises without stop—the deli a blue cloud. Big bag in arms, she stares outdoors, sighs despairingly, then waves at the deli.

—Is this where the society foregather and commingle here in Kathmandu? We *can't* be the only ones alive.

—You'll get used to it, I say and force a witty little smile. I like it.

—I think I am going to cry, L. says. Stamps out her cigarette. Would you hold this for a moment, she asks J. Hands him her groceries. Thanks, I need a cigarette for this trek.

J. watches her torch her Gaulois with a gold Dunhill.—May I see that? What's it burn?

—Compressed butane. Turn that nut and you can weld with it. Or burn down this whole village, ha ha. My God, I wish I were in Florence.

Then L. invites us to take her to her house facing the Hall of Phil. for some antipasto. So we guide her.

—This morning brilliance disorients me. I can't see where I'm going. I don't dig sunlight anyway. Well, on Corfu or Dhilos, one of those secluded, empty Ionian or Aegean beaches, okay. But Chautauqua beach? This is my first day in the States in two years. When is the next plane to Athens?

—King James can connect you with Buffalo, J. says, still holding her groceries.

—I can't make Buffalo. I may not make the Hall of Philosophy. Call me El Poopo. Let me lean on you, Jack. I need a seeing-eye saint —no brandy, thanks, I can't drink. Is this place mapped yet? You two are the first human beings I've seen since I left Corfu Thursday. Alitalia poisoned my spumante. I'm absolutely bereft. They won't let me back into Greece again, I'm banned from the Ionian *and* the Aegean. I'm too psychotic for the Greeks—and they invented me! I need help. I live in the four houses on Cookman Avenue across from the Hall of Philosophy. I'll reward you both handsomely. Antipasto, Gaulois, grape juice. You can stay for a snack, can't you? Stay for a week! You're really ready to *pop,* huh? I've had four. They're with their grandfather in Paris for a while.

—This is my third, I say, trying to catch up.

L. waves an arm at Bestor Plaza.

—Life is not what I'd hoped! I'm not getting that much out of it. So often it doesn't seem worth it. It's so much WORK! I can only hold together when I'm in motion. If I stop I come apart. It's a helluva way to stay sane. I can only keep adding to myself, houses, trips, people, parties, kids, places, clothes and pretty things—while what I really long for is utter rest. I'm always stirred up and ready for more! It's hell on my kids, you can imagine.

J. eyes me, Some rare bird this is!—You're independently wealthy?

—Oh, you dear man! L. weaves in mock shock. We pass the empty Refectory. The redbrick library is closed today. L. flaps her wings, skating on money, singing, *It's* SPRING *again! And* BIRDS *on the* WING *again!*

—Jack wants to be independently wealthy so he can write, I explain.

L. supports herself as a decorator. That's the only thing she does well, besides acting and having babies. Paint and redecorate. Rents, redecorates and sublets at twice the rent. As absentee landlord, she has 16 small caves in Lond. 7 Paris, and two young architecture students as her crew and rent collectors.

—Do I have problems? Do I have tenants? Do I need a Mafia hit squad on permanent payroll? It's an expanding madness.

Now she's inherited four houses at Chautauqua from her late husband, for child support. They're a business trust, no taxes. The only way she can support what she already has is to rent, redecorate and sublet still newer places for cash to keep everything floating, like a pyramid club.

—It's quasilegal. I'm in a sea of lawyers. I can't afford to keep *these* houses unless I turn them into white-elephant tax shelters.

—You mean you have to lose money on them? I ask.

—You're digging me.

—Christ, J. says. L. has him reeling. You have to rent these houses at a loss?

—Right! So I'm staying. *Me?* I mean, *me?*—at Chautauqua? a mobile manic-depressive with paranoid symptoms? Hey, I'll cheer up, Jack. I'm an advanced melancholiac on the mend. Dese bones gonna rise! I joined a nondrinkers bridge club on Corfu. If you can get sober in a foreign language, there's hope. I'm no alky. I'm a schiz who needs total abstinence. Crazy people shouldn't drink, not even sparkling wine.

She was in relapse on Alitalia, thought she'd ordered gelati and got served Asti spumante. Knew it was poisoned, gave it to the guy next to her. He passed right out.

—I hope he's still alive, he was a *Sicilian* lawyer. There I was, gang, hovering on hospitalization in Greece, and Greek asylums are 17th-c. at best. Greeks still see suicide as a mild anxiety attack that went too far. They were eying me for real psychosis on a Greek scale. Massive private vendetta and pistol-waving, a few bodies out of windows. That's the stuff they like in a nut. And I was a gravely crazy lady. For me even a *teensy* weensy retsina is too much booze. That stuff is like radiation poisoning to me, I mean evil. And since I've returned to Catholicism I really believe in the Devil. I'm not in good shape. I

haven't eaten since Roma. I'm getting low-blood-sugar blues. I hope
this antipasto will lure me back to life.

—Jack's A.A., I say.

—Really? He looks *very* sober. How long have you been in?

—I joined New Year's Eve. But I haven't had a drink in nine
months.

—Great. I've been dry one month. And am I happy I passed up that
sparkling arsenic on the plane. I got so scared that I've been drowning
my kidneys in Coke and mineral water for two days. Maybe I'll give
A.A. the tourist number. I'm a crazy sailor who can't drink in any
port. I've only been on this continent overnight and already have
asthma. Maybe I'm a hysteric, not a schiz at all. But I don't think so.
Even Chautauqua has me hyperventilating. Am I scared? The capital-
ist running-dog taxmen are after me. I've *GOT* to beat this depression!
I swear on my shrink's prescription pad (one gloved hand taking an
oath on the other) I'm going to climb out of this pit.

Real heroine-on-the-rapids drama. Something in her so appeals to
me. Like a word flying around the earth that finds you and explains so
much at once, makes it all half-bearable, while only deepening the
mystery. MOZART DISCOVERS BACH! Leopolda's part of some
big legend *out there* who has touched down where I am. Though no
matter how much gets explained, a sunny winter day only makes the
riddle more brilliant.

—What're you laughing at? L. asks me.

—Myself. I tell her I have to go back to the hospital to get my
medication balanced. After the baby. I'm quite sad about it.

—Yeah, that's too bad, but it'll do you good. Let me explain something, do you mind? When you laugh in someone's face, make it clear
you're not laughing at them. Or people get angry. You would, you
know? Take it from an older sister. All right?

—Okay. My face shrivels into the walk. Thanks.

As I say thanks, something vital floods me. I haven't just shrugged
her off with a swallowed frig you. A deep breath. I really feel good,
better about myself.

—Make it a habit, she adds.

—Yeah! Well, I'm trying to laugh more. I have no sense of humor.

—Great! Good for you. Breaking the ice is half the battle. You'll
laugh. Right, Jack?

—Curranne's always laughing. But like the Buddha's, you just can't hear it.

—Someday this'll all be over and where will we be? L. asks. Laugh Now, that's my motto.

—I'm too solemn.

—Money, huh? L. says. Don't mention finance. I go into instant catatonia.

—Things will get better, J. says.

—That sounds so sane. I surrender daily to God but I'm still warding off the Devil. Chautauqua's all Protestant, isn't it? I'll bet they don't even believe in the Devil here.

We stare about the snow white Devilless plaza.

L. whistles, head hanging in disbelief.—This isn't life, it's shredded wheat.

—Mother's Oats, I say.

—At least it's not Yugoslavia. Hey, you're not having twins, are you?

—Don't even suggest it! J. cries.

—Well, you'd know by now. Two fetal heartbeats are unmistakable.

L.'s a midwife. She's been in on fifty or sixty births on Corfu and the islands. Talk about primitive conditions! But going on birth calls helped her stay sane. For one thing, she didn't drink during a delivery, and sometimes they could last three or four days. Which also kept her apart from her second husband and kids, who have all packed up and gone to Paris. She repeats herself often, I find it very dramatic. She doesn't know if she's married or not. She's on lithium. Got a supply in Athens before she came but still needs checkups. Lithium not accepted here but is breakthrough drug in Europe, will be here sooner or later. She'll probably not get sick again, if she stays on the drug and off alcohol. Her depressive phase is lifting. She really may never have another attack.

She rubs my shoulder.—Anything you want to know about booze, babies or mind medications, just ask. I never charge.

—That's about what we could pay, J. says.

—Well, you're not going to pass up helping your wife through a delivery? This is when you really get married.

J. doesn't think they'll allow him in the delivery room.

—They won't, so don't ask. Hey, you two take all my sermonettes with a grain of salt, okay? I'm an incorrigible advice-giver. It's the only way I can damp down my doom and gloom. My analyst is always saying, Bring me a dream! I tell him, Life *is* a dream, let me bring you my bills. Have you ever had a bill-lifting spiritual experience? Seriously.

I tell L. about my spiritual experience and point out the bench.

—What was it like? L. asks.

—Salty blue, sort of sweet and sour. I could taste the current going through me. Could taste it for weeks. I can taste it right now.

—That beats electroshock, she says.

—Of course, we're facing the same old bills, J. says.

—And the car's depressed. But now I love this guy. Don't I?

—That's the miracle, J. says.

I think rebirth without love is only extending the misery. Why be reborn to stay in the same old ruts? Whole object of rebirth is to love.

Little miracle-moment on Cookman Avenue by L.'s porch: the day dampens, flakes sift down, the walks level with fresh snow. The frozen lake, in deep-feathered air. All is still. We alone move but for falling snow. Beside the classical, open-air Hall of Philosophy, all tall fluted pillars and Greek roof. Empty benches rifted. We go into its stone space to watch four pure curtains fall about us. J. steps onto the raised lectern and—hesitating for summer visitors not yet seated?—his breath spuming, addresses the empty benches something like this:

> My name is Ozymandias, king of kings!
> Look on my works, ye mighty, and despair!
> The leaves of life keep falling one by one!
> The Moving Finger writes!
> The Worldly Hope men set their Hearts upon
> Turns ashes!
> I Myself am Heav'n and Hell . . .
> Strike from the Calendar
> Unborn Tomorrow and dead Yesterday!
> Drink!—for once dead you never shall return!
> The Flower that once has blown forever dies!
> And lo! the wine is on the wing!

(Ha! Ledger-writing is more fun than writing poems.)

We clap as his voice fades.—Look! he says, pointing. Behind us lights come on in Unitarian House.

—Hey, I've got *neighbors?* L. says. Her house sides Unitarian

House. A pack of people on their porch applauds J. It's Reverend Christopher G. Jaspers, his haywire Cherokee wife Winnie and their five kids. Chris is black British West Indian who married us in King James three months ago. They are moving in, Chris says. Their trailer got repossessed. So they got permission from Boston to move in here.

One look at Winnie makes me heartsick. Not yet thirty, five living children (last year, twin stillbirths) and nameless mental problems. It's Chris who makes me heartsick. *Her* hard times are ahead. Winnie thinks stoic Indian composure will see her through; doesn't know how to help herself. To Chris, who avoids meeting her disturbances head on, she's a saint and all wrapped up in child-raising and housekeeping. While the bugs chew her brain out. It takes one to know one!—an hour with her takes my breath away for three days. Winnie's a small, dark-haired, beady-eyed self-tyrant who spends half the day talking with her ancestors, serving spirits, pouring herbal tea for folks not there. My urge is to belt her back into reality, a natural but very dumb urge (I shd. be a ranch foreman). Someday soon she'll be swept away from Chris and her kids for six months, get a braino flush and wake up. Maybe not enough though. I've left two sons & three husbands behind.

J. intro's Leopolda D., their new neighbor, just inherited these four cottages, moving in today, etc.

—I'm sorry to hear about your repossession muck-up, L. says, her accent chiming on his warmly clipped West Indian lilt. His tribe of British American Black Indians listen in wonder to her familiar but foreign tones.—We'll have to have a double housewarming. Do you have heat?

Chris has just lighted the gas heater and is letting water into the pipes. But it's not winterized.

J. says, It'll be paradise after that trailer, right, Winnie?

W. the statue says nothing. Time has no clock for her, the hours stream and explode, dimming in ripples.

—I'm embarrassed I haven't paid you that ten dollars yet for marrying us, J. says. He's red but gritting his teeth. I goon at the lake, mortified. I feel big, pregnant and bumbling before L. and, when he adds that we still don't have the cash, I punch his kidney. But Ch. tells him not to worry.

I see real concern for us in Chris's pale brown worry-waved face. At heart he's poleaxed with anxiety. And despite his warmth toward

Winnie, and what must be nervously prolific lovemaking, she too looks shredded. Stone-lonely. Maybe wise too, in a weird way, but that I doubt. I'll do anything to avoid her loneliness again. Chautauqua's silence refreshes, but loneliness can kill. Behind W.'s stiff front I hear bones breaking. Avoid loneliness like the plague! You can be alone and not lonely, or a rigid old swamp stump like her.

Since she's never been hospitalized, W.'s more fearful of me than I am of her—but we're attuned. I'll try to draw her out; kids aren't enough, or Chris. I watch W. try to sew up memory lapses, patch the gaps with hard stares. If I can't be friendly, I'm failing myself. W.'s on the edge of clinical breakdown, a state I can't help her with, but some caring words might just tip her back from falling. Maybe W. needs the crisis, a big poison release, so she can get through it and recover instead of going along in slow burnout. She thinks they can always go off to the reservation if necessary; that's her ace. Doesn't know she has to take herself with her. I want to help!—myself as much as W. Breaking out of habitual selfishness, it's overcoming a hundred muscle cramps when you feel knotted all over—and flaky! A great strain, Winnie Ice Maiden's awakening.

When Jack tells Chris *soon* about the money, Ch. waves it off, wipes his steamy brow with a knit hat.—Like I say, man.—He stands in Unitarian H's little archway, entry to the hollow church of his future. He's only thirty. Half bald, fringed with staticky frizz, cross-ribbed forehead befogged. Stunned ageless, straining to hear through mental mumble. White eyes signal myopia, our fellowship of the cracked. A minister accepts an impossibly boundless task, to mend the poor in spirit of his faith, lead the confused, make clear some soul-Word each hears differently if at all, while Chris himself is the lowliest and most unfocused member of his congregation. Asks far more of himself than his flock demands. Feels gifted (he tells me) with the power to see "heart outlines." He thinks Winnie would smile more but that she has gray, misshapen teeth. He enjoys Jack yet sees the heavy heart J. rarely shows me. He thinks I'm a screwball and withdrawn, but digs my cold-nosed mind. So muzzy and unintelligible to his congregation. Croons Bible texts with lyrical wrong emphases; his sermons peel off, go silent. Ch. is his church's poorest earner; his Sunday collections barely support the phone bill and cleaning—who pays for those glads and lilies? His flock never gives to the poor or bears charities. They are social Christians who don't believe in Christ. J. tells him—You should spew out those lukewarm pissants and go Episcopalian. Chris sticks it out, a Transcendental fruitcake, though even Emerson gave up on the U's and resigned his pulpit. Actually Chris has no place to go and dreamwalks through his role using defensive suffering to blind himself. The more he hurts the more he wraps himself in aerial makework, singsong gibberish, sermons with their little cries, catatonic caesuras. He may crack before she does. It's a strange race they're in, outslowing one another to the madhouse.

I try to help. Yesterday (Friday) I nailed Chris to Leopolda's kitchen table and sermonized him myself.

—You know what's wrong w/me? I'm grieving!

I ask for whom, who died?

—*I'm* dying. Can't you see Winnie's sick? I'm afraid of what's coming for me. You do know she's sick?

So? I say. The way he looks I don't want him slipping into breakdown.—Nothing she can't handle, do you think? She'll put out.

—Oh yeah? Maybe yes, maybe no. Meanwhile I'm paralyzed, waiting for her to hit the hospital or get better.

I tell him he's got to look out for himself. If he ties himself to her illness, and adjusts the whole household around her symptoms, trying to second-guess them, he'll get as sick as she is. That's not the way. He's got to detach! He'll get pissed off because she thinks he's indifferent. But that's the secret. He and the kids have to come first.

Chris fades out, trying to sweeten my pill. *Detach, huh?* Smiles disbelievingly, sly in stone. You may be right, but I'm not built that way. Whither thou goest I goest.

—Wow, that is sick. Martyrdom is sick, man.

—It's a sick world. Somebody's got to keep the folks pepped up and singing. Big shiggery sigh and shake—but still enstoned.

That's bullshit, I say. I'm three years older than this West Indian, so I swear freely.—Hey, Chris! We're talking.

—You don't think the world is sick?

—That's an abstraction. Did you get your sink unplugged?

—What's so abstract about a quarter of the world starving?

—It's there but I don't sentimentalize it. I can't help anyone else unless I help me first. You're starving too, you know?

Ch. rubs and hides his forehead.—I didn't notice.

—For reality, man, just like Winnie is. You spend half your life paralyzed by abstractions. So do I. Right now I'm working on how to boil an egg without falling into tears if the shell cracks.

Chris says, Shell cracks, huh? That can be helped. Start with cold water and vinegar. Suddenly he gasps, blows at the ceiling. Wide white eyes roll. I'm a spokesman! I can't bury my head in the sand while peoples starve. Anxiety is upward and rampant. I'm supposed to have the answers. It's the fifties, I keep up with current events, I read *Time* magazine faithfully. It's no abstraction that I can be defrocked if I don't show where my *head* is and what my *heart* is made of. That's a fact. *De*-frocked, woman.

—Defrocked? I ask. Because *Time* says Red China will have the bomb soon? I'm shaking in my boots about that. Meanwhile, my mother's hip is wasted by polio. There's a chance of cancer. I need drugs before my mind slips again. We're two months behind in the rent. The house is falling down around us, and we're stuck in the living room as if it were Rocky's bomb shelter. I'm talking about our house over on North Lake Drive. Do you hear what I'm saying?

—What?

—Are you listening to me?

He fixates guiltily on our *Time.*—Do you want to borrow that? I ask.

No! he shouts.

—I'm saying I'd be paralyzed if I didn't detach.

—Detach? (It's Greek?)

—From my daily household crises. When the rocks are coming down!

—I rely on my heart. All strength flows from that organ. I look at a man and I know right off what his heart is made of. I see heart outlines. You have a cold blue heart.

I ask, How'd I get that?

—That's for you to say, but I know you got your problems. He taps his head.

—Thanks. I do. What's my cold heart made of? Sticks and stones?

—A kind of piny wood with green needles and stiff gum all over it. (I don't want to misquote him!)

—Well! What's yours made of?

—African cedar. Cedar has a beautiful odor. So does pine, of course. Did that *Time* come today?

I tell him it's a month old. Stole it from my dentist. Chris moves his chair away but crafty, shrewd Henry Clay Alexander, President of Morgan Guaranty Bank, posing by a vault's big spiky hinges, creeps after him. Ch. stares at a poisonous yellow stripe: THE MONEY BUSINESS. Money business, I read that issue! *Time* is the favorite of the Unitarian community in Boston. You can't visit a house without seeing it.

—Detach from *Time* magazine, why don't you? I ask.

—*Self-Reliability* by Emerson. That's very germane. I've got to get home! Jumps up, shaking, his face orgasmic with guilt. Eisenhower calls, I wasn't here. I'll pray for you.

—Pray for me about what? I ask.

—Your polio of the genes. Aren't you worried? You should be! Frantic, Chris runs out. Fragmenting before my eyes.

So after some chat on the porch, the whole Jaspers tribe, Leopolda, Jack and I tramp through Unitarian H. for a look at the two floors and dormers. L. invites them to a buffet at her house when she's fixed it up, and we leave through dropping snow. It's noon but we can't see the lake from L.'s porch. Windless, the stillness builds white inches.

L. says she made a terrible mistake. She *came* here instead of renting these houses sight unseen through an agent. Now that she sees them, her decorator's instincts are aroused. Wants to knock all four into shape. Winnie arrives and stands in L.'s doorway, glaring accusingly. Chris thinks we might like to come to dinner tonight.

—Dinner? L. says. Oh, we couldn't. Not unless we bring it.

Winnie scowls.—You don't want to come?

—How about if we bring a big Greek salad? L. says.

W. says proudly, We don't eat rabbit food.

L. laughs. A rabbit wouldn't touch my Greek salad.

—We have red beans and rice. You don't want to come?

We'll come! Jack cries.

L. says, And we'll bring a salad. Thanks a lot.

I walk Winnie to the porch steps. Do you remember when we came to dinner in your trailer last fall? I was getting sick?

—No. Lips pressed tight, brown eyes wired to the steps.

You remember, I say. I said some pretty funny things.

I don't dare touch her or she'll bolt.

—Well, I was getting sicker by the day. I want to tell you something as a friend. I got very sick. Very disheartened, angry and depressed.

I see W.'s shocked and fearful. I'm too frank?

—I go. I have to unpack.

Wait one minute, I say. I was sick, mentally. I want to tell you I'm better now and that you don't have to be frightened of me. People like me can be scary, right?

W.'s dead pale.—Why tell me this?

—Because I want you to know. I'm very much better. I decided to help myself rather than just drift with my bugs and get worse.

W. looks away with *my* wooden smile. I'm lying to her? Well, I am. *I* didn't do anything, J. did it! I can't very well tell her to go out and *freeze* her bugs on a bench in Bestor Plaza, and wait for Chris to lift them.

I want to be your buddy, I say. I need a buddy and I'd like it to be you. I need help and encouragement and support. Not just from Jack, but from a woman. You have no idea how hard it is for me to say this. If you paid me to, I couldn't. But I'll do anything to stay sane and be a sane mother to this baby when it comes. You can understand that, can't you? You're a strong woman. You can help me, can't you?

—You have it easy, Winnie says. Why do you make a joke of me?

—I'm not making a joke. I know you're having hard times. So are we. But we can help each other, you and I. If you need anything, phone me or drop by my house. Okay?

Her deep sneer squashes me.—*You don't need me!*

My knuckles are white. W. digs her way home in her Norwegian reindeer sweater, denim skirt and wet sneakers. Black braids still maidenly, if not her gray teeth. Curranne the Martian! We'd hardly had one instant of eye contact. I'd been one lone emotional smear to her, a strange, threatening pregnant woman. And she may be right, I'm a threat to whatever balance she has. And I've never said one uncritical word about W. to Jack. Her avoiding eye contact was a kindness, since she can't lie or dissemble. Keeps as perspectiveless as a five-year-old. Say nothing, look nothing, be nothing. That sneer was deserved?? Or she was squashing herself?

Speaking to Winnie shakes me. An old person like me shouldn't be so open! I've never had anything but haywire, unstable friendships, though I'm open with Jack; less so with Dr. David. I had my heart in my throat with Winnie, but Leopolda looks hopeful as a buddy (detestable word!) Women are boring (sane ones), I lose interest as soon as their mouths open. L. rings a bell with me. I could share with her. (Sharing, ugh.) I feel *worth* being her friend. L. gives me whiffs of a life

I've never lived. It's a wipeout, having no professional life (not currently anyway). Poetry's no profession, but maybe I have a knack for stories. Even this little bit I've written feels real. J. hasn't written a word since we married. Too much criticism from me, *last May!* Righto, pound yourself for J.'s not writing. Funny, I have supernormal memory for itemizing my 10,001 failures, disasters, errors, justified criticisms, injuries, insults, those I took and those I gave, back to the cradle it seems. I'm outlandish, really grotesque. Judgment Day can hold no surprises—I'm so well prepared! But I dread PHZ. My brain turning to fleece. Suck away my gumption to write? C., you've slept away, blacked out, lost so much time. Now fight for every hour coming to you! Still not all that solidly joined. Sleep like the dead. And training myself to sleep lightly between feedings. But only half-awake feeding. So I won't think of money? Money I only hear about distantly, wind over a stovepipe. I ask J. if money's kept him from writing. He says no, he's looking for a subject, then creates make-work to keep from writing. He's interested in these few pages but I slap my hands over them. Refuses to read a word anyway, until it's done (whatever it is!) "and revised twice." He sees the filled pages turning. Coming right along, huh? I say, thumbing my start. Even a few pages feel thick to my thumb. I'm thick to my thumb, ha ha!

My Chaut. recovery is snail-paced mystical experience, starting with the big push on New Year's morning, then slowing down to one winter day at a time; then another big push from Little Pig. And now this big writing lift. I'm putting everything into this ledger that occurs to me. Fear no irrelevancies, J. says. They may turn out to be the most vital elements. I get a winged saving-my-ass feeling as I dig in. The truth, *so painful!* When I think about the pages so far, all I see is a catalogue of my black marks, or that's what I feel. But if I turn back a few pages I see I'm not *totally* centered on self-criticism. In fact, I feel pretty good. In fact, I feel superb! There's life in the old girl yet! I have the worst disease in the world, a mind turned on itself, and am overcoming it.

Well, back to my big day, last Saturday. L. shows us about her dark green cottage beside Unitarian House. Dim and cramped, with old wicker chairs and settee, ruffled organdy, dead ferns, an upright with ivory facings curling off the keys. Serves camomile, Italian bread and butter and unlids the antipasto. Soon we're collapsing over the dining-

room table as she mimics an Italian waiter stomping Spanish tourists.
—We no got sopa de pesca, we got anti da pasto!

That Winnie, I say. She had all those kids at home, and now refuses
to go to a gynecologist or a hospital.

—Hates doctors, huh? L. says. Why not?

As a full-blooded Cherokee, W.'d lose her self-respect exposing herself to some white doctor. She's made of steel when it comes to gyne-
cologists. Doesn't want to lose face with Great Spirit.

—Great Spirit! L. cries. What's *he* know about kids?

—She had stillborn twins last year, J. tells her.

—At *home?* Man, that's dumb.

—In a trailer, I say.

—A trailer can be messy. When there are two fetal heartbeats, the
mother should always deliver in the hospital. There might be complications. But two stillbirths! It couldn't have been the cord?

J. says, Who knows! I don't. I'd never dare ask.

—She's internalized the whole experience, I say.

—That's a terrible cliché, J. says.

I say, I mean she's swallowed two deaths without digesting them. Is
that better?

J. says, I get tired of this jargonizing of human experience.

—*Stop carping!*

—I plan to internalize that, J. says. You're sticking up for yourself
too much these days.

—Internalize *that,* L. tells me. Well, ten billion dollars' worth of
equipment wouldn't help with a stillbirth. There's nothing you can do
about a dead baby. And nobody's at fault. The big difficulty is *twins.*
You know a second baby is coming. Do you tell the mother the first is
dead and weaken her spirit for the second birth? You've got to be
honest with the woman. If she doesn't hear the birth cries and see the
living baby, you can't fake it. You have to go by the woman herself. Is
she a hysteric? How much prebirth talk did you have with her? Does
she trust you? The first shock can be harder on the midwife than on
the mother. Winnie didn't know she was having twins?

I shrug. Ask Chris. She was her usual stoic self.

Jack says, But she can't get the grief out.

—Ha, I say.

L. asks, What's funny?

—She thinks Chris thinks she's a cast-iron saint, and she won't do anything to disabuse him. Like busting loose. He actually thinks her mind has turned to Indian meal. Can we talk about something a little happier? I'm actually furious with Winnie when I think about her shitty cultural bias.

The noon is pinched and fuzzy. Snow falling by the windows. I'm in two worlds at once. Leopolda switches on the overhead bulb, faintly watering the dimness. The room sinks depressingly. L. grits her teeth, her pained coppery eyes pitying me.

—Curranne, she says, I hear you. But Winnie must feel on enemy turf. *I* started breaking down on Corfu. Suddenly . . . everything was Greek to me. Not just the Greeks but even the simplest shopping trip from my villa or caring for myself in any way. The world had lost its soul, if it ever had one. What I needed, I thought, was some ginger-bread Wundermensch to take care of me—somebody delicious I could take tiny bites out of—whose little tidbits and attentions would keep me all zaftig and glowy. *Mmmm!*

Her ecstaticized chatter rolls on around the bend.

Well! she says, coming down. You don't know any little old wizard I could hire, do you, to be my handyman and get these four houses in shape? I'll let him have one to live in. And there'll be a salary.

A twinge of eagerness stiffens J.—I know somebody, yes! Me. I don't know much about house repair but I can paint and rake and so on.

L. thinks that's an idea. But there'll be a lot of carpentry and plastering. Nothing elegant. J. has turned hard blue. He could get a *book* on plastering! And plumbing maybe? L. adds, the pipes have pneumonia. J. asks maybe we could hire a plumber, save on tools? L. agrees, we may need one or two guys extra to get everything up to snuff. Then J.'d only have to patch and mend. She could show him how. If he falls off a gable, her insurance will cover him. What do you think? he asks me. I see him ache to charge into the light at the end of the tunnel.

Manna from heaven! I tell L. But we've got to repair Mrs. Lancaster's first.

No problem, L. says. That's my specialty. What's wrong with the place?

J.'s eyes brim. Holding back. *A lot!* he whispers. To begin with, the pipes burst.

L. asks, Doesn't she have insurance?

She must! I cry.

I hadn't thought of that, Jack says, shocked. Does insurance cover house repairs? I could call her in Sarasota and ask. I'll feel like an ass but— . . . He grips his chair, about to float away. *Amazing!* Why didn't I think of her insurance? My brain must have crawled off to Chicago.

His lust for peace fills me too. I say nothing. That's when *it* begins. You took my mind away, I hear him say.—How could I have done that? I ask, prickling.—Done what?—Taken your mind away?—I didn't say that. I said my brain crawled off to Chicago.—Jack, I heard you say, "You took my mind away."—I didn't even *think* that, he says, and I don't think it.—Well, are you saying I'm hearing things? I ask and feel my mask forming, a smile stiffening in plastic. Quite ghastly, the will shrinking and no help for it.

—I'm not saying anything. He asks Leopolda, Did you hear me say that?

—You didn't. So skip it. Forget about it. Curranne, are you worried about something?

I stumble.—I'm upset about this snow. These little streets don't get plowed and the car could get snowed in. If I go into labor, how will I get to King James?

Leopolda nods.—Good question. How will you?

—I don't know. Is your mind back from Chicago yet?

J. says, It's okay.

—Well, let's keep in touch. I smile to show humor. That was a joke.

—Thank you for telling me.

—Am I a sourpuss?

—Not at all!

—Do you think I'm totally devoid of humor? I ask L.

—You're the life of the party! Isn't she?

—A laff-riot.

Stung, I bang the table.—Stop mocking me! You don't need me for a laughingstock when all Chautauqua knows you're the idiot who ruined Mrs. Lancaster's house.

—I thought I'd kept that a secret from them. Let's be buddies, huh?

—You don't need me at all, I say.

—Not when you're like this. But I do need you ninety-five percent of the time. That's the truth.

—That's a lie.

J. turns to Leopolda.—I really love her.

—Don't tell me, tell her, L. says.

—I love you, he says.

—Don't *look* at me! I say. I'd like to put your eyes out.

—It's really blooming, he says.

—You've thought I was a big pill from the first moment you met me. You'd dance a jig on my grave. *"Thank God it's over!"* Am I right? Isn't that true?

—I never argue. If that's what you think, so be it.

—You never argue? Why not? Do I have the plague? Ha ha ha, that's very funny! Now that is a real joke. I hope you can appreciate it.

—It's not funny to me, J. says. It's at your expense.

—Are you going to burst into tears about that?

He howls a big sad laugh.—No, I'm laughing. What else can I do?

—You have a fund of dumb questions.

L. says, I think this has gone on long enough. I have to go back to the deli for feta and anchovies. Did you think those Indians will eat anchovies?

—Ask him about his writing, I tell L. He'd create all this bizarre stuff to mask his instability. Jack has his problems. He's probably the sickest of the three of us. The first two months we went together he kept calling me his mother or his sister. Do you remember that? Your problem is transparent.

—I'm an open book to you.

—You look ready to cry, I sneer.

—I think *I* want to cry, Leopolda says.

—I thank God—*every day!*—that I've met you, J. says. You're the First Person I've ever got out of my shell to know.

—You can't say a single sincere word, can you? I ask. Oh, man, if I'd never met you, where would I be?

—A little less pregnant? L. asks.

—*No!* She likes being pregnant! Even by me.

—You're unreal. I must be a saint to put up with you, I say. The pressure of just being in your company day in, day out is incredible. Your constant insincerity would drive anyone tutti-frutti! Dig me?

—Sure, I dig you. I should be put away for your own good. Right?

—I didn't say that, I say.

—I caught on. But I'm not leaving. Does that sound sincere?

I sigh.—I can't fight you any longer. The mind can hold out only so long.

—I can stay? You'll allow it?

—You've beaten me! I surrender!

—I'm glad you feel better, Jack says, and tells L., Sorry about this.

Leopolda says, It's nice to clear the air before a birth. Everybody knows where they stand. No bullshit dropping down at the last moment.

J. offers to go to the store for her.

—Don't trust him w/money, I warn her.

—Don't confuse me with your father, J. says. She'll trust me or I can't buy anything.

—I know why you hate me. It's because I respect myself, I say, dissolving, but forcing myself on. You are livid with envy.

—Christ, I think you've hit it, J. says. Your big mistake was in not becoming an analyst. You'd be a natural.

—*And we'd both be rich ha ha ha ha!* I cry.

We all howl.

Wha ha ha ha!

—Of course, analysis may be just a fad, J. says. And die out among human beings . . . except for a last fifty years in Africa.

Leopolda says, Well, whales are big this year. Their brains are five times human size. Curranne could analyze whales.

Jack says, And hang out a stuffed whale brain for a shingle.

I love it! I say. I'll do it.

Leopolda says, Now you're swinging.

J. says, She's on the right track.

—Maybe I've had my last hospitalization, like Leopolda.

—Well, *one* more, J. says. Unless you plan to have Little Ikiru in a snowbank.

—Hospital feels poisonous already, I say. I hope they let me out in three days. They'd better or I'll ventilate the place.

L. says, Why go?

I tell her there isn't any midwife service in Mayville. I checked.

Jack says, You did? You didn't tell me.

—What do you know about midwives? How could you possibly be interested? I ask.

J. says, Oh, women's business, huh?

—Yes. What are you suggesting? I ask Leopolda.

L. says I can have the baby at home. Lots of local women must have babies at home.—It's not like giving birth in a barn, you know. It's the most comfortable way there is, farm women know that. You can't fool them about hospitals. Then everything is focused on the family, not on another factory delivery and unto us a baby Ford is born.

Boy, that chills me. I get sweaty just thinking about the hospital. Something bursts. The chair soaks warmly.—Jesus, my bag broke. I hope this isn't a valuable chair. All that damned laughing! My God, I need a towel.

Hallelujah! L. says, running for a towel. Don't worry, you have plenty of time.

J.'s eyes go white.—We'd better get home. Should I bring the car over?

—I can walk.

J. starts toward me, the door, the towel. But let's not take any chances! he cries.

—Right, L. says. Curranne, lie down while Jack gets the car. Hey, pretty exciting.

I take J.'s cold hand.—I'm going to be all right, Jack. I've been through this twice before.

—I'll buck up. This is our little anchor we're having. Just hang on. I'm dying of thirst and tell him to bring ORANGE JUICE.

—I'm off! J. is electric.

L. says, But don't break a leg.

J. stops, thinking.—Happens every day. Babies happen every day.

L. says, Maybe we should go with him. He needs support.

—Jack, I think I'll walk.

J. cries, That makes me useless! Let me get the car.

—Sit down, Jack, L. says. And as we all sit at the table again, she takes our hands. Let's join hands. Hers is strong. Let's have a little serenity around here. Dear Lord, grant us serenity. Help us each to get through this day in one piece.

—Two pieces for me! I say.

L. says, Two for her. Give us the wisdom to go forward one step at a time. Help us to keep our heads. Amen.

Jack begs, And help the motor to turn over.

—Don't bargain, L. says. He may not want the motor to turn over. You never know. He may want you to draw on other resources.

As we go out, holding Jack between us, I stop on the porch. The blank freshfallen street grips me. The day darkens.—Ohhh! that was it! I say.

J. asks, That was what?

—My first labor pain. *I-yi-yi,* here we go again.

Very strange to stand in sleepy snowfall, a blister of pain breaking and rippling up me.

J. asks, Are you timing your pains?

—You can't time *one* pain, Jack, I say. Suddenly the noon dark lifts on a gush of energy and at once a deep throb grips and releases me.— My God, that wasn't seven minutes! I've got to take a shower and get this muck off before it rots.

J. says, I think we should call Dr. Gogarty and go directly to the hospital.

—How far is the hospital? L. asks.

—About thirty miles, I say. Maybe a little more.

L. throws up her hands.—With these contractions you'll never make it. In fact, in this weather the doctor may not even make it out here for home delivery. Look, you've had two kids, I've had four, Winnie's had five successfully—that makes *eleven.* Why don't we get Winnie and just go into my house and have it? That can't be any more dangerous than driving to King James.

—What do you think? I ask J.

—I'm chicken either way! Why don't I just crawl under a snowbank until tomorrow?

L. says, Well, let me check my little bag. There may be some supplies I'm short of. She turns us about and marches me back to her house. They help me up the steps as she asks if I tore on either of my first two deliveries. Am I RH negative? Anemic? Diabetic? No hepatitis or hemorrhoids? How about allergies? (I *like* all these questions.) How's your heart? What kind of problems did I tell Dr. Gogarty about? Any abnormalities?

—I'm okay, I say. I could use a little Drano in my mental plumbing, but the rest works super. *Heavy-hoping sigh.* I'm sure the baby will stabilize me.

—Any abortions or miscarriages? L. asks. Problems in earlier deliveries? How was your head?

—Screwed on. Especially afterward. Afterward was a dream.

—I say, old sport, this looks like a jolly good time, L. says. We just have to keep a sterile atmosphere. Like that line from *The Story of Louis Pasteur*—"Still boiling milk? I say, Louis, all Paris is laughing at you!"

L. drags a black bag from among her suitcases and unsnaps it.
—Brimming! she says. This was her father's civilian kit before he went off to the R.A.F. They didn't have much use for obstetricians in Burma, so they made him a medical supplies officer.

J.'s distressed. His eyes pop under the heels of his palms.

—I want to have it *right away,* I tell him.

—Hold on, L. says. Why don't you take your shower while I tell Winnie what's up and Jack phones the doctor and we get a table set up in the bedroom for my kit.

J. looks wild. Honey, I say, run home and get the baby blankets. I never call him honey.

L. says, Jack's going to stay right in the bathroom with you while you shower. Now just a light soap and rinse. *Don't* put your fingers inside. What we will need, Jack, are some milk and honey and tea and fruit juices from the store. Curranne wants plenty of liquids. And I'll get more towels from Winnie.

I gasp at another cramp.

—Breathe deep. Was that back or front? L. asks.

—Front.

—That sounds as if you're serious. Remember, breathe with the contraction, good and deep. Don't hold back.

J. asks, Serious?

I grab his shoulders.—Jack! Jack! You're going to be all right!

L. clamps his shoulder.—I'm giving it to you straight, Jack. Everything is *not* hopeless. There is a strong possibility that you will survive this delivery and live to a ripe old age as a grandfather. *Relax!*

J. sits.—All right. I'm relaxed. What *method* are . . .

—The Dymphna method, L. says, clear and British. It's terribly dangerous on fathers, but I've never lost a mother yet.

He asks, What's it based on?

—You laugh a lot. Not enough to make you weak! But just enough to make the baby want to get out and join in. She laughs loudly. Afterward we sing a lot of Noel Coward and hop about like mad dogs.

That sounds great to me! But J.'s white and getting whiter. He sees right through my good humor. I send him to put on the teapot, but he's right back and sits down woozily, cradling his forehead.

I ask, What's wrong, little boy?

—I walked into the goddamn door frame.

—Oh, I'm so sorry.

—Don't ask if it hurts. Look—is that a lump?

—Let me get you some snow in a napkin, L. says.

He looks near tears with pain.—For God's sake, don't worry about
me!

L. packs his brow with a cold crunchy napkin. I hold his head but
suddenly flop onto his lap, clutch his shoulders and breathe deep and
steady.—See? I love you, I say, rippling.

J. hugs me.—*I know you do!* His cheeks run with snow or tears.

—All better? I ask.

He buries his head in my milk-to-be.

—This is the greatest day of my life, J. says.

—Don't smother.

—Mother Smother! he cries, digging in hard. I'm in heaven!

—I can see, I tell him. It's the last fully undivided moment he'll
ever get from me. Now, I've got to shower. You can help.

He's sobbing.—I'm so lucky! All this is a miracle.

But I can't wait for talk. I'm bent on having a baby and becoming
whole again. No backache, no brain ache. Even sane? How many
years since I knew halfway decent health? Somewhere within me a
whole woman is just sprouting. And a cracked woman rummages
about the attic looking for her lost megaphone.

Back muscles stiffen, curdle at the work ahead. I should know better—but it's fear, only fear. I'm mazy with it until L. breaks through,
her thumbs kneading my shoulders. She reads nerves. My muscles
unknot, bones crackle. Loosen up! she orders. Concentrate on re-
laxing. The day falls away in patches. Much harder to focus on what I
must endure. *I'm* the baby, tugged this way and that, drenched with
hope and fear at once, hot, cold, hot, cold, a mare shaking off flies.

Between pains something foams up within, waves of breaking bubbles deepening my relaxation, changing my breath. The wall flakes
and fades. I come to, here and there, under voices or in the stretch of a
pain. This is L.'s bedroom, she has a whole stack of patterned sheets
from Greece, blue and yellow cypress-leaf shapes too dizzying to look
at. W. spoons me chicken broth, I'm half-sitting, her dark eyes deep
and beady. She *knows* when I'm here and not here. Fibers attach me to
her and to the sea-green bureau, to papered walls and crooked roses of
the ceiling—the whole happy and suffering room. I don't miss the
hospital! Fat narcotic flakes drowse by the window, numbing me. I am

a mote on the white sea-silences of Chautauqua. Then rocking side to side, giving birth on damp leaves in a Brazilian rain forest.

A little less pain, please.

J. back from a cigarette, smelling of toothpaste. Biting back his fear like a Chicago gangster, not even a tiny smile at the corners. L. takes him back out for a whispery lecture. He's back again, grinning through shock. His eyes burn gas-blue, even in this light. L.'s moved two extra standing lamps into the bedroom. Dr. G.'s alerted and on his way. Between pains I sing a bit, or think I do, my body chiming like a slab of music. Evening is falling. J. holds my hand. Our eyes bind, break into the blind spot of the next moment. Baby, too, will bear that dark patch of unknowing at the center of things.

The black spot hangs in the middle of the room. I talk, hold back, calm myself with leisurely breaths. Inside I dig and scratch at the black spot. Wipe honey all over my face for Jack.

—You look like you've already delivered, he says.

—I'm in swell shape.

—Christ, yes. You're a marvel. Turns his face away; knuckling his nose. His voice catches hoarsely. I'm so happy, he tells L. Thank you.

—Don't thank me, thank her, L. says.

He grips my hand.—It's all true.

—What is?

—This is. It's like waking up and here it is, a moment I've waited for all my life. I love every minute of it. I'm only sorry about the pain.

L. says, Makes it worth it.

I drift.—What does?

—It's taking you where you want to go, L. says. The pain is a ferry. Go with it.

—I'm not fighting . . . and I'm not worried.

Ha! she laughs. Why should you be, with experts like us around? She hands me a pink vanity mirror. I inspect myself. Everything private is stretched and gross and swollen. Nice, huh? L. asks.

Super, Winnie says, mimicking me.

I've never heard an Indian mimic a white before. Her smile adds a wicked little private kicker. Study the mirror again. Coming right along, huh? I ask Jack.

J. is a stiff wavy mask of hysteria.—If you say so, he croaks.

W. takes J. out into the hall for a hissed lecture on stoicism. He returns, a billboard of good will, and shoots tense little Cupid looks

with all his tiny bow-strength. Veins rise and branch down my breasts.
Veer into blue tubes in my arms. He casts little love-darts at my breastbone.

—Stop that, I say. I'm turning to butter.

He embarrasses Winnie, so L. coaches him in breathing. J.'s a sport
and goes along.

—I feel better now, he says. Coughing and coughing into his lies.

—This exercise isn't for you, L. says. It's for her, so you'll be in
sync.

—In sync for what?

—For catching the baby, she says.

—Where's it going? J. asks.

—It's not going, it's coming, L. says. The doctor may not get here.
So I'm going to do the head and shoulders. You're going to catch.

—Happy to help. You want me behind Curranne? he asks.

—No. First I want you to laugh a bit.

—Ha.

—A leetle more, señor, L. says.

—Ha ha ha. He catches W. measuring him with disfavor. Is *she*
supposed to laugh too? he asks L.

—She doesn't have to, L. says. After the baby comes, Winnie will
dance the Dance of the Great Spirit.

I nod along.

J. is awed. In *here?* he asks W.

W. shrugs. I'll see how I feel.

—I'm part Indian myself, J. says. Five percent Iroquois.

W. snorts. Those loafers.

—I have Indian blood, J. insists. One drop goes a long way.

—That's why you don't work? she asks.

L. and I burst, our howls beating over J.

—Did *I* say something funny? he asks W.

—You couldn't have, she says. You're too sober to be an Iroquois.

J. says, I thought Indians were long-suffering, sober people.

—Not that sober.

—I don't hear you laughing, he says.

—You have slow ears. I laugh so fast you don't hear it, W. says, and
smiles from a very high place. I'm laughing right now.

—I didn't hear it, J. admits.

L. tells W., And you keep laughing. But don't overdo it.

I touch W.'s hand.—Thank you for being here.

—Did I give you the business? I'm sorry. It's hard to come down off the mountain, W. says.

—I push too hard. Bear with me, I ask her.

—I've forgotten it, she says.

L. says, Now, Jack, follow me closely. After the top of the head appears, Curranne will *push* on the next contraction. The baby's head will come out. She'll pant more slowly while I wipe off the head and suck the mouth and throat clean—with this little trap. On the next contraction and push, the shoulders will come through. My hands will be *here,* Jack, and your hands will be *there.* Like this, around the vagina. You will massage gently, like this. Soothes the strain. Then on the next big contraction the baby will slither out—don't look so shocked—

—It's not very mystical, is it, J. says.

—This will be the most mystical experience of your life! L. says. You will measure everything that ever happens to you by it. You're helping yourself be born, my lad.

—Nothing moves Jack, Winnie says.

J. cries, Yes, yes, yes! I can see how it will be! So what do I do next? Of course, Dr. Gogarty will get here, Curranne, don't worry about that. This is just backup.

I ask him, Jack, don't you want to catch?

—Want to? I thought I had to.

—But don't you want to? I ask.

—I'm getting dizzy. I need a cigarette.

—Give me your hand. I place his hand on my mound. At that second the baby kicks right into his palm.

—*Yehh!* I want to!

I say, I'll help you, you know. So will Leopolda.

W. says, We'll do everything we can to help you.

—I need all the help I can get, J. says.

L. says, First, relax. Go have a cigarette.

W. wipes me. My palms, my soles are damp. Wipes my legs and underarms. Looking into her eyes, I get a rush and then drop through an air pocket and it's *later,* my energy shot horribly. I've pancaked awake at such a low level, I'm alarmed at what I've spent or wasted. I read their fatigue and know the baby's dead. I start crying.

—Don't lie to me.

—I won't, J. says. The doctor's not here yet. But I want to catch! I plan to rush him right off to an Ozu.

Little Ikiru, still alive!

I'm still crying. Jack, I think he should eat first.

—I wouldn't deny him that, J. says. But Ozu will give him the hang of things.

W. asks, Who is Ozu?

—Japanese medicine man, J. says. Very big on home drama.

Anxiety sweeps her.—You think she's having a walrus? You can't take a new baby out into a blizzard!

I tell Little Ikiru, I guess you'll have to wait.

J. asks W., You don't dig Japanese medicine men?

He speaks with forked tongue, Leopolda warns her.

Winnie rises stiffly, writhes and glistens at the redheaded dog before her. This liar is fifty percent Iroquois!

L. draws her to the bed's foot. They lay out sheets and L.'s kit on the bureau. The black patch hangs unmoving among them. I watch their fishbowl gestures and think, Two nuts are delivering me.

—Two nuts and a drunk, I croak.

Winnie says, She's back.

L. asks, Have a nice little rest?

I'm back from somewhere, my energy flat as death. No, I whisper. I wasn't resting. I wasn't here.

L. wipes the bureau mirror. What?

—I wasn't here.

—Don't let it worry you. How do you feel?

—Not alive. Bury me at sea when the ice breaks.

—You'll buck up, she says, tilting the big mirror. How's that? See yourself?

Nod. I look different. Can't be me, that drained body.

The room floats in seaweed. Winnie damp-dusts dead flies from the sills, wipes the bedtables, the brass bed itself. Damps the floor with piny disinfectant she's found in the mop closet. I float on pine boughs. She wrings a cool cloth for my brow, not smiling. Away in some fear.

—What? W. asks me, lowering an ear.

—Keep hanging in there.

—I'll stick around.

—If you don't, I'll come back and haunt you.

I grab her fingers gently, suck their pinyness deep into my lungs.

Drowse, a pool of lazy electricity waiting to stab awake. Propped on an arm, Jack wilts in a wicker chair, one of L.'s birthing books on his lap, his head dropping again, again. A finger to my lips. His head falls back. W. catches the sliding book. Her long black braids sweep him. He doesn't wake. Her smile flickers. She glances at a picture in the book, then gives J. a lecturing glare. Snaps the book closed, puts it into L.'s kit.

Leopolda pulls the evening shade—my last glimpse of heavy snowfall. As if lifting off the Great Plains, the wind from lake ice grinds endlessly, cuts and strikes willy-nilly against house corners and roof. If we had candles this would all be a hundred years ago. Timeless people watch over me. I am moved.

—It's like a play, I whisper.

L. says, Play? Yeah, lotta fun. You having fun, Winnie?

W. eyes her with silent trust that she's not joking and nods her enjoyment. The room falls hushed but for the wind and J.'s snore. Then L.'s radio plays for a while. So inhuman, the mellow baritone announcer while I'm in labor. I've discovered the function of the orgasm, I think aloud—waking J. It's to make you forget this will ever happen.

Hey, Leopolda asks Winnie, does Great Spirit pull the wool over your eyes in the sack?

—Birth is a miracle, W. says sternly.

Blinking, J. claps his knees. I dig Great Orgasm. *I mean* Great Spirit.

—But Great Spirit's pain is so boring, I say. I'm a very sick puppy. The wind shreds and wails.—I'd rather be on Waikiki.

J. says, I'm just glad I don't have any oral magic and am really here experiencing this.

W. asks, Oral magic?

Firewater, Leopolda says.

—I'm an alcoholic, Jack tells Winnie.

—Now you are one hundred percent Iroquois, she says.

—Maybe they'll take me back! J. says. But I don't drink anymore. Does that count against me?

W. says, The way you work, you'll fit right in.

—Jack works like a dog, I say.

L. lowers her fetal stethoscope to Little Ikiru. Let's see how you're coming along. Ha! rat-tat-tat-tat! Sounds like a little gorilla pounding his chest in there. She hands it to J. He listens with surprise.

—You'd better get on your running shoes and take off, J. says. Little Barefoot's gonna leave you in the dust.

L. measures my cervix. Four fingers! Any time now.

A contraction gathers but my energy slips even lower. I can't muster a sob. As I come back, L.'s on the front-room phone. Agitated, pounding her foot. Pacing about, arguing, half enraged. Was that the doctor? I ask when she returns.—He's not here yet.—I meant on the phone.—The phone's not connected, she says.—Who were you shouting at?—I wasn't shouting. I was putting on chicken bouillon. You must have drifted off.

—You won't get away with it, I warn her. I'm going home. Where are my clothes? I'm getting outta here.

—Oh, really? L. says. Here, have some bouillon. You'll need strength for your walk.

—I don't want any. You know, there are federal regulations against this. It's a capital crime. You've heard of the Lindbergh Law?

—Have a sip.

—*No!* I know she's spiked it with . . .

L. says, Okay. When you get thirsty, speak up.

I'm gripped by a profound, unslakable thirst and give in. All right, *one* spoonful. Her henchman, a callow redhead, sits in his chair. He says, Do you want me to read to you?—Read what to me?—Well, there are only two books on the shelf. He lifts one. *Mystagogues of the Supreme Threshold* by Wheaton H. Hobbs—how's that grab you?—Why should they leave that behind? the tall Englishwoman asks.—Sounds like dope, her henchman says. And Dale Carnegie, *How to Win Friends and Influence People.* I know you dig that.

—Why should I?

He says, It's about role-playing.

I sneer but, perfectly reasonable, say, R-r-read me a few pages.

—Ingrid Bergman, he tells the tall woman. I feel halfway cozy, being recognized. He reads for a while. I finish the soup, measuring him. The strange little Indian woman listens intently too, to this spiritual seedwork of the White Man. Plainly it's having a profound effect on her. This is really quite interesting, I lie. You must like it, I tell him, with that little smile of yours.

He's off balance, I hope pleased. You like my smile? he asks.

—Read some more! It's fascinating, I say. I'll get this manly dolt to help me to the bathroom—then climb out the window.

Powerful American success stories fill the room. Suddenly I'm Lincoln and bighearted to "Two-Gun" Crowley, Al Capone and Dutch Schultz, killers all, who see themselves as public do-gooders.

—I forgive them and commute their sentences, I say. I don't want any arguments. They've suffered enough.

The Indian woman nods at the book, pleased and approving. I'm not sure where we are or what we're doing. Have we blessed the baby with our secret ceremonies?

The henchman reads on. Rockefeller feels important by giving money away, building a great new hospital for the poor in China. Dillinger sparkles at being Public Enemy Number One, crying proudly, *I'm Dillinger!* The book gives me an energy boost. I decide to take the hill on their ground.

—Which one of you is the leader? I ask. I'll deal with him or her.

The tall woman grins. Our leader? He's not here yet.

—She means the doctor, the Indian woman says, pulling up my sheet. I give her a punch that drives her into the wall and knocks a chair over.

—*No doctor, get it!* You call a doctor on me and I'll cut him to ribbons. That was just a taste. I am the greatest gymnast in Sweden. I have a knife under this sheet. Don't make me use it. You're not shuffling me into any funny farm. Get that out of your heads right now.

The tall woman helps the Indian up and rights the chair. Are you okay?

—*Whoo!* the Indian says.

The henchman holds me down while I rave on about the doctor and keep my eye out for chloroform.

—Why don't you go back to Chicago, Al? I ask him. Your whole gang couldn't feed me one drop of that chloral hydrate. You touch me again and you'll find you have an electric eel on your hands. Don't you understand that I'm indestructible? I am grounded on psychic energies from God. And *you* are a pipsqueak of a pipsqueak. Did you know that?

I'm half sitting as the bed starts breaking like thin ice beneath me and I balance myself with both hands to keep from sinking. They are shocked by the groan of fear I give, which is clearly not a labor pain. I am breaking down. I know I'm relapsing by the room's liquidity.

—Help me!

The tall woman sits by me, taking both my shoulders. Curranne, we can't have this.

—What?

—You know you're having a baby, don't you? she asks.

—It was never like this.

Right, she says. You're also going crazy. Curranne, I am Leopolda Dymphna, your midwife. I am in charge of this delivery. I want you to know that you can go crazy if you want to and it won't make a bit of difference with the baby. We will go right on having it without you here mentally. I'm not forbidding you to go crazy. You may feel safer over there. But it would be a helluva lot simpler if you stayed around and helped. We're all here to help you.

—Nelson Rockefeller wants my baby! You think I don't know he thinks it's his?

—And we're right here to see he doesn't get the baby.

—Who are they? I whisper, squinting.

—This is Jack and Winnie. They're not with Rockefeller.

—We'll blow the sonofabitch to pieces if he tries to walk in, J. says. That should help.

I shake my head no. All the pieces will just grow up again.

L. says, We're here to protect you. Do you want to have a breakdown?

—My God, no!

Good! L. says. I want you to know that if everything gets too rough —and it won't, you're having a perfectly lovely baby—you have my permission to leave us and have a breakdown. But we would all like it more if you would hang on. In another hour or so you're going to be holding and feeding your own new little baby. Now you *know* that baby would rather have you here than off on the moon. Right? When you think about it, you really want to stay here with us, don't you? Of course you do. We're nice people! But *we* don't even have a baby bottle.

I complain, Oooh! I cut my leg.

—How? she asks.

—On that knife.

—Let's see. That's quite a scratch. You must have a sharp toenail. Let's put some antiseptic on that. She tamps the blood off with a stinging swab. Let me clip your toenail while I'm at it.

J. cradles my shoulder. His other hand massages and lifts the small
of my back. My rear end is a hot frying pan. His comfort is immediate.
He has a lump on his brow.

I ask, Where did that come from?

—I skated into a doorway. Feel better?

Panic flash. The room glares. I'm crying, don't know why.

—I don't want to lose this child!

He asks, Why should you, it's *right there*. Everything's going fine.

Winnie eyes me with a rare shine. She grips my hand, her lips pale
buckskin, nearly white. Tremendous fingers lock me into the heavens.
Energy surges down her arm into mine. She nods at my awe.

—Great Spirit is with you now, Winnie says.

My jaw drops. I melt like pig iron. Instantly a contraction gathers.
Red radio-tube waves rise up me, rings crackling. A huge prickling
itch shudders over me, from scalp to soles, every inch of my skin a
glove of eczema. Am MAD to have the baby NOW so it won't catch
my rash and be a big bloody sore lump. There it is! inside me, safe in
hot brilliant chrome steel, slowly, pliantly turning about, its fingers
opening and closing in oil. My uterus is a woven-metal bag or mesh
purse, its neck open. The baby's crown inches down on grease and
fatty lumps. My cervix glows. I am wholly one with my three-dimen-
sional inner organs, alive to every beat and ripple. While I rove and
focus on each organ, a tennis match plays somewhere, two rackets
thwack solidly against a ball, back and forth, air whistling on catgut
thwomp . . . thwomp . . . thwomp . . . thwomp . . . My freckles
shine and prickle down my shoulders and breasts, stamping me with
fertility flowing from far sea-kings of the Irish coast. My energy
creams and shakes.

The man leaning between my legs has a raccoon mask of gangre-
nous fatigue glowing around his eyes. His breath smells of banana oil.
Has he been drinking extract? The yellow odor becomes banana panic,
my head fragrant with methyl fumes. Cartoon bananas with flapping
eyelashes are on the march. Little Ikiru in diapers crawls after them, a
corkscrew curl on his head. Now I lift loose and flatten to the ceiling,
floating above the pain while Leopolda urges me into panting grips, I
go with and breathe through heavy waves as they come. Winnie lifts
me from behind up the pillows. I watch L. massage and soften and
enlarge my lips with mineral oil, Jack beside her. My Marine!—his

bare arms glisten with antiseptic—ready for any beachhead. Drops fly
slowly as he claps his palms.

—Pass that ball, pass that ball!

The pressure on my opening startles me. Leopolda bucks me up.
Jack too keeps a steady flow of sweet talk, Honey, you are *in the
money!* while I whisper loudly, I am a sane maniac, I am a sane
maniac, I am a sane maniac!

—What beautiful hair! Jack cries. All I see is the hair, but it's
beautiful!

I haven't been shaved. Is he talking about me?

Leopolda slops on more oil, massaging, waiting for me to bear down
after the next wave. I *ride* the wave! Turn mercurial, am winged with
pain. Suddenly I am my grandmother and giving birth to my mother
who will also have births. At this clear vision all fear lifts. I am superhuman. My blood is liquid steel. I hunger to give strong birth, twins,
triplets, quads. Choral music lifts me, just tell me when to stop. *I can
do quints!*

—Who's playing the *Ninth?* I ask.

L. says, You're picking that up on your fillings.

—No, no! J. says. I was sort of humming it mentally.

—Is the magnet ready? I pant. I'm gonna let go. Be sure the magnet's on.

L. says, Switch on.

The magnet hums. If this is the worst, it's bearable. Waves reach
into me and grip the baby's head. With a deep breath I pop out the
head. A small face rebukes me. *Commuted!* I cry at the peppy little
face. L. leans quickly over it with the suction and clears its nose,
mouth and throat and wipes off mucus. The head tilts slightly. She
turns the baby easily on oil, reaches in with a finger and hooks out one
shoulder, then the other. The next wave comes as Jack's hands lift
with hers under the baby's head, *the wave* . . . passes and as I bear
down Winnie presses and *lifts* against my lower back and in a rosy
burst the baby slithers straight into Jack's arms and I am absolutely
refreshed.

—I can do it again! I pant. Do you want another?

As J. raises the baby with its cord, I ring with bliss and emit a
sheen. The baby is pale and coated with bits of fat. It makes a small
sucking falsetto cry, its small unmuscled limbs waving. How can anything so small be so much work?

Dizzy with smiles Jack says, This has to be a girl.

Leopolda says, Or else he's been cheated.

—My God, I've had a daughter, Jack says.

—Don't faint, chief, Winnie says.

L. quickly blankets the baby and lays it on my chest. The pale body is flooding pink. I snap to, my mind bright with oxygen. As my brain floods, I watch a rose flush rise over her skull and turn pink-purple. My red cells unleash quarts of iron into my blood.

—Wahoo! J. shouts. You're terrific!

—Oh, I've done it before, I explain. But not a girl, of course.

—Hey, it was easy for a guy like you, he says, kissing me. He's drunk or disoriented.

—It wasn't *that* easy.

—What a beauty! A girl, a girl . . .

L. says, Back to work.

I say, I didn't scream once.

—You were world-class, L. says. I can say that with authority.

Jack tells Winnie, Look at this little champion!

She shakes her head.—Too red for an Iroquois.

J.'s arm is around me, a hand on the baby. Little Ikiru's tiny face muscles stretch and yawn peacefully. Fingers blossoming and unknotting, testing the new air. Bluish lenses, suffused and unseeing, stare at me from the heart of life. She's a soft, musky ostrich feather under my fingers, much lighter than Matt or Mark. I suck the buoyancy of her little girl's frame into my heart and memory.

—Don't let her float away! I plead with Jack.

Heavy knockings sound from the front door. W. returns with steaming, huge Dr. Sweets Gogarty who fills the bedroom doorway, then sweeps in on cognac. A long slim bottleneck rises from his coat pocket. Dr. G. is redfaced and trimly mustached, his green eyes bloodshot and goggling.

—Greetings! It's Frosty the Snowman, he says hoarsely. What a divine drive!

His soaked face bends over the baby, a giant cold finger poking back the blanket. I reel under the brandy. Please, Jack, don't accept. W. leaves, holding her nose.

—But I see Mother Nature has progressed nicely without me. Hi, glamourpuss, what's your name? Maybe I'll just sit back and supervise the trimming. He goes to the door and calls after W., his huge palm planted on the wall, Any coffee in this roadhouse? I came the last ten miles on automatic pilot. My car's out at the gate. Give that beautiful mother some orange juice with honey, he tells L. Is din-din ready? Not mine, the baby's—that's about all I know about pediatrics. And the birds and the bees! I'm a mere thoracic surgeon, you know? I'm no big whiz at maternity followup, it's all a mystery to me. Sits heavily, the old mat seat wheezing. Winter nights must get lonely out here. There wasn't any tearing? I don't know why you needed me. Carry on.

The baby and the doctor nod off.

We hear cries outside. Leopolda lifts the front shade. She turns to me, white-eyed.

—My God, they're doing it!

Through the evening blizzard, flutes and tom toms whistle and beat from a circle of chanting phantoms who leap and howl on Cookman Avenue. Suddenly Chris presses his nose against the pane. His cheeks are streaked with paint. An eagle feather plumes his knit cap. Each fist against the glass shakes a feathered rattle.

Dr. G. sits up.—*What is that man doing?* his deep gargle whispers.

I tell him, It's for the baby.

—My heart's in my throat! he says, leaning to look. That sounds like a war dance.

Jack heads for the door.—I wonder if they'd let a soberfaced old Iroquois join in?

Leopolda says, Can't hurt to ask.

—Oh, hurry! I beg her. Turn off the lamps!

I watch Jack join Winnie and Chris and their kids. The sleeping baby stretches elastically, then folds her small face toward me. My milk drains into my breasts. I give her her first nipple. The calf-like strength of her suck shocks me as she swallows the whole ringing tip. My shoulders are fiery. The phantoms hop and bellow the Dance of the Great Spirit. My flow begins. In the dark I gladden like the sun.

PART EIGHT

Rainy Nights

S heets of rain falling all night. This morning, afternoon, evening. Digging at dirt gutters, gurgling in drainpipes. Flooding the Hall of Philosophy and howling downhill. Some crickets staked out under the kitchen floor, chigging and chirring. A moth is sunbathing in the floor lamp. My fingers sweetly acidic with orange peel. A webby, smutty mold smell rising from rotten porchboards. I'm alone. All day we work indoors, for two days now. Lightbulbs can't fight this darkness. This weather reminds me of our little house on Commercial Street in Provincetown, the long gray Cape springs with Jerry. The window-battering nor'westers, whole weeks of gray. I see Matt crawling to the sofa, pulling himself up and in surprise standing for the first time, the little bag between his legs swinging even at that age, his whole being ashine with wonder at this fresh new view of the living room. I feel nutty as a moth beating my brains out on a dim bulb.

Jack is hardening; sorta smooth too, ha ha. The houses are shaping. This one, Leopolda's, where we now live, is almost fully restored. When I returned from North Warren last week, Jack & Leopolda had prepared everything possible for me. I need help! With the feeding schedule, full rest seems impossible. But rest I must to avoid relapse. Really rest. Somewhere in all this care for me and Avon there must be room for Jack to find his writing voice again—whatever it will be. It's too easy for me to suck up every ounce of energy between us. That doesn't help me gain self-confidence and sterling health.

Today read through my early pages, meeting L., giving birth and so on, which I wrote for my present enjoyment, now that I'm back from No. Warren. Felt guilty with success, so am going on. J. laughs off his old black writing but can't find a voice to replace it. He's still grieving for it? Winnie's right, he's too sober. He and L. drive down to King James for A.A. almost daily, rain or shine. They make quite an uproar, trading their drinking tales. I stay home mainly and have time at last to devote to my own recovery by bringing my ledger up to date. J.'s typewriter hooded. Getting sober takes up plenty of time! he says. Not as much as drinking did, but plenty. Sometimes he feels like a rock-solid Puritan, and that's definitely no help. Mostly he just doesn't trust himself. His track record shows that he lets everything slide when he surrenders to writing. He says he writes best dead broke, with his back to the wall, and with a big lump in his throat about where the rent's coming from. And when he can't afford the slightest novelty or distraction.

Don't give me that dirty diaper, I tell him. We're that way now!

I don't care. Narcissistic writing like mine is sheer dope. I don't want to go down into a pit of whimsy and thumbsucking self-concern and leave you and Avon to shift for yourselves. I don't know, maybe I was bored stiff by my old writing and would do anything not to face it. So I had to be thriftless and penniless to get it done. Maybe I'm in mourning for my dead habits and the easy old days that were such hell. And remember that I'm caring for five houses, a retarded station wagon, a baby, and you. I'm not complaining, believe me! It's the best life I've ever had. Maybe it's too good and that's why I can't write. What do you think?

Jack, have you ever seen me out of my mind in public?

Yeah . . . So what?

Sometimes you make me feel like the Madwoman of Chautauqua, hidden away in Trueheart's Tower. Really, don't you think I'm doing damned well? Don't deny it, Jack. I am *on the mend*. I am doing my part. So remember—when you hear your violin start up—that you're also taking care of *yourself* too. That must be a strange new feeling.

Thank you for reminding me. It's so hard to believe!

Look at your own recovery, I say.

Oh, we're so *lucky* . . .

Just keep thinking that way. A swee-et smile.

That's so beautiful. Where did you find the canary?

The smile grows as I lay it on him.

That was a half-pound canary? Trueheart's Tower, huh, he says. You have a gift! Maybe you're the budding author of psychological romances. Have you thought of that?

Are you jealous that I'm writing, Jack?

I'm envious. But it's not too dramatic.

Not threatened? I ask.

I hope not. Am I?

How could I threaten you? You tell me.

He looks away, thinking. Only by not being here, he says.

I'll be here. Where would I go?

Clears his throat. Well, I missed you while you were away.

I missed you. But I'm back now. And locked in. I couldn't get away if I wanted to.

That's a blessing, isn't it? he asks.

Being chemically deprived of the power of choice? I ask.

Oh no, no! Before, your disorder didn't allow you power of choice. Now you have one. Stop taking your pills and see what happens to your power of choice.

You have a point. But it makes me so monotonous!

J. says, So does your disorder. When it's active, that's really monotonous. Think of the millions and millions of schizzes before you who never had a shot of PHZ. You're not in luck?

I had a really *vivid* sex dream last night. Maybe I'm waking up.

That's hopeful, J. says. What was it?

I can't remember. But you were dead. And then reborn. I could tell by your erection. It was shrinkwrapped and gleaming. When I unwrapped the cellophane, your erection was standing and pink and a daisy lifted straight out of the urethra, with a little sun in the center. That was all pretty interesting, but what captured me was your eyes. They'd been dead and now the film on them revived and got wet and gleamy. How's all that hit you?

Like Spanish fly. That was a pretty good dream.

D'ya think it's all this rain?

I think it's all this sanity. You're having your own little Mental Health Week celebration. May your dreams come true!

Jack, it's not that easy. I shut up.

It's true the trees don't melt or swim off to heaven or the ground break up beneath my feet. But recovery takes more than a thrice-daily pill and weekly support fuck, I mean visit to my analyst. First days at No. Warren left long scratches down my psyche. While the docs built up my tolerance for PHZ, then cut back to maintenance, I began bringing in weird chitchat. Nelson R. now owns all the radio and TV stations in America, there's no hiding from him. TV beams can look in on you anywhere. He's such a shithead. So bland and pasty and big-smiling, shows up at my door *aa*nytime, grabs me with his pasty fingers, rubs me up. Just because he fingered me when I was five or six, he thinks he owns all my children. The man's sick. Walks in without knocking, strolls about the apartment, talking and slowly stripping while secret agents sneak in the back window and stamp my kids all over with Nelson's invisible fingerprints that show up only under ultraviolet light. Halfway to his knees hangs the world's richest dick. What in God's name am I supposed to do with that? Shakes the dumb thing at me, still talking. Hiya, Peggy, you still in first grade? What are you wearing? Oh I *love* pink panties! Lemme show you my diddle finger. Skins it back, the head all purple. Watch out, Peggy, you'll start bawling. Feel a really good bawl coming on. That sticky paste of his drying on my arm. Like those invisible fingerprints, doesn't wash off. Nelson thinks it's too late, I'm past medication. Lemme rub that widdoo cut, make it aw better. Okay, two or three tears, that's enough. Let's move on, think of something else. I am ringing with unspent tears. Fortunately, I have a lot going for me with the walls back together. Avon, Jack, Leopolda, even Winnie and the houses. There's a real world waiting for me. I haven't slipped into hopelessness as after earlier commitments. I'm set on coming back two-handed and undespairing, despite Nelson's lock on world communications. There are still plenty of loose planks in my flooring, a few cracks and wavy boards, and a *lot* of third guesses. (Third? Ha! Fiftieth is my *speediest.*) Last night Leopolda cooked. I laid out four place settings.

Who else is coming? she asks. Avon?

I counted four chops in the pan.

Two for Jack.

Two for Jack! Oh, that's not fair, I say.

Then split the extra. I only want one. How do you feel?

Absolutely pitiful. Groan at the missetting. He can keep the extra. I'd eat a 5-lb London broil if we had it. But I don't want to put the weight back on I dropped at No. Warren.

Hey, better Happy Mother than Depressed Dieter, L. says. You can't afford depression.

Yeah? I want to be Svelte Wife too. When I start running, no more hunger. Funny, but running cuts my appetite. My whole body will straighten itself out. You'll see.

You *run?* I'll have to see that. Where will you run around here?

Oh, this is a wonderful place to run. You'd never get bored. But I'll probably stick to the fence and perimeter. That's only three miles.

Three miles! L. cries. You don't want to strain yourself, fella.

Ha! If I can't do that in 25 minutes, I'm sick. Anybody should be able to run for 25 minutes. I mean 25 *minutes?*

Not El Poopo.

I get stamina from Jack. He says he can't afford depression either. Meaning he can't let me catch it off him. He leaps Bestor Plaza at a single bound. He gives me iron salts for sanity; he's such a blood-builder.

We've been drenched all April. Chautauqua will never be the South of France, L. says, but sometimes I get hints of the summer ahead. The buds are out, the limbs vivid yellow-green in the rain. So healing, if still so sad, the grounds, where we live undersea. But with a big, vibrant spring on the way. I feel it pushing to get out and roil up! We watch big yellow forks of lightning dance on the hills beyond the lake. Every morning I feel my milk flow at Avon's first waking breath, and I am fluid boundless love for her. No regrets for Matt and Mark. I can't support sad thoughts. I fix on what I have now, the blue suns rising above her cheeks. Some demonically hungry-for-life little changeling drinks me dry while staring out of Avon's body. I have no spare love for another child, much less two. I'm only sad that she'll be raised as a singleton and not be learning from her two big half-brothers. I sit with my back to the window when I burp her, so she can see out. Hey, what's all that out there, snooks? *Ur-rup!* she tells me.

Higher Power, help me get well. Please let me have 20 years clean and bugless. Then Mr. Sturdy can survive me and go riding into the A.A. sunset with Avon and Leopolda. Ol' Jack, still losing weight, will never die. (He says neither of us will.) I get vitality even from his silences. When he's out of the house, I'm a bored robot. Sheer dependency? Maybe so. Even Avon sparks off of him. What I like best but find forbidding about him is that he gives me exact change in whatever comes up between us. He picked that up from me last year. Now I get it back with the convert's extra wallop. Sometimes he apes my gestures unknowingly, a way of sitting spreadlegged, elbows on knees, wise hands talking and all bones lightly braced for taking on the weight of the world. Or my turn of head, which was unnerving when its familiarity first struck me. When he talks his head arches just like mine! He really admires me, I don't know what's wrong with him. My mind turns him on.

Boy, I wish I could think in schiz, he says. Not all the time, of course. Just when I need it.

He digs your curve ball, L. says.

He doesn't know there's a killer X-ray side to him that discourages

schizy flippancies. Even his *hands* and *fingers* are rational. They smell
of sawn boards, plaster, wallpaper paste. His veins stand out now. His
fingerpads are like planking. He calls L. the most constructive person
he's ever met, a master of domestic particulars. I agree, she's amazing
in the kitchen. Knows everything, herbs, the works. Yesterday he
came home for supper like a minstrel in burnt cork. We cleaned four
chimneys! What bondage, I love it! Turns on the shower, the bathroom
door still open. And what learning the woman has. She's a genius, a
real liberator from stupidity. Some kind of Leopolda da Vinci of interior decoration. I feel moronic beside her.

I think she's splendid too, I shout. Stand in the doorway, watching
him through the curtain as he soaps himself. She may be my first real
friend.

I thought I was.

Well, I just wish we didn't have the money-tie dependency. It
hedges my spontaneity, which isn't all that hot anyway.

Put your hand in here. I'll show you something spontaneous.

Oh, super.

D'ya really think so? *Where are you going!*

MY FINGERS ARE ALL GARLIC—from the sink. And you'll
fall asleep over your dinner plate.

Well, that's the only part of me not in blackface. I think you're a
sociable maniac anyway.

What's that mean?

I mean you're spontaneous enough for me, kid. Even if you aren't
much in the shower. There it goes.

It'll be back.

You don't think I'll need a bicycle pump?

My God, Jack! Do you want to injure yourself?

L's "training" me in appropriate responses, right smiling and other
schiz etiquette. *The smile* comes when I think I could be happy crazy.
Each crazy is unique, but they all feel the tug to stay crazy. Mad
people adjust to madness, like alcoholics to their alcoholism, and carry
on. And it can feel safer than the straight world. Let's just check out.
Sometimes the deeper I know Jack the less I think I need others.
When you're lonely the bottom of the pond looks glamorous. Very
attractive, being alone. But I've got to reach out too. Sanity is other
people, L. says. The first *real* talk we had, she stiff-armed me with
Jack's Higher Power (she's Catholic, doesn't like buddy-buddy HP

phrase, wishes they'd called it Hidden Power—but J. says it's not all that hidden.)

If *you* don't think your HP is working for you, L. says, you're really certifiable. Rationality doesn't fill the hole (taps her heart). Time for a change, don't you think? What've you got to lose? Your mental health?

I sigh. I'm pretty rigid. I give it to her on the chin. Let me tell you, I *really* don't dig that shit. And do you realize that Nelson has his own church right there on Pocantico? That sonofabitch plays both sides against the middle every time.

I've heard enough about Nelson for today. He must be as popular as Jesus and Hitler in your state loonybins.

He's stronger than PHZ.

I guess you're stuck with his company.

Jesus and Hitler, huh? Hey, I don't want to *be* Nelson Rockefeller— or even in that big prick's company. If I thought I could escape him, I'd be begging for a lobotomy. But nothing helps. He just walks in and starts talking—and he's the most boring man on earth. Nothing touches him. A monkey in the zoo is more sensitive. He's all banality. Bottomless banality! And after he's really bored you stiff, I mean flattened you, he unzips this . . . thing.—*What thing?*—What would he unzip? Wave my hand. I sink when I see it. When he hauls it out it's like getting punched in the stomach. I want to knock myself out. The endless hours of servicing he needs just to get a few drops out. If you get even that. If you get anything at all. He's so divorced from his feelings that he can't focus even on ejaculating. Too numb to come! I *can't* call him sex mad. It's just that he talks me to ribbons—and then shreds some more. He comes in, takes my hand between his pasty palms across the kitchen table—*this table*. Starts to unburden himself of his enthusiasms. And it's as nullifying as being in bed with him. *Just good friends,* he tells me, patting away. *We're just good friends, aren't we?* What's worse is when he's really taking care of himself. Drops ten, fifteen pounds. Even twenty. He's still all flab. Doesn't have a muscle on him. But his *animation*—it's crushing. Massive little tête-à-têtes about dieting to get in touch with his feelings and improve his sexual performance. I could be mistress to a President, if I didn't let his rays bounce off of me. So, get it?—I can *easily* do without his companionship. But if he dies tomorrow, he'll be back to see me the day after. He can't stay away. Can't keep his hands off me. Can't keep his tongue out of my brain. He swears over and over and over we're history's perfect match. *I'll never leave you.* His feeling for me is stronger than death. *Just wantcha to know that, Peggy.*

If you went to the moon—

—he'd be waiting for me.

Well, money can't buy everything, can it!

Oh, he's crazy about Margaret Sullavan too. I don't know how she stands it.

I went to No. Warren a week after Avon was born. The other people there didn't work HP's magic on me. I expected to be back home in two weeks. It took five. The first half of March was full eclipse. *Zaput.* Then I found myself smelling fragrances of places I'd never lived but want to live. Sniffs of the future! Little patches of grass, patchouli in homey rooms. My *nose* was leading me! J.'s eucalyptus aftershave, and memories of fall leaf-burnings (but next fall's), my mind swaying with elms, maples, beeches. All these prickly smells reminded me that I have a lot of hopes planted back at Chautauqua. Funny, my nose waking me up, so that I wanted to get out and breathe again.

After all the bullshit, Leopolda says, HP heals those who heal themselves. He takes one long look at you and says, Move it!

While there I showed off Avon to Ed, who is the same struggling broken clock, his chin goofy as ever. Ziggy is the same sour brown lunatic, a haughty small Somerset Maugham weighing the minds of fellow lunatics. Ed wants to set up a Good Humor empire in No. Warren with Ziggy, who is a lawyer, as his business manager. Z.'s already typed a contract. Ed's designing ice-cream wagons and logos for umbrellas.

Ziggy urges, Show her the chart.

Ed unfolds three myopic typed pages full of deals and figures. It all hinges on my mother dying, he says.

She should, Z. says.

I see sixty grand for the house alone, Ed says. We'll sell everything. Z.'s in for 17%.

He shows me the tax stamps from Ziggy's cigarette packs, which are glued to Ed's proposal, validating it with the federal government. He flicks it significantly with a loud finger. I'm impressed! I hope they've affixed the right amount from their cigarette packs. I have a silver cheese foil from Denmark I keep folded in my pocket as my passport back to Chautauqua and show it to them. It's from a package

Jack brought and I've kept it faithfully and practically pray to it when I think about our home. It collects energy in my shoulder blades, circulates the orgone in my chest. Sometimes I hold it for hours, my heart with Jack.

J.'s first visit I had double-hearing. As he talked I heard a second voice speak from his stomach, complaining of life under an iron press. A flat, rumblingly deep voice I'd call The Melancholy Jack who wants to be writing and is kept under pressure. When I look out my windows, or step out for a cold breath, I see all the buildings and think of Pilgrim State and the vast horde of wards at Gallinger (35,000 patients at Saint!), then of all the buildings like these in every state, then on all the continents on the globe, then of all those who belong in these buildings but don't make it, and then of all the buildings it would take it they did, and then *my* Voice squeaks up, telling me, It's a very big disorder and you're a very small person. So, Jack, I know what an iron press is.

Why aren't you talking? he asks me.

You're talking.

Well, say *something.* I like your voice.

But I say nothing. I hear his iron press, its stomach groans.

At last he says, Getting a word out of you is psychodentistry.

I'll tell you, Jack, I say, tears springing. You make me feel utterly helpless. Just sitting there looking at me! SO judgmentally! It's like you're bringing the whole world to bear on my little back. I don't know what you expect of me. Can't you see that I'm a . . . rattle-pated addletrap?

A what?

Addlepated rattletrap. *A poor, helpless lunatic!*

Oh! That's just your character-armor coming loose.

My throat closes. I think I am going mute, I whisper.

I won't swallow that one either. This is one of the best talks we've ever had. You never tell me your symptoms. You must be better.

Well, since I'm already here I have nothing to lose, have I? Shake my head despairingly. You are so crazy, Jack. I don't see how they'll ever let you out the front gate again. Just hopeless! Keep your mouth *shut* and you may have a chance. Maybe you've been working too hard.

He stands looking out my wire-mesh window, fingers locked in the diamond grids. My ward is salmon-painted. The afternoon is salmon-painted. My mind is salmon-painted. Salmon is a shallow color.

You look like a Hopper that Jerry used to tack up first thing wherever we moved. A man half dead at a window. That should have told me something.

Well, I'm happy. You should be getting out soon. I'm very uplifted by this visit.

My God! How can you say that?

Hey, don't kid yourself. You're halfway home. You're *talking* to me, aren't you? Are you sitting off in your corner by yourself? In your own little psychodrama. Are you catatonic in front of the TV? Curranne, you're ready to pinch and kick. You tell me your symptoms. You *look* terrific. How are the other mothers in here? Do they know you'll be leaving so soon? Points to a shopping bag full of magazines. Leopolda sends these. Real time wasters, the kind you'd never buy for yourself. Wait till you see what we've done to the house! It's white as a Mississippi gambling boat. If you get home in time you can see it before it's painted cobalt blue.

Cobalt blue!

Leopolda's unhappy. It's the first one we've painted and it looks just like the rest of Chautauqua. Not distinguished. She's hiring a Mayville painter to slap on this deep Mediterranean blue. She needs the expense. Every penny spent is a penny saved. Are you gonna kiss me goodbye?

I'm not worth kissing, I mumble.

Funny, huh? I never pass up a chance to get a good grip on all these bones. Kisses me long and hard. Remember that, Slim. It may get you to the phone faster.

I hang on him, looking away. I am slim, I tell him. I feel it.

But still nicely organized.

Give me an answer. Am I more trouble to you at home or in the hospital?

Oh, you're a tremendous pain in the hospital. There's no question. I much prefer you on your high horse around the house.

Wave a fist in his face. But he grabs it, holding me. Suddenly, hard hands softly handle me, squeeze my breath out. Hold me all over.

Oh, don't touch me there! You may get what I have.

Would they let me stay?

Are you serious? Oh, I can't keep Avon here, I say. It's too gloomy.

I'm afraid this institutional atmosphere is going to seep into her. I know she needs you and misses you. I start crying. I don't want her to think you've abandoned her!

How could she think that?

She knows things! She reads me very deeply. And *you* held her first. She loves your hands. When you get up at night and bring her to me, she's quiet even before she gets the nipple. And your voice was the first she ever heard.

Ha! *Pass that ball!* Picks up Avon, nuzzling her. You smell like champagne and daisies to me. Or your hair does.

You idiot, that's milk bacteria.

I know what wine smells like. Whoops, ha ha! No, you *can't* fly out of here. You can't come home, Avon. Not until your mother promises to wash the veggies from now on without fail. Before she cooks them! I don't care about boiling water being perfectly hygienic.

I let Jack draggle on about bugs and poisons in the vegetables. How can I persuade a complete financial dunce that Nelson Rockefeller, Morgan Guar. Trust, Hartford Ins. and other big-money gangsters are after my mind as a sacrifice to the international usurers' cabal? Even I wonder, why *me?* I must be VERY important if they think they can get at each other through me. I mean, my mind is REALLY WORTH SOMETHING! Nothing else makes sense. I've known this for 15 years and watched its growth. Grown mighty lonely and cut off—especially from my babies! And from those innocents I've married. First converted on our roof at 18. Flooding conviction, a morning never to lose. Clear answer that meant everything sweeping into me. Illimitable tension springing from a few skimpy clouds at dawn. Blue of such brilliant crisp depth, sucking at my eyebrain. The power-melt of the rooftop, the tiles like isinglass not asphalt. The house lifting on unseen wings, every part of me ringing and being spent. Trees superdeep, their innerness thrice the innerness of normal trees. Intensity leagues beyond sex. More of a heavenly invasion, a cow's tongue going up my whole body, all my skin ecstaticizing me to eternal hardness. I would live forever. Deepest experience of my life, cold chills of being free. *Knowing at last!!* Was struck mute. Must always guard this moment from J., though he knows some details about it even better than I. Especially making love I might forget or be open to telepathic snooping. Block off for his own good, I shd. add. Just let me be, Jack, I can live w/it. You wouldn't want to know what Nelson has in store for me.

But I get broadcasts from Buffalo through my bedsprings and know he wants to use my brain—in tissue-thin slivers—to regenerate the market. Pump up prices. Get the presidency.

I will, I will, I will, I tell Jack about the veggie bugs. But Dr. David—

Dr. D. says you're over the hump and wants you home as fast as you can get there.—He does?—He thinks you've done fine. But he says this atmosphere is not one of the glories of the earth.—It's poisonous. Turn to the wall, finger a teddy bear decal. Will you be there? —Of course I'll be there! You think I'd go off somewhere and leave you and Avon with L.? That's what you think?—You might go with L., she's in good shape. I know you love the baby. But I wouldn't blame you.—Here, Jack says. Hands me Avon and the car keys. Crawls under my bed. Stretches out.—What're you doing!—*You* go home. You can sign yourself out. I'm staying here. I must be crazy putting up with you. All the time I think I'm your best friend and then you talk to me like this! I deserve to stay here.—All right, all right, you win. I'll *beg* for my papers. Soon!—Very good. Then I'll only stay overnight. Folds his arms, eyes closing. My God, do I need this rest. —Two can play at this, I say, and flop onto my bed.—*Ahh!* he sighs, fondling me through the mattress. Looking at you this way, I see why I miss you. It's your glorious bottom I most appreciate. *Just* the right weight and balance, really a wonderful match.—Lean over and glare down at him. You don't seem to know that this is a mental hospital. People are *sick* here!—Are they? I feel right at home.—With a little effort, you could get committed, Jack. I can see you have sexual problems.—Never denied 'em. I need fast relief, Doctor.—Have you tried pushups?—They're no fun alone, do you think?—Well, if you promise to be there when I come home, I'll take your case on.—I don't know if I can wait. But I'll be your eternal slave, Doctor.

His joking pulls me out of the blues. But after J. leaves, I let loose into my pillow. I want to be home! I spend the rest of the day stupid and puffy-eyed. As I stand in line for dinner, waves of self-pity start at my toes and rise through my scalp. I can't see my tray, only a steel glare. Skip the franks, pick at my beans.

(Rereading this, I see I leave out a ton of unglamorous stuff. I don't even sound sick! These events could happen more or less to normal people. J. says he could never describe the full shock of Marine Corps boot camp, the moral, muscular, mental revolution. I know nothing can describe the brute drudgery and dumbness I feel daily. Words and thoughts not taken in without repetition. J. knows perfectly when to repeat himself for me, but I can't bother with his repetitions here. I'm *still* too tender for such memories.)

My second week I was quite out of it but feeding Avon regularly. I came out of the mist on a Sunday night, gliding toward her cry. First time in days I knew who or where I was. Blackouts on the ward not as upsetting as at home, where the GUILT POURS DOWN. I shared a pale moonlit room with Eugenia Pratt and her baby woke up too. So we both sat nursing by the wire mesh in full moonlight. Having no idea who this stranger was. Our legs were quite close. When I changed breasts, she did too. Reached over, touched my knee and jumped back, gasping. I was real! Sometimes the babies would cry for awhile before E. or I could rouse each other from our PHZ fog or even choose the right baby. E. is a French teacher from King James Community College. 15 minutes (then 15 hours, 15 days) of her monologue is like six hundred Nembutals, or the whole *Temps Perdu* in one numbing gulp. I'd feel attacked and pound back a few fistfulls of orgone theory to spice things up. Her hair looked full of gnats in the moonlight (and at other times!) but I must say she absorbed all the orgone theory I could invent. If I'd had a box she'd have climbed right in for a treatment. She digs orgastic potency. Sometimes while nursing she'd go white and lean back against the wall. She didn't need the box. She was pretty heavy on the finger too as if I wasn't in the room. Overly finespun as she was, masturbation seemed a positive act, and maybe was. But she'd rubbed herself red as a carbuncle. With that kind of warning I chose abstinence. Got to like cold bathroom tile on my cheek when horny, though I must have looked as bombed as E., stoned on my tiles. Would feel joint pains, petit crucifixion. Writhe on the bathroom floor, weeping, *I don't have a prayer! I don't have a prayer!* I wonder what kind of waves Eugenia gave off to Maxwell, her baby. Fearful, I ignored her bad-mouthing her husband. But felt better when I could lift her spirits. Or made an effort to, if she wasn't off on the moon with Proust. The God of madhouses has an awful lot of interior territory to cover, down in the damage.

What strikes me hardest is the sudden adult look in Eugenia's face when the mist lifts for a moment and pain sweeps in. She ages right into her mother. Face muscles shrinking to the bone as time snaps back. She's weighing the immediately lost day, lost week. Talk about *Temps Perdu!* Looks like she's seen a python cross the room.

Well, now I find I can write one-handedly while feeding Avon.

Matt and Mark once got worms from unwashed vegetables, but I still forget to do it. If I only rinse, J. scrubs them. Wants those chemicals off! I do my best but I'm not Pasteur. There's too much I don't catch until he points it out. And points it out, again and again. But, man, am I brilliant at window washing—the second time around. I tend to make portholes.

We're making love again. Jack's passion lifts my skin a bit. Even crazy I attract him (though I'm not now). You smell like rising bread, he says. Sour, warm yeast, it's heavenly—makes my blood foam. I wanta gobble you up, *mia bambina,* starting right in this area. Okay, love my yeast—but don't pretend you're falling for my loony side! (What can that mean? He's never known me much else.) Anyway, my surrender is less provisional with him than it's ever been with anyone else. How well I know what I mean by that! What I'm really passionate about is lasting recovery, so that I can be a full wife and mother. Not this incomplete puzzleheaded person.

My first few days home I'd forgotten how to peel a potato or even an orange. Two days of blood in the sink. Not daring to tell Jack about this vicious blade. Why do Jack & Leopolda allow such instruments into the house? No way out?? Would boil a whole zucchini instead (brief triumph). Skin a banana, serve it on a platter. Leopolda now helps and I get little bumbling touches of heaven, especially when I remember the lows of Gallinger. Get a big wind of freedom—*fearful freedom!*—even in this rain. Dull girl masters sharp side of knife.

Crumb by crumb, minute by minute, we're actually turning into a family. Never despair, Jack says. His current makes me want to jump up and sing. He doesn't even know he has it. I get hard aching swings from poverty to confusion and happiness. It's like sweating for muscles. You go at it hot and bright and one day the energy is there—King Mist is dead. I was sharp all last summer and fall on pregnancy exercises. I get flashes of that sharpness now. (While a piercing foreboding plucks my heart out.) I see myself running and sweating, my brain squeezed beautifully bug-free. My heart gets raw, I crave Jack. Then the day bends; all my feelings filter through cotton and incompetence. Unbearably raw craving sweeps in but I'm too paralyzed to reach out. Washing one glass is like cleaning the whole bathroom, and I wonder why an earless glass won't hang with the cups. My arm sticks in midair as I count the cups and try to grasp why the glass won't hang there.

Jack, I need you.

Knowing he's not in the house, I can say this aloud for courage.

Even so, it's clear that the glass has gone crazy and should be thrown under the porch. I sneak out, throw it under.

When symptoms erupt they stand out and ache like prickly rash all over my back where I can't dig. I itch to boil dry and disappear. Steam to dream. Then there's no choice at all, none. Stress shoots through me like nitrous oxide and I could lose all my teeth without a whimper. I'm off with Pound in Bank of America beating up VPs and making rotten-hamburger deposits. Imagination gallops off on adrenaline wings. Hallucinations waltz in without a whisper. Symptoms turn fact. I sit through dinner, hair flying, trying not to eye the visitors in the living room, though I know each one has a special little salve tin of aches for my rashes.

When I get the poor-me's I must remember that I have the best shot of anyone in my family at a truly satisfying life (Jack says) and it's terrifying, that life can get better, despite the bottoms I bounce off of. I have no false hopes, just fears about what will happen when I reconnect—find the feelings to make me whole. Respond to real life, not the whimsies. I've never been here before; these bottoms are miracles beside my old fears. I face frightening sanity.

Some evenings I look up from my plate, or the couch, or come out of the bathroom and see Jack in work clothes, reading or asleep, some newly minted stranger (or am I the stranger?), his face aged and thinned, with friendly character lines, a mist having swept his identity out of mind. Am usually quite tired when this happens, no brainpower left. Scratchy, lecherous, diseased, sink into a stupor of whorish worthlessness. Why is a slut like me deceiving this warm soul with his God-given eyes? The whole living room vibrates to the God-given eyes watching me. Such a punch in the chest, I'm speechless. I can't even mask my senselessness. Or smile *the smile*—that tiresome response not in me. I don't want to dwell on this now. I'm only reminding myself how much I need J.'s gumption and common sense as a self-starter. He's a human provisions shelf; for me, at least. I want to imitate his recovery. I make daily efforts to boost his morale, when I can remember to. I don't always have something to boost with. But I learn, I bear up. I worm my way out of my blues. Still, I *love* a rainy night like tonight. Sunny days aren't everything. I'm not sad a jot right now (shaky maybe but not sad). Word by word I find peace in this writing. Though I face more than I have to, must learn to hold back from the edge a bit more. It's like praying. A ledger of those who love me, a people prayer.

I can't imagine having another friend like L. I did get to like Eugenia when we were less wacked out—especially during unguarded moments when a fearless adult appeared in her face. But Leopolda! How many friends deliver your baby the first day you meet? I get a flush thinking about L. What support! And yet . . . her begging, wounded, coppery eyes . . . an undiagnosable nuthouse all in one person . . . with a serene spot I'd die for. She'll be swamped, suicidal, unbearable, carrying her head under an arm, and then cheer up in five minutes by jumping into my problems or helping Winnie get back on the track. W. derails easily. She's worse since moving here, still Winnie One Note, with her sense of manic responsibility, as if the tribes of the earth pivot on her holding firm. All her judgments are off-center, but she answers at once to L.'s logic. L. was the first of us to come through. Whatever the way is, she knows it.

Here I sit in my pelvic girdle, thrice opened to deliver a child, my bottom half in touch with my brain, with some fifty or sixty small and large bones poised for writing down, or brain-fingering, the life of my mind in this sex machine. My mind slowly uncrippling its spirit-joints. Pages I stitch to catch a breeze. Because I have two friends! *Some miracle!!* All my life I've wanted a friend like Jack or Leopolda, and now I have two at once. Not that I sought being a loner or outsider. Or that Jerry and Ned weren't gems. But on the street, on a bus, sometimes even around the house, I radiate something unbearable. It's so unsettling. I get so hungry for a hand, a chat, small talk. Somebody to have a sandwich with. When I do I get hyper, or fearful, and hear my answers missing the mark. I have painfully stiff mental fingers, with only my spirit for a ball to grip. I go forward one feeling at a time. I have an illness that says I am supersensitive but unable to feel. Smile at that.

So now, Curranne has two-and-a-half friends, with Winnie (she's only half here). Ha! who am I to make such a judgment? Make that three full friends. I do get crushed thinking about her. Wanting to help but not being awake enough for the boost she needs. She resists me. I want to believe I can help. But she glazes over, can't speak sometimes for an hour. Wants a friend, I'm sure, but can't admit it. When I leave I was never there. Or when she visits me she may go blank and just walk out. I always check to make sure she goes next door to the church! She might forget the direction. But if she died tonight, some part of me that has roots in her would shrivel . . . my heart stink like a wet dog. I have a sense of vigil, of sitting up with her through deep darkness, even in daylight. What can I give her? I'm only groping myself. Sometimes she has a brain like a ringpost, a solid steel Indian for hitching horses. What can I possibly share with her? *Something* that keeps me from shrinking back into myself. Call it will to survive. She may have more will than I. But mine doesn't drift with every blow; I steer. I have a course. I see the fog roll back ten feet, my next steps clearing. For ten feet at a time, I sense profound order. A real rock to leap to. Could a schiz ask for more?

Last night Jack sat in his rocker, listening to the rain. His eyes shut, face moving. Muscles clicking or swimming.

What are you doing? I ask.

Telling God how good it is. He likes to hear that.

I feel envy. You're so *trusting*.

Yes, I am, J. says.

How do you know He hears you?

You're back, aren't you?

God-waves from his eyes pass through steel. The room afloat. His hard hands grip the rocker lightly. Please don't let those hands touch me. They can do anything imaginable. Hold my breath—don't attract tiny spark hanging from his finger. If it bursts in me I'll be Curranne the baboon and climbing the walls.

I think about my prayer (I don't have a prayer!) on the bathroom tiles in the new mothers' ward. Okay, the prayer I don't have is answered. For me—but not for how many others? For Eugenia? What superdisturbs me is J.'s power of example. *Something* works for him. I'm moved less by what happens to me than by what I see moving in him. He's a glove God puts His fingers into and moves, a handy puppet to look out of. The vibes are very catching, those God-given eyes. Living room quivers, I sit wavering, barely together. I want it— one pinhead of Jack's serenity. Or is it his *privacy* I envy? The Buffalo broadcasts have cut down but even one or two a day leaves me feeling porous. No borders! Somebody always listening to me think. Voices

spit through me like bad TV signals, voices on white noise. Everywhere little and big islands of mist drifting through bone—no privacy,
not for ten trillion dollars, not for a penny. Not for a prayer. Never
know when taffy-brain will strike—or leave. Then I look at Jack, his
privacy. He can leave everything behind, fly off like Peter Pan or
Shakespeare. No voices, nobody listening in. When he's in heaven like
that, I can't bear to touch him. Even with a word. So marvelously
alone, in the living room with me. I try to help him keep his silence. I
get such hope. It's possible for me too?

Maybe by mosmissis? ismossis? (look up)

Health, mental and otherwise, gobbles up the day. The rain has shut
down J & L's roofing just when they've finished the third roof. At
breakfast today she again launched into me for holding back on HP.

I see your problem, fella, she says. I have a black lawyer who
phones me—without benefit of the phone company—because the People of the State of New York, New York, are suing me for illegal rent
practices. Actually, he says "illogical" but I know what he means. I'm
the opposite of a slumlord, with my low-rent Kings Row.

Jack looks out the wet window. This voice comes down from the
clouds?

Huh? No, man, from my bones, L. says. When Mr. Bones lifts the
phone off the hook, every nerve lights up. Total switchboard panic.
But I don't show it.

That's good. Why answer?

You must be kidding, I tell him. I look at L. with affection. Loving
the wounds in her eyes, her flighty hands, the way her lips push out
words and smile and die and smile. All that spirit half-crushed half-
released by chatter and breastbeating. J. bears her monologues because
she's a fellow drunk. Sometimes down in King James she goes into
little street dances that could get her locked up. I bear her talk will-
ingly. Look at what she puts up with in me! She's even awakened me
enough to put up with *her.*

I don't overreact, she tells J. I ignore Mr. Bones's blaring away as
long as I can. But this shady snake uses subliminal advertising. He
gets his message across no matter what trick I use. The more I fight,
the stronger he gets. *Yakking shyster!* There, see? I'm weaker, he's
stronger.

You need lithium, I say. That's all you need.

Isn't it pretty to think so? L. says. Lithium's not much help for

voices. The visuals are gone, thank God, but the *melody* lingers on. I'd
rather talk to HP and be crazy than not talk to Him at all. I spent
years asking Why me? Why me, Lord? Never answered.

A blessing, huh? Jack says.

L. says, He don't plant 'taters and He don't answer folks who walk
around with their head under their arm crying *Why me, Lord? Why
me?* He's pissed by the why-me's. He talks only to a select list. You've
noticed He only speaks to saints? Come to think of it, He doesn't
answer them either. He sends Gabriel or some other angel. I think He
spoke to Moses and showed him His back parts, something like that.
Big voices are big phonies. You've got to get a strong grip on this fact.
If "someone's" talking, it's a gremlin.

J. laughs. What if it really is Gabriel!—not Brother Bones?

Horsefeathers, L. says. You can ship Bones back to Kenya, I want
Prince Charming. JC! But He's never there for me either. I'd sit
around Corfu for months in a gray funk. Talk about cancer of the
marrow and severe iron deficiency. Death looked like flying down to
Rio. What're we all after anyway? Money? Houses? Families? I've had
all that and they were too much strain to enjoy. I don't know what I
want. Sometime ago something got plucked out of me and never put
back. Now at least I have God. What I think I'd like is lasting mental
balance. That's my motto: SERENITY, SANITY, SOLVENCY. But
I don't damn myself for being a bedbug or look for a ball of cotton to
climb into. That's nice, you know, self-acceptance? Even a little bit is
nice.

I put spiritual recovery before mental, she says. That's just me, of
course. I'm not bugging you about anything, Curranne. If you need a
Higher Power you can feel unselfconscious about, take Beethoven.
He's peppy. Stronger than you are. You leaned on him when having
Avon. Me, I go straight to Mr. Wonderful. He organizes me around
what's really important for me.

I know there's something better than PHZ, I say.

There'd better be, L. says. What's not important are the daily disasters I struggle through. They're so boring. I always survive. Who can
get spiritual about beating the housing market? I need a maintenance
dose of people. Maybe I can help somebody get born, huh? If I'm
interested in people, I'm halfway home. My self-concern can absorb
any amount of time I want to give it. That's devitalizing. I mean
there's healthy self-concern and then there's self-obsession, right? So

far, Chautauqua is heaven. No Freud-fodder neurotics, just straight-
forward loonies. And I'm not running off to strange villages and hopping around the islands on birth calls. I'd lose three days to a week on
a delivery. Disaffecting for my husband and kids. They still wonder
what I was up to. What I was doing was not drinking. Keeping my
bugs at bay by not draining my defenses with alcohol. I could stay
sane three days in a row if I didn't drink. Pregnant women saved my
life by needing me. Helping me beat self-obsession. If I just relax and
follow HP's lead, I'll noodle my way into the Plan every time.

Plan? I say. I dig plans. What plan?

Oh, HP's got it *so* organized! Leopolda says. But I don't understand
a particle of it.

J. says, What's magnetic to me is feeblemindedness to you?

Right, she says.

Or paranoia, I say. Where's the plan?

The Plan is that HP *wants* us to recover. We weren't built to fall
apart. Of course, there are defectives, sports, blind alleys—going by
our terms, not His. Who knows what He's really got in mind? He may
be looking for His next big step in all us kooks. Maybe He's put us
into a walking half-sleep because He's working on our rebirth in the
Now. What's the first step? The sick person has to be willing to recover. Right, Jack? That's the hardest step. Who ever knew that? It
has to be repeated and repeated. Otherwise we'll just chase the bus
back to the funny farm at the first falling leaf. *A leaf fell! I'll never
make it!*

Hand Jack my hairbrush. That's what Goldbaum told me at Gallinger.

Hey! Out of the mouths of shrinks, spiritual responsibility, Leopolda says, and holds out a palm in the falling miracles. Will they
never cease, Lord? But dumb bunnies like us need more than miracles.
We needs lots of repetition and hammering. With us the Plan sinks in
for ten seconds and evaporates. We need big juju, brainwashing,
maybe wrist tattoos: BE WILLING! For you and me and Winnie and
Chris, everything is a little extra effort. Or more than a little. When I
put the Plan this way, it's not awfully exciting, is it? Well, we're slow,
folks! We don't crave raw excitement. Look how long it's taking to fix
these houses. I'm competent, but anybody else would've been done in
three weeks. She bats and dresses a Gaulois, lights it measuredly. Did

you ever watch Jack count his thumbs? He starts with his toes, just like one of us.

We both howl.

That was unkind, she says.

Brushing Curranne's hair or counting thumbs, Jack says, stroking my hair, I takes my time. Pulls my hair tight as I snap on my turquoise silver clasp. Kneels, slips off my shoe. But I'll count *yours* just to show how *fast* I can do it.

I sit on my hands. Jack, I don't keep my thumbs down there.

No . . . He smiles, tickling. But that's where you keep your orgones!

AGHH!—leap back.

Let's make Jack an honorary schiz, L. says. He really has sterling symptoms. Why do I feel drunk? Let's not work today. Let's just swill coffee and fight caffeine poisoning with orange juice. Let's bust loose! I want to dance until I faint. *Zorba! Come back, Zorba!* I love you, Zorba!

I feel like Hercules. I want to muck out some stables, J. says. I like mud and manure!

Fits right in! Don't you think? L. asks me. The windows are filthy, Jack. Why don't you go out and wash 'em?

And finish the roofing while you're at it, I add.

One last caffeine boost, J. says at the pot.

Leopolda looks out at her backyard willow. Those buds are glowing. What a green! I'm a watercolorist manqué, you know? Gazes at rainbeaten shrubs. Gray cloud and whips of yellowgreen neon buds. She pouts, waving her cigarette, How could all that be a big lie?

I'm so moved by L.! Feelings I couldn't give Eugenia Pratt in the ward—but which she awoke—I want to give to L. I just want to give! *It's spring!* Something in me wants to be *given*—like sperm. I say so.

Jack says, I can't identify with that.

Oh, you poor man! L. cries. You were doing so well . . .

He sighs helplessly. Maybe I can find a book to bone up on it.

That may be your problem, L. says. Too many books, not enough bones.

I'll bet you're right! I'm ready. I'll give up books for a real life of real flesh and hot blood. Cracks a walnut in the crook of his arm, then breaks it to bits between the heels of his palms. *Any ideas?* he asks me.

My God, those windows are filthy.

I'll get right at them. Although I think a rainy day is a nice time to rest and get your joints oiled.

I like a sunny day for that!

You've been sharpening your wits, my dear, J. says.

Yes, L. agrees. It shows.

I plan to lift all of our conversations to a higher plane. I ask L., Will you have trouble renting these houses?

Money and banking! Jack cries. What higher plane is there?

Heck, no, Currannie, L. says, I'm already agettin letters. These dingbats rent themselves. I'm already halfway to the bank.

They aren't dingbats, I say. They're *showpieces*.

Yeah, L. agrees cheerlessly. I'll *never* lose any money.

Maybe HP has something in mind, I say.

HP? Jack searches the ceiling. Who said that? Did the Pope pass through?

I didn't hear anything, L. says. Must have been a mouse.

Well, He *could* have something else in mind, you know, I say.

Leopolda's wide-eyed at Jack. Did you hear a squeak?

Oh, frig you both, I say.

Maybe He thinks she's had it too easy, L. suggests.

Something behind her words strikes me to the root. Too easy, huh? My eyes prickle. Milk drains into my breasts. The rain blooms, gray and flowery. L. takes my hand.

What's wrong?

Minor spiritual experience, I whisper.

What? Jack asks.

Lactation!

It's that painful? he asks.

I'm so *happy!* Despite the garbage.

Oh, is that all? L. says. A gratitude attack. Nice not being in North Warren, huh? Especially today. I dig.

Avon coughs. I look at Jack and he brings her to me. I've got two friends there I'd like to help, I say. I drop my flap and pop her the nipple. If I could. You two guys have A.A. I feel left out. I want to help some nuts and grow too.

Hey, it's not the same, she says. Leave the clinical cases to the clinics. You're doing fine with numero uno.

Yeah, J. says, nodding at Avon. You're doing beautifully.

Besides, I haven't seen any recovering nuts around here, L. says. You can't call Winnie recovering. She's not even on meds.

Ed and Ziggy are on Thorazine, I say.

They're basket cases, Jack says.

So was I! So were *you!* Or don't you remember? *I* do.

They're so adapted, they wouldn't leave, he says.

They'd leave for money, I say. That's all they talk about. When do the rentals start?

July, maybe late June, Leopolda says.

So there's May and June, I say. If we offered them rooms and small jobs, they might slip out from the hospital for two months and find they liked it. Give them some self-esteem. They might even want a shot at some kind of sanity and self-support again. They could help with repairs. They might even get the idea that the outside isn't so horrible. You know, we plant the seed. Maybe it doesn't take right away, but in a few months or a year or so, who knows? The urge might hit harder. To take a real shot at real life.

A half-real shot at a half-real life, Jack says. You couldn't get 'em past the gate without straitjackets.

I'd only have to swing Ed. Ziggy'd come along. He's got a weird idea Ed is his big meal ticket.

How would you talk Ed into it? L. asks. Even if I were ridiculous enough to agree.

That's just it! This place is a colony, not a town. It's another institution! Take 'em some pictures of the houses—*these* houses. What's forbidding about Cookman Avenue? It's not like living in a city. There's nobody here. Everything's protected and quiet. They could stroll around all these empty streets. Go fishing. Help *us*—I'll bet they're both manually skilled.

Jack blinds himself. One week with those two and you'd be back in North Warren.

Wouldn't know until I tried.

Well, I know, L. says. Stop and think. On top of Avon, you'd be doing their cooking and laundry, their dishes, maybe their beds, and your own housework. How long could you stand up to that and still get the rest you need?

You know what the Romans discovered? I ask. The way to get an arch to stand up is to increase the weight it bears.

You're not stone, J. says.

Or Roman, L. says.

Oh, all right. Forget it.

J. cries, People can't bear to look at Ed without his jaw. *I* can't bear to look at Ed!

Without his jaw? Leopolda asks.

That's really it, isn't it? I ask him. You can't bear to look at him? Even if everything else could be ironed out—

It's not easy.—Not that they're dangerous.

Of course they're not dangerous!

They're not dangerous, Leopolda informs Jack.

I tell her, These guys on the outside would be *less* dangerous than most civilians. They're insecure and timid. They want to be agreeable. Well, sort of. They're just like us, they'll do anything not to upset people. They'd be afraid of getting sent back. I sure am! Some days less so than others, okay. You know, the state pays their board at a halfway house. It's cheaper for Pennsylvania to board them out.

Even if they're across the state line in New York? Leopolda asks.

That's only paperwork, like picking up unemployment checks out of state. I'm not sure but you should get over a hundred dollars each for them. Tax-free. Weekly.

You don't say! she says.

AHH! I say.

Yeahhh! Tax-free? And working for the Lord at the same time? Oh, fuzz, I don't care about Ed's jaw. But will *they* want to go along?

I think they're half ready to split. Tomorrow's my day with Dr. David. Come with me, I say. I could get him to write me a recommendation. He's very impressed by you and Jack and A.A. He'd understand what we're doing. Especially if we stress the money angle. So we don't sound like a pair of knotheads.

Well, I could look these guys over, she says.

They're both bastards, Jack says.

Jack, are you testing my patience or my intelligence? I ask. I'll explain again. Ed and Ziggy would only be afraid that we'd dump them. Leopolda will always have the power to blow the whistle. Anyway, she could make pretzels out of either of them.

I'm not so sure about that, she says.

Jack goes to the window. And over sixteen hundred dollars tax free for eight weeks' room and board. That's not to be sneezed at.

Leopolda cries, Jack, you're a genius! You've figured it out already.

I'm glad you two ladies are thinking of the money and aren't a pair of batty altruists, he says. Forehead to the runny pane, eye fixed on clouds.

For that fee I'll bend a few pretzels. But these guys would have to be signed out to me, not to you, Curranne. You're too recent a member of their establishment.

What's that matter? I say. The main thing is helping them. I gotta get sane! I have to be a model of sanity so I can go back to work as a sub in King James. I can't be mentally unfit when I apply for reinstatement. People pick up instantly that you're wired on PHZ or lithium or anything else. They don't know what it is but they sense it. I want to hit that office drug-free, if possible, and look civilian.

What'll you do afterward? Jack asks.

I mean just for one day, Jack, while I get the job! I want to go in looking like a Maybelline ad. Not a cloud in sight.

Leopolda sighs. Peachy-keen again would be nice.

Someday, I say, out of the garbage. Once and for all!

Screw pills! L. agrees. Pills are for idiots.

Of course, Ed and Ziggy would be on 'em for life, I say.

We'll get by, L. says.

Now we're using our brains.

Why don't we all go swimming? Jack asks.

Boy, I'm glad I unburdened myself, I say. Talking it over with you, I feel on the mend again.

We're in the Plan, L. agrees.

My God, this is my *fourth try* at lasting mental competence, I say.

Getting your rocks together, Jack says.

I slap the table. I should know enough by now to do it right, don't you think?

We're really swinging, L. says. Jumps up, clapping her hands at the dancing weather outdoors. Let's go see your doctor right now.

I'll phone him!

Oh, don't bother, Jack says. Just drive out and surprise him.

Just drop in, huh? Leopolda ponders.

We weigh this seriously, then I do phone. Dr. David says he'll be delighted and greatly honored to meet Mrs. Dymphna tomorrow.

Write yourselves a note so you don't forget, Jack says.

As I continue this, it's now Avon's 2 A.M. feeding. I almost slept through. But my body heard her cough and I was dripping in my bra as I awoke. At 10:30 Jack & Leopolda returned in the rain from still another A.A. meeting. Of making many meetings, there is no end, he says. L. agrees: The whole idea is meeting people as daffy as you are. —Damaged, you mean, Jack says. Only the damage isn't irreversible. I've gone with them to three or four. Alcoholism seems so clean-cut and treatable, beside schiz, paranoia, manic depression and so on. Of course, alcoholism is a form of insanity. Once they get sober they all agree to having been insane. The world was too gray to live in without booze. They'd get insanely depressed and chase good cheer. Now instead of chemical good cheer they have fellowship. Those two sure cheer each other up. Always laughing about old insane behavior and drinking disasters. It's all meetings, meetings, meetings, people, people, people. I wish I could be helped that easily. And maybe that's just what we're going to do, what L. calls "milieu therapy." Start up our own little Halfway Happy House.

They'd talked about Ed and Ziggy. They parked by the lot at the gate, then ran home in the downpour. In the kitchen I heard them race in and strip their soaked clothes. The bulb brilliant in the wet air.

Well, here we all are again in Cocaine Kitchen, Leopolda says. We need a new shade for that bulb. It's driving me straight to bed. Good night, all.

Goodnight, El Poopo! Jack calls. Can you make it up?

Leopolda groans on the steep back stairs. I'm going to poop out right here. I like that nice washboard look when I wake up.

Hi-i, I drawl. (Working on my humor.)

It is I, Coyote Trueheart. How is woman?

Plenty wacked out.

Ah? Straight shooter tell Coyote.

I'm psyching myself up for Ed and Ziggy. Big moment of truth tomorrow when Leopolda and I make the pitch. I think the hospital director will be happy about a halfway house at Chautauqua.

He should be overjoyed just to say *adios* to that pair. They are ready for improvement. They haven't changed since the night we met. Kisses me in his shorts, races into the bedroom for his red velvet robe. But *you* sure have come out of that squirrel cage a changed woman.

How have I changed?

Leopolda's afraid you'll go off the deep end the other way. Super religious. A real tambourine rattler.

Never! I sit. I sigh. You know, that director? That bastard'll see I'm wired, first thing.

He'd better. It's his staff that wired you! If he thinks you're off your meds already, *forget it.* Anyway, he'll just see your emerald beauty.

Yeah—but what if he's heard about *us?* We made quite a pair last year! Maybe not so hot to run a halfway house?

What's he heard? That you're a madwoman of low morals, who wed and reformed? That I'm a drunk, now in A.A.? They *love* recoveries. Even with drugs, it's all mystical to them—who recovers, who doesn't. Ask Dr. David. They'll lap it up. Just sit there like a queen and let Leopolda talk. Anyway, how could he know?

How do I know what people know about me! These are two small towns, Jack. He's gonna see me walk in with a baby, and asking for still more *too-too*-toorouble from Ed and Ziggy. *Ed and Ziggy!* He'll think I'm really bent.

You're not going in rags, are you? Jack asks. Just gussy up. You're a head turner in your best threads. Very *compos mentis* in looks, like a college teacher. You can express a bottle of milk before you go, and I'll take care of Avon.

I don't have anything nice that fits yet.

Just flash that orgone-box smile. They'll think you're a sex instructor from Sweden. Hey, the rain's stopping.

The front porch lights up as if swept by headlights. It's the moon. He switches off the lamp and we go out on the porch. The full moon rides clear, then mists over again, like Moby Dick. Or HP. Spring wind sighs past, moving the skywrack. A great clearness falls on Cookman Avenue. We stand in the rising and passing brightness.

Jack hugs me softly. I know how you suffer.

The great hush gurgles and drips for blocks around. All Chautauqua a big shell. The lake smears white. Jack's eyes are liquid and slip into me. He really does know.

Thanks. Sometimes I think I'm not going to make it, I say. Not for me, not for you. Not even for Avon. It's such shit, never knowing if I'll . . . lose real things to guide myself by. When I was at North Warren and we'd go to the dining hall, I'd think I was a baboon in line with other baboons. Not a human being at all. That wasn't so long ago! I don't tell him how I repress my rage, feel self-estranged. Sense my genes ready to go alien. One prick more and the walls will wipe out. Maybe I don't have to tell him . . .

You'll make it. We're together, aren't we? And you want to be a pipeline for others. That's real recovery. Recovery is give it away or die. Just don't sit around sucking on your symptoms.

I'm weeping. I'm no pipeline! He cradles me as I lean on him. Sometimes I'm changing diapers or ironing and this mist hits. And I can*not* think! I might as well be in Africa. How can I give *anything* away?

Don't worry. You're a powerhouse.

Powerhouse!

The night drips and trickles, a mystery ready to burst.

You're all woman, Curranne. I watch you cross your legs or fold up onto the couch. I watch you nurse. I watch you chat with Leopolda with your hands speaking. Your eyes reach inside you—they dig right down. Every fiber of you bent on getting well and, man, I am struck dumb. You are so strong! Then I see this woman *in* you judging the woman who's acting, and she's so unforgiving. Trying to knife your self-confidence and let the steam out. Someday that shy little nitpicker is going to piss off and let you be the happy, active woman I see. How often do I tell you this?

Over and over. I sigh.

How often do you need to hear it?

Over and over and over.

I love you.

Put my arms around his neck, his knee slipping lightly between mine. You can tell me that over and over.

Oh, you'll get tired.

Never! It's just so hard to believe at times.

That's not true. You believe it.

But I feel undeserving, I say. I think you're lying, and don't know why you do it.

Maybe I'm after a fast little body and soul?

Nut! But I'm not even here such a lot of the time.

Not when you're off nitpicking.

Well, let's stop talking about me.

Oh sure. Hide.

I don't hide, but press into him hard. His kiss plays over my face and each eye. I drink it up! Then he really digs into me. I lift, flowing into his grip, and slip under his robe.

I know you like your little nightcap, Scarlett.

You going to carry me up the staircase?

You hold your horses. I like it out here. First I'll just kiss the brandy off your lips.

I swear he's tasting it, he kisses me so slowly. I surrender to dripping porch, lake, moon, pearl clouds.

Come on, Slim, he says.

Barefoot in red velvet Jack leads me into the wet street and over Clark Avenue to the Amphitheater. A marvelous breeze sweeps through Bestor Plaza. The Colonnade's lighted pillars shine. We dance on the grass, not a soul in sight. Shuck my shoes, turn and dance, toes in rich grass. So slim! Feel watched as my legs flash. The bare trees bud through the fallenness of things. The grass glows deep billiard-cloth green. Every night I go to bed still unsaved but for the uplift and rest my body gives me. I long to savor the even mental light Jack takes for granted. Somehow, my life has shrunk. Even from a year ago. And despite Avon. Every now and then my throat fumbles and strains for a word I can't spear, I mean speak *("too-too-*toorouble"*)*, and I die at the sound when it finally plops out. I fall apart, or slowly turn to stone. If Jack should die—chaos—just fearful! He's my gift from HP. Maybe I hinder my growth, wringing so much from him. I keep this heavy need to myself. My folly is to bind him to my body. And I do. Shamelessly! But how he takes to it. We really energize a bed! So much hunger and vigor and capacity to feel criminal. I know every nerve that stirs him. He's not a zealous lover, he's boundless. I'm always the one who calls a halt. Save something for the rest of your life, Jack. But he grabs a breast, You just go to sleep and let me enjoy myself.—I *am* asleep.—Ha, the moment I've been waiting for!—Well, set the clock. —Do you think I plan to go to sleep and miss all this even for a minute?

As we dance through the plaza, I scratch his back ever so slowly while his eyes whirl and teeth grind.

You're marking up the goods, he says. You'll have to keep me.

That's what I'm making sure of.

Sometimes our sex is like making love at the bottom of a well. His voice and breath are far above me, and I'm as long as Alice, stretching and stretching until I pull him down to me and the knots build and tension comes. The next time we make love I want to see his face light up again as it did when Avon *shushed* into his hands below me. Twisting and girlish, I'm getting slick as we dance. I have sexual love for his whole being. His hands and broad fingers, bone movement, muscles, thinking, gestures. The manhood in his face passes into me something rich, patient and male. The thickheadedness lifts from my eyes. My heart breathes. HP wants us joined, every cell, light to light.

And yet warning flashes hang over me daily. Don't hold on too tightly to things you may lose. Don't crush him with your needs. Hold onto yourself, not to him. But when he takes Avon from me to burp her, his hands like oak, or even when he brushes my hair too roughly, sending electricity straight to my pelvis, I know that my being bound to his maleness may be all there is—I'll be denied getting back into his world of even light—and that life without Jack would be just too overcast to bear.

Put some nice thoughts into my head, I beg in a whisper.

PART NINE

A Schizy Summer

U nearthly! What confusion at Casa Dymphna. Or the Blue Villa, as Leopolda calls it.

The summer heaven stops dead in August. New tenants in whipping rain slickers take over the Green Villa and the Red Villa. The Yellow Villa's Belvedere family has arrived and wetly decamped. Demanding his rent back, Carter Belvedere speaks to Leopolda only through his lawyer, though he lodges but three minutes away in the Athenaeum Hotel.

"He's set like steel," Leopolda tells Jack. "Breaks his lease and thinks I'm a millionaire! The whole family blames me for the weather. These houses aren't built for cold days. I'm not at fault."

"We forgot the roof," Jack reminds her.

"I thought that one didn't need it . . . *And it slipped my mind!* Is that a crime?"

"Be happy he's not suing for damages," Curranne says.

After a perfect July, the sun vanished, sucked up into windy gray drizzle seven days ago. Evilest weather since 1903, reports *The Chautauquan Daily*. High noon is a massive lead sheet, the plaza pole flagless. Trees bend and drone through the night. Damp brass in the Amphitheater's open-air Victor Herbert concert cough through the evening downpour. First light shows larger limbs fallen on roofs and smaller branches about the cobbles. The very birds starve in the nest, then blight the walks with drowned chicks. The Yellow Villa reeks of mildew when Jack runs in to empty pans and look for new leaks. On the second floor lost roof tiles leave the ceiling cheesy with glowing nail holes.

Each morning after breakfast Curranne collects Ed and Ziggy for Group with Leopolda and Winnie in Unitarian House. If Jack is not patching and repairing, he sits in too, but says little unless asked. Leopolda tells Chris not to sit in, allowing Winnie more freedom. But his office door stays ajar—perhaps he can siphon off a trickle of uplift for himself. He wants to get well without admitting he's sick. The group accepts his ruse, even Winnie, but at times Ziggy is stirred to whisper below Chris's hearing, or else to declaim and lard his *whereases* with Latin for Chris's hearing. Rules are few: no attacking fellow members, no touching, no liquids.

"The only oral gratification allowed is verbal," Leopolda says, but Ed and Ziggy smoke or they'd have stopped coming. At that, they try to avoid Group whenever possible, and take their seats in the circle with bemusement or mock disinterest. Actually this is the only activity that has engaged their souls for years, maybe decades. Surprising, the hungers it brings up among their winged anxieties.

This morning Curranne cannot get Ziggy up. She stands by his bed with the steaming coffee pot as bait.

"Let's go downstairs," she says.

"I can't go downstairs. Can't move. I'm in cold storage."

"Cold storage?"

"You the witch in charge of the back ward?"

"This isn't the back ward, Ziggy. This is Chautauqua."

His face a waxy sheen, Ziggy smiles at her ignorance. "You are some dummy, woman."

"You conked out after dinner last night. Didn't you sleep enough?"

"Sleep enough? No-o. The parade woke me up."

"What parade?"

"I don't know! I didn't get up. Them Islamites are too dumb to look at. Stuffed cabbages in fezzes. I avoid people bearing scimitars."

"Well, breakfast is on the table. Let's go down and eat it."

"You sure have funny ideas about me. I don't eat tables."

"Must've lost my marbles, Sigmund."

"I know you didn't have 'em when you came in. I think I heard 'em bounce down the stairs! I'm gettin afraid of you. Anyway it's too dark to get up. Still raining. My bulb's burnt out. I feel sapped already, just laying here. I must be a ghost."

"I'll have Jack change it."

"Won't help. This gate is rusted shut. I'm not moving. That floor isn't safe to walk on."

Ziggy is the only colored on the Chautauqua grounds, aside from some maids and chauffeurs he's glimpsed—but they're tucked away nightly in Phyllis Wheatley Cottage, which he's heard of but never seen. He peeks around the shade at his running window, then pulls the covers over his head. Curranne sends Jack up with a fresh bulb, which he leaves burning.

"Ed's watching the morning disasters," Jack says, closing the door.

"So am I"—under the sheet.

Working figures on the kitchen table, Ed feels useful to himself, numbers burning and eating his sheets.

"Interest rates have fallen," he tells Curranne. "Market looks strong."

She sets out his Grape Nuts box. "Are you buying or selling?"

"I may go public. Keep it under your hat."

Says this with a hint of swagger. He's deeply in love with her, shakes when she's near—her bust obsesses him. But Curranne, albeit obliviously, shares him with another. Ed pines for the vanished seventeen-year-old daughter of hack novelist Carter Belvedere who moved in a rage yesterday from the Yellow Villa next door. Did Diana spot him watching her window from his darkened bedroom? He fixes on the filled bowl on the Grape Nuts box. The bowl reminds him of a chipped dish he loved in childhood, his mother's hearty servings of oatmeal. The bowl radiates heartbroken glory.

"It wasn't modifiable," he tells Curranne.

"What wasn't?" she says, feeding Avon in the open bedroom. She's rapt, weighing her next pregnancy, as the baby digs at her fingers and finds the lost nipple. Ed goes for a glass of water, glances at her bare breast.

"My pitch."

"Oh?"

"It stung right through their mitts. After five innings the catcher's hand would swell up."

"I was almost not going to call you for breakfast. I saw your light come on and off at two when I got up for Avon."

"Oh, I'm hungry," he says. Looks about for Ziggy as he folds up his figures. Sitting, he follows his course of empire in a financial romance rippling from the Grape Nuts box.

Ed rarely steps onto the porch for fear his goddess will see him. His eye cocks steadily toward the front curtains in hopes she'll pass by. Unlikely she'd be attracted to the Hall of Philosophy lectures across the street. He's written her a deck of unsigned letters, mailed at the post office in the middle of the night. The empty Yellow Villa still holds an erotic glow. Last night he sneaked into her echoing bedroom, stood looking at the walls that had held her, his lungs stuffy and heavy. First he'd stood getting soaked in front of the house, then slipped through an unlocked porch window of the shrine, his heart beating and suffering, and tiptoed upstairs to the forbidden doorway. Stepping through it dizzied him. Every night, about eleven or earlier, she'd lie writing in her diary by candlelight. Did her ear catch his fond, loud throbbings? She seemed never to be reading his letters. Her memory hangs in candlelight, a white bottom in magic amber laid. He foresees a nationwide chain of ice cream parlors, his first coup, his bulk cartons bearing the trademark of slim-breasted Diana praising the sun. Faith floods him, power over money makes him all-wise. An ingenious trademark is half the fight. Clean, white sparkling parlors, untainted in any way and kept disinfected by Curranne, sell Ed's dairy goods to customers who have never seen a madman in their lives. His eyes rim wetly with a vision of life among the sane, a world worth any price.

Curranne comes down from making Ziggy's bed. For breakfast Ziggy has butterscotch ice cream, fat marshmallows and stale glazed doughnuts he squirrels away after getting Chris's oldest boy, Glenn, to buy them for him at the Refectory. Ed questions Ziggy about the ice cream, like a chemist, then lays the Grape Nuts box flat before him and pours milk onto the bowl in the picture.

"You put in too much," Ziggy says.

Ed pulls his deboned soft chin at the flooded table.

"That bowl only holds so much," Ziggy adds.

Curranne hands Ed a china bowl, tamps the box dry and sops up the milk.

"Don't cry over that," Ziggy tells her.

"Do I look like I'm crying?" she asks, filling Ed's bowl with cereal. "Say when."

Ziggy mushes a marshmallow into his ice cream. "You look like you're stewing over something."

Curranne, blank. "I'm just coping."

Ed pushes his Grape Nuts away. "What is this slop? I want eggnog. That's why I left the hospital! For my health, God damn it—for eggnog!"

Where is the Ed, she wonders, who looked like Emerson? The night they first met and he won the fruitcake . . .

Jack comes in the back door, pours a coffee and sits thoughtlessly at the table.

"What do you want for breakfast?" she asks beside him.

"Anything." His hidden palm rubs back inside her leg. "Fried-egg sandwich?"

Her knee tells him to knock it off. "Not fried," she says.

"What do you suggest? Poached egg sandwich?"

"You're not eating fried foods!" Curranne says. "I like you the way you are."

"*Ooh!* Then just give me Egg Sandwich Surprise. D'ya want me to make it?"

"That wouldn't be a surprise. Would it?"

Ed taps Jack's wrist. "I'm having eggnog sandwich."

"That'll be interesting," Ziggy says. Catches Ed eying his ice cream–mallow mush. "Have some?"

"Nah, nah. I just want to know how it could be better."

"This way," Ziggy says. Mashes in stale glazed doughnut chunks. "Real butterscotch topping would make it perfect."

Ed studies the Refectory's quart package. "I mean the ice cream itself."

"This is market research?" Jack asks.

"Don't laugh," Ed says. "The world is waiting for a better ice cream."

Ziggy snorts. "It's already too expensive."

"That's nothing," Ed says. "I could mass-market a top-quality product and keep the price down by big-volume sales."

"I appreciate that," Ziggy says. "But a quart's an arm and a leg now. I thought we wanted a low-cost custard."

"Cost is nothing. People will pay anything for an ice cream that gives them a sense of religious well-being. Like Coke for Christmas."

Jack watches Curranne loosen ice cubes under the tap. "What?"

"Real health!" Ed says. "Family warmth! Santa Claus and Thanksgiving. Think what an Easter ice cream could do in Easter week. Pink 'N Peach! Pistachio mint for St. Paddy's Day and Christmas."

"You want to shuck ice cream?" Jack asks. Curranne salts cubes in the sink.

"Jesus too." Ed is alight, his finger thudding the table. "You need a campaign to identify pink peach ice cream with Easter. Make special Christian cones like hot cross buns for Lent. Could be done."

"Yeah?" Curranne asks. Puts a fire under a panful of salted ice with two eggs on top.

"This is the sort of idea that could start in a tent," Ed says. Looks hopefully at the pan for his eggnog. "Then spread across the country, with the right stimulation."

Jack nods agreeably. "The Second Coming?"

Ed weighs the stimulation of the Second Coming on ice cream sales. "I mean something more like Shirley Temple dolls. You wouldn't remember that craze. A trademark that people love, like the Coke bottle —that's what moves product."

Jack asks, "People love Coke bottles?"

"Feels like a woman and a prick at the same time," Ed says.

"Those Shirley Temple dolls were sexy too," Ziggy says.

"Sexy Christian ice cream with family warmth! That would take Sinatra to sell," Curranne says. Is her skirt too short? Are her bare legs too stirring for Ed? She feels him undress her from behind.

Ed lays a finger against his nose. "Good idea. But mine's better and less costly."

"What's that?" she asks. "Not another Coke bottle, I hope."

"A fresh face. I'll say no more. Don't tell 'em."

Ziggy tongues his bowl, eying Jack and Curranne. "They'll never get it from me."

"A face fresh as dairy cream." Ed mutes his lips swiftly, glaring about. Fingers the empty Refectory quart. "How much you pay for this?"

"Five dollars."

"Five bucks!"

"I didn't get any change."

"But that's highway robbery!" Ed cries.

"He got a half-dozen glazed doughnuts and a box of marshmallows too," Curranne says. Will the eggs crack?

"Is that the way prices are these days?" Ed asks her.

Ziggy says, "Cheaper to be crazy."

Leopolda limps down the back stairs for her third coffee to go with her fourth prebreakfast cigarette. Her right big toe broke while kicking open the Yellow Villa's rainswollen back door. She too feels swollen shut. Looks out at the drenching wind, then at the filled breakfast table. Jack pulls up a chair for her with his foot.

"When will I ever have a croissant again?" she asks him. Drops her face into her fingers, with a sigh shy of sobbing. Implores the ceiling. "Lord, I've been in my room, reading Your good book. Isn't that good of me? I know You're not going to let all our plastering come loose in the Yaller Villa. It just looks that way. Your little joke. It's not *really* going to happen—is it??—You Ol' Sweetie! It's time something came Our Way, isn't it?"

Jack asks, "He bargains?"

"He doesn't have to," Leopolda says, spouting smoke. "This whole morning has already happened. There's nothing to bargain for."

Ziggy is shocked to deep seriousness. "When'd it happen?"

"In the past! And we're just sitting here. Can't you feel it? Every second we sit here is past. That's very comforting. This is all in the past. Right now, it's past! What a wise way to have made things—to have treated death and calamity. It's *so* wonderful to be rid of the present. Look how dark it is." Drags her Gaulois, hacking, then calls above. "Turn it up, I'm going blind!"

Despite her groanings, Leopolda is least like a bedeviled ex-nut. Jack knows she's a genius at repairs. She taught him to saw, hammer, drive screws, plaster, paint, paperhang, plumb and pipefit, rewire, fix lamps, strip, stain and restore furniture, make gas stoves and iceboxes work, caulk, fix toilets, replace rotted wood, build porch steps, lay rugs, roof and tar, glass cut, clear chimneys, garden, handle and keep tools and materials fresh and much more. Ed and Ziggy are useless. She's happy they have no breakdowns and tosses off their sulks. Neither is eager to go back to North Warren, if he must, when summer ends. Leopolda wants them to keep their benefits and is strict about medication, despite Ed's ruses. And she's open with her time, lessening their loneliness.

"Thank God this summer is all in the past," Leopolda says.

"So far," Ziggy says nervously. "More's coming."

"Somewhere it's still 1929," she says. "Last winter I was on Corfu. This fall I'll be in Paris. I feel my whole life was printed all at once."

She soaks in ferns and doilies and curtains. Ed is in Roosevelt's second administration, playing Monopoly, the strange new board game on the ward. Ziggy's in Erie.

Nine A.M. blooms radium gray. Curranne nurses in the bedroom. Avon keeps nodding off while suckling. The lot beyond the gale-beaten window lies gnarled and empty. Waving vines feast on the blue glare over Peck Street and Episcopal House. Staring into the vines she feels a wave return and pass through her. It lifts through her capillaries, brightens her brain, awakens her nerves from head to foot. The tragic vines make her suddenly and vastly aware of a murder she has committed. Who was the victim? She gazes at Avon. The baby jerks, her jaw shuddering as if still on the nipple.

"You're safe, little lump," Curranne says. Somewhere in a book, her own execution date is already set. She flattens her star-boned palm on the running pane. The budding willow beyond whips off globs of green halo. Supernatural agencies and energies, ignoring her absence as they do her presence, will zap the planet and Curranne not be here. Or in this universe. She is the sacrifice. And once you've been offered up, there's no one left. No prayer will reach her.

Already lawmen with high-frequency eyes are after her, sifting through old addresses. Ripping up rooms. Disheartening! Beyond any guilt she has ever known, the old punishing force seeks her out. When her mother hears of it, as soon she must, she will go gray instantly and reel into her grave. This is killing guilt. Curranne is wax. There is no flight, no cavern or sewer, no escape worth trying. Whatever it is, she has done it at last, her life hereafter forever charged with error. She hears her beating heart run out, the last thud stretch into nothingness. What has she done? She clutches Avon to keep her from floating off. The floor runs and bubbles with root beer. Deathfoam chills her ankles. Its herbs suck her mind out and leave sweet emptiness.

Last night a dream about her dead child-husband, David, alive and camping out. Under the covers with David she senses him to be twelve or thirteen. Since their wedding night he would come as soon as he saw her naked. Couldn't stop it, grabbing his boy's pink acorn to cap the gushing. And still again as he tried to enter her. Now she's very pleased to have another chance to help him grow up. But he really is twelve or thirteen. She no more than touches him than his youth pumps through her fingers. My God, how could she have forgotten that he'd first been married to her dullard older sister Carrie? Now wild Indians are in the woods and ready to kill her. She lies frozen as they attack and knife her, their blades shattering on her solid breasts of ice. She awakes relieved that she was actually overlooked in their butchery. But now she knows for certain that wild Indians roam Chautauqua. The house is not safe, not alone, or even with Ed and Ziggy. There's no place safe from the bristling Indians.

Ed's grating fathervoice growls from the kitchen that he will leave in September because she has driven him back to North Warren. Carter Belvedere's letter in *The Chautauquan Daily* exposes her for running a cathouse on the grounds. How can she be such a trial to her mother? Carol will wilt and suffer, come down with hip cancer. Curranne's only peace is foreseeing that her barred cell will be electrified and thoughts of escape denied. Neither Jack nor Leopolda can save her. She is beyond God's grace. No dim atom of blood in the next world waits to embrace her with sinlessness. Her slack jaw and taffy limbs aren't worth it. Aflow with guilt, she can barely breathe, the room drifting with loss. Life falls from the air. The day drowns, radium parting her to bits. How could she have been so stupid! From earliest memory she's known: Never kill a human being—or pay eternally. And now it's done. To whom? Someone faceless in a fog. But that means less than that the murder can't be turned about. Its finality forces her into life's last stage, a formless floating "I" never to be whole again. Jail is a comfort that grants her an ego. She sees her image as Radiant Patience. If she can just get into her cell, she'll relax into cocoa butter, make not one stupid move. Suffer in lifelong silence, and steep in the pain her thoughtless killing has brought to others. The pain will free her someday, but for now she must sit like a child in her cell. She promises never to smile again.

By the curtain a stem of Queen Anne's lace draws her agony into its flat white umbrella and purple bole. Envy of the weed's brainless vegetal being divides her flesh. She hears a glug. Avon lies back from a breast pumped dry, her mouth welling with milk. Curranne wipes and pities her, moving her to the other nipple. Who will make milk for you when I am gone? If she hides the baby under the bed or behind the sheets in the top of the closet, will Jack find her after Curranne is sped away in the police car? She feels the breast under her palps. Are bursting cancer fats spilling into Avon? When Jack walks in, Curranne cannot smile. What shall we do? her eyes ask. I've betrayed you.

"What's up?" he asks. Her face melts in running light. "You in mourning?"

Avon pulls loose with a pop, her eyes rolling toward Jack, as milk squirts over her face.

Curranne's guilt tightens and balls in her. He takes the baby. She can't move. Her self-rage rises into tears. Then Jack's hand on her shoulder brings a split second of safety and she jumps up as he guides her from the room. She chokes, seeing five feet of empty space in the kitchen floor. He pulls her across it in a lurch. Her knees wobble with fear and relief as she leaps into the living room, the breath shooting out of her. Ed and Ziggy look up from the couch, reading her eyes and heaving shoulders. It's nothing new. They get up and pop on their baseball caps.

Leopolda slips Curranne's poncho around her. She has the baby underneath as the house members race through rain to Unitarian House's back door. Leopolda limps behind in forsythia slicker and sou'wester. Next thing Curranne knows she's Dumb Cow, seated in Group. It's gone on for some time. The floor runs with great gaping two- and three-foot cracks, going down God knows where. The room savors of cooking chili. The group sits in a circle of uncurling wicker and rickety bridge chairs, on throw rugs dimmed by threadbare cara- vans in the Holy Land. The group's mind level is lowering and hope- less. Curranne hears the emptiness of its efforts. Worse than emptiness, its brain-sapping failure. Harsh as she is, she will miss it in her cell. Where are the police? Like hopping gnats, electric lawmen crowd the gate, bolt onto the grounds. Spread with drawn guns toward the Hall of Philosophy. She should just hand Avon to Jack and jump down a crack when they race in with straitjacket wide and bucket to cover her shameful head after she's bare-stripped. Who can help her? *Nobody loves a crazy!* Some'll think she's sexy in a straitjacket and rape her too, her arms in canvas. Pass her around in the wagon. Her grimace knots, she chooses her crack. Across from her sits Winnie, detached but scowling with interest, the medicine woman studying her clan and Curranne.

Leopolda seduced her into the group. First she gave a buffet in the Blue Villa, inviting the Jaspers tribe, then told her captives about a free self-help group she'd like to start up. But—hands stirring dis- tractedly—the Blue Villa was too small. She needed a larger place, not a hall exactly, but . . . No refreshments would be served or allowed . . . When the first meeting was held in Unitarian House she asked Winnie to lend a body. There'd be a feeling of more people, a real group. With Winnie, Ed, Ziggy, Jack, Curranne (and Avon) in her circle, Leopolda explained that Group would not deal in analysis or even each person's background but only in finding out how the group could help each member think better on his feet (though they'd be seated), be more at ease dealing with people by learning to deal with each other, and talk with folks on the outside without falling apart or clamming up. The way to start is by thinking and speaking among six people, so that one person will be a snap. The idea's to give each other heart. A lot of heart. Group heart.

"So what we're going to do," she said, "is talk about what we're feeling *right now.*" She fell silent.

After a while Winnie said, "I think I'll go make lunch."

"It's only nine o'clock," Leopolda said. "We really want you here. Why don't you wait? We all have a lot to give each other. Lunch will get made. We need you, Winnie."

"She doesn't wanta stay, don't make her," Ed said.

"I'll stay."

"Thank you, Winnie," Curranne said.

Whatever she gives in Group, Winnie at last retreats into her co- coon as the happy wife. Today she weighs all present, including Ed and Ziggy. Now that she knows their fears better, the Blue Villa seems clearly the end of the road for them. They'll soon be carted off, hope- less cases never to leave the hospital again. Ed and Ziggy sense and fear her reserve. She's a civilian, not even on meds. Her words have many times the power of theirs. Around her, Ed and Ziggy sound stupid and awkward to themselves and to each other. Without fresh bucking and pumping up, their sense drifts off into flurries and fanta- sies for the rest of the session. Then Ziggy will look about in surprise, jump up and pace, or sit cowed and talking with Victor, his cynical but loving dead brother who sports a smart Jamaican straw and tells him he's wasting his time trying to get his shingle back.

Winnie's kids, Maggie, Flossie, Eliot, Glenn and Judy, who are two, three, four, seven and nine, wander in and out of the group, and sometimes sit listening to the strange circle game. At times they go make their own circle and Glenn talks to his dead twin brothers, Tim and Derek, while the others listen. Tim and Derek would be one year old, if they'd lived, and harmonize well with the living kids who are all familiar with Ziggy's hallucinations, Chris's, and Winnie's. Winnie first began talking with the dead twins, then Chris and Glenn joined her. When he's pacing, Ziggy often winds up in the children's circle, sitting and listening to Glenn with the ghost-babies. Ziggy foresees endless riches in becoming Glenn's agent.

Avon awakes in Curranne's arms. Two-year-old Maggie, a pale- yellow-eyed dusky adult with red nail polish, gets up from Winnie's feet and looks at the baby. Small bending fingers reach out and dig Maggie's nose. Maggie jumps back.

"Mommy, Avon scratched my nose."

"I'll have to cut her nails again," Curranne says.

"Let me see," Winnie says. "Oh, that's not so bad. You'll live until lunch."

"She's a little monkey."

Jack asks Maggie, "Hey, do I look like a big ape?"

"No."

"Then how could I be father to a little monkey?"

Despite his joking, Jack resists bringing up his distress in Group. Curranne hovers on breakdown—he's fearful of exposing her and having her slip over. This morning anyone can see she's disturbed, her eyes remorseful and scattered. He does not hear her sirens. Her fear is the only fact she can grip. It is so fused to her that she is the fear, one moment crouching and crawling along the Institution's fence, the next sitting here, a rigid nonreasoning shadow-body laced with adrenaline and flattened by guilt. During a lull Ziggy returns to his seat. His haunted animal eyes catch Curranne's and pull her erect. She thinks it's her turn to speak and jumps in.

"Um, you can see how well I am, because I married this big ape. If I didn't have to feed his monkey, well, I might break. It's the truth. But after a few months I'll be left facing me again. I don't like that. I keep breaking in the same place. I'm quite brilliant for long periods, very capable, then the troopers come. Sitting in this room with you people is the only possible way I know of finding enough coherence to meet you."

"It's only one day at a time," Leopolda tells her. "You can't demand full recovery overnight, Curranne. You'll get well bit by bit, no matter what the troopers say. Forget about them for today. Today is all you've got. We're all here together and nobody's taking anybody away because we have Chris and Unitarian House is a sanctuary. Even with a warrant they can't arrest you in here. That's a relief, isn't it! We're all safe here."

"You're doing a lot right," Jack adds.

"What?" Curranne asks.

"You're not alone," he says. "You're involved with the group. You've got tremendous high energy that you keep focused constructively. And you're not at all suicidal." Jack clears his throat. "Are you?"

"No."

Leopolda adds, "You're not killing yourself with overactivity and stress. You don't talk in circles about how bad or hopeless you feel. You don't express feelings of unworthiness. You're content as a mother. Are you hearing voices?"

"No. And I refuse to be a compensatory stereotype."

"Don't worry about being rehospitalized," Leopolda says.

"You're a very ardent woman," Ed says. "First thing I noticed about you."

"Then why can't she say what's bothering her?" Ziggy asks Ed.

"She just did."

"No she didn't."

Leopolda says, "Ask Curranne that, Ziggy, not Ed. But ask it helpfully."

"Oh? Okay. I'd like to know what's bothering you, and why I suddenly have to worry about the police coming here."

"The police aren't coming here," Leopolda tells him. "Don't you know what a sanctuary is?"

"Of course I know what a sanctuary is. I am a member of the New York Bar Association! My clients include Duke Ellington. I defended Orson Welles for his invasion from Mars. I am in steady correspondence with Vice President Nixon about the Communist infiltration of the American Federation of Musicians and the California Orange Growers Association. Don't ask me if I know what immunity from arrest in churches is. It's a concept that has never been tested in the Supreme Court, that's what sanctuary is. A warrant is a warrant!"

"Thank you, that's very helpful," Leopolda says. "But that works for us too, since it's never been tested and they have no precedent. Curranne, your friends would like to know what's bothering you."

Curranne breathes heavily. "I'm afraid to say anything that will hurt the group."

"You can't hurt the group," Jack says. "You couldn't hurt the group if you tried. The group is stronger than anything you can say or do."

"It's easier to feel rotten than to ask for help, isn't it?" Leopolda asks.

Curranne's eyes well. She whispers, "I can't say it."

"When you're ready," Leopolda says.

Curranne's eyes run constrainedly. She does not have a great venting, since she is slowly feeling better.

After a silence Jack says, "It doesn't matter what you say. It's the spirit, not the content, that matters."

Winnie nods hard at Curranne.

"We're here to build up our spirits, aren't we?—not our intellects or analytic powers," Jack says. "To get faith in ourselves! If the group really works, we'll feel more self-worthy and worthy of being loved by someone else. If the group loves us, then maybe one other person can too. But as long as we hold back on admitting our feelings, then the less we're helping the group help us." Jack swallows hard, his stomach fluttering. "I have *very* definite feelings of lack of self-worth. I wouldn't know where to begin describing them. But I'm not after any little verbal victories over my weaknesses. Don't I want a kind of self-assurance at depth which releases me from lack of self-worth? Somehow nature has devised the group as a way of healing weak egos. I can't rebuild myself alone, I know I can't. I've tried and failed too many times. Only when I open myself up to this healing force from other people do I feel really alive. And sane."

But even as he says these things, Jack half realizes that he can not expect the group to help him with his own deepest confusions. Or does not expect it. He has already revealed his more obvious strikeouts, during earlier sessions. Those about his low earnings (he earns less than ever, though his needs are met) and his not having published anything or even having written a satisfying work to strengthen his faith in his writing—here he is, past thirty! Nearly everyone he admires had published some kind of masterpiece, a great poem or piece of music, or was embarked on a large work by thirty. Or even had died by then. What's grating is that his skill is unsuitable for writing a talented moneymaker to help get by while working at something deeper. These are lighter, more manageable problems he has thrown out to the group without embarrassment. The embarrassment came when Leopolda told him they didn't apply to what the group felt at the moment. He skipped the next meeting, pleading work, but Leopolda sent Glenn to the Red Villa after him. Work could wait.

What Jack can't admit are his dizzying urges, which come even in Group. Erotic daydreams about Avon, pleasurable thoughts about Curranne dying and his running off to the Caribbean or the South Pacific for naughty idylls with his unmarriageable but nubby-breasted daughter. Who has just been born! Is he to have these daydreams forever? He's already threaded with dreams about a shadowy second woman in his bed, dreams from which he wakes edging into wet climax. Or she slips into him when he's half awake in his rocker and stiff with desire. Much like slippery love yearnings he had toward his mother and sister while falling about his bedroom drunk. Now the alcohol has gone but the passions still mushroom unwilled, if only in sleep. He often slips, calling Curranne Liz. And when he speaks with loony frankness about desserts or begs for a dollar or compares marriage to his bursting young manhood in fresh white shirts and machine-pressed suits, she tells him acidly, Jack, I'm not your mother. Pennilessness with Curranne echoes his dumb powerlessness to save his mother from the raving Irish drunk they lived with; he's still moneyless in steel wristlocks. Even daydreams of running off with Curranne, or rather Avon, find him in a hut as a carefree beachcomber with his bare-breasted mate. Last night, the house in shadow, he lay naked on the living-room rug waiting for his shadowy girl to come out of the shower to him. Then he noticed Curranne was awake beside him on the bed and naked in shadow. The girl came out of the bath in the dark, towel to her breasts, and smiled down at them. "Oh, this is how you want to entice me," she said, smiling at their nakedness, and dropped the towel to join them. Enjoying her visit he could not foretell Curranne's answer to this loveknot and woke up irresistibly, against his will and *tense*. That shadowy girl, Winnie at sixteen? Curranne lay half awake feeding Avon. Stiff, he fit himself spoon-fashion to her, reaching around for the free breast and then down her. She was wet, her sheath within rigid. Hard as stone he entered from the back, finger still stroking her cleft, and brought her to a gasping chill, the baby on her nipple as he pumped and fingered her. Fervently, he sucked at his dream-feelings, feeding himself into Avon through her mother and drawing her whole love into him, his daughter no baby but a potent bare salmon-leaping female like her mother. In his loving, even the baby was aroused and sensitive. Jack shakes, all cock, guilty and marvelous, his gush coming from toes and fingertips, as the night rises to mind in Group. My God, that was something, Curranne had whispered, still streamy with rising and fiery-fountaining nightsparks. Their embrace lingered, Jack waking from fathomless fathering, and then, whatever this had had to do with his revered Life Force, he forgave himself, slipping off.

He sits, genial and unhappy, mask tight, dismissing his weird roil of shadowy dallying. He wonders, even so, who is the girl from the bath?

A sane mate, closer to his heart's desire, now that he's more sober? It's nothing to talk over in the group. Certainly not today! He curbs daily an impulse to urge Curranne into habits he thinks will help her re-create herself as the bold, free laughing woman he imagines he desires. He wants to graft on fingers where she is all thumbs, rush her recovery, force the bloom of sanity into her face. The old shining eyes, with their play and bite, the smile that cut to the quick, can they ever be restored? He's framed both copies of his magnificent photograph of her from Love School, one for each bedstand—stereoscopic sanity, Jack says, I love it! Cruel reminders?

As Group goes on, Curranne's moods race. She is damaged and cunning, brave, angry, shamed, a self-sufficient vixen. Her pores flood with cold fear, its heady choking stink rising in cypress waves. She plans to wipe off her marriage and child and become a waitress. Her scalp and brow drip salt into her eyes. Her back and chest are damp in the wet airlessness. The straitjacket racing toward her is stinging tear gas. If she can get out through a hole she knows under the fence, near the practice shacks that give her the willies, she'll catch the Buffalo noon bus *(Oh, God, let me get on it, let me make it!)*. Nothing in her change purse, give the driver her wedding ring. Hole up, change her name. So stuffy, breathless the room she's taken—can she really bear it? She looks about, shocked to be still in Group, sirens on the lawn. How to make it safely to the bus, through the wild Indians skulking near the shacks? Wolves roam the grounds. Packs loose in the ravine, sneaking on their stomachs under rainy firs. How to find comfort, run to happiness, better herself. *Better herself!?* Successfully fake it as an analyst or surgeon—life is too unjust to expect such conceits of fate in her favor. Her guard is up, her smile mocks *anyone's* self-control. She has no faith in Jack, the group, Leopolda, Dr. David, phenothiazine or herself. Weighs robbing a Buffalo bank, since she is already under sentence. But bank robbery is too meager a crime for her guilt. Where buy a gun? At a pawnshop? Pistol in hand, she holds up the teller—but the grip rots in her palm. Whole witless fiasco goes off in her face like a firecracker. Blushing bungler looks up at the group, blindingly relieved after that dumb bank robbery by a second chance at financing her getaway. Wise up, knothead, let's avoid jail, the wards again. Let Jack guide her down this slippery path, though he's the one she's abandoning. To live alone and worthless, earn her board in big-city namelessness, hide and become a rebuilt person, is not alluring. Suicide more attractive, almost equal to her guilt. She resists both its hardship and the unbearable insult of failure. She still cherishes some small part of her consciousness. Her sex last night with Jack drove her into self-love near torment, an awakening, brightening self-assurance that ensteeled her right to life. Anyone gifted with her world-melting vividness, the supernormal erotic upwelling that parts her every bone from its neighbor, is wired for long life. Surely the drive in her blood, some still untapped hormonal energy, will grant her a life worth all the mad agony she is passing through. There must be a winner's circle even for schizzes.

She already cuts her nerve-ties to Avon. Just when Jack has helped release her emotional life, she must take scissors to all the small fibers pulsing between them, snip mercilessly. Let him think her dead, when she's gone. She radios that thought now: BE HAPPY I'M DEAD. Her limbo widens, deepens. She sees Jack drained and glowy with her death. We're all corpses anyway, Jack. Mortality settles on the children's group and Avon. Will Jack take Leopolda as Avon's stepmother? Not another nut! Too cruel. Regret floods her. She's too weak and unteachable for the group. Fondly, she recalls Jack's swatches of advice last winter, on the art of high spirits without finance. She misses the uplift of his old pep talks! In his new restraint, he treats her as a fellow recoverer and enthusiast in the wiles of self-brainwashing. While still on the *Sun* he'd once phoned her pelvis and told it that it was the most sane, dependable and brilliant pelvis he'd ever spoken with. She's already bereft. Give up Jack? She feels half created by him and his selfless craft. How deeply he has shaped her! She's learned to give, become desirous of giving, less self-obsessed—isn't the group her idea? Still so much of her is such a big muddle nothing can be done about. How can Jack love a mist? A mind that rises like a nine-hundred-pound cow, bone by bone, hind end first. She sits sobbing and suckling, then sees that Jack has the baby. He hooks her bra cup.

Ed is talking. She hears sounds of her lost father, whom she drove from home to his death, though here he sits. So she needs orange juice, PHZ, shock. Oh, a few kicks and punches too. No escape? If she gets her hand stamped with ultraviolet ink, she can ride any bus in the country free. Should she take Ed? *Why not?* she hears Jack say, Save Those Symptoms, Curranne. Ed'll help her to get iron cells from her childhood sins, conserve the plasma of original guilt. Treat *him* well! But won't his picture do? Surely be easier to keep track of than with that loony loose in Buffalo, maybe even taking up alcohol. Okay, she'll give him the Blue Villa instead. This offer redeems her, in part, from the wounds she gave him when she was a nutty kid, wounds she gave she can recall hurt by hurt. But what really should be done is that she and Jack should adopt Ed and Ziggy. Rosy visions of legal adoption arise, papers drawn up by Ziggy. Jobs bloom for all. The very walls of the cottage enwomb them. They walk fearlessly about the unpeopled grounds. Ed and Ziggy have full lives at last with marriages in sight. A spirit-family! The grounds quiver with goodness, hope breathes in every tree. On every breeze, old age beckons warmly to all.

Watching Ed and Ziggy makes Jack more lively than ever in bed, always eager to drop his book and talk or draw out and win from Curranne the feedback he can't get from their squeezed unelectric eyes. He respects her every word, but may not catch its secret source until a week later. He never argues, while she may come around on her own. Since Avon's birth she's hungry for praise of her body and never tires of his bottomless outpourings.

Kissing each breast. "Is this one strawberry or vanilla?"

"If she doesn't wake up pretty soon, I'd say watermelon."

He needs her badly. No one can replace her. She is queen, Jack her adoring prince consort and empire. Curranne is the only fulfillment he needs for now. She has fewer pettish, cross, thoughtless moments. He never suggests his importance to her, but her grim self-involvement is lessening to where she can be teased by thoughts of Jack reentering the outer world. She foresees herself as the wife who completes a potent and successful author. Let him pave the way for her works. She inhales the money and recognition flowing about their Manhattan town house, the estate in Virginia—Ed and Ziggy now stablemates. Blue grass sweeps to the portico. Smell the jasmine! She drinks druggy thoughts and consolations without a hint of reason to despoil their logic. The tall, great-windowed rooms looming before them become her secret, cloudborne and smiling, enspiriting her. She knows, she knows. Knows Jack sees something she knows but has never told him. Until the money comes, her little secret will stay put as her ace in the clouds.

Every other day, when she thinks of their future, she gives him an enslaving kiss, putting her bust and everything else into it, pelvis and tongue, her hands in his hair, eyes dancing with secrets, then throws in a hip rub as she turns away. Her other strategy is to fight off his hungry feelers.

"Stop coaxing. *I'm* cooking, Jack, what're *you* doing? Make the beds!"

Sliding to his knees, cheek against her. "Just let me rest here for *cinco minutos.*"

"I *know* you didn't get enough sleep last night. I sure didn't. *Hey!* somebody'll see you doing that."

"I'm researching my next novel."

"I'd say it's not going to be very literary."

"I'm not the big literary type you think I am."

"I'd hoped you were getting in training for the Great American Novel."

"Oh, that. I'm storing up for it."

"How long will you be? We need the money."

"A week? I could do it in three days but it'd look sloppy."

"Take a week, Jack."

These little tennis matches throughout the day boost her hugely. Her midafternoon feedings often end with her beating—or kicking—him off. He gets excited and wants as much attention as Avon. He undresses and stretches out beside her on the bed, stiff. If she's excited, she strips while he burps Avon and puts her in her crib. Afternoon lovemaking untapes her brain, leaves her skin silken, giving off warm-stove waves. Waves and waves of heat, so demisting and self-assuring, Curranne giving and taking whole-personed love. Some days her brain smarts, bitten alert, enlarged and enriched by flooding stinging secretions that sweep over her back, open her unbearably, until she is nipping and foxy, her body a snug little den for her husband.

And now, choked and lumpy, if she stays at Chautauqua her guilt will break up the planet. New York State heaves and buckles, magnetic winds pour down, the lake lifts from its bed. A skyey wave bends over the Institution. Only if she moves to Buffalo—or is buried, a shovel patting down her earth, fall leaves blowing—can mankind be saved. Amazing that solar ions haven't enough force already to set up crackling killer radiation around Unitarian House. The space shot will save a remnant of mankind should she choose to stay and die at Chautauqua. Her ear canals wash with static, a blue flare *whooses,* dripping, through her brain. She coughs and looks about calmly, tilting onto Jack.

"Like some orange juice?" he asks.

"Orange juice?"

"I think you would," he says. "Did you take your niacin?"

She doesn't know.

"I'll bring you some."

"I've got the rent for the ticket," she explains. "I'm going to give them my wedding ring."

"I'll give you a few dollars. How much do you need?"

"I didn't ask yet."

"Do you want to rest?" he asks.

"That's totally unnecessary." Dying for oblivion.

"Backinaminute."

She focuses on the blue halo around Ed, who is an early thirties bubblegum card ballplayer, big and hamfisted, not unfamiliar with cathouses and squirting into bar pickups with his Coke-bottle cock. "That girl knew how to drink," his eyes tell Curranne, a leer suggesting bed play. So, even in the thirties he was *sick!* He's on a bed with a bimbo, cracking her thighs with his steamball pitch. She's so stuck to him she overlooks his lapses. Curranne, Leopolda and Winnie are whores idly looked over by johns, repeats with half-familiar faces. She radios Ed some come-hither filth he ignores. In Ed she sees her mother's older sister Charlene's son Eddie. A few years older than Curranne, tough cousin Eddie has remote popping blue eyes that study her from an unapproachable branch at Chicago family reunions. Opalescently sexual, he carries his sports-tightened body with nonchalance oiled by money. Curranne too is sports-loving, a little hothead given to dares. One summer evening, her family visiting Charlene's, Curranne found Eddie and his sidelipped buddies in a nearby deserted lot. Eddie dared her into a small shack the gang had built, lighted a candle and, all of them hunched in a circle, unfolded his hardening untrimmed prick. She feigned looking away as he pounded himself. Her sight shot red when almost at once white juice surfed across the shack. She jumped out the door, ran through the lot to Charlene's and, whirly-eyed in a freezing white sweat, was put into a tub by Carol. As her mother scrubbed her in yellow light, Curranne slipped a finger down her hairless fork and started to rub. Carol's voice slapped the bathroom. Young lady, just what do you think you're doing? That part of you isn't meant to be played with. You will please to desist that practice now and forever. Carol's brown eyes clouded yellow. Splitting shock deviled Curranne. Shame clamped down. A veil rose between her and Carol. Thereafter, dawdling about her father, she allowed no sister to share his lap or threw a red fit, an encircling of Ed that also kept out Carol, whom she'd hit if Carol neared Ed affectionately. Still more father-crazy in her teens, she spurned fellow adolescents of either sex, seeing herself already a woman who'd grasped life's big secret. Alone, she rubs her butt around daddy's lap. He calls her to him, hands outstretched, for cuddles while reading. Gay moments, but those years are vague. Daddy died earlier, didn't he?

"It's really wonderful how we're all protecting the group by keeping unpleasant feelings to ourselves," Leopolda says. "Nice, huh? Sunshine and song!"

Curranne glares at her. "I won't apologize."

"Apologize for what?" Ed asks.

"For what? You should know!"

Ziggy says, "We should have a musicale."

She sees herself washing dishes, giving Ed a hip rub and turning away, her eyes dancing with secrets. Turning thirteen?—definitely past eleven. But his face is *so clear!*—Ed's past face more vivid than Ed's now. I didn't rub him there—did I? I couldn't have. She drowns the half-memory, humming. But the memory returns, his bone against her hip. So shocking. She shivers.

Jack hands her a tall orange juice and niacin. "This'll get you walking easy."

"Super," she whispers.

"The group can't support a really heavy blow? It will fall apart?" Leopolda says. "There are a thousand reasons why this group is useless, and we've heard half of them. There's one reason why we keep coming to it. We feel better, taking an action. Even if nothing gets through, we feel more clear-headed after each session. We feel less hopeless. Talk about fears. My worst is that the board of trustees will find out we have this halfway house through the season and zap my four leases."

"I'll take care of that," Ziggy says. "Keep cool."

"Well, I worry daily! I wake up swearing in the middle of the night. Is it worth the agony? When I look down the hill at that bloody lake, I have to admit this is not the Aegean. Or the Ionian. I get this big tug for Greece, paradise at five dollars a day including tips. Ceylon?—ducky. Who needs these four cottages? Here's Carter Belvedere yapping about legal threats against me. My wiring won't pass inspection, maybe? How do I know what he's spreading about me all over the Athenaeum? I'm not trying to frighten you folks. I'm saying flat out we're on thin ice. I'm warning everyone. Get ready to swim like rats if the ship goes down."

Winnie whispers, "I don't want to leave."

"Who wants to go!" Leopolda cries. "Did I say that?"

Winnie smiles knowingly. "You will save us."

"Ha! I don't have any miracles up my sleeve."

"Then there will always be someone," Winnie says. She swallows her lip. "Okay, I am craziest and most likely to give the group away with my behavior. You wish I weren't in the group. I am afraid you will move the group to your house and throw me out. Then you will say you don't know me. Never knew me!"

"That's crazy," Leopolda says.

"I didn't say I wasn't crazy. I only said the truth."

Ziggy asks, "Who wants you out of the group?"

"Everyone!"

"Well, I'll defend you." Ziggy turns about restlessly. "Fact is, I'm the one should go. I'm really crazy." He sags. A light leaves him. As he looks about the circle, he sees the prison of the wards. "You think I got no consideration for anyone, staying here. Enjoying the comforts. But I don't want to go back. It's a lot easier back there some ways. Out here I have to grapple with myself. I don't even dare step onto the porch. I know I stand out! People wonder what's a black man like me doing here? I see it in their eyes. Maybe if I had a chauffeur's outfit . . . but even then they don't want me here. They think they can send me back. Well, I'm not going. If that's inconsiderate, so be it. Shouldn't have brought me out in the first place."

"That's marvelous," Leopolda says. "You laid out your feelings clear as a bell."

Jack says, "Who wants you to go? I don't."

"I feel responsible for our trouble. I also feel like suing this damn Institution. I got my right to be here same as anyone else."

"That's the kind of talk I like to hear," Leopolda says. "We're with you, Ziggy. And I wouldn't worry about being crazy. Not here, not among all the fading folks I see shuffling about."

"Maybe so. But I'm different." He sighs hard. "I'm twisted."

"You're also a great guy and everybody likes you," Leopolda says.

"You never had better friends than this crew of loonies. Even when you were stable you were a loner, right? Here you've got friends who dig you for what you are."

Ed grunts. "Whatever that is!"

Ziggy smiles weakly. "You don't know me," he tells her.

Winnie declares from on high, "We all like you. Same skin as my kids."

"There! How do you feel about being accepted?" Leopolda asks.

"Nervous. In the ward I was strong. Out here I feel so worthless I should be whipped."

"Hey, wonderful, Ziggy. That took real courage to say," Leopolda says. "Keep it up."

"I'm hopeless. I am going to spend the entire rest of my life crazy!" Ziggy begins tearing and wipes his droopy eyes. "God damn it, I didn't mean to say that. You know what I'd like to be? A ho-mo-sexual! At least that would be a step up from a mo-no-sexual."

"Yeah, you want someone else in your life. Is that it?" she asks. "Seven years in a single bed isn't living."

"But who'd ever be ignorant enough to get into bed with an old black shoe what talks to itself half the night and hardly knows you're there? With effort I think I could know somebody was there and really hang onto that person." Ziggy tears heavily, punches his knee. "Damn dumb idiot!"

Against his will, Jack says hoarsely, "I love you, Ziggy."

"You don't know me! You knew me you'd run out the door!" Ziggy twists, pale with shame. "I fucks myself up the ass with clotheshangers! *Have since I was a kid.*"

"Do you enjoy it?" Leopolda asks.

He stares at her. His face falls away. He is fifteen.

"Then go ahead and do it," she says. "You got our permission. We don't care. Enjoy yourself."

"Yeah? Well, maybe I'll stop."

"Don't stop for us," she says. "Stop for yourself. If you want to stop."

Winnie reddens, bug-eyed and rigid.

"You still like me?" Ziggy whispers.

"I think we should skip all this talk," she says.

"Skip me too, huh?" Ziggy asks.

Curranne asks him, "Who hasn't used foreign objects on himself?"

"Not clotheshangers!" he says.

"Well, washrags or pillows. So what?" Curranne asks.

"Candles," Leopolda says.

"What is this?" Ed asks. "Crazy day at the nuthouse?"

"What's wrong?" Leopolda asks. "You shocked about something? You've seen everything there is to see at North Warren, haven't you?"

"Perverts, sure. Couldn't count 'em all."

"I'm no pervert!" Ziggy tells him.

"Well, you want to be! You just said so."

"That's something else. I want a friend."

"Ed's your friend," Curranne says. "Aren't you here together?"

"He wants a friend he can hug," Winnie says. "He can't hug Ed."

Ed laughs. "You're right there, sister."

"I don't like sister. My name is Winnie."

"Sure, Redwing. Or is it Winniehaha? I'll remember," Ed says.

Leopolda asks Ziggy, "Do you think he should apologize to you?"

"Yes, I do."

"Tell him so," she says.

"I think you should apologize to me."

"What for?" Ed asks.

"For insinuating I'm a pervert."

Ed says, "I don't know what else to call a guy who stuffs coathangers up his bunghole and wants to switch to fag."

"Whereas, Ed, I was born and here I am, but I'm not a fag. Not yet. Maybe I want a man for respect because a woman won't look at me."

Winnie says, "I want him to apologize for calling me Redwing and Minniehaha. That's like Rastus or Pocahontas."

"Tell him so," Leopolda says. "He'll never learn otherwise."

"I feel you should apologize for sneering at me for being Indian."

The group stiffens electrically, waiting for Ed's apologies. Jack and Curranne look away from him.

"Speak up," Leopolda orders Ed, easing him into speech. "You can do it. You can say I'm sorry that I sneered at your feelings or sneered at your race. You are, aren't you?"

"Why should I be?"

"Because I don't like you to speak to our members that way. We're not a ball club and we're not here to attack each other. We're here to support, not to make jokes at each other's expense. Who else thinks Ed should apologize to Ziggy and Winnie?"

Jack and Curranne nod.

"I do," says Maggie, standing beside Ed.

Ed looks down. "What do you know about it, half-pint?" He laughs. Others join in. "All right, I'm a shit, I apologize. I don't believe it! But I want this bunghole brigade to move on." Smiles at his morale-booster.

"You don't care whom you hurt, do you?" Leopolda says.

Ed shrugs. "Not much. You're all against me anyway."

"Well, I want to forgive you for your attack on us just now," she says. "I think you should apologize to all of us, and to say it right to Winnie and Ziggy. You can start by wiping that smile off your face."

Ed looks dazed. "Zinnie and Wiggy?"

"Start by saying you're sorry for insulting the group," she says.

"All right, all right. I'm sorry." Winnie's drugless civilian glare withers Ed. "I apologize to the group for calling it a bunghole brigade. I *meant* an endearment!" Looks about for understanding.

"Accepted," Leopolda says. "Speaking for myself, not for the group. And remember that you're lucky to be sitting here with us. Please be earnest and give your best. Now Winnie and Ziggy."

"Well, I—" Ed says. "I reapologize."

"Thank you," Winnie says.

"That's okay," Ziggy says. Wipes his eyes hard until the hoods stretch. "No harm done. I just wish I'd kept all that to myself."

"We'll forget every word," Ed says—but smiles slyly.

Ed can afford to be generous. He will be the first person to receive the bromide of mercury cure for schizophrenia when it's perfected, and then he can leave these losers behind as he builds his chain of parlors. But Leopolda overtakes him again.

"How do you feel about the group asking you to apologize twice?" she asks.

"I just want everything on an even keel," Ed says.

"So?"

"So I apologized, didn't I?"

"But how do you feel right now?"

"Everybody makes mistakes."

"That's great," she says. "We're happy you want to be gracious and contribute."

"Oh, I do."

"You're always here on time," she says. "You always have something to say. You're vital to us."

"If you say so. I like to feel I am. I'll pitch a few."

"How do you like being here?"

"At Chautauqua?"

"Well, yes. And right in this room," Leopolda asks.

"It's a room."

"How do you feel about it? Does it make you happy?"

"This room? Not really."

"Why not?"

"I don't like the rugs. Picture rugs are sappy. Pretty soon I'll be seeing rabbits. Who are all these people on camels?"

"I'm sorry you don't like the rugs. Do you like sitting in this circle?"

"It's all right."

"Does it give you any uplift?"

Ed clears his throat. "I like it. It makes me sad," he says without thinking.

"What's sad about it?" Leopolda asks.

"Some rooms I like make me sad."

"Why's that?"

"This one reminds me of schools and rooms I lived in growing up."

"Did you like those rooms?"

"Very much."

"What makes you sad about this room?"

"I don't know. I'm going to lose it."

"You're going to lose this room?" Leopolda asks.

"Well, I am," he says. "I've been sitting here for months now. Maybe I shouldn't enjoy it so much."

"How about the people in it?" she asks.

"What about 'em?"

"What's going to happen?"

"I'm going to lose them and this room." Ed's soft jaw quivers. He wipes his mouth.

"Does the thought of losing the group make you sad?" she asks.

"I don't know why it should! What've you ever done for me? You're trying to confuse me, that's what. You're trying to get me to say something that isn't true and I won't say it. *I won't say it!*"

"Why should we do anything to confuse you?" Leopolda asks.

"You want me to say what's going on in my mind. You want me to get angry and blow up. You want my secrets! I'm going to be an ice-cream millionaire and you think you can get my secret formula and trademark."

"I think it's wonderful that you have a secret formula and real plans for your future," Leopolda says. "Why will you be sad to miss us— and this room?"

Ed is silent, his face sucked into his throat. "I've lost everything! I have nothing! I'm not here. I'm dead and sitting here. I've been dead a quarter of a century and hung around like a ghost. You're making me say this! I won't say it! I will not explode! *I won't say it!* You think I'm full of all sorts of sex urges like that fag Ziggy! I don't have any feelings. Ha! I'm sexless! I'm—I'm—I can't raise it up! I don't have any feelings. Ha! *There!!* You want it, there it is! God damn it! But don't think I don't have *feelings.* I'm full of feelings. I'm the world's greatest love-letter writer."

"We're all glad you have feelings and write such great love letters. Whom do you write them to?"

"That's for me to know."

"Well, maybe when she accepts you, you'll be able to raise it up again," she says.

"Don't say that . . . She's too young for that kind of fooling around. I couldn't do that. I'm going to put my girl's picture on my ice-cream cartons. This isn't sex. It's being a success like in *Fortune* magazine. They'll write me up after my first million. Then I'll show her the article."

Jack asks, "Won't she already have seen her picture on the carton?"

"You shut your eyes or I'll put your mouth out," Ed says.

"You'll put my *eyes* out?"

"This is shocking," Leopolda tells Ed softly. "We're not here to attack anyone. We're here to support each other."

"Then stop him from trying to confuse me! He can't trick me."

"Trick you?" she asks.

"I will not blow up! Tell this jerk to watch his step."—kicking his leg toward Jack.

"Don't try to push me around," Jack says, red-faced. "One more fucking threat out of you this morning and we're going outside. I don't care if you are thirty years older than I am."

"Jack, why are you threatening Ed?" Leopolda asks.

"He can't threaten *me* in front of my wife! You all think I'm some kind of hired doormat! *Jesus Christ!* And he wants to put my eyes out? How the hell am I supposed to sleep at night after a statement like that from a lunatic?"

"Proves everything I said," Ed says.

"Ed, *look!* You've upset Jack," Leopolda says. "Winnie, what do you think about all this shouting?"

"It's not good for the children," Winnie says. "And it makes me frightened so I want to go to the plaza even in the rain until it's all over. We will get bad reports from the people on the street and get thrown out, like you say."

"I am so fucking angry!" Jack whispers, giving Curranne the baby.

"Why don't you tell Winnie how you feel, Jack," Leopolda says. "She's very frightened. Maybe you can calm her down."

"I'm very upset, Winnie," Jack says. "Maybe I mean frightened."

"I can see that," she says. "Be strong."

"Strong? *Strong?* That's all I am is strong! I'm strong twenty-four hours a day. I need to be weak once in a while. I feel like Atlas cracking to pieces with all nine planets on his back. I get arthritic pains in my knees from what I've got on my shoulders. The weight, the money, the loonies. I shouldn't say that?"

"I feel the same weight," Winnie says. "All day, all night. Seven days a week, month after month, year after year. You've only had one year like this. You aren't even loony yet."

"Don't even suggest that," Jack says quietly.

"Summer isn't over yet," Ziggy says.

Jack throws up a hand. "This has been the happiest year of my life," he tells Winnie. "And the worst, bar none. I never thought I could be so happily married. I thought I was incapable of putting aside self-interest for more than twenty-four hours. Now I've been doing it I don't know how long and have happiness I never dreamed of. What's excruciating is the sheer misery that goes along with it. My life is a swamp I can't begin to drain. There's no dry ground anywhere. I don't see one ray of sunshine that outlasts five minutes. And yet one day at a time I have something that's worth everything it costs me to sit here with you."

Ziggy is uncomfortable. "What makes you miserable? The rain and all them dead birds?"

"He's not writing," Curranne says. She gives Avon a nipple under her shawl.

"I'm not writing," Jack says. "I know there are worse things—like mental illness—but *this* is my misery. This room, I memorize every chair and rug for a paragraph I may never write. I feel I'm wide awake in a dark place that keeps flowing away from me and doesn't get written about. I feel overalert inside some big memory memorizing me. I see all of us in double focus, our faces past and present—only the past is right now, like Leopolda says."

"I don't understand any of this," Winnie says. "You are not talking to me. I don't know who you talk to."

Ed snorts, turning from Jack and Winnie.

"This is an inappropriate response?" Jack asks Leopolda.

"Do you think it is? I know I got lost. Maybe I'm tired, but it's still early morning. Why don't you tell Curranne how you feel right now?"

"Oh, don't tell me," Curranne says.

"Why shouldn't I tell you?"

"Well, I already know. So why don't you tell Winnie or Ziggy?"

"You don't want to hear how I feel right now?" Jack asks.

"Boo hoo," Ed says.

"Well, you'll be too ideational with me. I already understand you. It's the others who need explanations."

"I'm not explaining ideas, I'm saying how I feel. What do you mean ideational? I don't even understand the word."

"I mean how you *think*. Don't I?" Searches the rain on the roof for succor. "Oh, go ahead, tell me. Just don't upset the baby."

"Wait a minute," Jack says. "Is upsetting the baby more important than how I feel in Group? Am I supposed to remain mute every time the baby is nursing? Just dish you verbal Jell-O because baby's at your breast?"

"I'm very confused, Jack. Just tell me how you feel and I'll sort it out."

"Sort it out? More jargon. *Thanks*. I feel lousy. I was threatened by Ed. Winnie can't understand why I'm leaking blood about not writing. And you want to tune out on anything upsetting, or maybe dangerous."

Curranne says, "What could be more dangerous between us, I don't know."

"I think I'll just drift on," Jack says. "I get no sympathy from you."

"Jack, just tell us how you feel," Leopolda says. "And don't worry. You couldn't say anything dangerous if you tried."

"You don't think so?" Jack asks.

"We've heard everything dangerous that could ever be said to us," Leopolda says. "We've heard it over and over until by now it's as safe to swallow as mother's milk. The things we tell ourselves daily, and I mean you too, are far worse than anything anyone else could say."

"Amen," Ed says.

"I didn't know you were religious," Jack says.

"I'm very religious," Ed says. He pulls a red kerchief from his hip and spits out a cud of snuff. Takes out his tin and restuffs his mouth.

"Well!" Jack says.

"I must be or I wouldn't have left the hospital. Don't think I don't have religion. What else could have made me give up my free room and meals to try to make it out here?"

"Okay, I'm sorry," Jack says. "Glad to hear about your Higher Power."

"That's what it is. It's spiritual. Don't knock it," Ed says. "You got no higher power."

Jack reddens but stays silent. At last he says, "Maybe you should apologize to me for that. Or is arguing with a mental patient like hitting a drunk? I shouldn't do it. But don't tell me I don't have a higher power. Please."

Ed floats on fresh snuff. "I apologize."

"I really liked what Jack said," Winnie says.

"What you would like even better is what he didn't say and is hiding," Leopolda says.

"I feel I'm being judged," Jack says.

"Never say I don't judge!" Leopolda cries. "I judge constantly."

"No wonder I feel I'm found wanting when I speak!" Jack says.

"Oh, that's your own opinion," she says. "You couldn't get a remark like that out of me. Never. Not in a million years. I support people, I help. I wouldn't tell a dog it was found wanting. But judge, yes, that I admit. I have to. I have the worst problems. I'm responsible. Without me we wouldn't be here, you said so yourself. I stand to lose money, property, and maybe even my mind if we don't act judiciously *every moment.* Two minutes of mayhem and the roof could come down. We'd all be camping out in Bestor Plaza under our gate passes to keep off el drip. Sure I judge. Now get on with what you weren't saying."

"I'm too amazed. I don't remember."

"All right. We're patient," Leopolda says. "But don't take forever. We may not be here when you finally get ready. Curranne, how do you feel about Jack's bad memory? Relieved?"

"Oh, he's wonderful, you know that. He'll remember."

"No, that's not enough," Leopolda says. "Are you disappointed? Aren't you at all interested in what he might throw up?"

"I suppose I am," Curranne says.

"But not very much, huh?" Leopolda asks.

"Well, I *live* with him. Nothing he'd say would surprise me."

"You mean, everything he says surprises you?" Leopolda asks. "Or that you wouldn't be deeply moved by whatever he might reveal of his feelings?"

"Yes. No. It'd all depend. Wouldn't it? I know he wouldn't say anything—" At a loss, Curranne waves her hand.

"Ungentlemanly?" Leopolda asks. "He wouldn't say anything that might wound you in public? In the group? Tell me, why do you have to defend him from himself? We all know Jack is a gentleman. Well-mannered, well-spoken, et cetera. In fact, very capable of speaking for himself. And he might even do that if you didn't issue your little insurances of gentlemanliness. I think I mean *in*surances. Are you afraid he might hurt you? Damage your marriage? Maybe even drive you bats? Could he do that? If he really set out to?"

Curranne slips behind a hand on her brow. "A lot of people could drive me over the edge," she tells Avon.

"That's no answer," Leopolda says. "Could Jack?"

"I can't answer," Curranne says.

"He'd have to be pretty ingenious to do it, wouldn't he?" Leopolda says. "You're a pretty strong-minded person, aren't you? That's what I see. If you set out to, you could probably cut Jack to ribbons in quite a few of your discussions. But you don't do that, do you? You hold back. Correct me if I'm wrong."

"She's granite," Jack says.

Curranne swallows hard. "No. I mean yes. Yes, I'm strong-minded. No, he couldn't drive me bats."

"Then what are you afraid of? Are you defending Jack or yourself when you pour cream all over his reactions in the group?"

"I don't know," Curranne says.

"Think about it," Leopolda says. "You know, all of us here have our lives on the line. We're eager to know what you feel."

"What I think," Curranne whispers.

"No, what you feel. We'll forget what you think. We'll remember what you feel. Nobody ever helped a schiz by filling him up with facts. What we all need is support. Feelings. We want to walk out of Group when the season ends stronger than we were July first. We're not here to become intellectuals. You know all this. I'm just talking to give you time to look at your fears of the group."

"I'm not afraid!"

"Well, that makes you unique," Leopolda says. "You've graduated. You can leave the group now. Do you want to leave?"

Curranne waves her hands, smiles pointlessly, falls silent again. Slumping backward, rewrapping the baby. Her head drops.

"I really don't know Jack," she says.

"You're married to him," Leopolda says.

"Yes, but I don't know why he can't speak in the group."

"He talks quite a bit," Leopolda says.

"But he never says anything," Curranne says.

"How do you mean that?" Leopolda asks. "That's pretty strong."

"I don't know! Maybe he's always secretly defending himself, I mean me."

"Jack's afraid he'll drive you into relapse, that it?" Leopolda asks.

"You'll have to ask him."

"Of course I'm afraid of that," Jack says.

"That's perfectly natural," Leopolda assures him. "But, Curranne, don't you feel that his fear makes you act out just what he's fearing? That he's got you living and hiding in a stereotype? A crazy-doll's house?"

"I hadn't thought of it that way. I don't think I even understand your question."

"Well, don't you resent it?" Leopolda asks.

"Resent what?" Curranne asks.

"That his fear keeps you his captive and makes you feel weaker than you are?"

"No."

"Why not?"

"Because I'm as weak as he thinks I am. I'm very weak! I don't know why I'm not in the hospital!" She breaks into silent, restrained sobs. Her breathlessness and watering eyes are the only signs of distress as the group supports her wordlessly. She experiences its binding sympathy just by being there, herself having comforted others with a kind of Quaker wordlessness. She tries to speak but is tongue-tied.

"Do you want to wait until you finish nursing?" Leopolda asks.

"Yes!"

"That's all right. You've already said the worst of it," Leopolda says.

Curranne stares at her speechlessly, through tears. Then bursts with relief and laughter. The others chuckle, if still unsure what's ahead.

"I'm very sick! I really am. I must be," Curranne says.

"You're sick if you keep it to yourself," Leopolda says.

"Boy, am I disorganized."

"Ho, you thought *that* was a secret!" Leopolda asks. She smiles around the group. "Takes one to know one, doesn't it?"

"But I still can't talk about it!" Curranne says. "I really don't know what it is I can't talk about. I wish we could drop it for now. Just drop it!"

"Drop it where?" Leopolda asks. "Into the lake? Off Third Street Bridge? Wouldn't that be nice if we could just drop it. Are you having a breakdown, Curranne?"

"I don't know. I don't feel so hot."

"We don't want to go on if you feel the slightest stress that isn't a pleasurable stress," Leopolda says. "Whatever you say, feel strong for saying it. Or keep it to yourself until you feel better."

"I'm frightened," Jack says. "Don't push her. Mostly she's perfectly all right. But I don't think she should chance a relapse."

"Curranne thinks she's already having a relapse, Jack," Leopolda says. "We just want to help drain off some of her fears for right now. For this moment. There's nothing the group can do one way or the other if she *is* having a relapse. We can only be here, and let her know we're here and waiting to help."

"I won't be alone," Curranne tells him—a hard-won gritty little smile.

"That doesn't seem enough," Jack says.

"What do you want to do? Call an ambulance?" Leopolda asks. "Call an ambulance, if it will make you feel better. But she may not want to get into it—or even look like she needs it when it gets here."

"This is so fucking dangerous!" Jack cries. "Have you been taking your meds?"

Curranne nods yes.

"Faithfully?"

She nods.

"Those pills don't work for everyone," Ed says. "I never noticed they did me any good."

"You're on the outside, aren't you?" Ziggy asks.

"They coulda let me out years ago," Ed says. "They just didn't know how together I was."

"If you call your last seven years together, you must be crazy," Ziggy says.

"Don't push me. My insight is that I never saw a single person besides us leave the hospital who was on Thorazine."

"You got no insight at all," Ziggy says. "You thought that if anyone left it was because he wasn't like you and skipped his pills. That isn't the same thing."

"Yeah? I know plenty about what's wrong with everyone in this room, meds or no meds," Ed says, his fist a light ball pounding into a mitt. "I'd tell you what's wrong with you but it wouldn't do any good. Water off a duck's back."

"This is pitiful," Curranne says. Watching his fists clench the phantom ball, pity for Ed's thirty years on the wards—and for the cocky hopeless courage of his new freedom—wrenches her. "I want to hold you, Poppa."

Only Ed seems to hear Curranne and eyes her curiously. His daughter? The middle kid walked in her sleep, maybe wasn't all there.

"You're right, Ed," Leopolda says. "The five greatest analysts alive could sit down with Ziggy—or with any of us—and give him the works: all his symptoms, what they mean, insight after insight that would amaze Ziggy. For five minutes! Then he'd fall right back into the same state as before they told him. We're not here for insights. They're no help to people like us. They drip right off of us. We're here to learn how to get out of ourselves and connect with other people and have a real exchange with the world. Have feelings! I repeat myself, but I have to keep reminding me why I'm sitting here. What's wrong with us is fear. We're paralyzed by the thought of other people—they might find out how weak and confused we are. Why can't Curranne talk? Because she's afraid to join the group. Really join and open up to us. Instead she gives us wonderful Jack so that we won't know how weak and sick she thinks she is. We saw this pattern start the first day the group met. Now we have a breakthrough. After thirty days Curranne is actually frightened enough of herself to ask the group for help. Or I think she's doing that. Here we sit, waiting on Avon. Meanwhile Jack has told us how much he loves Curranne and Avon and how terrified he is that their lives may fall apart in the next five minutes. This is extremely commendable! He revealed that bouncing off of us, *he's* become as weak and ineffectual as *we* secretly think *we* are. That took courage. What's wonderful is that we're all here to help Jack crack through his strong man's mask—*Hey, Zampano!*—and recover his wits. Am I explaining this clearly? Are there any questions? Ed, are you happy here? You've expressed a lot of anger and anxiety today."

"I'm okay, boss," Ed says.

"Maybe you said some things you wish you hadn't. Believe me, your secret is safe with us. Everything you say in this room is absolutely confidential. Of course, we're all psychotics. Sometimes we aren't responsible for what we say. But that's the chance you take. Curranne, hasn't Avon had enough?"

Jack takes Curranne's shawl onto his shoulder and begins burping the baby. Curranne digs into herself.

"This morning while I was feeding the baby—"

"Skip this morning," Leopolda says. "That's the dead past. Archeology. We don't need what you felt this morning. What do you feel right now, in Group?"

"Well!" Curranne says. "I think you have no right to treat us like this! Any of us!"

"Terrific. We're happy to hear something spontaneous. What's your gripe?"

"We're all sitting here falling apart," Curranne says. "And you carry on an Inquisition. You don't show any sympathy at all!"

"That's very serious," Leopolda says. "Thank you for pointing it out. If you feel it, it must be a fact. To you, at least. Winnie, do I fail to give you sympathy and support?"

Winnie shakes her head no. Instantly she stands to declare yes. But sits again, shaking her head no.

"Ziggy, how about you? Do I run you down and weaken your self-image?" Leopolda asks.

"Not that I notice! But I feel like the real nut in this nest and that you're trying to hatch a wooden egg in warming me up. I'm a certified pecan! I'll never get wings."

"I don't agree," she says.

"I don't either. You're going to be a powerhouse for sanity when you get all connected up, Ziggy," Jack says. "Are you stronger than HP? If He wants you out spreading the message, He'll damn well grow wings on solid mahogany."

"I don't have the message yet," Ziggy says. "Or HP."

"You'll get it," Leopolda says. "You're well on your way. Ed, do you feel I've put you through an Inquisition? I *know* you've been very angry today. Are you angry with me?"

"No. Why should I be?"

"Jack, what's Curranne talking about? You like to defend her. Explain her position to us," Leopolda says. "In your usual nice way. Or be critical, I don't care! But be supportive."

"I detest that jargon. Let's say supporting, not supportive."

"All right. Be supporting."

"Thank you. Curranne doesn't want to tell us something, so she's attacking you," Jack says. "Takes the crunch off her."

"Amazing. I felt that too. Curranne, what do you feel about Jack's statement?" Leopolda asks.

"That's what he thinks!"

"But do you feel deserted by him?" Leopolda asks.

"No. He's saying what he has to."

"That's good, isn't it? Instead of his protecting you from the rest of us?" Leopolda asks. "Don't you respect him more for being more mature about you and not casting you into a stereotype?"

She nods. "Yeah. But I don't feel good. Really, I think I'm going to pieces. I don't think I can go on like this."

"Like what?" Leopolda asks.

"You're all turning on me so that you won't have to admit you're all failures with me—and that the group is powerless in my case. *'Not interested.'* "

"The group is against you?" Leopolda asks.

"Yeah—and it always has been!"

"It hasn't helped you before?" Leopolda asks.

"Not once. Since the day we started I've known you all thought I was hopeless and would turn against me. I don't know why I'm sitting here! I know I should drop out! How did I ever think you could help me? Every time I speak you all tune out. You can't bear what I say. You think it's all phony. That I don't have any feelings or center! Don't mean what I say! That I sound as bad as some cheap B-picture tramp who can't act! I loathe sitting here! If you think I enjoy this group you're all hideously mistaken! I have to fight my way here every morning. I shit on these sessions! For Christ's sake, I'm a college graduate—I have a degree! I'm a *Ph-f-f-Phi Bete!* What am I doing here?"

"You think the group is below your intellectual level?" Leopolda asks.

"Ha!"

"You feel frustrated having to associate with people more poorly educated than yourself?" Leopolda asks.

Tossing her head smartly—"Yeah, it's frustrating."

"Let me ask you. How did you feel about Ezra Pound's intellectual level when you visited him at St. Elizabeths?" Leopolda asks.

"He was crazy!"

"Well, was his intellectual level helpful to his recovery?"

"He didn't recover. They just let him go," Curranne says. "And without stinking meds!"

"Would our group ever have been of any value to Ezra Pound—I mean if he'd been a member?"

"Absolutely none," Curranne says. "He wouldn't have set foot in the room."

"Well, what if we went and asked him to join us?"

"He'd've thrown his table at us."

"Who is Ezzard Pound?" Ziggy asks.

"Ezra," Curranne says. "He's a great American poet, falsely accused of being a traitor during World War II, and then thrown into St. Elizabeths to save him from the firing squad."

"And he was crazy?" Ziggy asks.

"Paranoid schiz," Curranne says loftily.

"If he were in our group," Leopolda asks, "how would he act?"

"He'd make speeches like Jack," Curranne says. "From that balcony."

"You don't think he'd be a constructive member?" Leopolda asks.

"Not at all."

"Why not?"

"He was completely insulated by words. Talked constantly," Curranne says.

"Then he didn't want help, did he?" Leopolda asks.

"You couldn't have opened his mind with dynamite," Curranne says.

"Would you say he wanted to hang on to his illness? Say, that he cherished his own little world of visitors like yourself who didn't threaten him, and that he excluded everyone or anyone who might have wanted to help him?" Leopolda asks.

"Yeah."

"Would it be fair to say that he thought himself intellectually above anyone who tried to help him with his mental problems?"

"But he really *was* their superior!" Curranne says.

"Except in sanity?" Leopolda asks.

"Yeah. *They* could go home nights."

"So then, is it safe to say that he had no desire to have a manageable mind?" Leopolda asks.

"I guess it would be."

"Then we wouldn't want him in the group, would we? We'd catch on right away that he wants to stay sick, and make speeches and rant and rave. Wouldn't we?"

"Well, he was a wonderful poet, even crazy," Curranne says. "He wrote a lot of great lines in Saint."

"You're not answering me."

"No, we wouldn't want him."

"I don't want him," Ed says. "Does he want to join us?"

"He's gone to Italy," Curranne says.

"Good riddance," Ed says.

"Okay," Leopolda says. "Here's a man you really admire—"

"He knows all about what's wrong with credit and usury," Curranne says.

"—a poet who is one of the most educated men alive, gifted, a genius—right?—who has only one flaw. He's a paranoid with no desire to let go of his fears, those that he might, who prefers to stay in a pumped-up paradise of words and intellectual politics. One last question. If he was your father, how would you feel about his choice to stay sick?"

"If he was my father?"

"Yes."

Curranne sags unhappily. "I'd make every effort to help him."

"He doesn't deserve it," Ed says. "He's hopeless."

"You're not hopeless!" Curranne cries fiercely at Ed. "You've got a scheme to become an ice-cream millionaire."

"Just as soon as my mother dies and I get my credit together," Ed says. "One loan will do it."

"So you've got a way out, haven't you?" Curranne asks. "Well, he has an epic poem he's writing to work his way out. I think it's terrible of you to say he's hopeless. I really resent that. You should stick up for the sick and crazy! You above anyone! Why can't you stick up for a man as sick as you are?"

"He's sicker than I am," Ed says.

"He's *out,* isn't he?" Curranne asks.

"The point is," Leopolda tells Curranne, "that you can express deep feelings for a man you think is a truly miserable paranoiac—you even got up a tear or two for him—who is not in the room. But you can't do the same for some equally sick people with a desire to get well who are sitting here with their empty hands out to you. Is this a true description?"

Curranne nods mutely.

"I want you to understand we're not interested in your analysis with Dr. David. That's all between you and him. We're after something else you have to give us. But you can't give it because you're a Phi Beta Kappa. You're very proud of your intellect, aren't you? Right? That's no sin, is it?"

"No. I mean yes."

"It's a sin?" Leopolda asks. "I don't think so. It's natural to be happy you're gifted. But you're proud of it too. Aren't you, Curranne?"

"Yes. I mean no. I mean—I suppose I am."

"That's okay. That's an honest admission. We won't hold it against you. Will we, Ziggy?"

"Nah. I read lots of classics. In Latin, too. I have a Latin gift."

Curranne flushes.

"Now cool down," Leopolda tells her. "This Inquisition is all to a purpose, ha ha."

"I wish you wouldn't laugh, Curranne. I mean, Leopolda," Curranne says.

"Does it offend you? Do you feel belittled by it? It's just a disarming little laugh. To help your temper cool off."

"Don't be obvious with me." She's sitting up, interested.

"All right. I'll be reserved," Leopolda says. "I don't want you sneering at me as if you were Ezra Pound. So let me ask you. Pound is still a pretty good poet, isn't he? In some few narrow ways, his brain is still okay, despite the bugs. By his brain I mean his mind."

"So what?"

"So essentially then, for all his weird ideas—"

"They're not weird. And I wish you wouldn't say they were, without studying them."

"Fine, fine!" Leopolda says. "I'm not attacking his ideas—or yours. I don't attack anyone. Life's too short to waste it on changing people's politics. For all his unusual ideas, we might say that his brain is still in relative working order. He might actually be able to hold down the poetry chair at Oxford if his brain were all that was called for. Right? Do you agree? Okay. Then it must not be his brain that's sick. Or his intellect. But they could probably work better than they do, couldn't they—if he wasn't sick? He's confused a lot of the time, wouldn't you say? I mean, if you think he'd throw a table at us. So he must be sick someplace else maybe. Where do you think he's really sick? Tell us."

Curranne thinks. "He's frightened."

"What's he frightened of?" Leopolda asks.

"I don't know."

"I'll put it another way. Why is he a compulsive talker? Whom is he so frightened of hearing make a cogent remark about his illness that he can't let one word through his defenses?"

"Himself," Curranne says.

"Not the fascists and usurers?" Leopolda asks.

"I don't like this," Curranne says.

"Well, he's frightened of his feelings. Isn't he? Doesn't he need the whole literary world to defend him against himself? If he ever stops talking and writing, what will happen to him?"

"I don't know."

"Won't he lapse into a reverse state?" Leopolda suggests. "He may be struck mute. A kind of verbal catatonia. Still just as much fear as when he was hiding behind words, but now hiding behind silence. Alert as ever, of course. You know about catatonia. You've been there. What do you think about when you're like that?"

"I don't think."

"What do you do?"

"I feel."

"And what do you feel?" Leopolda asks. "Do you mind if I answer for you? You feel every destructive impulse you've ever feared in yourself. You're sitting on an erupting volcano. Aren't you?"

Curranne nods. "Something like that."

"Horrible, isn't it. We've all been there. None of us wants to go back. No one in his right mind would. Do you know anything worse than to have fears you can't name blowing you apart? It's something like being driven against a wall by a firehose, isn't it? No intellectual defense is possible. You can throw your Phi Bete key out the window, right? How could a flimsy little intellectual certification like that help you? Not when your fears are gushing. Or not when mine are. Wouldn't you say we're all equals in this room, when it comes to fear?"

"Yes," Curranne whispers.

"How may I help you?"

"Don't let him rape me," Curranne whispers.

"Who?" Leopolda asks.

"Eddie."

"Ed is impotent," Leopolda says.

"I'm an old softy, kid."

"That's a lie. I know he isn't. He showed me his thing."

"That's a lie," Ed says uncertainly.

"It doesn't matter if it's true or not, Ed," Leopolda says. "It's a fact to Curranne. Give her your word you'll respect her."

"Respect her! I treat her like my own daughter—and she comes up with this!"

"Your daughters are dead and buried!" Curranne cries. "You told us the first night we met. Just throw the dirt on them!"

"Jesus, listen to that," Ed says.

"More beer and pussy on the way!" Curranne says.

"Oh well, now! What can I promise her? I'll tell you both something. I'm *cursed*. I will probably go to my grave without one hump for the rest of my life. Tell her that calling me a rapist is like handing me a medal as I'm drowning."

"Don't tell me, tell her," Leopolda says.

"I swear I'll never interfere with you. I am a businessman! Young girl—I mean Diana—I mean young woman—you have no conception of what my net worth is going to be just twelve months from now. I will not jeopardize a great American fortune for one piece of—for one diddle. That crazy I am not. I give you my solemn promise, right here in public, that I will go to bed with Ziggy before I consider your charms in any manner whatsoever."

"Well!" Leopolda says. "Did you hear that, Curranne?"

Ziggy says, "I heard it and didn't like it."

Curranne turns aside. "Hear what?"

"Ed has promised never to assault you. We all heard his promise." Leopolda asks Ed, "Don't you think you should tell her you're sorry she's afraid of you?"

"I'm sorry you're crazy," he tells Curranne. "The fact is, I'm promised in marriage to a woman I can't marry for three years."

"You are? Why can't you?" she asks.

"I've taken an oath. She's not of age yet." Ed's lips mush in shock.

"You mean she's fifteen?" Ziggy asks.

"I didn't say that," Ed says.

"I don't predict much for that marriage," Ziggy says.

"What do you mean?" Ed asks. "I'm founding a dynasty. A lot you know about the great families that run this country."

"Do you feel more comfortable?" Leopolda asks Curranne.

"I don't know what I feel with this nut loose in the house."

"Winnie, wake up," Leopolda says. "Falling asleep in Group is an act of aggression against the members. Curranne just started to give us a few of her feelings about the group."

"What?" Curranne says. Cousin Eddie, beating off in Chicago, his hard circle of buddies tightening. Her heart beats, it was only ten minutes ago. "Stay away from me!" she cries across the circle at Ed.

"When you're ready," Leopolda says. "We're all sorry you identify your fears with Ed, because we all like Ed and wish him well. And don't find anything frightening about him. But you were fearful a long time before you met Ed, weren't you? We were wondering if you might not feel a little more outgoing and really ready to join the group. We want what you have to give."

"I don't have anything left to give," Curranne's small voice says.

"Don't you feel that some of the pressure on you has been removed?" Leopolda asks. "This might be a good time for you to speak up for yourself and tell us what you hope to get out of the group."

Curranne looks about unhappily. "I can't relate to the group. I'm too bored with myself. I'm bored with my illness, bored with your illness. Bored with your ideas! I've never heard such feeble concentration in my life. I wish to God I'd never started this group."

"Jack," Leopolda says. "Why do you think Curranne is bored with us?"

"She's not bored with the group, she's angry," Jack says.

"Why is that?" Leopolda asks.

"The group has failed to defend her from herself," Jack says.

"Defend *me!*" Curranne cries. "I don't need to be defended from myself, I need to be defended from this damned cottage fever and rain and being cramped up with schizzes twenty-four hours a day! Ed and Ziggy never go out. *I* never go out, I don't dare. I might come home and find the stove on fire with some garbage they forgot they were eating. I don't hear three sane sentences a day—even from myself! I didn't know what I was getting into when I invited these nuts to stay here. There, I've said it! And if I'm not suffocating in *my* house, I'm *over here* swimming in lunatics. Who needs it? Maybe I'm not clear. Maybe nobody understands me. *I'm trapped!* Don't you see how I feel? I want to give up this whole business. This group has got me coming apart! I want to close my door on everybody here and be left alone. *Close the door??* I *dream* of it. I need a vacation from schizophrenia! I've been drowning in it since I was a child and too young to know it. I want to wake up sane some morning and talk to absolutely sane healthy people for one whole day—a whole month. Two months, for God's sake, like a trip to France! Or the Greek isles! Everybody gets a vacation *sometime!* Where's mine? Year in, year out I'm either drowning or floating on a lifesaver temporarily or drowning again! That's how I feel about being in the group. That's why I shove everything off on Jack. I don't want to be here. I don't want to care! If I were really sane I'd see how crazy I was! I'm choking to death in this frigging room. *I'd like to chuck you all into the lake!*"

The children have fallen silent.

"Where would you rather be?" Winnie asks.

"Sane!"

"Marvelous," Leopolda says. "Ziggy, are you upset by Curranne's feelings?"

"Music to my ears!" Ziggy says. "I was happy to hear her let it out."

"Ed, are you upset by her angry outburst?" Leopolda asks.

"Nah. That's what we're here for. Spring training. I'll forget what she said if she'll forget what I said. If she can. I've already forgotten."

"Winnie, are you upset?" Leopolda asks.

"Curranne told the story of my life," Winnie says. "Me too, I hate being with nuts night and day. I feel hopeless. I understand. I feel sorry for *her* since I feel too worthless to feel sorry for myself."

"What about you, Jack?" Leopolda asks.

"I wish she'd spoken up sooner. She's kept it all under a blanket, even to me. Of course, she's done that before—right up to the night we got engaged on her front porch. Or was it in Fulmer's Dairy?"

"Third Street Bridge!"—punching his shoulder hard for forgetting.

Well! She has some legitimate complaints that make her want to close the door on the group."

"Of course she does!" Leopolda says. "We all deserve better. But what have we *got?* We've got each other. And that's where the hope is. Every day each of us thinks he's crazy as a bedbug. The floor wobbles, the walls wobble. How can we let off the pressure? Somehow we've got to outlive our guilt and fear by talking out our worst anxieties and getting fellowship and encouragement from people as sick as we are. This summer is passing like a bolt of lightning. Where will this group be in September? Wherever we are, maybe we'll be stronger. We'll have known each other. We'll not have lived every single moment of these two months alone and fighting destructive self-images and urges. I think each of us will have just a little more faith in himself and a lot less fear. The first step is having faith in yourself. Getting some horse-power in your spine. Then when the fudge hits the fan and your fears try to shake that faith, you have the group to help prick those fears. The group or HP. Prick them, not analyze them. For us, recovery from schiz, even partway, is not an intellectual problem. What do we need? We gotta have heart, gang, that's what! See you all same time tomorrow. My God, do I need some coffee."

Ed reads a dark green caravan underfoot in the rug. Spreads his feet, trying to make out the hooded faces. But the misty pilgrims resist his probing.

"Nice session," he tells Ziggy.

"Groovy," Ziggy says.

PART TEN

The Higher Power

H̲ey, my voice sounds pretty good! Curranne tells herself. Her hot brow steams and drips. The ball of her foot groans onto her mother's tub. While running her morning bath, she's had a hectic chat with Dr. David. Her voice strumming with health, firmness, a sunny bounce. Slept rottenly but a deep-running hot sweat has her fit as a bowstring.

Nine o'clock October sun falls straight into the tub. She is rising cream and fat, hot and afloat in a deep heart of sunlight. She dips her freckles neckdeep into steam. Slides side to side, flushed and splotchy, breasts waving. Energies buzz, hum in her limbs. Her throat is ready for grand opera. The red air speckles with pollen. Her tongue tastes of butter. Triumphant and lazy, she feels the ease of earned rest. No blues today! Not in this cool red October furnace of rising sun. Her closed lids burn. The light bakes her soul pleasantly. Her spirit enlarges. Heat gathers in her lower lips, runs up her spine. Her eyes open, half-liddedly gray-green, spermy, slick with life. She dreams thoughtlessly in sun, her life a seed she fingers in her palm.

Rested or not, Curranne rises at seven to feed Avon and have her mother baby-sit for an hour—before limping to her real estate office—while she stretches in the backyard and runs to Lincoln Junior High's cinder track and back. She's building a new HP through thirty-minute sweats, and tries to recover body rhythms set up after her earlier pregnancies. Her strongest morning impulse is toward freedom from Avon and the luxury of Carol bathing and grooming her grandchild. One brief hour daily Curranne devotes wholly to herself and working up a glow in the brilliant fall chill.

She stifles her severe disregard for Carol as a mother. Curranne's earlier intense self-concern and secret lovelessness toward Avon, whose care might betray her and be a source of failure, have waned. She has at last forgiven Jack's empty fathering of the child on her through his drunken lack of a rubber. She often faces down this hard fact against him. His slippery act has impelled her to review herself and become a different woman, more giving, surrendering of self-concern. She's grown obsessive about not neglecting Avon or exposing her to drafts, bugs, dogs, or even other babies who might have "diseases." But the pain, boredom and well-being of exercise, a hangover from junior high days as a track star, allow her new physical ease and gratitude in mothering. Sweating for HP, Curranne feels whole, a full woman, a swimmer in the blue.

Exercise began in earnest at Chautauqua. Pacing the lake, the bell tower and practice shacks, the fence. But nothing is certain about her health. She strives to avoid losing her third baby and having it sent back. This fear bloomed in September when Jack got a job as day manager of Fulmer's Dairy: he works sandwich board during noon rush, keeps up fountain and bulk ice cream inventories, roasts nuts, makes out the work sheet, and hires and fires. At first he drove down to King James and back to the cottage daily, and on nights when working split shift as night manager slept over at his mother's. Curranne kept the Blue Villa going for Ed and Ziggy, while Leopolda took wing and now gathers new leases for her London and Paris caves before wintering on Corfu. Ironically, the Institution cracked down on the halfway house only after season's end when the year-round folk complained of a strange eruption of standout nuts that threatened to go through the winter. But at his business manager's urging, Ed wrote his first letter home in a decade and found that he'd inherited his mother's house in Olean. Ed and Ziggy have lighted out to see about selling it and garnering Ed's windfall for a Dairy Queen franchise. Curranne soaked up her empty house, happy alone with the Jaspers next door. Loneliness was maple syrup. With the year rounding out, she felt a seasoned Chautauquan, her heart soft toward the great family of houses, the old trees, her whole body swelling to the deep tug of the lake in all weathers.

But fears bubble. Earlier husbands drifted away, through the pull of work, and now the young waitresses Jack manages tweak her jealousy. After a weak spat he agreed to move into her mother's with her, since Carol is a built-in baby-sitter. They might even see people again together. Working around ice cream and still vexed by not writing, he's put on weight, while she diets and exercises as if for both. She works up racy good looks and is at ease hauling Avon about in a sling (the first ever seen in baby-carriage King James) and feels above the waitresses when she stops by once a day or so for a free orange juice from Jack. What do these waitresses know about HP? Curranne's inner brightness at the dairy gives her skin a spearing high ruddiness. While Avon's drinking eyes attract *oohs* and *aahs,* Curranne is a cat at the cream. She's becoming a star.

Today she'll drive to North Warren to see Dr. David. She has two dreams for him. Strange how dreams rise from bottom darkness, cling like static to her waking mind, and await the descent of Dr. David before they burst into sense. Usually he ignores the dreams she tempts him with, and leans more on strengthening her grip on daily life. He's frank, since she's quite knowing. "If we take away your fear, you might fly apart. Look how well you've adjusted. Say we lift out the center pin, your fear of your father and abandonment. What will we replace it with?" "The Higher Power?" "Do you believe that?" "I'm working on it!" "I think you need a very strong belief first. Let's be patient." "Well, I'm bent on full recovery, Dr. David." "Wonderful!"

In the tub she's piqued by Ed's remark last summer that a Coke bottle is both a prick and a woman. Then she foresees her return from North Warren today and the refreshment of her orange juice at the end of Jack's noon rush. This pleasure brings to mind her rich hopes after Matthew was born and thoughts about raising the boy in an artistic household, the oils and watercolors she and Matt would sit for as they aged. Not one appeared, and after her breakdown she'd not the patience (and wouldn't have dared) to sit for a portrait, even if asked. Then Mark came, another breakdown, divorce. She'd reawakened in second marriage, longed for a television home diary starring her and the growing boys. But she'd never seen herself on a TV screen even once. Not up to facing a camera anyway (or had Ned spared her some harsh unveiling?), although she admired the vision of raising sons in Ned's TV uproar. She recalls her two days in a tub as a teenager, when Carol had lied to her about Ed's return. During that bath episode she'd come apart, her arms floating about the room looking for her father. Then her legs fell into pieces in the tub. Her floating head peered down at the parts. She has never dismissed this event. Each part of her in the tub pulsed with worthlessness, a wracking horror of bones unlocking, muscle bands slipping, her whole body unhinging, joint by joint. No escape, dismembered in a porcelain womb. Slowly the thought fades before her assured stardom in today's King James. So it's not Chicago or Manhattan or Cape Cod. It's *now,* with Slim Trueheart vividly worth being, admired, loved, distantly envied. Pleasure opens her, sweeping her limbs. She watches her breasts rise and nipples stiffen.

She soaps her brown-spreading rings, happy they aren't crinkly and used-looking. During the summer her whole case felt crinkly as used chamois. Now new capillaries flush rosily all over, reddening her breastbone and shoulders, patching her arms and flanks and cheekbones. All from running. Her gray-green eyes sometimes deepen to hazel. Funny the rubber body (or blown-up balloon) she'd felt she was when pregnant. Why should a dummy need dentistry? She's ended her dental work; now the *bill* is in massive decay. Some hopes are set aside. Ledger misplaced (!), she's resigned to poetry, at least for the next year, and will go back to subbing and sobbing (something she'd not told Jack about), if not into real estate with Carol. If her mother will have her. She notes a growing number of jerks on the street, a few faces from North Warren, and does not want to echo their loud derailed voices in supermarkets. Lessening what she's always expected of herself makes fuller recovery seem more possible. She's fishing for a cottage in one of the breezy country villages outside King James. Jack talks longingly of Manhattan, but thinks she's not up to it. He sees less and less reason to stay in King James, since Stella is selling her big rooming house and moving to Florida. Curranne sorts these cravings, soaps and fondles her womanshape breasts. So nice, alone in the house. Avon sunken to China in her crib downstairs. She feels muscular, focused, well-bound, lean, and aroused.

Carol cracks the door. "I'm leaving."

Curranne blushes violently, sitting up. "I thought you'd gone. Is Avon awake?"

"She's having a long talk with someone. I threw your togs in with her sheets and diapers. Will you put them into the dryer before you leave? If you have the time?"

"I don't know. I'll try. It depends."

"Try."

"I said I would."

"Are you fixing supper or should I?"

"Mother, I don't know. That's a *thousand* hours away. I haven't even had breakfast yet! Anyway, today is Jack's payday. If I can get to the bank with his dick, I mean his check, we may eat out."

"Then I'll hold off shopping."

Curranne sighs. "Stop pestering me."

"I'm not pestering. I'm trying to help."

"I can handle dinner. I'd like to be alone, if you don't mind."

"I don't mind. Give me a call if you decide to eat home."

"Get out!" Blood drains her head white as she gives Carol her stone-turning Medusa stare.

"I'm not *in.*"

"Then stop looking at me and close the door."

"As you wish. Enjoy yourself."

"I'm going to drown myself!"—both fists striking the water.

Her mother limps downstairs. Curranne stares red-faced at her hard nipples, sensing a panic that leaps back years, young Carol shaming her about fingering her crotch in the tub. Curranne stops soaping, rinses herself angrily. She loves a good lathery rub and quiet five minutes with her finger, though running has dimmed her once strong hunger for formal daily hand sex. Starting with soapy shoulders and arms, the full sculpting. She's mad with wonder (really pissed) that Carol doesn't see the star athlete she's become in rising above daily self-abuse. What does her mother think she did in all those hospitals? Prepare for the veil? For God's sake, even as a girl she'd never been *bad,* only stormy. Not immoral or a lying thief. But Carol thinks the worst of her. Curranne imagines herself as a very bad child. But there are no details, only shame for namelessly vile feelings. The rest is fog. Now what does her convert mother expect of her? Virgin births? She can never live up to that! Curranne wonders what she expects of herself, or how she'll fully divorce her finger, now that Jack's working. Maybe she'll have to get him to bed a half-hour earlier each night. She can't *not* wash her lips and nipples—and can't help her orgasms—she's going through hormonal changes, for God's sake! The lightest touch and a mild, mild pleasure hooks her and then the urge to give love freely to herself is too overwhelming to forbear. There's no injury. She's not cheating on Jack, it only makes her hungrier for him. It's even ego-building! she tells herself, drying off, giving pink face a detached smile before she turns from the mirror and digs herself dry. All right, maybe I was bad in my heart, a really bad child. Somewhere back then she'd turned off Carol, freezing herself into mortal sin, no rejoining possible for them. She hates being obliged by her mother's love. Such quicksand! I should have been a lesbian, we'd have got along much better. Somehow, her mother could have accepted that. It

would have hurt and terrifically cooled her but it was something Carol
might understand and, in a settled Curranne, even welcome.

There'd always been a sexual suggestion hanging over her athletic
skills. Sometimes she thought herself a lost butch. Too late now, but
the half-life of the dyke has its attractions. Not much is expected of
you, just basic give and take. She smiles at the thought that her high
school yearbook's desert island dreamgirl was secretly an unfledged
bull dyke. That desert island was a horrible forecast. How many years,
all told, has she lived outside society? Even so, a lesbian tag offers
specific self-naming to live by, a post in the fog. Strap on a dildo and
let her harsh rubber-man feelings out on a woman. She'd rather finger
herself than *take* such abuse. Imagining a warm and delicately loving
woman unfolding to her in bed sickens her. She has too much invested
in motherhood to idealize lesbians or to fear her strong interest in men
and fake a blissful indifference to males. Men are her staff, in every
way. She'd fail as a sobby little sex-object for a woman. She roughs up
Jack in bed at times, pinning him with her knees. She likes him fully
awake making love, not dreaming he's somewhere else. Hey! where are
you? I'm here too, remember? Not much love recently though, with
his tensions about managing the dairy while Wes Fulmer's off on vacation. Or is it something in her? All her womanly warmth comes from
being struck against flint. She has nothing to give a woman. It would
take a gray day in limbo for her to try. She feels acute distaste for
working the wiles of her tongue on a woman. She loves herself too
much to do that, give that much. I must be going sane, she laughs.

Brushes her reddish-blond mane and cinches it in her silver turquoise clasp. More gray? Jack might miss it among the blond. And
what does it matter? It's so dangerous, loving him! Her belly ripples
about what might happen if he loses interest or someone steals him
from her. She'll be sucked apart. No more Curranne, a ghost! *Love* is
courting suicide. How can she do it? Swaying, she grips the sink at her
madness. Much better to love some abstraction, her dead husband or
Marlon Brando, who can't shrink her to utter nothingness. In fact, is
Jack worth such a star, gray hairs notwithstanding? She dresses in a
brown turtleneck, a tan tweed suit, hose and pumps, her regular fall
analyst-going wear. It hypes the recovery self-image she's urging herself into. She surely doesn't ape waitresses; she apes Manhattan lady
analysts, their quiet British cuts, trim as an almond. Nobody's overlooking this Phi Bete—quality is all.

Dressing, she reruns her morning run for ideas on bettering her time. She sees herself pacing through Baker Park, down to Third Street Bridge, across to Armory Hill and the fort and up to Lincoln Junior High, once around the track, and then downhill to the bridge, across the huge sunstruck gorge with toy houses far below, electric plant and Chadakoin, uphill to Baker Park and home. She often walks up Armory Hill. Tomorrow she'll run the first half. She checks her mother's mirror before going down to breakfast. Human adult on mercury, gray-green eyes shimmering. Is this life?

"You're getting better and better, and pretty soon you're going to be unbearable, and then you're going to get better than that."

In her running, daily improvement is clear and measurable, weekly improvement dramatic. When she started she got winded halfway over the bridge and had to walk all the way to the cinder track. Two weeks ago she became disoriented and began running uplake to Chautauqua, begged a phone call at a Lakewood grocery and asked Carol to come and get her. Driving back she was more panicky than Carol. That was disheartening but that afternoon she walked the right course with Avon in her sling, and next day bettered all earlier runs, pacing perfectly. The run to Lakewood had been five miles and set her up for the much shorter round to the cinder track and back. At 8:30 A.M., returning from Lincoln, she really is a star, passing among schoolbound kids on the bridge or running against bridge traffic. She still has straight rippling legs, long flanks and balled calves, with few broken capillaries despite three pregnancies, and marvelous arches for fleetness. Only her bosom's lift and fall embarrasses her among schoolkids . . . some familiar faces she's taught (and cried over). Her hard stare freezes catcalls. She knows many men and women drivers (they're all Martians) go to work and mention her as a kind of morning show. Curranne is the only runner in King James. By now, the streets are real to her feet, the bricks, the asphalt waking before her in deep October morninglight. She is not from Mars. Of course, Nelson R. owns King James, and his agents tag her through every street and park. Even so, this spying is better than Manhattan's, where he's wired every brick and window. Does that billionaire fathead want to get his hands on her! Wiring bricks??—so stupid. And every window on the island. Christ, he's so rich he could wire the clouds, the moon —and maybe has! She can breathe in King James, though the move back from Chautauqua shocks her with fresh inward pressures. She'll get along—but behind her every thought, about Jack or Avon or a job, or even which heels to wear, she's alert to NR's eye in the woodwork, the whispered Hiya hanging in the air, his smile unseen behind her ear. She reads in the *Sun* about his big parties and art collection, a world staged to make her feel left out. She's not lonely! Still, she tells Jack nothing of all this. Nobody loves a brain-picked victim who has nothing left to love. How unhinged is she by these ever present eavesdroppers? There's no measuring. But she's fearless about keeping in shape—screw the spies. Flattens her turtleneck, inhaling, look at those monsters. A strain, this completely secret life, but it must stay hidden if she's to keep Jack.

She goes down, squeezes four oranges, drinks eight ounces of whole milk, packs Avon into "Broken Bucket" and starts for North Warren, singing. She sings past the secret camera planted in Johnny's Texas Hots, but her anger heaves as she spots it. This is not the kind of star she wants to be. The anger must be pressed down, not show for a second. Even a tiny bit can light the fuse that blows her to bits. Instead, she thinks gratefully about an iron bar on her Manhattan police lock and how she once doubled it over her knee. If she had it now she'd stop at Johnny's and give his hots a glass sauce, a little powdered window. Or in Brooklyn Square tie the bar into a loveknot for the hidden camera watching her leave town. Don't bug me, I'm Popeye and I eats me spinach! *"Chicago! Chicago! Wonderful town!"* she sings as she drives. It's her front—but they are *not* going to cut her up. She's got Jack. And moxie, as her father used to say. She lapses into space, typing a letter to the *Post-Journal,* denouncing Johnny's Texas Hots.

The star Curranne is becoming is Margaret Sullavan, another Irish Margaret as is Curranne. After the ruck of Chautauqua, and her return to regular analysis with Dr. David, she decided to give herself goals, look smart, and trim herself to Sullavan's image. Sullavan's much older but has had three kids and looks terrific. Curranne doesn't mimic Sullavan's cracked throaty voice (her actress sister Cornelle does that already), she's after her poise, well-to-do flirty blitheness, and show of biting into life by intensely mirroring her wavering lovers. Curranne longs to engage and love broadly. This big stride out of herself must be made if she's ever to sub again, and to demand more from life. What she admires is that Sullavan listens to others more intensely than any human being Curranne knows, then reacts with radiance and spirit. She's also a genius at tearjerking. Her sheer womanly force strikes Curranne as the deepest possible commitment to life and willingness to sacrifice herself to it. It's a great way to go, to die in Sullavan's wardrobe. In Sullavan's last picture she gave her husband to Viveca Lindfors and died of cancer. No sad songs for Maggie.

"I will never be poor and fat," she tells the rear-view mirror.

She has gone to many more A.A. meetings with Jack, hoping for the uplift of their Chautauqua group. The clubhouse meetings feel homey, and she enjoys Jack's laughter there. Two members are familiar North Warrenites, wired nuts who look sober and half-sane. Touched by HP? Many drunks are. Still, she is not a drunk and Jack's meetings are not feeling-strippers for her like the old group's. What she likes best is their intense grip on reality. These are the most real people in King James, and they accept her. They tap the Higher Power, without PHZ. A few standouts even have "star power"—a red-faced fireman with faroff eyes like Swedenborg's, an oxlike bus driver who speaks small smoky words that carry her upward, a violin teacher with six fingers on each hand who now has sparkling ease before pupils. Sometimes in the clubhouse she gets the sweet taste of real time, the Now, not schiz time or nerves juicy with tomorrow and obsessed with fears of the office party next New Year's. Some kind of eternity, each meeting a subtly unfolding rosette of the present. No one there is forcing or tricking her into an angry outburst. Her big fear is not of car accidents or cancer. It's that she will vent herself in the wrong place. Atomic anger in a kindergarten is a scene she replays all too often, to stomach-falling horror. She listens at A.A. with all her Sullavan deeps, the smile that goes to the heart of things.

Sullavan is deaf, almost completely. She's not made a film in nine years, and three years ago committed herself to a sanitarium. Now the gallant woman's on a stage comeback. Curranne's parting from Matthew and Mark puts her in Sullavan's league, she thinks, as a world-class sufferer who still puts on a blithe smile and listens with absolute concern. Her mirror smile trembling as her all-aware and pitying eye seeks out suffering, takes it into herself. Chin-high, reborn and deaf.

Curranne recalls early stardom as she drives. Walking on her hands for her father. Sighs at what life gave that little girl to hurdle. But then, on to middle age with Jack. Their fine country house when his book comes in, the fireplace, her wardrobe. Lives a passionate accomplishment. She ambles through the living room to phone her daughter, now married in Virginia, and sits on the satin sofa, giving advice into the ivory receiver, engaged in Avon's problems and high with grand good will—the very interest she missed as a daughter. Never had it but, by God, can't wait to overflow with motherly wit for Avon. This vision of wisdom and giving invades her head and shoulders and breath. Waves wet her eyes. She glances at the sleeping baby—too long —gravel hoarse under the tires until she recovers the road. Still big-hearted, she has so much to tell the doctor.

Curranne arrives early, to nurse and change Avon in the car, and rehearse what she will tell Dr. David. His house sits on an elm-lined side street now red and gold with falling leaves. Bloody maples scuttle and crunch underfoot in the glorious dead yard. Stand on the porch with baby, shield her from blowy grit. The doctor's Jamaican servant girl lets her into the small waiting room with its books and original paintings. Her nipples still swell and stick as she sits waiting, weakly aware that she is more than half-aroused. Her stiffly risen breasts in the bathtub still need to be spent . . . a need at odds with her mask-like smile as she waits. The mask she relaxes into is not the Curranne who burned with self-praise in her mother's mirror an hour ago. Her face is sleek and silken. Can't quite make out the words but surely she hears Dr. David laughing under his breath. Right through the wall, telling a male patient about her ungovernable lusts, her carbuncular clitoris at North Warren—*that was* Eugenia, *not me!* Wasn't it? Well, you can't tell a man anything. Even a doctor! Or especially. Men are so unreliable. So unfaithful. They just don't have a woman's powerful idealism or sense of sacrifice. She serves the nest while he goes off on his daily little business trip. Dr. David, it's clear, told her mother to spy on her through the bathroom door. Curranne decides to run again this afternoon and clear herself of all these lecturing psychotics she puts up with. The sweat and oxygen refresh and patch her up with blushing capillaries. She checks her hose. Droopy hose is such a give-away.

She sits now fully alert, sworn to her regimen. Emotions trickle down through her. Fixes her bangs, unfriendly to Dr. David already. He spends half of each session fishing for reasons to keep her coming back when she already feels healthy enough to break loose from him and spawn with HP. And how pleasant to wound him by not re-turning! Partly she returns so that Jack and Carol, who support her, will know the inner work she puts into recovery. But this too is a mask. She's quite strong. Simply running has given her a fresh wind and mental zip. She's flushed out her voices and hallucinations. Strange that her brilliance is invaded by mourning, a sense of tragic victimization always ready to sweep her into full atomic dispersal if even for one blink she's unwary. Warding off defeat is hard vigil. Being unrested and overtired is her worst enemy. Sleep is a rich buddy with plenty to spend on her: MOROCCAN PRINCE BAGS GLAMOROUS SCREWBALL. Partly she returns to Dr. David to sidestep despair, convince herself of her worth in seeing herself through times of "realistic" hopelessness. She must sleep for rest, not flight from herself. Losing consciousness to avoid pain is a little suicide. She does not come back to North Warren for the baby and to be a better mother. It's more a habit or recovery rhythm she thinks HP demands of her, as if going for vitamin shots or sunlamp treatments. This waiting room is *such a bore!* The impulse to leave has her on her feet just as the doctor's door opens and he escorts his patient to the front porch with a few jovial shafts into the blue. As if this stooge is really leaving!

What am I doing here? she cries to herself. THIS IS SO STUPID! If I say the wrong thing, he can commit me right up the hill. She's in a panic to defend herself.

"Well, my dear, how are you today?" Dr. David calls out. "You look splendid! And how are *you?*" he asks Avon. "I see. She's not talking yet?" Babies are rare beings to him.

"Ha ha, not quite yet, Dr. David!" Curranne listens intently to his heartbeat (she *thinks* it's his), whose nuances can give him away. "Not since our last session."

"Come in, come in, Mrs. Trueheart!" Without touching her, he ushers her to a chair by his desk. "Can I get you or the baby anything? A glass of milk, perhaps?" A glass for Avon? Weird idea! What would be in it?

"No, no." Curranne looks past him at the silver-blue aluminum heavens, knowing a huge pull toward a flagstoned patio and cocktails in Connecticut with Sullavan and her crowd. "I do have to go to the bathroom though. May I just lay the baby on the couch?" Slips off her sling.

"By heavens, she's an intelligent little creature," the doctor says.

"Oh, that's *your* brow."

Sits by Avon, studying her. "I see it!"—playing along?

The small smart bathroom is beside the office. As she empties herself swiftly, she hopes the doctor will not give Avon a secret injection of fluids he's drawn off from himself. She's not hoodwinked by his good cheer, though his magic is hard to resist. Their sessions are more like duels with mirrors than searches for cure. Was his earlier patient a cohort from the hospital, now waiting out front for him to send her back? Opening the bathroom door, she sneaks to the closed front door and glances out. The sky is unbearable, its suck upward. Desire to live overwhelms and stiffens her. With closed eyes she mouths a wordless garble of prayer. She listens to the Jamaican house girl in the kitchen, surely a ward nurse in disguise who knows all the holds. She's ready to burst out to the car but can't leave Avon, and with a barking wounded sigh returns to the office.

Seated silently beside the baby on his couch, Dr. David appears to be waiting for Avon to sing. He is lively and late middle-aged, white-haired; his eyes, an Olympian blue, swell in rimless glasses. A warm, high-minded face, mouth thin and voice crisp and Southern. Curranne has read a book of his on genius and creative intelligence and knows he is at work on an endless volume about what he calls metabiology. It has little to do, he says, with the nuts and bolts of schizophrenia and paranoia, but will bear witness to the martyrs of madness and divinity. She weighs his ongoing interest in her—is she a case for his book? How could that be? She's not dead. Does he need a dead female martyr?

"I didn't bring you any dead martyrs, uh, dreams." She holds Avon in her lap. "I mean dead dreams."

"I see. Have you been dreaming?" Dips his pen.

"I don't know."

"You don't know or don't remember?"

"I have a vivid imagination," Curranne says, biting her lip.

"What are you telling me?"

"Oh? My daydreams are much, much stronger than my sleep dreams. My sleep dreams are a relief. Going to bed is like having a beach holiday where you sleep under the stars."

"How interesting! You've never put it quite that way before. This is a great advance. It tells me a lot. Could you describe the difference a little more clearly?"

"I can guide my daydreams—if they don't run off with me! In my sleep dreams I'm the goat for anyone who wants to cut my throat," she says. "And goats are all throat. You know that?"

"Aren't they! How awful for you. But I should think that would be more discomforting than a daydream."

"No. In sleep dreams you've surrendered to your fate. In daydreams you struggle. The agony is . . . sometimes you're ready to go out the highest window."

"Could you give me a dream that's typical of each kind?"

"No." She looks at the baby. "Well, I'll try. Driving over here I daydreamed about what I was going to say in this session. I got so emotional I nearly drove off the road."

"Well, well! Were you thinking what an old bastard I am?"

Rises back, ready for any hard word.

"Ha! No. I had a lot of good things to tell you. I got very carried away by them."

"How splendid. But you must be very careful about daydreaming while driving."

"Well, Dr. David, that's a new warning. I'll remember it, if my mind permits."

"Please do. You have a wonderful mind."

"What?" Leaning toward him.

"I said you have a wonderful mind."

"I'm sorry. I seem to be going deaf in that ear."

"Perhaps you should have it looked at."

"Do you think so?" she asks. "How is your hearing?"

"Much better, thank you. I've been seeing a homeopath."

"A nature doctor!" she asks.

"He's worked wonders. I don't even need my hearing aid. And I've had Ménière's disease for two years."

"That's very impressive. I'm not worried about mine yet. I rather like it," Curranne says.

"You like partial deafness? My, my."

"Maybe it's from running. Maybe I've burst something. I'm not worried. Margaret Sullavan is deaf, but she's going back on stage."

"How very noble of her."

"She could flop. It must be a different world, acting as if you *actually* hear people," Curranne says. "But she knows what they're saying from the script."

"Amazing. You admire her greatly?"

"Well, having a script! Hey, what a way to live! She's my favorite."

"I see. What is it about her you admire? I'm not sure I follow you. Surely not her deafness."

"Her strength," Curranne says. "She's always rising above tragedy. Well, if you can call them tragedies. And her ability to listen. She listens harder than any actress on earth."

"Well, now she has to," he says.

"She has to go through a whole play acting as if she knows what people are saying to her and then reacting to them."

"You identify with that?"

Curranne nods. The sky, the sky!

Dr. David thinks this over. "That's quite moving," he says, dipping his pen. "You always surprise me. But you don't think going deaf will give a learning advantage, or strengthen you the way you think it does Margaret Sullavan? I can assure you from personal experience that being even half deaf is no advantage at all."

"It's not like that," Curranne says. "What I admire is her presence. She's really *there* every second."

"You mean fully involved?"

"Every second."

"And you aren't?"

"How could I be? I still get slugged with gaposis now and then."

"I see. Tell me about your sleep dreams," he says.

"I can't tell you. They're too dumb and depressing."

"Well. We can wait. Maybe we shouldn't bother anyway."

She looks at Avon, her little dream bank. "All right. I had several dreams last night. Jack and I were at the beach at Chautauqua. We were talking about getting health insurance. He was very upset, wondering where the payments would come from. He's never had insurance. This was a terrible argument. He had a big spoon or spatula. I was standing there frozen."

"You were cold?"

"No, I couldn't move. Jack had made me out of sand. Then the tide came in and I tipped over. Couldn't stand up any longer. Then he made me all over again. And I knew I couldn't stand and would fall over."

"How did Jack react?"

"Oh, he was relentless. He kept crying, *'You know me, I don't give a frig about money!'* I couldn't stand up for him. The last time he made me out of ice cream from the dairy where he works. With the spatula.

I was very cold and tried to stand up but I was leaking blood from my rectum and kept melting. It was an awful feeling."

"Melting?"

"While trying to stand up," she says. "I've felt that before!—only it was the floor and walls too."

"How did this make you feel about Jack?"

"I was tremendously disappointed in him that he didn't think enough of me to take out insurance. Not that we had the money! But we could have taken out a loan for the insurance. He didn't want to do even that. He has a horrid prejudice against insurance companies. He thought I was just projecting big fears at him. Of course I knew that he'd come around in the end. I guess there's no other way to live."

"You guess?" Dr. David asks.

"Pound would never bother with insurance. Meanwhile he was trying to have erotic contact with me but I was runny milk all over and too slippery for him to stay in me. And my rectum hurt. He got angrier and angrier until he was punching holes in me with a bottle. He didn't have a penis, he had a bottle."

"Well, well. What do you make of that?"

"Well, I thought maybe he wants to drink and he doesn't because of me."

"It was a whiskey bottle? A beer or wine bottle?"

"No, a Coke bottle. That's why I couldn't believe he was mad at me about alcohol. I think he was just infatuated with his bottle."

"Are you sure it was Jack then?"

A staticky stuffiness takes her breath away. Lungs humid with charged atoms. Looks out at the sky. Tension knots her stomach.

"Now I don't know. The last time he made me, out of ice cream, I was so frightened of failing him that I tried to run away but I couldn't move and just eroded into the sand. He was looking down at me, very angry as if ready to electrocute me. He was mad as Zeus in Walt Disney's *Fantasia*. Did you ever see that?"

"I believe I did. With Stokowski?"

"That was the last picture my father took the whole family to before he left for the North Atlantic with the merchant marine. I remember all five of us sitting there in a row. Zeus throwing thunderbolts in the Beethoven."

"Did that frighten you?"

"My father frightened me."

"How did he do that?"

"He looked like he was dead. A drowned body or corpse. Not obviously drowned but just bloodless."

"How old were you?"

"Fourteen. I'd just won a race that day. I'd got a blue ribbon and he took us to the movies to celebrate. I couldn't sit still and began crying because I couldn't sit next to him. He was on the aisle, to stretch his legs, and my mother sat next to him. I got so angry I began stamping my feet. Then he got so angry he leaned over and slapped my leg. Hard! So I threw a tantrum and had to be taken outdoors by him during the Pastoral Symphony. I was screaming that *I'd* won the ribbon and should sit next to him. So when we came back, my mother moved over and I got my way."

"Did that make you happy?"

"Not at all. That's when he looked dead. When we left he pretended I was invisible. I was so frightened by this that I wet my pants. He was past being dead. He wasn't even there—or I wasn't."

"I see. Well, we'll talk about this later."

"Do you believe in a bolt from the blue?" Curranne asks.

"A sudden thought or intuition? Of course I do."

"I don't think I mean that. Have you ever heard of ions collecting and attracting lightning on a perfectly clear day?"

"Well, I suppose it happens. Are you afraid of that happening?"

She looks at the pure blue sky. "It could happen today."

"What could happen?"

"I don't know. It's like I feel primed for a second treatment from HP."

"A second treatment?"

"I think I need another."

"Another what?"

"Laying on of hands."

He's silent. Quietly breathing, made of sand. He has all eternity.

"But now I'm afraid of it."

"Was that the end of your dream?"

"I've got to stand up for myself," Curranne says suddenly. "I can't be afraid."

"Good for you!"

"I'll bet St. Paul felt it in the air."

"Felt what?"

"The intuition. When he was Saul and became Paul. Maybe he knew all morning! One moment he was a raging Roman, and the next he was a Christian. The Higher Power must have emptied all of his bugs out at once. Spontaneous remission, wouldn't you say?"

"I wouldn't know," Dr. David says testily. "I don't read that part of the Bible. He might have been in a highly suggestible state. Do you think Saul was crazy?"

"Schizophrenic?" She shrugs. "The other Saul was. From your part of the Bible."

"He sounds clinical, yes. The one David played for? But he was never a Roman psychopath."

"Was *he* ever healed?" she asks.

"I don't remember." He's silent. "Shall we get back to your dream? Was that the end of it?"

"No. I was in a *paroxysm* of bodiless anxiety. Jack dug around in the sand looking for me. I was there somewhere but he couldn't find me. I could feel myself draining away into darkness through the sand."

"Well, maybe we shouldn't go on."

Curranne sighs hard. "It's just as well."

"Don't you feel well?"

"I don't want to offend you with my other dream."

"By heavens! We've come all this way into forbidden territory together and now you don't want to offend me. So you *do* think I'm an old bastard and sonofabitch?"

"I'm afraid if I tell you you won't want to see me again." Her eyes drip. She straightens against the high chair back, her cheeks running. "I'll be sent back!" she sobs.

"Sent back where?" Doctor David asks.

"Up the hill! To the wards!"

"For a mere dream?" he asks. "Never. Not for a dream, my dear woman. Anyway, I can't send you back, you know that. You'd have to commit yourself and you're not thinking of doing that. Are you, Curranne?"

"No!" she sobs. "I'm never going back! Ever."

"Good for you! I don't think you are either."

"Don't you?"

"Of course not. You're coming along splendidly. Your capacity for insight has improved a hundredfold since our first session."

She's silent, verging on her Medusa stare. "That's such a lie!" She turns in her seat, not facing him.

"I see I've offended you."

"When we first met I was immensely stronger than I am now. I could leap tall buildings. I was teaching! I felt permanently whole. And you think I have more insight than I ever did? Just let me go, if that's what you think. You think I can't feel . . . *things giving away?* I can't bear to listen to such a twisted misdiagnosis. *Just lies!* Pump, pump, pump the lies in! Give the poor cow all she'll hold! That's all you can do, isn't it? Why don't you tell me I'm hopeless and let me face the truth for one whole day? Can't you see how much the truth means to me?"

"My dear, I *know* you've improved a hundredfold. That little revelation tells me so. When I first met you a year ago, you were breaking down visibly session by session and couldn't admit it. Now you're knitting visibly, session by session, and can't admit it."

Curranne whispers, "Do you really think so?"

"I know so!" He berates himself. "I shouldn't have asked you about that dream. You warned me not to. I must listen to you very closely."

"Oh, Doctor, I had to tell you. I was going to pour out such awful happycrap all over you, that's what I planned, and keep the dreams to myself."

"That's quite normal, my dear."

"I was going to be so gay, like Margaret Sullavan. Quite blithe and above it all. You know, she committed herself three years ago."

"Really? No, I didn't."

"In Austen Riggs, up in Stockbridge."

"You know a lot about her."

"I had an acquaintance at Gallinger who was in Riggs with her."

"Margaret Sullavan is a schizophrenic?" he asks.

"I don't know. I think she was a hysteric."

"I see. Well, she was something or she wouldn't have been there. Is her deafness real or a hysterical condition? Sometimes we hide behind assumed physical defects, such as asthma or deafness."

"It's real to me, Doctor. I mean to her."

He blows at the ceiling. "I'm so piqued!" he cries. "I want you to tell me your terrible dream about me. It may have—" But he covers his mouth.

"I really shouldn't," Curranne says. "But I don't want to stay asleep."

"Asleep?"

"It could be a mistake. But I'd rather be wrong than stay asleep."

"Do you feel you're asleep, Curranne?"

"Not when I'm me. Anyway, dreams aren't sins! Yes, I'm asleep, right now! Can't you see it? I don't know anybody who isn't. People are big dolls that get up in the morning and walk around without the slightest idea they're . . . missing. Copulation's just rubber valves getting hot by friction. I don't see why they have to feel guilty about what they do to themselves. What does it matter what a doll does? On the wards all the dolls are dizzy or twisted . . . or *misted*. Where's the dollmaker gone? I don't know anybody who's awake. It would be amazing to wake up. But everyone's as asleep as I am. You talk to anyone more than five seconds and you see it. People asleep with their eyes open." She shakes both hands at the sky. *"Anything* can happen to *anybody*, Doctor!" Tapping her skull. "The ground open right up and down you go. Valve wear, a bearing giving out, aneurysm, stroke, schiz . . ." Her lip quivers. "Schizophrenia. Schiz, schiz, schiz. I had my first breakdown at eighteen, doctor! I'd give *anything* for five minutes of real life. *HP! Give me five bug-free minutes!*" She waits. "He must not think I'm worth it, Dr. David."

"You're His image."

"He's a woman!"

"Your mind, my dear. Everyone's mind. Consciousness is His mirror. He's looking at you through your consciousness and you're looking at Him. And when you're asleep, too. He has to rest, you know? That's when He goes back into His greater rhythm and refreshes Himself. Some mornings, don't you wake up feeling like a god?"

"Not until I stretch. And hit my second wind. Why would God want to live in dolls?"

"When you were a child you put your imagination into your dolls and enjoyed it, didn't you? Now you're older and you have to bear the tragic side as well. Only, if you're self-willed, arrogant and cut yourself off, He's powerless to help you. Without you He's weak as a worm! He needs all the spirit you can give Him. Your strong right arm." Not at all as detached as his words, the doctor speaks with such quiet force that he loses his voice. Quickly he takes out a handkerchief and tamps saliva from his chin. "Maybe I shouldn't be saying these things. You have my deepest sympathy. I know what you're feeling. And I know the spirit you're looking for."

"Thank you, Doctor. But I can't give Him my strong right arm. All too often I can't tell my right arm from my left arm. He never comes to North Warren, does He? Or I've never seen Him. We're cut off by something He can't reach through. But if He did come He'd blow all this mist away. It's not demons and swine, Doctor, it's mist. But you don't read that part of the book. Do you? Hey-y, He comes for the *drunks,* Doctor! Why should He come for the drunks and not for me?"

"I thought He had."

"Well, I need a second treatment. And now I *can't* tempt you with my dream!" she says. "It wouldn't be good for either of us. I don't think we'd find anything worth going over all that again."

"Going over all what again?" he asks.

She smiles, disbelieving Dr. David doesn't know her dream already. Doesn't he read her mind when she's asleep? Didn't he have carnal knowledge of her last winter while she was still pregnant? She's under his thumb, no argument. He's lord and master. Lets her out on a string to Jack. As his concubine she should surrender everything in her mind to him. He has full rights to her inner life.

"Is the girl listening?" she asks.

"What girl?"

She nods toward the door. "Marbella. You tell her everything, don't you?"

"Marbella's my maid. I doubt that she's read five books in her life. Why would I tell her anything?"

"Well, she'll have to go. I wish I had some sherry," Curranne says, unfolding some sheets from her purse. "Something to make it easier."

"Is that your dream?" He tries to turn away but his heart rate rises, as she hears. Her fingers in the papers seem to fondle him.

"I made some notes."

"May I see them? . . . Very interesting. It's in code?"

"This has to be! It's reverse shorthand I do with my hand mirror. I have to have some secrets. Even from you. Shall I read it?"

"Only if you feel up to it, my dear. If you feel at all upset, we'll stop. Go ahead."

"Don't worry, it's just a dream," she tells him. "I was twelve or thirteen and home alone after school. In my parents' bureau I found my father's bathing suit and jock strap. I was naked and put the strap on, looking at myself in my mother's shadowy vanity mirror. Then I stuffed the strap with handkerchiefs and walked around like a man. Then I stuffed a soda bottle in and that was exciting. Suddenly the bottle and the resistance of the elastic in the jock let me know what it felt like to have an erection."

"I follow you," he says. His hooded eyes half-lidded.

"Next I was still in my father's jock and waiting with Jack in your waiting room. My session was coming up. I could see Jack was uneasy because I didn't have a bra on. He wanted Marbella to serve him sherry. She brought him ginger beer instead. 'Does this have any alcohol in it?' he asked her. She didn't know but Jack and I could see that against the window light she didn't have a slip or panties on and was smiling at us provocatively. I think she wanted some kind of foursome. I was definitely not interested, so that wasn't important."

"I see. Why wasn't it important?"

"I'm not a lesbian. I have no leanings that way, Doctor. You must have called me in because I was sitting here in only that strap and nursing the baby. Through the wall I could hear Jack talking with Marbella. He was saying, 'Yes, psychoanalysis has had its heyday and is on its way out, but Dr. David is great in just being David.'" Curranne blushes boilingly and sits dry-mouthed. "You overheard this and had a ferocious smile, I mean some kind of enormous, mysterious pleasure, and then your eyes became green snaky slits and you went into a coma. You were sliding out of your chair with ecstasy or sublimity or something and I helped you onto the couch. And then you had an uncommonly tall erection, it wasn't human, and were in, hm, oh Christ, spiritual ecstasy while I masturbated you and Avon lay on the chair watching."

Dr. David writes furiously, catching up. His writing is as unreadable as Curranne's code.

"I can see why you didn't want to tell me!" he says. "This is a very important dream, I'm afraid. Don't you feel it? Thank you for telling me. You were carried away while you were speaking. So was I! What do you make of it? Was that all? How did you feel when you woke up?"

"I thought it was time I gave up breast-feeding."

"My, my! I'm not sure I see the connection."

"Well, if I hadn't been nursing in front of you, it would never have happened. And I do do that, you know. Maybe you think of it as provocative. Do you? You didn't seem shocked the first time I did it."

"Well, perhaps surprised, just a little. You're my first patient who nursed during a session. But it's perfectly natural and I've gotten used to it."

"Then you don't mind?" Curranne asks. "You don't think of it as provocative?"

"Not a bit. Do you?"

"I haven't decided. I could always express milk before I come and feed her from a bottle."

"It's up to you. Is that all that you think your dream is about?" he asks. "I really don't want to push you if you feel at all upset, my dear. But this has been a most unusual morning so far. Really a red-letter day."

"Well, it's not like our usual session where we play obvious games with mirrors. I say, 'I don't want to come anymore' and you say '*I* don't want to come anymore.' As if you had a choice! I mean this is your business. Boy, I envy you. Just sitting there listening and then running off to the bank. Do you have any sherry?"

"You're not drinking alcohol!"

"No! I don't feel well. I thought it might help."

"Would you like a glass of milk?" he asks.

"No, I'll wait."

"It's no trouble. I just have to buzz and Marbella will bring it."

"Well, all right. Thank you. I'm really thirsty. I've got this craving for liquids after I run. It's like a rage. I think I have to go to the bathroom again."

When Curranne returns a tall milk awaits her on the tray by her chair.

"Thank you." Drinks it off, her head tilting back.

"My, my! Let me order another!"

"No, thank you. My own milk is coming. I feel it. It shouldn't be, but it is. Or something is. Do you mind?"

"Of course not. Go right ahead. Nursing calms you, doesn't it?"

"Sort of. Sure. But this room feels like a bowl of static."

Actually her milk isn't flowing but she wants to show Dr. David her skillful mothering and the baby at her nipple. She lifts Avon, pulls up her brown turtleneck and unflaps her nursing bra.

"That's better," Curranne says. "I have to watch out that Jack doesn't attack me when I'm nursing."

The room is even more electric.

"I admire you greatly for the effort you've put into your recovery," he says. "You're a wonderful mother, I'm sure."

"I have moments when I hate it. But I do my best. My mother helps. I wish we had an arbor out back so I could sit in it with Avon." Curranne is in the arbor. He sees her drift right out of the room.

"It's rather blowy right now," he says.

Lazing backward, she sees leaves whipping under eager blue. "I love raking and burning leaves. Don't you?"

"That's quite beyond me. I haven't raked a leaf in sixty-five years. I have no abilities with my hands. Not that gardening wouldn't be a great joy to me. I dream of being able to drive a car, or to garden, or maybe even typewrite for myself. But that's what I have to pay for being me. It is exquisite torture! If I want to hear a symphony I have to ask Marbella to find it and put it on for me. It goes without saying, I can't cook. I do shave myself, but quite badly. I *can* find a book. But all told I'm a totally useless member of society. Except, of course, for one thing."

"Analysis?"

"Oh, heavens no! All that listening gave me Ménière's disease, made me quite unbalanced. Though I'm better now, thank you. *To be apart* is to suffer. Without relief. Without end. Do you follow me? Good. Do you still run daily?"

"I sure do. It helps me keep a grip on things. If I can run well and really give myself a workout, everything else is easier. I mean running is what I do absolutely best. I've won prizes for running. After I knock myself out running, anything else I do seems simple."

"You don't feel—well, eccentric—running on the streets?"

"I'm used to that. It's envy, all those housewives stuck in their stereotypes. Screw 'em! If they try to have me arrested, I'll sue. I know my rights. A lot of people would like to have me sent back. Or Avon."

"Avon?"

"Sent back," Curranne says. "They want to take her away from me because I'm a bad mother. I run on the streets. People don't know what to make of that. Some guy bugs me, I give him the finger. Bad Mother loves to run in the rain. That's my favorite running weather! I can double my distance. I put on Jack's oilskin jacket and take off.

There's no one out. The streets are deserted. I can run to my heart's content. But I keep waiting for the police to pick me up. I'm ready for 'em. They spy on me with cameras, but I know my Bill of Rights. They'll find they're picking on the wrong woman. It will cost them a *ton* of paper to keep me off the streets."

"But the rain, my dear! Aren't you afraid of catching cold?"

"Doctor, for God's sake! You don't know anything about it. I'm at my peak running. I couldn't catch a cold in the rain if I ran stark naked."

"Well, I hope you won't do that to prove it to me."

"My metabolic function is enormous. When I finish I glow like a stove. My chest, my whole body is pink. Rosy! New capillaries everywhere. You should see me, Doctor. Jack is amazed. He calls me Athena."

"I see. Wonderful. You're not afraid of becoming too muscular?"

"Too muscular? A woman? That's not possible, like a man getting too pregnant. I'm afraid of not losing fat. If I don't wear it off now, and readjust my metabolism, it'll be ten times harder later."

"But don't you need fat nursing?"

"Not this much!"

"But you're not fat at all."

"Oh yes I am. Look at this monster. You just can't see the rest of me. Besides, I'm giving up breast-feeding. That'll make Jack unhappy, but he'll like me slim too. Next spring you'll be calling me Slim Trueheart, ha ha ha!"

"Do you want to tell me any more about your dream last night? Aside from giving up nursing?"

"I suppose some of the people weren't who I thought they were," she says.

"How very interesting."

"You were my father. In my ice-cream dream my father had sodomized me sometime earlier and I was bleeding while Jack was trying to rebuild me and getting frustrated. In the second dream—the sex dream—I was Avon. Jock strap equals diaper. Avon had taken over my body with which to seduce you. And I was tempting you through my daughter to take away my bugs. I was trying to give her to you, as if she were your granddaughter by me. If you took away my bugs your granddaughter wouldn't have them either. It's so dumb, pinning down dreams."

". . . Go on."

"I wanted to offer myself both as mother and virgin."

"But the male athletic support . . ." the doctor says.

"That's only Athena the athlete. No matter how incestuous I was, I was also a superb athlete, should be forgiven and not sent back."

"Amazing. You see that right off."

"Why shouldn't I? Fifteen years on the couch?—I should have some power of intuition. Vague, maybe, but operating." She licks the last drop from her milk glass. "Don't you ever want to dream the things you can imagine while you're still awake? When I'm sickest, Doctor, daydreams are facts. More vivid than facts!"

"Was your sleeping dream last night a fact?"

"It was more powerful than fact. I've never experienced sucking a man the way I did in this dream. I couldn't have daydreamed or willed it because I didn't know it existed or could exist quite this way."

"I'm not sure," he says, "just what was so special about it? Was it the dream's feeling-tone?"

"Yes. I've left that out pretty much. Your eyes were snaky green, then you collapsed into a spiritual coma and I took advantage of you. It's as if you'd come home drunk and I'd sneaked into your bedroom and blew you. And you couldn't believe it, it was the most spiritual experience of your life. Like the incest of the gods. That seems to be how half of the Greek gods were born. I've known all about that since my earliest reading in Compton's Children's Encyclopedia. The Greeks really must have loved incest. And attributed it to their gods to justify their own acts, don't you think?"

"You really are a Ph.D., aren't you!" He laughs. "In spirit, if not fact."

"We can exchange Phi Bete keys, Dr. David. If we ever get romantic with each other." There's Margaret Sullavan!

"Thank you! I'll remember that. But I never accepted their invitation, my dear. I am a poor plebeian when it comes to fraternity keys. Before we end this session, have you left anything *more* out of that dream? It sort of *leaped* from masturbation to fellatio."

"It was like blowing God."

"*Well!* But I'm still a little confused by it. This dream has so many levels! Almost too many, as if there might be something simpler at the heart of it. What was your feeling when you woke up?"

"At first I was happy."

"About the dream?"

"No, to wake up. In my dream the penis was cold, like ice cream, and even though it was marble and Zeus-like, it was melting. Then my mouth suddenly filled with sherry. I despise that taste and couldn't swallow. I simply hadn't expected anything like that to happen. I mean warm sherry's not all that different from urine. I was gagging on it and there was no place to spit it out without Jack seeing and smelling it and knowing what I'd been doing. Sucking chromosomatic protein out of a cock. For rebuilding genes. I thought God's sperm would blow all my bugs out."

"*Unh!* Let me ask again. Was your father a drinker?"

"Only what you might expect from an Irish-American sailor with Welsh genes, Doctor."

"I see. Did it disturb the house?"

"It disturbed everything," Curranne says. "He was two fathers. One of them abandoned me. I mean us."

"I'm so sorry for you. But this has been the most extraordinary morning for me. I've never had a schizophrenic patient with your insight. You are very rare, my dear. Some doctors retire from practice never having had a patient of your caliber. You must tell John I think he's a most fortunate husband. I mean that most sincerely. Someone like you makes my efforts in this whole dismal field worthwhile. You really inspire me."

"Well! Thank you, I'll tell him. You're not going to send me back?"

"I know you're jesting."

"Did you read my paper?" she asks, hooking her bra flap over the popped nipple. The nipple spits static down her back and bottom.

"My heavens! We didn't get around to that. Most extraordinary. And here I meant to get to it first thing. But we got sidetracked, didn't we? Most wonderfully."

"Did you enjoy it?" she asks. "The paper?"

"Enjoy it? Well, yes, I didn't miss the artistic qualities. I was quite moved, my dear. Perhaps more than I should say. I was most interested by your description of rebirth. There is something absolutely convincing, really very fine indeed, about it, especially your physiological details in coming back to life. Of course, I've talked with John about it when he came in for his visit. But your viewpoint, waking up on that bench—for me it went beyond mere history of a psychotic episode. Or my offices as a doctor. We'll talk about it next time."

"Jack thinks it was a miracle."

"So you said. My dear, I look forward eagerly to our next session when we can discuss it. Now I must get a half-hour's rest before my next patient. And we have not got to the bottom of these dreams, I'm sure you realize. By heavens, we went way over today, didn't we? I must keep my eye on the clock with you or we'll talk for two hours. But then, this was the most valuable session we've had. I'm certain of that."

"Well, I still have my lapses."

"So have I!"

But when he rises, good cheer turns to purposeful impulse. Like a lover, he cannot stop himself. Looking down on Curranne in her chair, the baby in her lap, Curranne's naked face upturned to him, his hooded blue eyes suck the balled static from her stomach. It is like Jack's laying on of hands, but that Dr. David gulps her discharge into himself. She sits back suddenly as if on a live wire. Her windpipe sears, lungs gushing burnt air. Her nipples sting dizzyingly, but pain fades. It has happened!—his wondrous chair is *everything* she described to Jack last winter. Why had she been so fearful? The afterimage of a large near star lingers, blue and heavenly, in the tender deeps of an after-shower twilight. Then he slaps his palm, waking her.

Curranne rises in a room less vivid than the one she entered. Unlike his usual farewell at the closing screen door, he walks her and Avon onto the porch. With a start, she realizes that this is the first time she has ever seen him outdoors. The porch needs paint. The glory of the yard is dimmed. The leaves are plain and dusty. His face, shockingly close at her own level, smiles-and-does-not-smile directly at her. In his close-shaven cheeks, the set of his firm mouth, the light on his sharp temples and sheen of his tissues she reads supernatural wisdom set into human flesh.

"Thank you for everything, Dr. David," she says. He grips her from a distance. He never touches her, but is absolutely sure of her unfearfulness this once. So unwired, her rich white eyes. She nuzzles him swiftly before she can stop herself.

"Why, thank you, Curranne," he says. She takes his arm as she steps sideways down the porch stairs, looking carefully around the baby sling, and holds on through the leafy walk to the station wagon. He does not open the door for her.

"It looks a wreck but it's useful," she says.

Two minutes have passed since the ball of static left her stomach and lungs. She feels in her pumps the weight of her body and Avon. Half-lidded in the soft blow, her long fingers shielding Avon's eyes, she is whole. The madhouse sits on the hill. The world is undramatic. She cranks down the handle and lays Avon in her basket, then circles the wagon for flats.

"Talk about miracles!" she says, kicking the front left.

He hacks into his hand. "I seem to have burnt my throat." Then, as she rolls down her window to say goodbye, he turns about on his walk, his arms lifted forcefully, and shakes them at his maple.

"What a heaven-sent day!" he cries, half reeling, and wipes spittle from his chin. Leans down to the window. "And what a heaven-sent patient. Most fortuitous, our meeting. When I think of what one of my lamentable colleagues would make of you! I can't help but feel divine intervention at work. I'd swear you sprang from my own brow—a daughter!—that we're of the same blood. It's your intelligence. It's in your eyes—*the spirit.* You know I need you? Have a wonderful drive home, my dear. *Look at those clouds!* But no woolgathering, please. Leave that to me, and come back safely. I am sure you have a splendid future ahead of you. Goodbye, Princess Avon. Goodbye, Mrs. True-heart. I must go in now. Even this much heaven makes me giddy."

PART ELEVEN

Falling Star

S he drives back, breathing deeply of the greatest well-being of her womanhood. Noon treads on giant light over the Alleghenies. The sun soaks into October rust on the hills. The blue sky draws up memories of the wet blue of early Kodachromes of her many families. She has too many pasts. Stood squinting in too many Kodachromes at too many ages in too many hairstyles in too many bodies with too many families. Now they all go at once. The past fades, yearning for more purpose. For many minutes, driving, she floats on sensations of the now. She is Now. She trusts the wheel in her hands. The car feels faithful as never before. Her heart rises to the loyal hum of the motor. Her full tank gives bite to the tires. The needles assure her. She is not riding on empty.

Is all this the Higher Power?

Leopolda gazes at willow buds aglow in the rainy yard. "How can all that be a big lie?"

This world and car, body and baby, and mind? This must be HP. No romance, Curranne Trueheart, this is it. You've made it! Her spirit chokes her. She must hurry to Jack.

Sane at last, fear plucked out!

The sky is flush with invisible Being, the Ever-Arriving. It fills each nerve with an itch to be. Eternal light bears down, breathes its white heart into her core, its brilliance pulsing in her pulse. She is one with the hills and like the hills how much light can she hold, how hard burn? Great unseen hands pull her from a womb, she shudders at the first print of existence on her skin. Once more Dr. David slaps his palm. Her lungs gasp, flooding. She is tearful with shock. Memory loses its shadows, every crevice brightens with immanent victory. She is a new woman, ageless, with no hint of wilt. Illness dies from her eye before the Ever-Arriving. Her flesh, the bones grasping the wheel, are heavenmade, her mind His being. She stares as a virgin at the road ahead. She is an experiencing spark that knows it can never die.

High noon slowly closes its focus and dims. Only the highway lies brilliant before her, a tunnel of light she drives into. Avon, strapped into her seat crib, has begun to get carsick and bubble curds. Eyes on the road, Curranne strokes her. The baby sucks air, crying chokingly. Her heart leaping, Curranne just misses a gray-haired hitchhiker.

"Now, now . . . You'll be all right, Little Smarty."

But Avon cries wrackingly until Curranne pulls into a boarded-up Dairy Queen and fondles and burps her, then changes her diapers, and fondles her a bit more, chatting with her. The close hard light brings back her earliest Warner Brothers road movies. Her blood cancer is in remission, Margaret Sullavan will keep her husband and not die after all. The next thing she knows she is driving down the road and the seat crib is empty. Stabbed, Curranne pulls onto the shoulder and looks through the wagon, even dashing to the back door and lifting it. Turn around, speed back up the road, looking for Avon. She spots a county police car parked by the Dairy Queen and pulls in to report a kidnapping. That gray-haired hitchhiker? A lone traffic cop has Avon in his arm on his front seat and talks into his mike. Is this sunny dead Dairy Queen his outpost? Curranne at her wheel fights hysteria . . .

The trooper hooks his mike to the radio and gets out.

"Is this your child, ma'am?"

. . . nods dumbly, glancing up once, then not looking at him.

He says nothing, studying her.

"May I have her back?" she asks in a small voice.

"Are you all right, ma'am?"

"I think so. I'm better now, thank you."

"May I see your driver's license, please?"

"Certainly."

As she digs it out, he eyes the inside for a bottle and leans close to her window, sniffing.

"That's cologne," she whispers, half-strangling in her turtleneck. "Isn't it?"

She hands him her license and at last sees his strong-boned face and smoky gray-blue eyes. He's very young.

"Would you get out of your wagon, please, Mrs. Trueheart?"

Hair neat, suit trim, well shod, she stands beside "Broken Bucket," trembling for her baby. Her heart sucks her throat dry. Her calf muscles clench to keep her from fainting.

"What happened?" he asks, shifting the baby.

She smiles brilliantly, lips sealed. Truth chokes her breathless. She reaches for support to her open window, then snaps her arm back. "I went out of my mind!" Curranne says, nodding hard.

As he studies her license for violations and restrictions, her hands hunger for Avon. Her quivering legs turn to water. Does the license *say* she's mad? She's forgotten! At his silence she gags on fear. He watches her gag.

"Are you an outpatient of the mental hospital?"

Stares at him, her vocal cords ready to snap. Her toes cringe in her pumps. Now her mouth stiffens past any pretense of smiling. She locks her hands on her pelvis and stands fast for her sanity.

"I am a former lunatic. I was released."

"When?" he asks.

"Eighteen months ago. Though I went back this year to get my medication balanced."

"You're on medication now?"

"Yes. I'm sane today."

"You live in King James, I see." Shifts Avon as he reads. His eye is beyond appeal. "What were you doing in Warren?"

"I was visiting my doctor whom I see weekly. Apparently I was upset by my visit. Though I didn't think so at the time. I blacked out driving home."

"Thank you. Who is your doctor?"

Shaking hard, she gives Dr. David's name and address. Will he send her back? Daylight pierces her every sin. "Would you like his phone number?"

"Not yet. Please be calm. You're not the first person in or out of a blackout I've run into in this area."

"You mean mental patient?"

"Right."

She reads his smoky eyes for second meanings. His hard, bright youth is a legal mask. Which gate of the law does he guard? Child abandonment?

"How are you feeling now?"

"Much, much better. Thank you."

"Do you think you could drive home safely?"

Avon sucks the officer's badge.

"Yes!"

"Very good. What is Dr. David's phone number?"

She gives it to him. "He should be awake now."

Still holding Avon, he notes the number on a pad. "Awake?"

"He lay down to rest for a half hour when I left him."

"When did you leave him?"

"About twelve-thirty?" she asks.

"Well, it's five of one and you're only a few miles out of the city."

"Yes. I don't speed."

"May I ask what your child was doing here?"

"I stopped to change her diapers. Then I forgot to put her back in the car. It may have been my medication."

"But why did you take her out of the car to change her diapers?"

"I don't know. I suppose the crib was in the way and it was . . . easier? . . ." She waves at the stone stoop under a boarded door, where she must have changed the diapers. The stoop is grim with murder. "I really don't know."

"You weren't just abandoning her?"

"I would never abandon a child." She squints with quiet force. "I'm sure I blacked out."

"You're very sure, Mrs. Trueheart?"

"I blacked out. That's why I'm back here. How could I tell my husband that I'd abandoned our daughter at a Dairy Queen? Most lunatic Phi Betes can think better than that, Officer. If I may have my baby back, I promise . . . that"—her smile begs confidence—"I'll never go out of my mind again!"

His eyes tighten. He thinks twice, long and hard.

"I think that would be easiest on everybody," he says, and hands her the baby.

"Thank you!" she whispers. Her eyes well at the light piece of herself she'd lost. "What's your name?"

"Trooper Pierson, ma'am."

"Thank you. You're very kind. Do you have children?"

"Three."

"So have I."

They weigh their bond. His fearful eyes, the round stab of an angel.

"I do wish you well," she says.

Down the road she pulls off, shaking with delayed shock. Ahead, the gray hitchhiker she earlier just missed turns to eye the pulled-over station wagon. Wrinkles crinkling, he takes off his fancy fedora. She sees a huge sideswept frizz of curls, a small pointed beard. Intense slitted eyes feed on her. He wears a tattered GI overcoat, its collar up like a dandy's, baggy tan trousers and carpet slippers. His parted thin lips are mute. He looks like salt, age after age worked into his lines and creases, his skin unearthly as Methuselah's on his last day. *But you're in Pisa or Venice!* Straightening haughtily, he turns out a thumb by his coat pocket.

By King James Curranne is still too shaken to face Jack for lunch. She drives down to Steele Street, parks under Third Street Bridge and, Avon in her sling, walks under the span to the river. She gazes up the leaf-strewn slope of Armory Hill at the fort's solemn redbrick fantasy, then out at the gliding Chadakoin. Bridge pillars rise above, bracing the span. Their plain science and engineering intrigue her. She loves this bridge. Joining far-apart valley walls, it is King James's most fulfilling structure. Walking the span always calms her. Simply to be on it is to hang in a dream. Up there, there's no place in King James where the round sky offers greater deeps of blue or bloom of cloud. Or draws wonder from a farther earth-line. An aura of binding gritty miracle sits on real roofs and streets below, of an earth created and threaded by spiritual intelligence.

Suddenly she chokes. Someone will think she's going to throw Avon in the river and report her. Maybe they have already. She hurries back to the station wagon and drives home.

As she unlocks the empty house and goes in, the phone rings.

"Are you coming down?" Jack asks. "I'm ready for my lunch hour."

"I'll be right there. I'm walking," she says in a small voice.

"Is Avon asleep?"

"She says no."

"Well, if she starts crying in the store, it upsets me."

"I won't come if you don't want me to."

"Of course I want you to. That's why I'm phoning. Hey! I don't believe my eyes. Ed and Ziggy just walked in the front door."

"I'll take Avon into the cellar if she cries."

"What cellar?"

"I mean into the john," she says. He hangs up. She stands, phone frozen in hand, as her father walks down from the second floor. "Or on the roof," she tells the humming receiver. Trying to ride over cresting gooseflesh. Her father is four or five years younger than she is now. He's naked and staggering, his wee-wee wobbling stiffly. He comes into the front room, throws himself heavily into a stuffed chair, then runs the palps of his fingers over his arms and chest and thighs and, looking out at the street, begins stroking his wee-wee as if she's not there when he knows she is. After a moment he goes back to the stairs. Perhaps he doesn't want Carol to catch him disobeying her edict about walking around naked in a houseful of girls. She hears him flop onto the bed with a sigh that lifts through the house. Springs creak; fall silent; creak more. Curranne slips out of her sling, lays Avon on the couch, and on tiptoe mounts the stairs. The bedroom melts with oven heat. He is sunny with summer sweat, half out of it, his wee-wee lying nearly to his bellybutton. Sailorly underarm sourness reaches to the hallway. He's such a young man! She breaks into sweat. His rough, curly, beautiful ease and forbidden body, unbearable. She turns and sits on the top stair, rocking. Her head swells with hunger—but he's not himself. He's in the sick state the whole family hates and that he promises each of them he won't get into. Each has had a touch of him privately in this state. Even so, this is her great chance to displace Carol by leading him from his sick state. Curranne really does not want to win him like this when the bedroom reeks of armpit and wine and yeasty, sour father-crotch. Perhaps if she just lay beside him, stiff as wax, she would not have to sacrifice herself further. She rocks harder. If only he weren't so stinking when sick!

"Come on in, I won't bite," he calls out.

She lies fully dressed beside him, not having moved from the step. He has her in one arm but is quite still, his pores fruity as rotten rind.

"See? Isn't this fun? A little cuddle never hurt anyone." He turns her to him. "Sometimes when a daddy's at sea for months on end, he needs extra loving when he gets home." Bends her waxen fingers down to place them on his soft long wee-wee. "Just leave that there."

This come-on comes in woolly waves and grunts and rumbles from his mind, not his mouth. Slowly, the blood drains from his face, his sweat cools to a sheen, his hair curdles white before her eyes. His face is melting. His chin and mouth shrivel into rubbery folds. His jaw is gone. She stares at Ed.

"This bone is where you sprang from."

She drowns with unhappiness. Now she will have to take her mother's place and going gray with Ed face an eternity of housework. He's so unreliable! No joy in life will ever be possible for her with her mother's pisspot husband. Carol says he'd drink his own piss. More than once Curranne's watched him wee-wee off the back porch after dark, the family listening from the kitchen, Carol calling, "Curranne, come in here before you're arrested along with your father." Her vision of self-sacrifice stones her with panic past tears. She should never have married him!

Avon is sobbing. The phone, ringing. She awakes on the stairs.

"Hey, where are you? My lunch hour's half over."

"What? Who is this?"

"This is Jack!"

"How are you, Jack?" she asks timidly. Who's he in the yearbook?

"What?"

"How have you been?"

"How have I been? What's wrong with Avon?"

"She's sleeping just now. Why don't you call her later?"

"Sleeping! Curranne, just wait there. I'll be right home. Do you hear me? Just sit down and wait for me. Five minutes."

The line hums. She hangs up. Sits deaf as Sullavan to Avon's sobs. Sees a baby hand wave and clutch.

"Now, now, Smartypants, you'll learn," Curranne calls over. "I know that you want me to leave so that you can take care of your father. You must think I'm Bad Mother. Someday you'll know everything I've done for you. I'm here, right? Have I left? Am I sunning myself at North Warren? I am not. You're acting mighty peculiar for someone your age. What've you been up to, my dear?"

"What's going on? How are you?" Jack asks, panting, still in his long apron. "I just ran five blocks and I'm too fat."

"This young woman tried to run away. I was about to call the police. There isn't a thing I can do with her. Maybe she wants to join the beatniks, she hasn't an ounce of sense. Just temper, temper, temper. See if you can reason with her. I give up."

"You *did* see Dr. David today, didn't you?" Jack asks. Flushed and still panting, fingers sweat from his eyes. "Christ, now I know how you feel after thirty minutes on these hills."

"Of course I saw him. But he's forgotten all about it. You can phone him and ask. He won't remember it. I think he's going senile."

"Senile, huh?" Jack walks the baby, talking to her.

Over the sobbing Curranne says, "That's a form of dementia, you know!"

"He seems of sound mind to me."

"It's all a mask, Jack. Believe me, I know. I'll say no more. How was school today?"

"Work's fine. Say no more about what?"

"I can't imagine why you allow me to be alone with that old man."

"He's not so old," Jack says.

"He exposed himself to me today. Took *everything* right out. I was really shocked."

"Oh? You don't sound all that shocked."

She collapses onto an elbow, hands talking. "You think I should be in *high dudgeon?* I'm more mature than that. It's not as if I've never seen the works before."

"No, I'm sure it isn't. I'm glad you're so sensible. Maybe she's hungry."

"Jack, she wouldn't come in for her sandwich. Really, I've nothing left to give. I've given her everything I have. I'm spent. Mothers run out of gas like anyone else, you know."

"Well, maybe you should try. You must have some milk. You can't bring her down to the dairy if she's having a hunger fit, Curranne."

"She's not having a fit. Those are guilt pains. Maybe she'll remember what I'm worth the next time she tries to run away. About five more minutes of this, Little Sticky, and you'll be sent back."

Jack is thoughtful. She sounds about twenty-one, if not nineteen. "How would you like to rest this afternoon? Why don't we drive over to my mother's and leave *her* there with a bottle until I get out of work?"

"Does she know how to care for a baby?"

"Are you asking *me? I* don't remember. But I think she does."

"All right. She must know the basics. I need a little vacation. I think Eisenhower's getting on my nerves. Nixon too."

"That's too bad."

"They're just patting Rocky's hand until he takes over."

"You'll like a little time off. You have a lot of coping. You shouldn't work yourself to pieces."

Jack changes the baby and gathers diapers while Curranne presses milk into a boiled bottle.

Curranne sighs. "Somebody screamed at me on the street. Or on the highway. That was it."

"Who?"

"Some crazy hitchhiker this morning. Some jerk."

"Christ, I miss the group."

"Pretending to be Ezra Pound."

"Somebody from North Warren?"

"Oh, this guy was too far gone for North Warren. Wearing carpet slippers on the highway! I mean *really* bugs."

"It's saddening to hear. But they're actively crazy, and you're not. That's a blessing. So keep smiling."

She changes breasts. "I'm always smiling."

"You sure are. Laughing at depression is half the battle."

"Sometimes I just want out of it. Oblivion, ever heard of it?"

"I know all about oblivion." Jack phones his mother, then says, "Ready? Let's go, honey."

She stops in the doorway. "Did you bring the police with you?"

"Me? No. Why?"

She goes out with him. "I could walk through police fire anyway."

"Well, we shouldn't meet any." Jack hands her the baby and closes her car door. *The Red Shoes*—should he park her at the Wintergarden for the afternoon?

"Did you wash your check yet?" she asks. "Oh, shit!" she cries and opens her door. "I've got to switch the wash to the dryer. I promised my mother. Don't leave without me."

Jack sits crying in the car. Wipes his eyes, waiting for her. At last she gets in, slamming the door.

"Lock it." Hands her his check. "I couldn't get to the bank."

"Well, let's drive by. I'll run in."

Jack swallows hard, thinking. "Okay."

They drive silently. Abruptly her hand clasps his wrist, her thumb chafing it warmly. Partners, her thumb smiles, rain or shine. Her eyes are oystershell-white, slick, loamy with chest-thoughts. No schiz smile, mouth relaxed utterly. Has she sensed his tears? She looks ahead, her knees crooked and frame set with a womanliness that lifts him—even her bones make him mute. How many billions of women have had these bones? What perilous luck, what agony, to possess such a goddess-creature, her moods so winged, wise, faltering, rapid, threatening, secret. His eye catches the bank below through a cat's cradle of wires and traffic lamps. Jack turns down North Main in dread.

"I never blew Ezra Pound."

His nerves charge. "I never thought you did."

"I don't want you to have any dismal ideas about that."

"Never crossed my mind." Now it does, brilliantly. He grips himself. "I think of you growing. I have very positive feelings."

"Jack, I know when you're lying."

"You're doing fabulously. You have some bad days. That's natural, isn't it? But every day you're a little healthier, a little stronger, more self-composed. And some fine day—not so far off maybe—you'll be everything you want to be. Just keep your goal in mind and things will shift your way."

"HP, huh?"

"Sure."

"Dreamer." She gives a feeble little breath for HP, and ties it into a scornful little remark. "Of course, he wanted me to. He was quite disgusting. He stuck out his thumb in front of his pants."

Fist in her lap, thumb up. Her prick makes his scalp race.

"Pound? When did he do that?"

"This morning! He wanted me to pull off the road and just do it."

Jack signs his check at the red light. No place to double park in front of First National.

"I'll drive around the block and pick you up," he says. "I hope there's no line."

Curranne smiles from above. "There won't be."

She gets out and as Jack drives on, crosses the street to Kresge's Five-and-Ten and goes in to the toy counter. A colored counter doll in a copper beehive wig, her wig and brain storing waves from Buffalo, turns to her with charged eyes.

"How much is a baseball bat?" Curranne asks.

The girl leads her down the counter to shrinkwrapped plastic bats and balls. Her voice comes from a far bass speaker in a large hall. "These sets are three ninety-five."

"This is a toy. I want a real bat."

"Well, you hafta go to a sporting-goods store for that."

"I don't have time. The bank is going to close."

"I'm sorry. I can't help you."

"That's very clear." Leaving, Curranne eyes the copper beehive. "You should learn to relate to reality."

Since Jack will be back shortly, she gives up and goes into First National batless. She's no sooner inside than airless narrow walls close in and quietly choke her breathless. Philip Falcone, the fag druggist at

Jack's long ago *Hamlet* and sharp cheese, stands ahead of her in line. The line feels rigid with endless mannikins; she's instantly impatient with him and three customers ahead. Curranne turns and walks up to a swell-faced young fop at a desk, a man with droopy blond hair she deplores and sin-puffy eyes. Her chin juts manfully at him.

"I must see a swish banker," she announces.

"A what?" he asks, startled.

"A Swiss banker! I need immediate service. I am on a mission for Nelson Rockefeller."

"Governor Rockefeller?"

"He is waiting outside in a motorcade for me to cash this check."

"Good heavens," the young man says. Stands, glancing at the front windows. "Why doesn't he go to his own banks?"

"I don't know. But please cash this immediately or I shall raise a stink in this bank that won't air out for a month of Sundays."

"May I see it?—Are you Mrs. Trueheart?"

"I am." Digs out her wallet. "I have a baseball bat in my purse."

He tries to swallow a smile, which Curranne catches. She reddens.

"If you don't cash that check at once, I intend to strike with all the force at my command." She hefts her purse threateningly, eying each streetwindow.

"Well, I'm sorry. I'm afraid you'll have to wait in line, ma'am."

"I am Mrs. Rockefeller!"

"You're not Mrs. John Trueheart?"

"Are you trying to tell me I don't know who I am?" She glitters, moving past his desk toward the window beside it.

"No, no, I'm sure you know who you are," he says loudly. Backs away, scared of a nut, waving for the elderly guard up front. She looks at the old man hurrying toward them, and laughs.

"Ohh, you pisspot, ha ha ha! You prissy little ninny—you're going to hide behind that old man?"

Curranne's shoulder bag swings overhead, flies, bounces off the heavy glass. The bank goes silent. Suddenly Philip Falcone stands beside her.

"How are you today, Mrs. Chaplin? I'm next in line at the second teller. Why don't you take my place?"

"Thank you, I will!"

"You seem to have dropped your bag," Falcone says, taking it from the guard. Hands it to her. As he walks her to his line, a lone woman steps aside, saying, "Go right ahead." Curranne marches up to the teller, Philip at her side. Shoves check and wallet under the grill.

"I won't need that." The woman teller quickly shoves back the wallet. Counts out bills.

Philip does not wait but walks Curranne to the front door, where the young man talks with the white-eyed old guard. He turns to her nervously.

"Good day, Mrs. *Chaplin.*"

"Mrs. John Chaplin Trueheart Rockefeller," she corrects and goes out to the waiting car.

"Good to see you," Jack tells Philip.

"I'm very happy to see you and your lovely bride," Philip says. "And your beautiful daughter. See you at the clubhouse tonight?"

"Heck, yes," Jack says. "I need a meeting. Christ, you're looking great."

"I feel five years younger since January first," Philip Falcone says. "Cheers."

"Cheers," Jack says, driving off. "God, I like him. He came into the Program same day as me. We'll share our First Birthday together on New Year's Day."

"Doesn't he know we're married?"

"The fog doesn't lift overnight."

She hands him the bills. "Was I long?"

"Not at all. Any problems?"

"No. Philip gave me his place in line."

"Well, that was nice of him!"

"HP?" Curranne suggests. Smoothing her skirt. "Grows little miracles where you need 'em."

"Big ones too."

Jack turns up to his mother's on Rose Alley and parks.

"I hope Stella doesn't mind," Curranne says, brushing and reclasping her hair. Touches up her mouth.

"Oh no. She's happy to be asked."

"This is the first time. Tell her we won't make a habit of it."

Curranne carries Avon while Jack brings the big baby basket from the wagon's cabin. Curranne checks Avon to make sure her wings are well-hidden, if not fully drawn into her back. One afternoon last week, after her nap, Curranne was staggered to find the baby in the next bedroom. Had this completely unfamiliar being flown in the window?

Only when her overfull breasts throbbed did she divine Avon was hers. Or possibly hers. Who was its father? Such a slamming depression, to find herself saddled forever with a strange child. In a snap! Puffy from tears, she said nothing to Jack and then Carol came home and treated the baby as a creature natural to the house. So Curranne accepts her motherhood while reviewing possible fathers. Only yesterday did she agree that Jack Trueheart, who works long hours and is hippity-hop when not sexless in bed, is the lawful father. Undrugged and overly sensitive, he sighs that she's too sexy and beautiful for an assistant soda-fountain manager. She misses *any* joke about this, with her energies risen mercilessly from running and exercise. Hormonal overflow is one more weight—along with renewed motherhood, a lecherous father, Dr. David and dirty old Pound—she must bear under HP's fierce vexation with her.

"We're lucky we weren't given a pig," she tells Jack.

Jack opens the porch door. "A pig?"

"You know, the Duchess's baby in *Alice*. I can't *read* that book!"

She eyes Jack, his hair fallen, blood high, and reads his unwary love for her. No matter his hanging hair and disorders, when she least expects it, his tireless helping hand and unwearying earnestness for her well-being do break through her fears and find their own way to move her. Her Jack could save the earth itself from acts of God or, given the need, atomic warfare. She's never seen him do it but he leaps over houses, as he quite likely did today hurrying home to her from the fountain. Once more, as after the bath this morning, a spark in her rises to him. He is so male and whole. No abstraction! This pull toward a real person is such a risk (but she's pulled into it daily) and surrender so damaging should he be driven off by her quirks, that fear keeps her just this side of turning into gas, drifting off into particles. Only below words do the habit of daily surrender and the power of love invade and grip and rebind the particles back into her original spark of being. At moments—on a day her PHZ level has popped the distorting bubble around her, and the real and unreal are not washing together into a new actuality, say when she may be taking down fall blankets for their bed, or wavering half asleep on the steeps of Armory Hill with Avon beside her—the feelings she and Jack have traded and built up over the past eighteen months destroy her with grieving tenderness for that very hour not shared. She has lost so many hours, or had so few sane ones. Her waking, long-delayed first love for Jack overlaps a backed-up crush of feelings about child-sharing, homemaking, bodily rapture, and being each other's best friend, as well as more nameless soul ties. All these breathe and boil about in a rage for release and speech, while fear warns her of their power to vaporize her. But now she sniffs the small vacation of the afternoon ahead—it's spring in October! Her sense of eternal support from Jack gives her courage. She wants to *spend feelings.* Today. She's ready to turn and run downtown, *now.*

They go into the rose-papered living room, with the basket and baby like offerings. Jack feels a lift at Curranne's brushed hair and trim brown outfit, her rising glow.

"Well, look who's here!" Stella cries, hands on hips and rocking half comically. "This little person hasn't been to visit me in nearly two weeks. My God, I think she's grown."

Jack is suddenly aware that he's still in his stained sandwich-board apron.

"She'll be no trouble." Curranne holds up the bottle. "I'll put this in the icebox. You don't have to heat it when she wants it."

"I don't?"

"She'll drink it straight from the fridge, Stella. Warm milk is a myth," Curranne says.

"Well, I don't mind heating it," Stella says as Curranne goes into the kitchen. She looks at Jack meaningfully. *Is she off again?*

"She's all right," Jack mutters.

"You shouldn't wear that apron on the street—*ugh!!* What's wrong with your eyes? They're swollen."

"Hay fever," Jack husks—but she doesn't believe him.

Curranne returns. "If you're going to watch television, take her out of the living room. The cathode rays give rashes."

"I didn't know that," Stella says. "Is this something new?"

"I think she's very susceptible. In fact, I'm sure of it. That's the only explanation."

"Avon has a rash?"

"It hasn't shown up yet. But my mother turned on the set last night before we could get out of the room. It may have altered her mind. She may want to kill us."

"Your mother?" Stella asks, shocked. "I wouldn't think that of Carol."

"Not Carol, Avon," Curranne says. Jack looks away from her. "She was very naughty this morning. She nearly gave me a heart attack."

"Good heavens," Stella says.

"She tried to run away from home."

Jack walks to a french window and looks out at the finely raked brown lawn, his back to the talk.

"You're not suggesting that I'll have to chase her down the street?"

Curranne sighs. "That wouldn't help."

"Why not?"

"She has wings."

"Wings?"

"She just disappears." Snaps her thumb. "One moment you're holding her and the next she's gone. Crib and all."

Jack says hoarsely, "What should Mother do then?"

"She'll show up. Or if she's really naughty and is gone too long, well, call the police. They're used to her antics. I had the county troopers out after her this morning. They're very helpful. Actually, quite kind. But probably none of this will happen." Bends over the crib. Avon looks at her intently. Behind the baby's still smile the mouth muscles slowly spasm as if suckling. *"Will it?* You've got to be better, haven't you? Your very best for Grandmother Stella."

Stella watches heavy snowfall fill her living-room roses.

"I need some water," Jack croaks and goes into the kitchen. He runs cold water, grips the sink with both hands. Eyes shut, his face ripples like the baby's. He hears his mad wife dialing the living-room phone. Stella comes into the kitchen. Jack stiffens, red and breathless, unable to lift his filled glass.

"My son, I can't help myself. You deserve better!"

"I have the best," Jack says. "You don't know her."

"Oh my God. I can hear with my own ears, can't I?"

"But you can't hear with my ears." He hears Curranne shut herself into the hallway bathroom. "When she's logical she's very wise indeed. She's the wisest woman I've ever met."

"Well, maybe she's too smart."

Jack shrugs. "May well be."

"I know you're very bright, John. But are you trying to tell me she's not out of her mind?"

"Sure she is, off and on. But I live with her. When she's okay, she's everything I could want. More than everything! There *are* islands, you know, where she's almost sane. I mean it's like paradise at my finger-tips! . . ." He turns, sobbing, and splashes himself violently from the tap. Catching his breath as he hears the far bathroom open. "I *have* to let her make mistakes and learn. I can't undermine her with advice. None unless she asks for it."

"I think she's beyond advice."

"So am I," Jack says. "I live one hour at a time. I can manage that much. Just about."

He finds Curranne in half-collapse on the couch, hands cupped between splayed knee bones. Her eyes are dead celluloid in a doll's head. Her mortality—all that spirit stilled to plaster and celluloid—knifes him. He sits by her, waking her hand.

"Through?" she asks.

Jack blushes. "How was the doctor?"

"Had a patient. I'll call him later. I charged it to our phone."

"Well, you didn't have to," Stella says.

"Thank you very much," Jack tells her. Looks down at his mother-offending outfit. Would Hemingway be seen running the streets in a tomato-stained apron? "I know you have work to do. I'll pick her up right after I get out."

"Don't fret one minute. I'll take care of that little lady as if she were queen of England."

Curranne smiles wordlessly. Avon sneezes. "Maybe there's too much carpet dust in here," Curranne says.

"That's not very likely," Stella says.

"I wasn't thinking," Curranne says.

"Maybe you need a rest," Stella says.

Curranne turns toward her free afternoon. "What I need is a good run."

Stella tries hopelessly to hide her dismay at her daughter-in-law's enthusiasms. She's driven past her accidentally, more than once, on the bridge or by Baker Park, and had to pull over in a burning blush. Clearly even binding wouldn't stop that flapping and flopping.

"See you later," Jack tells Avon.

"Alligator," Curranne chimes, with a little growl. "My God, I'm hungry! I can't even think. Let's go." She bats his shoulder with buoyant whimsical arrogance. Dressed like this, Stella thinks, she doesn't look a bit eccentric.

Curranne smiles to herself as Jack parks outside the dairy. Even wolf-cheeked, she looks sleek and bright to him. Reddish-blond hair foxy with womanly cunning, eyes zingy and gay. She jumps out of "Broken Bucket" and stands straight as a bowstring in chill sunlight. She squints in the October blowiness, stretching and pulling as if for a run. In the blue shine and clouds of the dairy window, her eager glance catches Jack's face plunged into the street and sidewalk. Curranne has already decided—on the short ride down—to lock into her good feelings and leave Jack and Fulmer's (as much for his sake as hers) for Dr. David's in Warren. It's a choice so right she wants to burst. *Chicago! Chicago!* After all these years, to plug straight into HP. Super, man.

Ed and Ziggy wait in the round booth at the back, joined by Jack's old friend Frank Brinks. Frank and Jack were soda jerks at Fulmer's fifteen years ago. Since then Frank's been hospitalized twice at North Warren, and married twice. His second wife, Beverly, was a patient he met there in his Jesus phase. "I wasn't a religious Jesus," he explains, "I just liked wearing the bedsheet." Their first two children were put up for adoption, at Beverly's urging. Beverly's now heavy with child again. With the death of his mother, he has come into forty thousand dollars—"A fortune in King James!" he assures his mad wife—quit his chores as a social worker and bought a rambling manse on Swede Hill. Since blooming with money, he's grown into a rambling manse himself, on time-release phenothiazine shots and an enlarging gorge. He's sharp as a playboy today, in a blue pinstripe and robin's-egg homburg. He loves its high crown and stiff curled brim, its blue Easter brilliance. "Matches my eyes, don'tcha think?" he asks, blinking his Dutch blues. Jack thinks Frank is one of the wonders of research, a madman who conducts himself with the aplomb of sanity while happy as a child. He is aglow at Jack's return with his knockout cuckoo wife.

"Hi!" Curranne says to all. "What a bunch of ugly mugs. Shove over!"

"We don't mind, Curranne," Frank says.

"Don't mind?"

"Join us!" Frank says loudly. "Ours is an assembly of Rockefellers."

She eyes Ed and Ziggy. "Will you look what the cat dragged in? How are you bums?"

"We're not bums!" Ziggy cries. "Never have been, never will be."

"We're socking Elsie the Cow where it hurts," Ed says.

"That would be the udder," Frank says. "I don't see the significance."

"Borden's trademark," Ed says. *"We're* going with Dairy Queen."

"You look wonderful!" Curranne says. "New duds, huh?"

"A few threads from *Esquire,"* Ziggy says.

"I haven't seen these two guys since I left North Warren six years ago," Frank says. "That hospital, so boring—it was like Cleveland with water around it. And now here they are. Just back from Olean, independently wealthy, and ready to go into business. And they're friends of you and Jack! It's a small world, as we say in 'The Twilight Zone.' They were just telling me about their wonderful educational summer at Chautauqua. I didn't know you'd all had a *villa* up there! I'm amazed. I'm thunderstruck. And I haven't had a beer. Good to see you. How's the baby?"

"She's running away from home already," Curranne says. "I have to keep a sharp eye on her."

"Wow," Frank says. "Our latest is trying to kick loose too."

"Prenatally?" Jack asks.

Frank sighs dramatically. "I fear she takes after me already."

"She?" Curranne asks. "You know?"

"We're *hoping* for a girl this time. Beverly picks up signals from Venus, by way of our new microwave oven. There's not much question it's a girl. The signal's so strong it cuts right through her meds." Motions to the waitress. "Are you eating, gents? Curranne? What'll you have? On me, you're all my guests, here in little old Vienna. You look like something out of the movies, Curranne. Motherhood really agrees with you."

"Well, I run."

"Run? You mean like jog?"

"A little harder than that. I couldn't work up a real sweat anymore jogging."

"I'm very impressed. Maybe I'll take it up next spring. Perhaps." Frank studies the menu. "Today is not a good day."

She eyes the *Esquire* duo (though Frank is massively well-trimmed himself). "How're you guys? What's happening?"

Natty Ed sucks an unlighted cigar. Ziggy has a burgundy silk rising from his vest and bulky brown fuzz suit. Jack rejoins the table, hair drenched and combed, as the waitress arrives. She's in her early twenties, older than the other girls and fuller-figured in her blue uniform.

She's Becky Normstrand, and her jokes make Jack blush. Ed and Ziggy quietly shrink away from her.

"What'll ya have?" she asks.

Curranne throws herself back. "I'd *like* raw beets and carrots with some raisins thrown in."

"Hey, Curranne, the *ge*vegetable stand's on the corner," Becky says, with a laugh. She never inquires about the baby.

"Maybe I'll have a liquid lunch. I'll start with a large orange juice, please."

"That's not enough," Frank says. "You gotta have *food*, Curranne. What star-worthy dish is on this menu, Jack?"

"Maybe I'll have a sliced tomato with it. Thank you, Becky."

"Don't thank me, thank Wes Fulmer," Becky says. "He started this zit factory."

"Where *is* old Wes?" Frank asks.

"On vacation in Canada," Jack says. "Took his whole family and left me to whip the help into shape."

"Ha!" Becky cries. "Is that your big dream? Thanks for the tip. Are you eating or just renting the napkin?"

"Melted cheese with bacon and a lime phosphate," Jack says. "And a scoop of vanilla, plain."

"Now that's real food," Frank tells Curranne. "Have some topping, Jack, it's on me."

"It's my lunch, Frank. It's free."

"That's too bad. I hate to see you *deny* yourself, Jack. What'll you tycoons have?"

"Double cherry Coke," Ziggy says. "With a squirt of phosphate and heavy on the cherry. And a ham on rye with pickle and tomato."

"How about some lettuce too?" Frank says.

"Yeah, lettuce. And toast it."

"Hey, man, we don't toast lettuce," Becky says.

Ziggy shrivels. Why did he ask for toasted lettuce?

"This gentleman would like the rye bread toasted," Frank explains. "Mayo, Ziggy?"

Ziggy shakes no.

"Of course he wants mayo," Frank says. "And butter. Marvelous. Ed, eat up. I'm buying."

"Yeah!" Ed nods to Becky.

"Yeah, what?" she asks.

"He'll have the same, right, Ed?" Frank says. "I read minds."

"You can have my job if you want it," Becky tells Frank.

"No, no. I'm in temporary retirement, my dear. Don't you see my hat?" Flicks the blue beauty. "Is this a businessman's *chapeau?*"

"You look rather young to be retired," Becky says. "What did you used to sell?"

"I sold faith in the system." Frank laughs *hoo! hoo! hoo!* deep and happy, a Halloween pumpkin. "I sold a little piece of blue sky to folks on welfare. And a mere fifteen years ago I used to work in this very store. While you were still sitting in your red wagon. Jack and I stood side by side packing bulk until our arms ached and our knuckles were skinned bloody. And now Jack has worked his way up to store manager—"

"In only fifteen years," Becky says.

"That's excellent," Ziggy whispers.

"It's the American way," Ed says.

"That's right," Ziggy says. "Shows it can be done."

"It's never too late in the dairy business," Ed says. "Milk is a steady seller. It's like an economy outside the economy."

"By heaven, I am astounded at your grasp of the American business ethic," Frank says. He tells Becky, "Do you realize that these two well-dressed tycoons are themselves entering the ice-cream business?"

Ziggy spreads a piano run, sagely settling the world's problems. Blushing, Ed ducks his chin and flashes a satyr glint.

"They may have a place for you," Frank says.

"Come back when you're ready to open. What'll you have, Nelson?"

"Frank," Frank says.

"Oh, I thought you were the Governor."

"No, I'm Frank Brinks. I'm sad to say that Governor Rockefeller couldn't make this august gathering. I am his brother, known as Half-Nelson, because I'm only half here half the time. Or am I Quarter-Nelson? My dear, I'll have two scoops of walnut chip in a pool of hot butterscotch—extra topping, please. Money is no object. Add some walnuts." Raps the table. "Let's not stint on a day like this!"

"Who'd you rob?" she asks, and hips off.

"A noble Amazon," Frank says. "Well, Your Eminence, how are you?"

"Plugging along," Jack says. "How are you?"

"Fine, fine. I'm feeling fine, Jack. Like Pierre in *War and Peace.* He inherited a third of the wealth of Russia," Frank tells Ziggy.

.Ziggy is not cowed. Ed absorbs Pierre's third with ease.

"For a buggy King James musician, a bit of fantasy on a Tolstoyan scale. Right, Jack?" Frank asks.

"Life imitates art."

"Well, I didn't inherit a third of Russia. How's your writing?"

"I've got some ideas."

"You always did. Do you know," Frank tells Curranne, "when we used to close this store on Saturday nights, Jack would bring his trumpet and I'd have my tenor and we'd blow in here until the wee hours. We saw many a dawn through that front window. When the police would knock on the door with complaints, we'd feed them big buckets of sundaes drooling with sauce and covered with a half pound of pecans. Those were the days, Jack."

"I was a lot sadder then than I am now," Jack says. "Not that I didn't enjoy them."

"You'll just have to make do with the dregs," Curranne says. A little joke; she's already half sad at leaving Fulmer's for staid North Warren. She likes the dairy—and so, often knocks it since *she,* worthless woman, likes it. Now that she's leaving, her true feelings rise free. Yes, she's half in love with the dairy. More than half!

Frank asks Jack, "Have these two fortune hunters told you about their prospects?"

"What are you up to?" Jack asks Ed.

"We're holding our own," Ed says.

"We've taken options on three Dairy Queen franchises," Ziggy says.

"Not one—*three!*" Frank cries. Rubs his palms in glee.

"Do you have the money?" Jack asks.

"Options aren't much," Ed says. "They're just to hold the franchises while Dairy Queen looks into our background."

"That's it," Ziggy says. "All we need is a business manager for front."

"While we bring in the backup cash," Ed says. "This is just a beginning. First we get these three off the ground, then we expand."

"But how are you going to buy equipment?" Jack asks.

"We don't care about equipment," Ed says. "Dairy Queen supplies that. We're not actually going to open these pig troughs."

"Nah," Ziggy says. "That's for dumb fruits."

"Courteous countermen." Ed sneers.

Jack blushes.

"That's beneath us," Ziggy says.

"We're going to lock up options and then broker the options ourselves," Ed says. "At a sweet little profit."

"Very sweet," Ziggy assures Jack. "That's why we need a front man who looks like he knows the ice cream business and could actually run a Dairy Queen."

"Yeah, it's like Leopolda with her apartments," Ed says. "Once we have the franchises, we sublet."

"And never get our fingers dirty," Ziggy says.

"You wouldn't want any spots on that suit," Frank agrees.

"Never touch ice cream," Ed warns.

"Why not?" Curranne asks.

"Oh, it carries terrible plagues," Ed says.

"Well, not if it's pasteurized," she says.

"Pasteurized ice cream isn't fit for dogs," Ed says. "I would only eat real ice cream. But most of that is filled with typhoid. Ice cream is for mo-norons."

"Morons," Ziggy says.

"Typhoid?" Frank asks.

"It's in the bubbles," Ed explains. "That's where the bugs incubate. My mother used to work in a dairy when I was a kid. I know all about it."

"Are these options legal?" Jack asks.

"Sure they're legal," Ed says. "We're buying up leases. We've already locked up Chautauqua Lake. We've got options on the Bemus Point, Celeron and Lakewood franchises. No competition. That's all the franchises Dairy Queen will allow in this area for five years. That's why we need you for a partner and front. We don't want to face the public ourselves."

"Or the business community," Ziggy says. "We can't stand much investigation."

"You are the front and we are your silent backers," Ed says. "You have the expertise and I put the cash into your bank account. They investigate you, not us."

"What! No, no," Jack says. "I can't even think of this. Anyway, you two guys have the options, I don't. They'd smell something dirty."

"No problem," Ed says.

"You wouldn't even have to leave your job here," Ziggy says. "This is all taking place on paper."

"You don't actually *do* anything," Ed says. "This is big finance, Jack. Money doesn't enter into it. It's all credit."

Ziggy says, "When you got credit you gotta run with it."

"This is fabulous," Frank says. Heavy with respect. "And it's only the beginning. I wish I knew more about the ice cream business, I'd go in myself."

Jack cries, "Dairy Queen doesn't even sell ice cream, they sell custard!"

Curranne grips Jack's redgold forelock. Terrible eyes shake him, their gray-green shine superhuman. "Will you listen to them! Didn't you learn *anything* from Leopolda?"

"Yeah, *roofing!*"

"Look where she is today subletting leases," Curranne says. "Next week she's going to Corfu until April."

"The frozen custard business is *very* sweet right now, Jack," Frank says. "Growing by leaps and bounds. People love cold custard. I love it!"

"Well, I don't," Jack says. "Tastes like plastic. Don't tell me any more."

"You think this is a harebrained scheme, don't you?" Frank says. "I think it's brilliant—ingenious! Frankly, Jack, I'm surprised at your shortsightedness. Ah!" he cries at his pool of nutted hot butterscotch. "Nectar! Look at this stuff, Jack. All nature is addicted to it. Butterflies spend their whole day of life eating pollen, flower after flower, and impregnating nature along the way. All of organic nature works on sweets, glucose, nitrogen, sap. Even sex is some form of glucose attack on the brain. I see it!—hormones going mad in ginger sauce. You know all that. What could be a more perfect business investment than to lock into the sugar cycle? Even corn syrup, you can't fail, man. Sugar is bigger than alcohol! There's no end to consumer appetite. And Dairy Queen is just getting off the ground. You guys will be millionaires in five years. This could dwarf life insurance and the Church."

Ziggy suggests, "If Jack doesn't want to join us, maybe you would."

"I'm retired." Hard sigh. "But if Jack is pussyfooted, I'll give it my earnest consideration."

"Can you stand a minor financial investigation?" Ed asks. "This thing is going to grow."

"Can I? Sure I can," Frank says. "Isn't it legitimate already?"

"Oh sure!" Ed says. "I mean in the long run I want to go into a national-brand ice cream. Make it ourselves, bug-free. The real money's in that Dairy Queen formula, not the leases. I have my own ice cream formula. It's a secret. We need a spotless front."

Frank spoons in rapture. "Magnificent." Raises his dish toward Becky, appraising her as she passes. "*Magnifique!* Well, Jack, what do you say? I feel very secure about this. I feel good. It's your shot at the big time. You can always write books after you make some dinero to tide you over."

"Mucho moola," Curranne says.

"What do you think?" Ed asks Jack.

"You don't have to do much. Just sign some papers," Ziggy says.

"We'll all be friends—practically brothers—and own the whole world," Ed implores hoarsely. "On credit."

"Kings of the earth," Ziggy says.

Frank throws up his hands. "I find this all very moving."

"Jack doesn't want to stay a dairy manager the rest of his life, believe me," Curranne says.

"I'll speak for myself, thank you," Jack says. "Don't you speak for yourself?"

"Oh, it's not the same. You need someone to push you. You need something to build on. Think of Avon if you can't think of yourself. And setting aside her college money."

"Jack, doesn't this appeal to your Napoleonic side?" Frank asks. "It does to mine. Even the Rockefellers had to start somewhere."

Curranne slaps the table. "They sure did!"

"You hate the Rockefellers," Jack reminds her.

"Money is money," she says. "In this case it's security. You know what drives more people crazy than anything else? Financial stress. If there was enough money for everyone there'd be a lot less schizophrenia and depression."

"You can't blame all madness on money," Jack says. "Every crazy is crazy his own way."

Curranne says, "I agree with Frank. Sugar is big bucks. Where is Wes Fulmer today, who owns this sugar shop? He's off in Canada with his family! Where are you? *Plugging along.* You have to think of yourself, Jack, aside from your family. Hey, I'm really excited for you!"

"I can see."

"Look at it this way," Frank says. "Financial anxiety is a prime factor in stomach and bowel cancer."

"Jack's half crazy from money. He wants to move out of *my mother's* someday. Don't you?"

Frank says, "What do you make here, Jack? As much as on the *Sun,* may I ask?"

Stress brightens Jack's bowels. He can't answer.

"Can you meet your bills?" Frank the social worker asks.

"I'm getting very depressed," Jack says.

"Let's change the subject, right?" Curranne says. "Just when we're getting somewhere."

"I don't want to dampen you two guys' enthusiasm," Jack says. "My ex-brother-in-law is a lawyer. Why don't I ask him for advice before I say a flat yes or no?"

"Ziggy Scott, sitting right here, *is* a lawyer," Ed says.

Ziggy nods. "Still have my shingle."

"*I* wouldn't run into anything like a crazy man!" Ed says, wide-eyed.

"Wants a second opinion," Ziggy says. "Perfectly natural."

"No offense meant," Jack says.

Ed says, "Just be honest. Say what *you* think." Eyes plead, a wounded dog.

"We spent all summer together getting our heads straight, didn't we?" Ziggy asks. "What's your frank opinion?"

"I don't know enough about it."

"Off the top of your head, Jack!" Frank cries. "Nobody's going to bite you."

"This is ridiculous. I can't commit myself one way or the other, and I refuse to throw cold water on the project. That's not my business."

"Let's go," Ed urges Ziggy. "He's not going to say anything."

"Okay! Jack has forgotten all about Leopolda."

"Who's this Leopolda?" Frank asks.

"A venturesome woman," Jack says.

"A dame with guts," Ed says.

"One of us," Curranne says.

"Which Jack here isn't," Ed says.

Ziggy rises with Ed. "We haven't paid yet."

"He's paying," Ed says at Frank. *"Jesus!"*

"I'm not him anymore," Frank says. "But my party, gents. You guys have a card? We might get together yet."

"We're at the Hotel Samuels," Ziggy says. "See you folks."

Jack's amazed Ziggy said goodbye. "No hard feelings?"

"None at all," Ed says. "We're upward mobile."

"Hard feelings only hold us back," Ziggy says. "Ill will is for idiots."

Jack watches Ed and Ziggy walk outside and stand talking in sunlight at the front window.

"Those guys are in the flow," Frank says. "If you'd ever seen them at North Warren, you wouldn't believe the recovery they've made. Businessmen!"

"They're crazy as bedbugs," Jack says.

"At last! An opinion," Curranne says. "I thought you were their friend?"

"I am, aren't I?"

"Stop that!"—shining-eyed. Jack jumps. "If you're their friend you'd have spoken up! You think Ed can't take it? Or Ziggy? You should lay it into them, if that's what you feel. Really warn them! What kind of friend are you? They really ask and you sit there looking out for Jack!"

"Jesus Christ, I can't win today."

"You can't, my son," Frank says.

She sees Jack weakening. "If you're their friend, march out there and announce your doubts. Tell *them* to wait for a second opinion from your brother-in-law." His hands knot. Again she grips his forelock. *"Will you listen to me?"*

"Please let go of my hair, Curranne."

"Listen to me!"—shaking him.

Jack's fear rises. "All right, I'll listen. That means you'll listen to me too, right?"

"Of course I'll listen—though it's not the same thing. Now get out there! They respect you. They came here wanting your frank opinion."

"Well, I don't think they're acting honorably with Dairy Queen."

"Honorably? Jack, this is business." Frank waves at heaven. "I don't know, maybe you are one of us. Too bad I turned in my bedsheet."

"I don't care," Jack says. "If they act out of a mean and dishonest motive, they're setting themselves up to fall apart again."

"Why is that?" With his mind at full power, Frank weighs Jack's sanity. "That's the way the world is. I'd say it's the sanest thing they can do."

"No, they're undermining their recoveries. Ed even thinks it's a typhoid product."

"But do *you* really think so?" Frank says. "Or should they go into instant chicken broth?"

"Go ahead," Curranne says, nudging Jack.

Jack stands slowly. "What shall I say?"

"Ask them which is more important, sanity or money," Curranne says.

"They'll stomp all over him." Frank laughs as Jack goes out. "Those two guys are still un poco loco, huh?"

"They'll listen," Curranne says. "They admire Jack."

She watches Jack in his apron talk with Ed and Ziggy in gusty sunlight. All their hair flying, even Ziggy's tarp. Leopolda stands among them, listening with sympathetic horror. *How's Diana Belvedere?* her lips ask Ed. He turns from her, red-faced, swallowing his lower lip. She vanishes. Curranne yearns to be with her in London and Paris and Corfu. Dr. David surely has the money. She'll put some *zip* into that recluse!

"They're listening," she says. "It'd be harder on Jack if he said nothing. Do you know anything about musical instruments?"

"I am a musician, Curranne! Why?"

"I want to buy Jack a trumpet."

"He has a trumpet, hasn't he?"

"It's hocked. He hasn't played since last Christmas. I'd like to get him a new one for a present. Something special to remember me by."

"Are you going somewhere, Curranne?"

"What? I'm deaf in that ear."

"You know, you have such clear eyes! I asked are you going somewhere?"

"I don't know. We never do, do we?"

Frank shrugs. "I get my booster of phenothiazine in the ass once a month and don't worry. Did I tell you, I'm part of a study program? It's my wife who skips her pills and gets flaky. Are you worried about a relapse?"

"It's always possible."

"That's realistic. Good for you."

"But I get terribly sad. Don't you?"

"*Me,* sad? Ha! Never."

". . . Not even about Beverly?"

"You're right, she upsets me tremendously. I don't know what to do about her. She's six months pregnant and keeps telling her doctor she's well and doesn't need her pills. If she skips them for a few days she thinks the Mexican Army's charging up Swede Hill to rape her. Among the pleasanter activities they have planned for her. Maybe you should talk to her. She idealizes you terribly. Getting pregnant. She might listen."

"Why doesn't she take a shot like you do?"

"Well, she's taking a new drug. It's ten times stronger than mine. She's needle-shy of anything that strong. Do you take your Thorazine regularly?"

"What?" She bends to him.

He looks about and asks quietly, "Do you take your pills regularly?"

She nods. "The phenothiazines don't work for everyone though. The symptoms can persist at any dosage."

"How are your symptoms?"

Curranne masks. "Manageable."

"So are mine—not that I believe you. What's wrong?"

"Nothing! Maybe you'd help me buy Jack a horn?"

"My great pleasure. I'm in the book. You look very downcast. Are you sure you're all right?"

"I need to run." Looks about unhappily, then asks in a small voice, "May I tell you something? Someone should know in case I disappear."

"Disappear! Where? What are you saying?"

"I think I'm in love," she says timidly.

Frank's stare says he clearly doesn't think she knows what love is. "Ah! You mean not with Jack?"

"Jack? *I love Jack.* I have to leave him before I drive him off. *You* understand that. If I leave first, I still have a chance."

"No. I'm not following you."

"Everybody leaves me. In the end, they cut loose. They can't bear me any longer."

"Wow."

"I've lost three husbands." Her eyes close. She chokes. "And then I break down!"

"But if you love Jack . . ."

"It's so dangerous! He's the worst thing that ever happened to me! I'm so dependent! And my recovery's being constantly measured—against every meal I cook—bed I make. The ring in the tub! I love him but I want to kill Jack. He's the Marine sergeant guiding me through boot camp. I have to wipe every table twice or he'll come right after me with his own rag. He can't bear the way I wash dishes. I'm not allowed to. I'm wasteful. I squirt soap all over the plates instead of into the sponge. You're not like that, are you?"

"Uhhh . . . nothing like that. We're big on frozen dinners."

"Oh, he'd never allow that. He's not one of us. There's only so much he'll take. I've got to leave before he does, for my own *sanity*. What would happen to Beverly if you left her? She's so superdependent on you, Frank. I know she is. I'd find that extremely discouraging to my recovery."

"I see what you mean. But you want to run off with someone else?"

She nods. "I think I should. He's twice my age, maybe more. He *may* want to elope."

"Well-l . . . I'm not sure I want to know about this. Doesn't he love you?"

"Jack's mad about me! He worships me. I'm everything to him. The poor guy lives at my feet."

"Of course, you're a wonderful woman. But what about this other gent?"

"I haven't asked him. I feel he's the only man alive who can save me. I really feel it. I'm absolutely certain he's my only lifeline to a normal life."

"A normal life? What's a normal life? You mean without drugs?"

"I'll take drugs!" Her eyes mist. "I'll do anything to have a normal life. Then sometime, when he dies, I can come back to Jack. Worth more and . . . normal."

"How can you ever be normal?"

"I don't want to wind up crapping all over myself in some back ward for twenty years! Not because I can't *unscum* a bathtub! Worthless as I am, I think more of myself than that!"

Plunged into the ward, she feels cold disappointment half pleasantly camphorate her breast. She looks at the three men beyond in windy sunlight. The very street and daylight about to be torn from her again? Eternity bursts inward.

"You're telling me I have breast cancer! I mean brain cancer?"

"What? Of course not! Hey, buck up," Frank urges. "Nothing's that desperate. Just stay balanced on the old Thorazine saddle and you'll have a normal life—whatever that is. I've never met a normal adult human being. May I ask, what does this old man do?"

"What old man?"

"Your lover. I mean your lifeline."

"He's my analyst."

"Maybe *I'm* going deaf. Did you say your analyst?"

Nods. "He wants to marry me. I know he does. He lives alone with a Jamaican housekeeper. I think he wants to have a real life. He needs someone to shine his shoes and change his phonograph records. And garden and rake and typewrite."

Frank shakes his head. "Curranne, I'm amazed. I'm thunderstruck. Don't you know anything about analysis? You're supposed to hate your analyst, not love him. I mean if you ever expect to have a normal life, he's the last person on earth to have it with."

"But he's HP!"

"I don't know who he is! But *we* are funny people. We hate the people who help us most. They just show us how weak we are without them. You're destroying your treatment by marrying your analyst! He can't go on analyzing you if you've married him, you know. That's not ethical. It's like teaching your wife how to drive—*never* attempt it. I speak from dread experience."

"That doesn't make sense!" she whimpers.

"It does to me." Frank shrugs. "Why do you think Beverly resists absolutely everything I do for her? She's a paranoid schiz. I expect it of her! Resistance is her identity."

"That really sounds hopeless," Curranne says.

"I didn't mean it to. I don't want to depress you. Of course, I hurt, and she hurts. But that's the way it is. I'm sure your old doctor loves you—"

"He wants me!"

"Of course! But not in bed. He could lose his license just for putting his finger on your kneebone. Does he ever hug you? Put his arm

around your shoulder? Buck you up like some garden-variety neurotic? Even shake your hand?"

"He's never touched me in any way. Well, today he gripped my
shoulder."

"He shouldn't have done that!"

"And I nuzzled him."

"You *nuzzled* him?? Were you out of your mind? That's very dangerous. But you did it, not him. You're a paranoid schiz. He's afraid
you'd burn his house down if you tripped on his doorstep. You've been
reading him all wrong, my dear."

A long god lies dead in the dairy. Electric bulbs fight the darkened
day. She watches Becky slap a metal shake can onto a mixer in the
straight world. Her back crawls with otherness.

"Feeling better?" Frank asks.

"That frigging bastard is trying to kill me."

"Wonderful!"—health stickered all over her.

"I mean that."

"Call him up and tell him. He'll flip with happiness."

"He'll get what he deserves. I don't know how!" Double-fisted. "I'm
going to put it to him. Take my word, buster. I'm going to save all this
up. My next session! *He'll never know what hit him."*

"Ho ho ho, I wish I could be there!"

Over Frank's shoulder she sees Ed grab Jack in a bear hug, bend
him back. Jack stands resistless, at last pushes Ed away. But Ed picks
him up again. Jack bounces off the front window, his arm sliding up
quivering glass. Walking away, Ed shakes a fist at him. Curranne slaps
her brow with shock. Jack marches back in a huge burn and sits.

"Thanks!" he tells Curranne.

"What for?"

"They abused me until I thought I was going to melt into the sidewalk."

Frank winks at Curranne. "They're mad at you, Jack?"

"They never want to see me again. They think I'm a menace and
Ziggy's going to report me to the Food and Drug Administration. I
thought Ed would throw me through the front window. The fuckhead
tried hard enough. Can you believe it?"

"What went wrong?" Curranne asks.

"I'm a widely known voyeur and abuser of children and young girls
and a potential rapist. The police are already onto my unhealthy prac-

tices and watching me day and night. And if they weren't they will be, after everything said out there in public. Actually, I'm lucky I'm not sitting here full of glass. I could be dead right now! *Jesus Christ!* I must have been out of my mind to try to wake them up."

"Actually they may have believed you and are reconsidering everything right now," Frank says. Jack eyes him weighingly. "Trust me. I've been there."

"I'm sorry they got angry," Curranne says timidly.

"What've you got to do with it? It's me. I did the absolutely stupidest thing for the right reason."

"I saw him," she says. "Ed really tried to hurt you!"

"It's not your fault, Curranne," Frank says. "But I'm sorry you're not going to make that million, Jack. Did you blow your top?"

"Would I hit a drunk?"

"Jack loves them," Curranne says. "He didn't, but he does."

"Well, Ziggy was pretty nice," Frank says. "I liked his suit. But Ed scared me. You understand that they're not friends, don't you? If they split this moment, there'd be no feelings lost. I saw that right away. How can you love a pair of nuts like that? That's Christian charity carried above and beyond the call of duty. They're hopeless."

"They're in hell," Jack says.

"Let's have something more to eat," Frank says. "Curranne, my dear, you haven't touched your tomato."

"I'm not hungry," she whispers.

"Don't worry about those guys, they'll get along," Frank says. "I know something about where they are, Jack. They've already got about a hundred years of insanity between them, haven't they? They can take care of themselves . . . Jack, what are you writing?"

"Writing?" Cradles his forehead, eyes closed. Still can't breathe.

"Jack's a great writer," Frank tells her. His big Dutch blues brighten. "Have you read any of his Prometheus novel?"

She nods.

Frank tempers his delight. "It's going to make him someday."

"I've got an idea for a novel in which no one's face is described," Jack says.

"I don't like not seeing faces." Curranne turns, half poisoned. "Please don't show it to me if you do write it."

"Did you ever see anyone without a face?" Frank asks her.

Curranne is silent.

"Not a happy sight. God, I feel drunk. I must be in butterscotch shock. So what happens?"

"The heroine's an owl," Jack says.

"A novel about an owless!" Frank says. "That sounds daring. What's the point of it?"

"She's this spectral creature God intends to see with in the dark."

Frank says, "God is the dark. He sees everything."

"Zeus couldn't," Jack says. "That's why he popped Athena from his brow. So he could see in the dark. She's the goddess of owls."

"I don't like this story," she says.

"Why not, Curranne?" Frank asks.

"I can't even see in the daylight."

"Neither can an owl!" Frank laughs. "You're a solemn old owl. Come on, laugh a bit."

She flashes a Gorgon mask that freezes Frank. "Ed nearly threw Jack through the front window, Frank. I saw it."

"I'm sorry," he says. "I heard a funny sound—"

"May I ask you something?" she asks him. All World War II in her eye.

Frank's still chilled. His arms ripple with dread. "Be my guest."

"Why did you and Beverly decide to have a third child? You're both schizzes and have already given up two children. That seems like too much weight to drop on a baby."

"Yeah, I know. Genetically." Two hard sighs. Warped genes *are* a weight. "We thought of that. A lot! All we can do is pray, right?"

"You think praying will help?" Curranne asks.

"It'll help *us.* Only God can say what He's going to do genetically." Frank is quiet. "If He knows. Right, Jack? We try not to be paranoid about our genes. It takes blind faith."

"If you'll pardon me, it sounds like blind selfishness," Curranne says.

"We wanted our baby," Frank says. "Didn't you?"

Curranne is silent and guarded.

"Was Avon an accident or a choice?" he asks her.

"She flew in the window."

"Well, I mean we're having ours on purpose. We waited two years after giving our last child away before we got up the courage to try again. Maybe I'm selfish. Maybe Beverly's selfish. But we're both self-ish together for the same thing and that makes us very, very close. We really like each other for going through with this, despite the fears. The children have never been at fault, as far as we know. They seemed like sound kids to us. We were the ones who kept breaking down, not our kids. Now we're older and wiser and we like each other more than ever. When the money came, there was nothing to hold us back. We decided to take a shot and run with our hopes. Life got worth living. Really intense!"

"You mean in the sack?" Curranne asks.

"Where else? How much closer to heaven can you get? It's the opposite of suffering, isn't it?"

"It's the big carrot," Curranne says.

"Maybe for God too," Frank says. "He must like sex."

"And taking chances, huh?"

"Sure, He's subject to chance. Isn't chance part of things?" Frank asks. "If He didn't have chance, He'd be bored with empty powers. 'Let's do this, let's do that'—everything always going His way."

"You're talking with the ex-Messiah of North Warren," Jack reminds her. "I like your hat."

Frank ticks his robin's-egg brim. "Custom made at Jay Lord's."

Curranne is rueful. Eyes the hat unhappily. "You're a pretty fanciful guy."

Frank laughs. "My tragic flaw!"

"I'm sorry I said that about you and Beverly. I mean, asking questions. Who am I to say you haven't made the right choice?"

"You were just curious," Frank says.

"No, I see you better now. You really are a kind fellow and not trying to buy friendships, as I thought you were doing. I didn't understand you before."

"I'll be frank. I have to be! I have a very weak ego. I *was* trying to hide behind money."

"No, you have a very big heart," she says. "That's your weakness."

"Well, thank you," Frank says. "I'm sure no one else ever saw it that way."

"I-I . . ." Curranne clears her voice twice. Holds her hand over the table. "Shake?"

Frank looks both ways frantically, the squinting, elephantine paranoiac. Presses far away with a long fearful face. Still timidly backpedaling, he clutches his wrist, yanks it over the table and offers her a hand.

"So happy to meet you!" he whines brokenly. With beleaguered little yelpings.

Curranne bursts, howling at his mockery. Collapses over the table. As she raises back, her howl echoes throughout the dairy, open and joyous. Jack grabs her. Frank too howls. Jack's dairy tensions burst, he rolls sideways. As Frank beats his head against the wall, his hat drops off. Curranne grabs and jams it down over her ears. Frank pounds his leg, tears running, pointing at her. Her eye chisels his brain open. She lectures him with a Hitlerian finger, her jaw jutting under the blue homburg. They both grab the table and pull long serious faces, glaring with self-control. He lets her arrange his tie again. Jack is blind with tears. He rolls and sobs with joy. Their howls rise as he slips onto the concrete. Curranne half stands, tips the hat at stunned counter customers and, starting to hand it to Frank, instead climbs onto her bench seat and sails the hat the length of the dairy—into the front window.

"We're howling maniacs!" Frank cries, jiggling in his seat.

Jack climbs back halfway, choking, his head fallen into Curranne's lap. Her gaiety breaks above him, unbridled. Her eyes are unstuck of everything, pained only by joy.

Walking home for her run, she feels purged by prickling October leafsmoke hanging over the streets. There is a space in her where something has died and fallen away, past recall even by leafsmoke. Something once paralyzing is gone. Utterly. What, she doesn't know, but the strings of her being ease gently as she looks upward and plucks at her thoughts. Four-thirty in King James. A red sun burns at low slant through Baker Park. Blazes in half-stripped tree limbs. Lies molten on scorched leaves. First twilight deepens. Drinks her into its watery rich azure. Her heart mirrors a world beyond hovering on the sky's edge. The deep blue sucks at her wind. In memory she walks huge floating hills full of yellow schoolrooms. She is alone. A far dog barks after a breeze-tail of leaves. Late robins hop about before sleeptime. Then all together the park streetlamps blurt false blue light. Her spirit opens. A ghost hangs before her in the evening air.

He has a face at last. Not the face of the helpless drunk upstairs in her mother's bedroom. She has no homefear of the living–corpse face of drowned Daddy at *Fantasia*. Her fear of him is plucked out. Only now does she know at depth this loss of fear which began when HP

lifted it this morning at Dr. David's office. Granting for a short space
ease from her endless yearning. Mental peace, full recovery, she'd been
there!—her self-trust as steeled as her grip on "Broken Bucket." And
then blacked out while driving, her lost fears leaving a vacuum she
couldn't bear. An infinite rebalancing she hadn't the strength to support. She is moved, seeing the old doctor as she tempts him with her
dreams. His ecstatic saliva. Then his eyes above her, his untouching
hands imitating Jack's laying on. Research for his book? Or couldn't
he help himself? She sees his pale, dead yard. Enters the swelling light
on the hills. Tastes again a gigantic peace, lets it spread through her.
Taking a chance on God. Her two miracles, welcome healing events,
not the supereggbeater explosions, the wallbenders she's familiar with.
A little peace itself can pack a wallop of hope, strength and courage.

Even her father's drowning, his abandonment forgiven. He was sick!
That's clearer than ever from what she hears at A.A. Anyway, he'd
been a superb swimmer, as she'd always known, since the family's
earliest picnics on Lake Michigan. She remembers being on the beach
with him even before Cornelle's birth, in the earliest days of the Depression. He'd wear a long black bathing suit that clung to his
bunched genitals when wet. She remembers rinsing sand from their
suits and his hairy muscular swimmer's thighs in the kitchen bathtub
at home. His witty eye and curly-headed square features so like pictures of Zeus and Hercules. His prick a twisty branch, shrunken and
pointed on its tight bag. With a clutch she sees his soberest smile, its
intense questioning cut, firmness, quick lift of pleasure. And then the
smileless smile of the man who was not where, while drinking, who
was instead a glassy-eyed braggart corpse. She remembers the cinnamon of her first adolescent daydreams about him. Daydreams stealing
upon her with the force of fact. Of giving him pleasure during Carol's
cold spells, their King James house under days of heavy frost. The
dreams themselves are vague. Only their forbidden stir has power and
the memory of guilt spreading fear in room after room of the house.
Only a narrow path through the rooms for her to ropewalk with
safety. After he died her last refuge was the crypt of the bathtub.
Envying no-nonsense older sister Carrie's role as daddy's lookalike but
not her boring middle-class poise. Now, as she turns the corner to the
house, he will not be waiting for her on her mother's bed.

She runs onto the porch, rehearsing what she will say to Dr. David.
She will lay it out plain. She must replace Marbella the slut and be-

come his live-in mistress (his housekeeper-slut? *Ugh!*), saving everyone money including poor Jack. She sees herself as a fourteen-foot-high Alice-ogre lecturing Dr. David in his bath, bending down to tie his laces, boil his oatmeal in a tiny kitchen. Spiritual evenings, editing for him and typing his vast manuscript. Mystical voyages to Egyptian star-planes. Or else she will arrange with Alma Anderson of the *Post-Journal* to expose Dr. David's licentious life-style and malpractices. Ousting Marbella—with Curranne moving in by force. She'd like a loving household under her steel hand. Marbella, whose hated face Curranne now sees as Becky Normstrand's at Fulmer's, must be displaced. If she can squeeze into place this last piece in the arch, she will be stone sane. Cured! If she is not cured already, as she feels. Indeed, she is hugely healthy. Powerful. Almost lantern-jawed with wisdom. The thought blows into her, nearly lifting her off her feet, that she is the wisest, most learned, eloquent and healthy woman on earth. Who matches her? No one she can see, looking about, her jaw weighted and wise. She strides about the living and dining rooms, shaking with supernormal brilliance.

Fearlessly, she runs upstairs, snorting at her mother's empty bedroom. Changes into her shirt and running shoes. As she starts down to the phone she sees she's forgotten her shorts. Tearing open the wrong bureau drawer, she finds Jack's bathing suit and jock strap. She takes out the jock and straps it on. Maleness floods her. Struts about, snapping the strap. Balls two handkerchiefs into the pouch, swaggers up and down the hall like a cowboy in bootheels. Back in the bedroom she shucks her shirt and digs out a tee shirt of Jack's. It hangs halfway down her thighs. In her mother's mirror she draws the shirt tight, over the bulging jock. Too droopy. Safety-pins a fold into the strap. Now arms akimbo in the shadowy mirror, she's not happy with her hair. She razors a sweatband from a bath towel, then stuffs her ponytail under and knots the band lightly. This will have to do.

And now, the joining with Dr. Zeus, who wants her as bride, daughter and guide. *Ha!* she cries, fist up. Dashes down to the living room phone, hangs over it in a muddle. The phone is too slow, she'll run to North Warren. Better still she'll radio him. She strides to the dining room table. Sits. Slaps her palms down.

"David! Dr. David! I know you've been listening to every word I've thought."

"Yes, Mrs. Trueheart?" But what a huge sigh! To disarm her?

"Let's not beat around the bush. I want an answer."

"I can't answer."

"Then I won't be responsible. Don't you want to see me cured? Do you want me to be your slave forever?"

"The fact is, Curranne, you are cured."

"*I* know that. How did you find out?"

"The cure is . . ."

She jumps, shocked. His deep-chested voice, now heavy waves from ceiling, walls and floor, shivers the table. Mouth ajar, Curranne eyes the voice–vibrating walls and ceiling and floor. She hangs onto the table, a raft in heavy seas.

". . . that you can speak freely to me. You've discharged your fears."

"You want a punch in the nose? Don't hand me that b.s." The deep-polished mahogany table brings in a huge TV face of Dr. David. She snatches a long dinner candle from its holder and raps him. "You're so superior! Are you saying I haven't always been free with you?"

His voice grows softer, turning down, but is now loftier and threatening in its quiet near-whisper. "Not before today! Today was our breakthrough."

She sighs at the face in the table. "You're leaving me no choice."

"Your *lasting* cure is just around the corner. Just around the corner! You are breaking through at this very moment, Curranne."

"I know I am. I can feel it, I'm getting ready to fly. I'm probably an angel or goddess. Oh, of course! I have a little secret, David. I sprang from the brow of Zeus. You thought I didn't know that, didn't you?"

"Why don't you go out for your run?"

"You're going to see what a real bitch is. I eat little mice like you."

"It's getting quite dark. I'll come along and we can talk on the way."

"You'll never keep up." The Gorgon trickster, she flashes her owl face at him, rejoices in his shock. *"Caught you!"* she screeches, and laughs unpleasantly. Her big yellow eyes grow round, glow in the dimness. Her owlness hollows her bones, tufts her arms. Her eyes are circled by disks of small feathers. Her head twists in short stiff jerks, taking in bit after bit of the evening. She feels the gravity of dark earth beneath her, awaiting her winged glide on the currents of night.

"Think you can keep up?"

"Well, I'll do my best."

"You can't *stop* an owl. Even eagles are afraid of an owl. Next time I see you I just may tear your heart out. When you're least alert. You won't even hear me coming! Only my screech as I hit your breast."

She hoots a tremendous falling wail straight into his face—HOO-*OOO-OOO-ooo-ooo!* then carves violently into the finish with her candle:

ATHENA

Candle in hand, Curranne slams out the front door. Floats off the porch. As she does Jack drives up, watches her pace over Sixth under lamplight and up Jefferson to Baker Park. He gets out to take the crib into the dark house. It's quite forbidding. She's been in here in the dark? Then the image of Curranne's odd running outfit shakes him. She'd looked naked under one of his tee shirts. His skin shudders. She could get arrested for that outfit. He gets back in and drives after her, thanking God for the early darkness masking her costume. The candle's something new.

As he reaches Baker Park he sees her round the dry fountain in blue lamplight, then stop, dance about on one leg, remove a strange loose strap and ball it under some leaves in the fountain. Under spare black limbs she paces half bare-assed to Fourth. Easier for him to miss the one-way streets if he goes to Third and catches up there. His palms sweat. His shins are tingling. Street nudity is unheard of in King James.

Her feet are winged. She runs too fast, forcing the pace before her second wind. Suddenly she hears David's great rustling wings beat behind her. She lengthens her stride.

"Sometimes you're just senseless," David says from above. "You shouldn't fall in love and have children. You're smart enough to know that. *Falling in love!*" He sneers. "You belong in an asylum. A nice, quiet place."

"Like your house?"

"We're both exiles, aren't we?"

Her mouth tastes of roasted chestnuts. Fateful with huge yearning, she sees a Chicago corner from her childhood flash before her. The family buys heady finger-burning chestnuts from an Italian vendor. A heart-piercing nutty sweetness flows from the image . . . of a time before tears . . . before the first fingerings of fear, bone-squeezings of

threatening voices. Her hard little body racy as a tadpole—and her
mind!

"Safe and cared for. Though you may be unhappy for a while. Or
forever! Apartness is eternal suffering."

Curranne is past answering. The voice melts into flowing pain, short
little bursts buoyant with agony.

"Things will be easier for you there. A lifelong commitment. Cared
for. Flowers in your room. It's best you do it yourself. Before they
deport you. Just come. No more hope. You'll be home at last!"

His soft thunder shines with logic. She has always fought her voices
with abuse or filth or cunning silence. This voice's strength, greater
than any, reaches weakeningly into her very muscles. It has taken the
most frightening tack of all. It's on her side.

The temptation to give in, her eyes waxed with surrender, final
commitment, her own room and flowers and safety—what *mercies* the
voice offers! All for you, Curranne, no more struggle.

She paces onto Third Street Bridge. The Chadakoin Valley widens
before her, billowing with high cloud in evening blue. Beyond the hill
trees sits Lincoln High where—twenty years ago, perhaps on this very
day!—her father watched her race. But even after her victory, she
recalls unhappily, her school counselor wrote to Ed and Carol about
her uneven temper. By high school she'd learned to hide its flaring
behind her Gorgon mask that stiffened the unwary to stone. An amus-
ing power, but saddening. Jack alone has learned how to mirror it
back by polished and loathsome indifference.

As he pulls onto the bridge Jack sees her far ahead on the facing
walk. With two-lane traffic he must pass her and wait at the far end.
Even from here he can see she's ragged. But the bridge is empty of
footwalkers who might report her undress.

Her father's sunstruck face, vivid, big and welcoming, on the day at
the cinder track. Once more she outdistances the pack by thirty yards,
sees them far behind on the final lap. He dances a little jig, her miler's
blue ribbon in his fingers. His smiling eyes forgive all. She's in tears,
surging with happiness but maddened at not being his favorite. Self-
possessed Cornelle wins that trophy without running a yard. Yet on
this brilliant fall morning, for one split second, she denies Cornelle her
place and is queen absolute, spent fully and ringing with joy, his fathering sunflow seeking her every part and crevice. Must this joy ever
lessen?

"I knew you'd do it!" he says. "You're the fastest thing on two feet on the whole earth, Curranne, my moxie!"

Curranne my moxie! Happy pistol shots into her breast. She dies for his love.

The evening squeezes into a tunnel. She focuses on the sidewalk ahead. Running into soft pearl light and deepening blackness. Heels thudding, soles gripping grit. Gasping, Curranne fixes on her wind. An upward glance shows the bridge melting and stretching like taffy. The asphalt bubbles burnt electrical discharge into the air, that taste that dried her tongue at Dr. David's laying on of hands. Her muscles burn with discharge. Are old ropes, frayed wires. She cannot cough out the foulness choking her. Curranne is sure she will faint from lack of oxygen before reaching midbridge. The sweatband's bind strains her head. Her being stops, starts, stops, strains against concrete. Knots tense in her brain. If only she could drain herself of herself and—a tadpole again—start fresh! She owes all she is to others and now has nothing left to give. Every cell is bankrupt. The bound goat kicking on the altar, she longs to slice open her bindings, her windpipe, let up-ward floods of air, gushes of blood. What mingling! What fulfillment! Pumping, she runs in the silence of the deaf, hearing only the heavy bird-thud of her heart.

Jack finds he is the lone car on the bridge. He slows twenty feet behind her. Usually he admires her straight spine and striding thighs, the set of her hips. But all that ordered energy flags. Her legs are naked. She runs on sheer will. He rolls down his window to call to her.

At midbridge Curranne falls choked against the concrete rail. Her face is drawn dark blue in lampglare. Her veins are dark lines under blue skin. Slowly spreading, a terrible purpose shines from every bone in her grip. She punches the air in triumph, looks over the rail. The Chadakoin winds in silver. A train *chunks* far below, metal smiting as cars couple on moonbright tracks. She climbs onto the rail, unaware of Jack's screech, and leaps without a thought. The owl is off and gone. Looping the hard breezes, the redbrick fort scribbled with skyglow. Her spirit-rags whip with new life. She is of the sky, fearless and wise, her pulse bird-spirited in the blue. Noiselessly she sweeps down on Steele Street. A ghost plugging her throat pops. Her chest unbinds and sucks in a ravishing full breath. Her flesh floods with its mission. Terrible-eyed, her clear mind courses the shadow-valley to-ward North Warren and Dr. David.

At the last second her body charges with shock, waking her. It's no dream, she's falling. *Stupid woman!* A life's error blazes up, blistering. Betrayed again! All is stolen, Jack, Avon, her boys. Grief fills the falling Margaret. She shrieks with pity for the waxen girl lifted from her roof by firemen.

Whose hand will save me now?

Peace bursts, spreading through earth and sky. She is at one with the great smacking force of the All-mighty hand closing on her. Her spark rests unmarred in His palm. His power fills her boundlessly, forever.

Epilogue

Don't go through hard times alone. I tried, and it doesn't work. My mourning lasted a year. The fits of anguish, even longer. My heart would drift off and break. I'd come to on my couch with a scream, clutching my nuts in horror, then feel her hand withdraw from mine, finger by finger, each finger whispering, *Let go.*

That was not easy. Not in cramped King James, on streets livid with the stigma of suicide. I don't think of Curranne as a suicide (not in her character), only as a woman who lost her wits. By trying too hard.

What was most unnerving was that I might follow her if I lost my own wits. That fear drove me further into my fellowship with recovering drunks. Fear of death-by-impulse was driven out by giving strength to others. But I'm no saint, please.

Still, I wouldn't have written this if I'd not been obsessed by her. Some years more than others. Parts of her story I've had to imagine, more than you might think. I hope I've avoided melodrama. Maybe I should have left out entirely her inner experience. But once I put in her first thought, I had to go on and make reasons for her looking and acting as she did. And I wanted to. I wanted to live over our lost days together, hold all of her before me. Fondle her again. I wanted to touch her everywhere.

Where do people go when they die? Into dreams, and some profounder part of you where they live on quite unbound by your life. They come back, self-possessed, smiling. Wondering how you're doing, what you're up to. You talk with them, or I do—I don't sit around knocking God. He'd already given her back to me, and my unborn Avon, that New Year's morning I found them frozen on the bench. I saw His hand raise the dead. If only to allow one flowering. When He did take her He spared her a lot of hardship. She wasn't getting well. For all I know, if she were alive today she'd be sharing space on some ward. Perhaps the full reach of her miracle is the space she shares here. Here she shares the overflowing womanhood her illness denied her sharing in life.

Goodbye, Curranne, my hard, splendid, mad wife, whom I've made up out of the piece of you that walks about in me. Floats up, speaking wordlessly with warm glances, urging me on at these pages. What a warmth I get from you now, right here most of all! What is it you offer me? When I die, will we mingle and be happy together? Will I find the heart I fought for so hard? Know your fullness at last, every finger of you? The undistracted creature itself? Keep your memory of me *green,* my dear. Remember all of our homes together, the rooms, the walks. The days at the lake, when we were so alive (dance for me on the grass once more!). So alive. Even in sorrow, so bright-boned and eager for our recoveries. Crazy or not, lapping up our good health. I think we may have matched our cracks better than we knew! Whatever the pains were, once again I've had joy in your company and would do it *all* over. We were luckier than we could ever believe. The bonds of love are worth any price, even grief. That fades. Life heals the hardest death. The power that rekindled you on that winter bench still enspirits our wildflower daughter. When I see her wise gray-green eyes, and watch your tender Chaplin-grin—my God, I want you back. How much more I could give you now! But only your smiling strength remains.

January 1, 1985
Greenwich Village